D0951870

BY SUSAN VREELAND

Girl in Hyacinth Blue

The Passion of Artemisia

The Forest Lover

Life Studies

Luncheon of the Boating Party

Clara and Mr. Tiffany

What Love Sees

LISETTE'S LIST

LISETTE'S LIST

.

A Novel

SUSAN VREELAND

RANDOM HOUSE

NEW YORK

Copyright © 2014 by Susan Vreeland

All rights reserved.

Published in the United States by Random House,
an imprint and division of Random House LLC,
a Penguin Random House Company, New York.

RANDOM HOUSE and the HOUSE colophon
are registered trademarks of Random House LLC.

LIBRARY OF CONGRESS CATALOGING-IN-PUBLICATION DATA
Vreeland, Susan.
Lisette's list : a novel / Susan Vreeland.
pages cm
ISBN 978-1-4000-6817-3
eBook ISBN 978-0-8129-9685-2
1. Young women—Fiction. 2. Art—Psychological aspects—Fiction.
3. Provence (France)—Fiction. 4. France—History—German occupation,
1940–1945—Fiction. 5. World War, 1939–1945—France—Fiction. I. Title.
PS3572.R34L57 2014
813'.54—dc23
2014001952

Printed in the United States of America on acid-free paper

www.atrandom.com

2 4 6 8 9 7 5 3 1

FIRST EDITION

Book design by Barbara M. Bachman

FOR
Jane von Mehren

In our life there is a single color, as on an artist's palette, which provides the meaning of life and art. It is the color of love.

—MARC CHAGALL

BOOK I

ROAD TO ROUSSILLON

1937

AMID THE CROWD OF TRAVELERS DARTING IN FRONT OF THE Avignon train station, the delivery boys on ancient bicycles swerving between children and horse carts, and the automobile drivers honking their horns, André stood relaxed, eating an apple from a fruit stand. Meanwhile, I paced in a tight circle around our carpetbags, our valises, and our crates filled with everything we could take with us from our apartment in Paris, plus the tools from his workshop, plus the dream of my life sacrificed.

"Are you sure we're in the right place?" I asked.

"Yes, Lisette." André plucked a broad leaf off a nearby plane tree and laid it on a cobblestone. He touched my nose with his index finger and then pointed to the leaf. "He'll park right there. On that cobblestone. Just watch." He squeezed my hand. "In the south of France, things happen as they should."

But apparently in the south of France, buses didn't operate on schedule, as they did in Paris. Nor did the light have the same effect as it did there. Here, the light singed the eye, wrapped itself around edges, intensified colors, ignited the spine. If it were otherwise, I would not have recognized the loveliness in a bare square that was not Paris, but there it was—a shimmering watercolor of fathers and grandfathers sitting under the plane tree, their white shirts blued by the cornflower sky, which found openings in the foliage, the men eating almonds from a paper bag, passing it from one end of the bench to the other and back again, perhaps talking of better days. They looked content, sitting there, while I withdrew my hand from André's and made another senseless circuit around the modest pile of our belongings, feeling his gaze following me.

"Look at them," André said in a low voice. "All members of the Honorary Order of Beret Wearers." He chuckled at his own invention.

Eventually a boxy little bus, a faded relic once painted orange beneath its rust, sputtered to a stop, the right front wheel crushing the leaf on the cobblestone. André tipped his head and gave me an excusably smug but tender smile.

The stocky driver bounded down the steps, nimble-footed, pointing his toes outward as weighty people do to keep their balance. He hailed André by name, reached his thick arm up to slap him on the back, and said he was glad to see him.

"How's Pascal doing?" André asked.

"He gets around all right most days. Louise takes him his meals or he eats with us."

The driver bowed to me with exaggerated courtliness.

"Adieu, madame. I am Maurice, *un chevalier de Provence*. A knight of the roads. Not, however, Maurice Chevalier, who is a knight of the stage." He sent André a wink. "Your wife, she is more beautiful than Eleanor of Aquitaine."

Foolishness. I would not fall for it.

Had he said *Adieu*? *"Bonjour, monsieur,"* I responded properly.

I was amused by his attire—a red cravat above his undershirt, the only shirt he wore, which dipped in front to show his woolly chest; a red sash tied as a belt; his round head topped by a black beret. Black hair curled out from his armpits, a detail I could have done without noticing, but I am, thanks to Sister Marie Pierre, the noticing type.

He placed a hand over his fleshy bosom. "I deliver ladies in distress. *Enchanté,* madame."

I gave André a doleful look. I was in distress that very moment, already missing the life we had left behind.

"*Vite! Vite! Vite!*" The driver circled his arm around our bags in three quick movements, urging us to move quickly, quickly, quickly. "We leave in two minutes." Then he was gone.

"One *vite* was enough, don't you think?"

With a wry twist of his mouth, André said, "People in Provence speak robustly. They live robustly too. Especially Maurice." André began loading our bags and crates. "He's a good friend. I've known him ever since I was a boy, when Pascal used to take me to visit Roussillon."

"What's the red sash for?"

"It's a *taillole.* It signifies that he's a native son, a patriot of Provence."

We waited ten minutes. Two men took seats in the back of the bus. Soon I heard robust snoring.

Our self-proclaimed chevalier finally scurried back. "Sorry, sorry. I saw a friend," he said, working every feature of his round face, even his wide nostrils, into a smile of innocence, as though having seen a friend naturally justified the delay. He pumped up the tires with a hand pump—robustly, I observed—and started the engine, which choked in resistance, then lurched us ahead under the stone arch spanning the ramparts and out into the countryside to the east.

The road to Roussillon between two mountain ranges, the Monts de Vaucluse to the north and the Luberons to the south, kept me glued to the window. I had never been to the south of France.

"Stop here!" André ordered. The bus came to a shuddering stop and André hopped out, plucked a fistful of lavender growing wild along the roadside, climbed back in, and presented it to me. "To welcome you to Provence. I'm sorry it's not in its full purple bloom yet. In July you'll be astonished."

A sweet gesture, sweet as the fragrance itself.

"How far is it to this Roussillon place?" I asked the driver as we started down the road again.

"Forty-five beautiful kilometers, madame."

"Look. I think those are strawberry fields," André said. "You love strawberries."

"And melons," Maurice added with a nasal twang. "The best melons in France are grown right here in the valleys of the Vaucluse. And asparagus, lettuce, carrots, cabbages, celery, artichokes—"

"Yes, yes," I said. "I get the idea."

He would not be *yes-yessed*. "Spinach, peas, beets. On higher ground, our famous fruit trees, vineyards, and olive groves."

He pronounced every syllable, even the normally mute *e* at the ends of some words, which made the language into something energetic, decorated, and bouncy instead of smoothly gliding, as it is in Paris.

"Apricots. You love them too," André said. "You are entering the Garden of Eden."

"I see one snake and I'm taking the next train back to Paris."

I had to admit that the fruit trees, laden with spring blossoms, exuded a heavenly fragrance. The grapevines were sprouting small chartreuse leaves, wild red poppies decorated the roadside, and the sun promised warmth, so welcome after a frigid winter in Paris.

But to live here for God knows how long—I had more than misgivings. For me to surrender the possibility of becoming an apprentice in the Galerie Laforgue, the chance of a lifetime for a woman of twenty with no formal education, had already caused resentment to surface in me. When André had made what seemed an impulsive decision to leave Paris and live in a remote village just because his grandfather had appealed to him to keep him company in his failing health, I'd been shocked. That he would so easily abandon his position as an officer of the Guild of Encadreurs, the association of picture-frame craftsmen, a prestigious position for a man of twenty-three, was inconceivable to me.

I had gone crying to Sister Marie Pierre at the Daughters of Saint-Vincent-de-Paul, the orphanage where I had been raised, complaining that he was shortsighted and selfish, but she had given me little sympathy. "Judge not, Lisette. See him in the best light, not the worst," she'd said. And so here I was, bumping along in clouds of dust, despairing that I wasn't in Paris, city of my birth, my happiness, my soul.

Following Sister Marie Pierre's advice to try to see the situation in the best light, I ventured a possibility. "Tell me, monsieur. Does this town of yours have an art gallery?"

"A what?" he screeched.

"A place where original paintings are sold?"

He howled a laugh from his belly. "*Non,* madame. It is a *village.*"

His laughter cut deeply. My yearning for art was nothing casual or recent. Even when I was a little girl, this longing had been a palpable force every time I stole into the chapel of the Daughters of Saint-Vincent-de-Paul to look at the painting of the Madonna and Child. How a human being, not a god, could re-create reality so accurately, how the deep blue of her cloak and the rich red of her dress could put me, a young orphan without a sou to my name, in touch with all that was fine and noble, how such beauty could stir something in me so deep that it must have been what Sister Marie Pierre called soul—such things drenched me with wonder.

André jiggled my arm and pointed out a cluster of red geraniums spilling over the window box of a stone farmhouse. "Don't worry. You're going to like it here, *ma petite.*"

Because of geraniums?

"*Certainement,* she will," Maurice chimed in from behind the wheel. "Once she becomes accustomed to *les quatre vérités.*"

Four truths? "And what might they be, monsieur?"

"You see three of them right here." He took his arm off the steering wheel to wave vaguely at the countryside, apparently able to drive and listen and talk and gesture all at once. Presumably that was a skill of living robustly. "The mountains, the water, the sun."

True enough. The sunlight made the snow on the peak of a mountain to the north blindingly white. It shone on a river to the south in dancing specks of brilliance and turned the canals into iridescent silver-green ribbons.

"And what's the fourth, monsieur?"

"It can't be seen, and yet its mark is everywhere."

"A riddle. You're telling me a riddle."

"No, madame. I'm telling you a truth. André, he knows."

I turned to André, who tipped his head toward the window and said, "Think and look. Look and think."

I studied the landscape for some mark.

"Does it have to do with those stone walls?" They were actually only remnants of walls, piles of flat stones forming barriers nearly a meter thick, some with wayside niches for figures of saints, I presumed, although I hadn't seen any.

"No, madame. Those were built in the Middle Ages to keep out the plague."

"Not a comforting thought, monsieur. Neither is that scraping noise. Is there something wrong with your brakes?"

"No, madame. You are hearing the sound of *cigales*. Insects that make their mating calls when the temperature gets warm."

Definitely something I would have to get used to. Thickly planted cypress trees lined the north sides of the vegetable fields. Their pointed shadows stretched toward us like witches' gray fingers.

Looking from side to side, I noticed another peculiarity. "Why don't the houses on the right side have windows facing the road, while the ones on the left side do?"

"Now you're thinking. Look. They all have windows on three sides, but not on the north."

But why? Did the sun glare through north windows too strongly? No. It would shine from the south, giving light to only half of the house. The other half would be dark and gloomy.

When I asked André for a hint, he told me to look at the roofs. They were terra-cotta tiles, long, tubular, and overlapping. Flat stones had been placed at their northern edges.

"Wind!" I shouted.

The snorer in the back of the bus woke up with a snort.

"The mistral," Maurice intoned in a deep voice. "Dry but cold. Oh, the mistral, it is fierce, madame. It comes three days at a time, in winter. Sometimes six. Sometimes nine."

"Don't delude her. It comes in the fall and spring too."

"That's almost all year!" I wailed.

Maurice explained that the highest mountain to the north was the southernmost mountain of the Alps. The mistral winds tore south out of Siberia, then leapt over the Alps to Mont Ventoux, which he called the Giant of Provence, and then arrived here.

"Windy Mountain is its actual name?"

"Yes. Now you'll notice that the olive trees bend to the south."

We passed several vegetable fields being tended. "Old farmers bend to the south too," I remarked.

I could always stay inside for three days, couldn't I? But what about nine? Despite my good intentions to be a compliant wife, reasons I would not like this place arranged themselves in a private list:

1.   Cold wind for nine days straight.
2.   Half of the house always in darkness.
3.   It wasn't Paris.

The two men in the back of the bus got off in the town of Coustellet. Soon after, the pavement ended, and an old woman at the roadside in front of a farmhouse waved both arms urgently.

"Ah, my first lady in distress!" Maurice brought the bus to a bumpy halt and scrambled down the steps to help her up. "Adieu, madame."

"*Non, non,* Maurice. I'm not getting on," she said. "Just take my duck and deliver it to Madame Pottier in les Imberts. She will be waiting by her olive tree."

"What duck?"

"You have to catch him first," she said.

The pen had a chicken-wire covering, so Maurice had to crouch down to waddle after the creature. He did his best to avoid muddy areas and splats of duck droppings, his thick arms stretching out to both sides, his stubby legs spread wide, his heels close together like a circus clown's. Getting red in the face, waving his beret to shoo the duck into a corner, he crooned, "Come to Papa."

André leapt off the bus to help him. With André barring any escape, Maurice flopped his body onto the duck, which caused a desperate quacking beneath his stomach until the angry duck squirmed its way out, right into André's waiting hands.

The farmwife deftly tied the duck's wings against its body and wrapped the twine around its two feet. André put the bewildered duck into the bus, whereupon it fell over. André righted it and said, "Enjoy the ride. Lovely scenery."

Maurice tied the other end of the twine to a seat leg and bopped the poor duck on the head with his index finger. "You are going into the oven, so accept your fate like a man," he told it.

The duck quacked.

"You've insulted him," I said.

Maurice corrected himself. "Er, like a duck."

Down the road, a matronly woman wearing an apron and a white kerchief hailed us.

"There's your second lady in distress," André said.

Maurice brought the bus to a halt and opened the door. "Adieu, madame. At your service." He handed her the duck through the open door.

She took it in both hands. "This fellow's going to be *pâté de canard* in a few days. I'll save you some. Does your wife still want the feathers?"

"Yes. For a pillow. Adieu, madame."

And the bus bounced back into action.

"Why do you greet someone with *adieu* instead of *bonjour*?" I asked.

He shrugged. "Think of 'à Dieu,' madame. It's the Provençal way to wish a person to be with God when you meet him as well as when you leave him."

A satisfactory answer, although I suspected that other Provençal ways were backward as well.

We stopped for a girl who was crossing the road while flicking a willow wand at half a dozen goats, then for an old man who was piling broken-off branches into his donkey cart—picturesque enough for a painting.

The road climbed steeply on switchbacks through terraces of orchards. Maurice identified the trees as pear trees. That sent me back to the painting of the Madonna in the chapel of the orphanage. A golden pear rested by itself on a railing in the foreground. Countless times I had asked Sister Marie Pierre why it was there, but she'd never answered me. All she said was to love the Virgin Mary and I wouldn't miss the mother I barely remembered. Her response never satisfied me. As I grew older I recognized that Mary was wrapped in her own thoughts, unconscious of the child she was holding, an assessment that may have had more to do with my mother's abandonment of me than with what the artist had intended to portray.

It was only a copy, but it was by an Italian named Giovanni Bellini, which made it all the more exotic. The chapel had only one painting. That was enough for me, then.

Maurice's voice swearing an oath as he ground the gears brought me out of my reverie. Just below a hill town topped by a castle and a church, he set the brake.

"Roussillon?"

"Gordes," he corrected. "I have to make a delivery here."

I looked around inside the bus. "What do you have to deliver?"

"Pastis. From the glass to my throat. It is the first *apéritif* hour. Come. I will initiate you, madame."

We picked our way up a long, uneven stone stairway to a café in the square. Maurice greeted the people he knew with more *adieu*s and ordered a pastis for each of us. The tall slim glasses held only a couple of centimeters of clear liquid, a disappointment until Maurice poured water into his glass, which turned the pastis cloudy.

André prepared my drink along with his. "Ah," he murmured. "One of the pleasures of the south. I've been waiting for this."

"*Santé.*" Maurice held up his glass and took a drink, then carefully wiped his trimmed mustache and the short whiskers of his white goatee, which, oddly, didn't match his bushy black eyebrows.

"I like the aroma." I took a sip, then another, then a gulp.

"It pleases you?" He raised his eyebrows. "The mix of anise and other herbs?"

"Very nice."

"Beware, Lise," André said. "It creeps up on you. Pour in more water if you feel . . ." He swiveled his hand in a circle.

"To suit yourself and the weather," Maurice said. "A true Provençal drink."

"And you are a true Provençal chevalier, monsieur. But please, tell me your surname."

"Chevet, madame." He put his hand out palm down about a meter above the floor. "*Un petit chevalier,*" he said, chuckling at his own joke.

As we descended the long stretch of stone steps to the bus, I felt pleasantly dizzy.

"Hold on to her, André. The steps can be treacherous."

"I am. I will never let her go."

"Your grandfather Pascal, he will be furious with me if I deliver her to Roussillon with a sprained ankle. When my friends learn

that I have brought a *Parisienne* to live in Roussillon—*oh là là!*—
they will be so proud. But I wonder. Can a *Parisienne* ever become
a *Roussillonnaise?*"

Would any *Parisienne* ever want to?

"Depends on how much we love her," André said as we boarded
the bus.

"Me, I love her already!" Maurice declared.

"You are too kind, monsieur. Is this town of yours nearby?" I
asked.

"Just down and up. Look for a sickle stuck in a fence post."

We had bounced along for a kilometer or so when I noticed a
curious-looking group of stone huts in the shape of beehives. "I
hope *that*'s not Roussillon." I giggled. "Is it?"

"No, madame. They are only bories. They're scattered all over
the Vaucluse. Some say the older ones were built a thousand years
before Christ. Others say two. Because these are more intact than
ruins elsewhere, we think they are more recent."

Eventually I saw the sickle protruding out of a post like a giant
comma. "What is it doing there?"

"Waiting for its owner, who left it there a few years ago."

"A very patient sickle. More patient than I am."

That wasn't quite right. It wasn't impatience I felt. It was dis-
may. All I might be able to see would be folk artists who carved
ducks at country fairs. I turned to André. "How are we going to
survive in a town without a gallery?"

"I can do other work."

"I didn't mean *survive* that way."

"But, Lise, you'll be *living* in a gallery. Pascal's seven paintings."

I had never seen them. Pascal had left Paris and had moved back
to Roussillon before I met André. All I had heard was stories. Would
these paintings be enough to compensate for the pleasure of working in a Paris gallery someday? I could feel that dream shrinking to
a crevice of a shop in this village: LISETTE'S DUCK FEATHER PILLOWS
AND PÂTÉ. Meanwhile, Monsieur Laforgue would train someone

else as an assistant while I would be stuck here taking care of an old man I didn't even know.

André grew quiet and restless. I placed my hand on his thigh.

"Pascal made a train for me when I was a very little boy," André murmured. "Out of wood, it was. I learned to count with that train. As he made each new wagon, he taught me a new number. He carved the numbers on the wagons. He'll remember that. He has an incredible memory."

"That's a lovely story."

After a period of silence, he said, "I just hope he hasn't lost his spirit."

I reached for his hand. "I do too, dear."

Soon I saw in the distance what André had described—a village of yellow-ochre, coral, rose, and salmon perched atop a mountain and skirted by deep green pine forest, houses all in harmonious warm colors stepping up to the summit like a pyramid of blocks, as if inhabited by fairy godmothers, tale-telling godfathers, and elfin children. Below it, in the same colors, rutted cliffs and warty-fingered pinnacles gave it support, altogether like some fantasy kingdom from a child's folk legend, altogether dazzling.

"*Voilà, madame!*" Maurice announced. "There you see it—the village of Roussillon, queen of the *commune de Roussillon, canton de Gordes, arrondissement d'Apt, département du Vaucluse, région de Provence, nation de France*"—all of this delivered with the pride of a patriot. I felt his spirit beguiling me.

I chuckled. "Pascal certainly chose a hard place to get to."

"Three hundred meters up," Maurice said. "He didn't choose it. He was born here. Just like me. Who would have guessed when we took up our fathers' pickaxes and went to work in the ochre mine that he would become *un amateur d'art,* a devoted lover of paint-ings, and would bring home a collection. From Paris, no less." He shook his head in amazement. "That Pascal. But no matter all the great things he's seen in Paris, I can still make him bite the dust at *boules.*"

André laughed. "He says the same about you."

As for a list of what I *would* like in Roussillon, I was sure of only two items so far: Maurice and pastis.

"Ah, yes, dear madame. I suppose there is one more truth beyond *les quatre vérités*. Love. We struggle, we complain, we grumble, but we love, more fiercely than the mistral blows. You'll see."

CHAPTER TWO

THIS VILLAGE,
THIS MAN

1937

MAURICE PARKED THE BUS IN THE LOWER PART OF ROUS-sillon, in a tree-shaded square he called place du Pas-quier, at the edge of a cliff. He insisted that we stroll through the village for my first glimpse of it, saying he would deliver the crates later.

I had to squint in the brightness that bounced off the buildings as we walked up the incline of the main street—or was it the only street?—and passed a humble post office, a *boulangerie* sending out the homey aroma of fresh bread, a small *épicerie* offering a smattering of groceries, and a *boucherie,* where a lamb rump covered with flies and a spread-eagled calf with a red rose planted impishly in its anus hung in the window. A blacksmith clanged away at his anvil, his open-air shop tucked tightly between houses. I held my breath until we passed, hoping that André wouldn't say that one of those houses was Pascal's.

An upper square bore a sign identifying it as place de la Mairie, and indeed, a mildly imposing stone-and-stucco building looking very much like a town hall did have the word MAIRIE carved in its lintel. Next to it, people sat outside a café. Beyond that, *grâce à Dieu,* a hair salon. Opposite it a water faucet dripped into a large shell-shaped stone bowl attached to a building. Was that where the hairdresser washed hair? Farther up the street, a belfry stood alongside an impressive Gothic arch of honey-colored stone.

An upper and a lower road continued onward from the arch into a residential area. What we had passed was apparently all there was to the village center.

André directed me to take the upper road. "It's called rue de la Porte Heureuse."

Street of the Happy Door. "Sounds cheerful," I remarked, but I was afraid my voice revealed otherwise.

The array of houses smoothly stuccoed in the ochre colors of the bright Roussillon earth and accented by vivid blue shutters and window frames and ruby oleanders leapt straight out at me, as if from a Van Gogh painting. Houses had their doors right on the street, some draped with ivy or grapevines. One doorframe was garlanded with green beans. How convenient. From the vine to the cook pot in two seconds.

Pascal's house was a two-story dwelling of cracked rosy ochre stucco. There were no windows that I could see. Apparently this was the north side. A sparse vine crept over the doorway, and a jardiniere surrounded by a fringe of weeds held a withered lavender plant. The door was unlocked, so we entered, and André called, "Pascal?"

No one answered.

Paintings surrounded me. I whistled out my astonishment, counting seven paintings in this isolated village!

A plain little one of a simple building in the countryside hung between two windows opposite the front door. Behind me, on the wall without windows, four landscapes hung in a row. On the left, a panorama of fields with a bridge in the distance and a mountain beyond, then a girl with a goat on a yellow path, then autumn trees with red-orange leaves in front of houses, and on the far right, a pile of large, squared-off rocks in front of a mountain. Puzzling. To the right of the stairway, a still life with fruits, and to the left—oh, *mon Dieu*! Bodiless heads with noses flattened to the side, dark lines around the eyes, mouths only black slits. Spooky.

"What's *that*?" I cried.

"Pascal?" André called.

"That one looks like it was painted by an angry child."

I caught only a glimpse of the paintings because André pulled me upstairs, again calling, "Pascal?"

The two bedrooms were both empty, although one bed appeared to have been slept in.

"Where could he be?" I asked. I had expected him to be moaning beneath a quilt.

André headed downstairs, toward the door, to search for him. I held him back. "I have to pee."

His face looked ashen. "We don't have a toilet."

"No toilet! What do you mean? What do you expect me to do?"

"We'll get a nice chamber pot for our bedroom," he offered with a grimace. "We'll toss the contents over the cliff. Or you can use a public toilet. There's one to the left of place de la Mairie beyond the water faucet, near the *boules* court."

"And I have to live like this? You didn't *tell* me!"

Now I really *was* a lady in distress. I nearly ran downhill, with André trotting close behind, exasperation at this situation exploding in my mind. To be confined in a village a day and a half from Paris; to stay indoors for nine days at a stretch, a prisoner in my own house while the wind usurped my freedom, going wherever *it* wanted, blowing everything to smithereens; to live in such a backward place that they said goodbye when they meant hello; to forgo window-shopping, cabaret hopping, gallery gazing; to become stale of fashion, destitute of culture, starved for art; to have my dream postponed, my ambition annihilated, my soul shriveled; and as if those circumstances weren't enough, to be forced to advertise my private bodily functions by clattering downhill at breakneck speed before an embarrassing public catastrophe overtook me, to reach a public toilet conveniently situated—by men, no doubt—

adjacent to the *boules* court: *Adieu, monsieurs, pay me no mind, I'm just going to pee.*

From the street, the outhouse looked clean enough, a lovely urine-ochre stucco, but inside I found only a hole in the cement and a raw beam about knee height over which I was supposed to hang my derrière. Even at the orphanage of the Daughters of Charity, we'd had porcelain toilets with oval wooden seats, and they were flushed from a water box mounted on the wall.

When I came out and faced the spectators in the *boules* court, I could do no more than greet them with a witless smile, then give André a look that conveyed unmistakably the impossibility of the situation.

"Oh, André" was all I could manage.

"I'll build you a toilet. Don't worry."

He turned to the *boules* court, where a man flung a fist-sized steel ball.

"Pascal!" André shouted.

"Ah, quelle surprise! Adieu! Adieu!" cried a man whose wrinkled trousers and shirt matched his wrinkled skin. Seeing me, he slapped his hand on his head, on a worn yellowed chamois cap with a narrow rolled brim that sat on his skull like a second skin.

He held his arms out wide. "So this is the legendary Lisette. André, you should be ashamed. She is far more beautiful than you led me to believe."

Pascal kissed me on my cheeks three times, once more than was customary in Paris, his drooping mustache scratching away at me.

When he approached André to do the same, André grasped him by the shoulders with a quick shake. "What in the world are you doing out here? Are you crazy? You should be in bed!"

"I didn't know when you would come. Or *if* you would come. Ah, but I'm so glad you are here."

"Playing *boules*! You write that you see death lurking around the corner, and you plead for us to come and take care of you in your last days, so we pack up everything, let our apartment go, abandon my position in the guild and my thriving business with nine steady painters, pry my wife away from Paris for some isolated village she knows she won't like—all because you say you're dying. And here we find you playing *boules*!"

"Oh, please, André. Don't be angry." He clasped his palms together in front of his chest and shook them as a beggar would.

"What do you expect me to be?"

"I just wanted so much to have you here with me."

He whined the words and made such a piteous face that it was almost humorous, except for the fact that it was dire. We had made a grave mistake, throwing away our future for an old man's fancy. It wasn't likely that the guild would reinstall André as an officer. The position would have already gone to someone else. The same with my hoped-for gallery apprenticeship. If Pascal didn't feel sick, I certainly did.

"Besides, how could an old man like me get my wood in for winter? Do you want me to freeze to death?"

"I'm of a mind to turn right around and go back. Lisette would love that."

"*Non, non, non.* I *am* sick. I only play every other day."

"You're sick every other day?" André's voice thundered, harsh and accusatory.

"Some days I am only *un peu fatigué,* a little tired. Other days I am *fatigué.* Then I stay in bed. On my worst days, I am *bien fatigué* and . . . and frightened." He crossed his arms over his chest and hunched his shoulders. "Would you much rather have found me on such a day? That's when I wrote you. Today I am"—he held up his index finger and thumb a centimeter apart—"*un peu fatigué.*"

"So you rest every other day," I offered.

"See? She understands. I don't play *boules* when I am *fatigué.* But sometimes, after I rest all day, I get out of bed to play just one hand of *belote* in the café. Some days two."

"You've done a deceitful thing, *Grandpère.*"

"Please, please don't be upset with me." His forehead contorted with the pain of contrition. "It's shameful for an old man to have his grandson be angry with him."

Despite my own frustration, I agreed. André and Pascal were each other's only living blood relative. Pascal had lost his wife two years before I met André, whose own mother had died in childbirth. Pascal's only son, Jules, was killed in the Great War when André was six. So there was a missing generation, which made the two of them very close. Pascal and his wife had raised André in Paris, and Pascal had taught him his trade. Even though I didn't know this man, and as angry as I was, I hated to see André berate him so.

A tall, wiry player with a wide dragoon's mustache approached us at the edge of the *terrain de boules*. "Excuse me, Pascal, but it's your turn."

"In a moment, Aimé. This is my family, come from Paris to live with me." He turned back to André, and the man withdrew. "We'll talk about it tonight, and you'll see. Everything will be all right, eh?" He held out both hands to me. "Lisette, you look fresh as a new lily after a long ride. You'll be happy here, I promise."

"Pascal!" shouted Raoul, a player wearing a farmer's straw hat.

"I am obliged," Pascal said with a slight bow to us. "Just one turn, and we'll be finished."

He swaggered over to the dirt court with surprising energy.

"I'm sorry, Lisette. I didn't expect this." André crossed his arms, made a fist, and battered at his chin with it.

Despite what was most on our minds, André's attention was being drawn into the game. Pascal and his teammates, Aimé and the farmer, Raoul, circled the playing field, studying the position of eleven—I counted—steel balls and one smaller cork ball.

"*Alors*, point or fire?" Aimé asked Pascal.

André explained. "Each team tries to get its *boules* closer to the cork ball than the other team's closest *boule*. Point means to roll a *boule* directly at the cork. Fire means to throw a *boule* at a *boule* of the other team in order to knock it away from the cork. Or you can fire at the cork, to knock it away from a *boule* of the other team, or to knock it closer to a *boule* of your team."

"Fire," Pascal said. "Definitely."

"You're a fool!" said the farmer. "It's too far."

There erupted a heated argument among players and spectators as to how he should play his turn, some contending for pointing, others for firing, citing the pebbles on the court, the slope of the ground, the inaccuracy of Pascal's aim, the strength or weakness of his arm, the unsteadiness of his balance. Some resorted to name-calling. His teammate Aimé pretended to throw a *boule,* trotting with his arm arced above his head to show the route of the ball in the air, advising some backspin, pointing along the ground to the cork. Everyone shouted robustly, agreeing there was no safe way to play it, everyone definitely having a fine time.

Raoul began to sweep the pebbles away with his boot, which brought an outcry of "Against the rules!" The other team rushed in to put the pebbles back, and the argument exploded again as to their exact places.

"Forget the stones," Pascal called. "I'm going to fire."

"Bon Dieu," André whispered to me with a tinge of disgust. "He's trying to show off for you, to win us over."

How endearing, an old man trying to impress me with his skill.

"Tell him to point it, Aimé," an opposing team member said. "You know he's afraid to fire."

"You don't know what you're talking about," Pascal grumbled. He chewed on his mustache with his yellowed bottom teeth. "All right. Have it your way. I'll point it!"

"A safer shot," André said to me, "but he got credit for wanting to risk firing. It's all strategy, bluster, and drama."

Everyone was respectfully silent. I held my breath, wanting the old man to win the point. His knees cracked as he bent to play the shot. His *boule* landed at the spot where Aimé had pointed, rolled toward the cork, but it hit a stone and veered left, coming to rest a meter away. I felt betrayed by a pebble.

The other team had won the game and the tournament. There was no cheering, no animated analysis. Oddly, the other team and the spectators turned to head for the café in near silence.

"I should have fired it like I wanted to," Pascal muttered.

"Don't go blaming us," Aimé said. "If you had fired, you would have missed for sure."

"Set them up again," Pascal said. "I bet you a packet of cigarettes I can do it."

The entire procession came to a halt and turned back toward Pascal.

Aimé placed his *boule* where Raoul's had been, and the farmer placed the cork where it had been. Pascal threw high, his arm gracefully suspended in the air long after his *boule* left his hand. The ball spun like a silver planet and landed like a meteor, knocking Aimé's *boule* away with a clunk and settling right next to the cork, as he had claimed it would.

"Just like two peas in a pod," he said with smug self-satisfaction, to which no spectator responded, no hand slapped his back in congratulation, no applause hung in the air, except my own robust clapping.

Only Aimé said quietly, earnestly, "*Formidable,* old man."

A surprising streak of pride rioted within me. "Bravo, Pascal."

"It *was* just one turn," he said sheepishly. "*Eh bien, ma minette douce,* you are here at last." Trying to make peace by calling me a charming kitten, he offered me his arm, and we began trudging uphill toward home, his breathing labored as he leaned against my shoulder.

CHAPTER THREE

THE PARIS
WE KNEW

1937

"WE'LL GO TO THE MEDITERRANEAN SEA AFTER THIS IS over," André whispered against the pillow that first night in Roussillon.

But for now, what? Was I to wish that Pascal would die soon so that we could go on holiday and then restart our lovely life in Paris? How unconscionable to think that. I nestled closer to André's chest so he wouldn't read that very thought on my face.

"I can imagine it," I said. "So vast, the sea so clear at my feet, so richly dark farther out. The lustrous blue as exotic as the peacocks' necks in the Jardin des Plantes."

He knew what I was thinking: No public gardens in this scrap of a village. No opera. No cabarets. No jazz at La Coupole. No Folies Bergère. No dance bands like Ray Ventura's. No cinema. No street musicians. No Guignol puppet shows. No department stores. No sculptures. And not a single gallery. I would wither away.

"The moonlight coming in the window makes your skin glow like pearls." He was trying with all his might to diminish my despair. "My Lise. *Fleur-de-lis de la mer,* with wet hair clinging to two sea-glazed nipples. That's what you'll be. A water nymph. A dark-haired beauty. A Cleopatra. A Greek siren. You'll sing to me, and I will forever adore you."

And I did feel supremely adored, and I adored him in return. But when he had fallen asleep, and the village fell silent except for the occasional hoot of an owl, I thought of what we could be doing if we were still in Paris.

We could be lingering along the shadowy quay below the Conciergerie on Île de la Cité among loving couples cooing in soft voices in a circle of yellow lamplight. Or we could be taking one of our favorite promenades, up to Montmartre to see the spread of rooftops from the vantage point of Sacré-Coeur.

Once, early in our friendship, before we had so much as touched hands, he insisted that I ride the carousel in place des Abbesses in lower Montmartre. Afterward, he lifted me off the platform and swung me around until I was so dizzy I had to hold on to him. His grin told me he had planned it. Then we took the funicular up to place du Tertre, the high square on Montmartre where artists sold small paintings to tourists and where there was always accordion music. André gallantly paid a man to cut out a silhouette of me in black paper laid on white. "A treasure," André had said, "deserving of my most elegant frame."

I especially loved our Saturday morning gallery tours to see new paintings hanging in André's carved frames. He felt no more proud than I did when we spotted one. By making beautiful paintings even more beautiful, he contributed to the rich world of art in Paris, and as his wife, I basked in the glory he created.

On Sundays we often went to the Bois de Boulogne and took out a rowboat to commemorate a certain Sunday afternoon in the summer of 1935. We had been rowing in the upper lake that day, and I happened to mention that the park had once been the hunting grounds of kings, while he said it was a promenade for queens.

"You are the queen of my heart. Lise, *la reine de mon coeur,*" he had said in a liquid voice as he rowed slowly. "Will you be my queen for life?"

"Yes," I said. "Yes, I will. Yes."

I hadn't considered it a serious promise of marriage, only a flirtation, but, acting quickly, André told me he loved me on the point of Île de la Cité, proposed formally on Pont Neuf, and by year's end we were married under the dome of Église Saint-Vincent-de-Paul in the motherhouse of Daughters of Charity, although he would have been happier with just a civil ceremony conducted by a magistrate. I was eighteen and in love.

He was a romantic as much as I, which showed itself when we took our walks. The first time we'd passed by a *confiserie* and smelled the almond and vanilla candies, I had tugged on André's arm to stop and look at the brightly colored marzipans laid out in neat rows. Little apples, green with red streaks; strawberries with flecks of black; peaches with candied skins blending golden yellow to orange to deep rose at the stem. Miniature works of art they were. André had just sold an expensive frame carved with interlocking arabesques, so he tried to guess which piece I would like in order to buy it for me. Cherry, he had said, but I chose a peach, just to tease him, laughing that I had fooled him. He called me Lise, my precious peach. Lise, the strawberry of my heart. Lise, the succulent melon of my life. Lise of the lavender eyes. Lise with skin like blushing ivory. Lise, my own true love, my life. Hearing him say extravagant things like that as we walked along holding hands made me feel that I was the luckiest girl in Paris.

That's what you did in Paris. You walked and you looked and you posed for the other people looking, and you pretended not to hear their conversations, and it was all a pageant of color and laughter. And through all this walking and looking, I heard Sister Marie Pierre calling after me as I left the orphanage, "Find some beauty along the way. Tell me in picture words."

Nibbling that marzipan, we walked until our feet ached, then stopped at a *pâtisserie* and had a *café crème* and shared a *palmier,* a flat, flaky leaf-shaped pastry drizzled with caramel. All over Paris, lovers fed morsels to each other, just as we did.

We often arranged to meet Maxime Legrand, André's good friend, the art dealer who had asked his employer, Monsieur Laforgue, to consider taking me on as an apprentice. Whenever André and Maxime were together, they were exuberant, gesturing in broad arcs, Maxime taking stairs two at a time, long-legged André taking three. They fed each other's spontaneity, bowed to old women, called them a breath of spring, danced in the streets with little girls, and sang Maurice Chevalier's "Louise" or "Valentine" while their mothers beamed.

In summer we three often sat outside at Café de la Rotonde to watch the parade of people. André and Maxime wore straw *canotiers,* and Maxime sported a white carnation in his buttonhole and striped trousers and white spats. But in winter we met him in the Closerie des Lilas, where it was warm and where the Montparnasse painters came to have a *café* and talk about each other's work.

Coming inside all smiles one afternoon in his beaver-collared overcoat, Maxime exuded an infinitude of charm—*infinitude,* a word I learned from Sister Marie Pierre. She loved teaching me words, and I liked to surprise André and Maxime with them, so that day I said, "I am experiencing an infinitude of elation in your presence," and then giggled at my affectation. On hearing cups and saucers being stacked by waiters, I said, "Listen to the infinitude of clamoring." She had also taught me to describe things by calling them something else, so I told them that the voices I heard singing in Notre Dame were "a brotherhood of seraphim," which delighted them both.

Maxime discreetly tipped his head toward some painter at a distant table and whispered, "Fernand Léger." When no one was within earshot, Maxime spun a tale of a wealthy art buyer assessing Léger's paintings in the Galerie Laforgue, where, as Monsieur Laforgue's protégé, he was learning how to praise a certain passage of painted light, or a strong, unifying diagonal, or an inventive composition. Maxime dropped casual comments about this rising star or that, and who was buying what, and how much the buyer had paid, and how one particular painting, newly arrived from the painter's studio, though a few centimeters smaller, was more exquisite in a number of ways, a vastly superior purchase to a larger canvas. I lapped up his stories like a starving cat.

"Why don't you ever have a lady friend with you?" I asked.

"I would be forced to ignore her in your presence. My devotion to you is a million times stronger."

I threw my shoulders back, sucked in my stomach, and laughed at his exaggeration, tossing it off as though it were a fallen leaf, yet all the while waiting for his next murmur of flattery, hoping for a private glance that would say he meant it. This easy talk, in a way, I think, charmed André as much as it did me.

"It's a good thing André is taking you away from Paris," Maxime said the last time the three of us met before our departure. "I would have pestered you until it became dangerous."

I knew beyond any doubt that he was only half teasing.

But I was André's. From the first time I saw him, I was his. He had found me on boulevard Saint-Germain at rue de Seine as I was hurrying home from picking up an herbal remedy for Sister Marie Pierre at the *boutique d'herboriste*. I was drenched with rain, and he held his umbrella over me. I took sly, sideways glances at his profile—his long neck, angled jaw, and dark brown eyes, whose mysteries I could not decipher, though I learned his name: André Honoré Roux. We walked the lengths of a few streets together, and when he had to turn onto rue des Saints-Pères and I had to continue straight toward rue du Bac, he wrapped my fingers around the handle and, with a blithe *"Enchanté, mademoiselle,"* turned the corner and was gone.

The next day my search for the tall stranger in the streets of Saint-Germain-des-Prés began.

CHAPTER FOUR

PASCAL'S
NEGOTIATION

1937, 1874

THE MORNING AFTER WE ARRIVED, ANDRÉ AND I WERE awakened by roosters, the first morning in my life that I had ever heard their raucous cackle. Apparently the roosters of Roussillon had a robust language too. We left Pascal snoring in rhythm with the roosters and with the *cigales'* scraping calls, harsher than a chirp, maddening in their incessant repetition.

André peered down a side street. "A sawmill. That's good. I'll need lumber to build sawhorses and a plywood work table."

I gave him an apprehensive look. Who would buy a frame in a village that had no gallery?

In the *boulangerie,* a middle-aged proprietress who introduced herself as Odette wore a white daisy in her hair and a beauty mark made by twisting the point of an eyebrow pencil on her right cheekbone, a practice five years out of date.

"So Pascal prevailed upon you to come. This must be—"

"Lisette. My lovely, lovable, smart, spirited—"

"André, stop. You're embarrassing me."

"Wife."

Looking me over, she said, "Your *Parisian* wife." She shouted into the kitchen, "René, come take a look at André's wife."

Superb. What was I? A department store mannequin?

His cheeks and hands dusted with flour, the baker poked his head through the doorway, greeted us, and disappeared.

As a gesture of welcome, Odette refused payment for the two baguettes we wanted, something that would never happen in Paris.

At home we found Pascal sitting at the table in the *salle,* which served as living room, dining room, and kitchen, his elbows on the oilcloth in a posture of despair. He apologized again and said for the sixth time how happy he was that we had come.

André merely said, "We know" and left to go to the sawmill.

I looked for a place to sit and realized that there were no cushioned armchairs, only a bare wooden settee that demanded erect posture, a backless bench pushed against a wall, and four ladder-back chairs at the table. It would be a long time before I could make cushions if I had to wait for every duck in the countryside to be caught by Maurice and plucked for its feathers.

"All the years that you grew up here, no one thought to put cushions on the chairs?" I asked.

He shook his head in the most dejected manner. "We *Roussillonnais* do not care much about comfort of the buttocks."

"Where do people go to buy things?" I asked to distract him from my rudeness.

"There's a big Saturday market in Apt, eleven kilometers from here, and we have our own smaller one on Thursdays."

He pointed to a pine cabinet fastened to the wall near the sink, which had a drain but no water faucet. The cabinet had ornamental openwork to allow air passage and elaborately carved double doors.

"It's a *panetière,* for bread, one of our traditional crafts in Provence. My uncle and I made it for my mother. I remember she said, '*Poésie bien provençale,*' which I took to mean poetry in wood, a high compliment. I must have been fifteen, but that made me feel like a man. I've made others too."

"It's lovely." I opened the doors and put the second baguette inside.

"We made that piece of furniture under it, too. It's a *pétrin*, for kneading the dough."

I stroked the rough wood marred by years of use as a cutting board as well. How long would it take for him to realize that I would never use it for kneading dough when there was a bakery here?

"I hope you will like living with the paintings."

"*That* I definitely will."

I walked from one to another hanging in a row on the north wall and stopped at each one, pretending I was in a gallery. Maxime had only just begun to instruct me in how to look at a painting. I had been overwhelmed by what there was to learn. Nevertheless, in front of a broad panorama of tilled fields with a distant mountain, I gathered the courage to ask, "Cézanne?"

Pascal grinned and nodded.

I was elated. In front of a soft-colored country scene with a girl in blue and a goat, I ventured, "Monet?"

"Pissarro," he corrected.

I sank into inadequacy.

Before a grouping of red-roofed houses seen through autumn trees, I guessed, "Either Monet or Sisley or Pissarro again."

"Pissarro."

Standing before the next one, I had no idea what painter would paint flat slabs of rock. "Who?" I had to ask.

"Cézanne. It's a quarry."

Beside the stairway hung a still life of fruit. "Oh, this could be anyone. Manet?"

He shook his head.

"Gauguin?"

He shook his head again.

"Fantin-Latour?" I felt proud to name a lesser-known artist.

"*Non.*"

"Renoir."

"*Non encore.*"

"Then it must be Cézanne."

"You're right! It can't be anybody else."

"But that awful one. Who would paint faces without bodies?"

He shrugged and held out his arm for me to come to him. In a plaintive voice he asked, "Do you want to know the real reason I wrote that desperate letter to André?"

"Yes, I most certainly do."

"I want to tell you and André everything about these paintings and the men who created them while I still have time, while I can still remember. I've been afraid I would forget if I waited"—he broke off for a few moments before he added—"until the end. I want you to understand how important they are so you will care for them. Those painters used the ochres we mine here."

"Were you a miner? With Maurice?"

"When I was young and spry."

"You were pretty spry yesterday, lunging to toss that *boule*."

"It's the getting up that's hard. I am not strong. Then I was strong. Going down into the mine at daybreak and working until nightfall, never feeling the sun on my face, damp to my bones, coughing all the time—what kind of a life was that? I begged to be allowed to work in the ochre drying beds as a washer, like I had done as a child. A child, Lisette. Fourteen years old. The *chef des opérations* wouldn't hear of it. I had to put in more time in the mine before he moved me to the factory furnaces. They weren't much better. We breathed dust and got so covered with ochre powder that it lodged in our pores. Walking home with our lunch tins, we looked like the ochre pinnacles in the canyons. I couldn't accept that I had been put on earth for that."

"So how did you get out of it?"

"I was young and brash and full of big ideas. I bragged that I could double the sales of our pigments in Paris by making calls on art supply stores. I had this crazy notion that they would buy more from a true *Roussillonnais* who had dug the ores with a pickax." Here Pascal chuckled. "I kept pestering the *chef* until he relented, saying that I was a thorn in his side.

"It wasn't long before I knew which color suppliers still sold powdered pigments for artists to mix into paint, and which dealers sold only oil paint in tubes. Julien Tanguy sold both."

"But how did you become a frame maker?"

"That happened in Julien's shop. He was a pudgy little man with one eye much larger than the other, homely but amusing. I liked him because he was a provincial too, from Brittany, and wore a straw farmer's hat. I appreciated his politics. He had been a Communard, had gone to prison for it. Artists adored him. They called him Père Tanguy because he slipped tubes of paint into the satchels of the poor ones whose talents he believed in when his eagle-eyed wife wasn't looking. And he hung their paintings on his walls to try to sell them in his shop. He's gone now, of course, but that shop still bears his name."

"I remember it. On rue Clauzel. It's bright blue."

"When I came through the doorway to his shop once, the little bell rang merrily, but I saw a sobering sight—a grown man, bearded, wearing a worn suit of black, weeping. No sound, but his eyes were soaked with sorrow. He was telling Tanguy how he and his wife had just buried their young daughter. Her name was Jeanne, my mother's name. Amazing that a person can remember such a little thing."

"How old were you?"

He thought a while and scratched his bald spot, round as a monk's tonsure. "I've got to write these things down. There's so much to tell you. It must have been around 1874 or 1875, whatever was the year of the first Impressionist exposition, so I would have been twenty-two or so. What a marvelous time to be young and in Paris."

Pascal seemed to retreat from the present moment. I thought he had finished, so I stood to wash the dishes. His hand shot out to stay me.

"I'll never forget the way the painter's clasped hands shook, so full of anguish he was. 'Such a thing,' the man mutters, 'just before our first big exposition. I need frames. I can't hang my pictures without frames. That would disgrace my friends' paintings.'"

I could tell by the softening of his voice that Pascal had stepped into the past with both feet. He told how a painting leaning against a cabinet had caught his eye.

"It was that one." He looked at it hanging in the row of four. Cottages, a vegetable garden, a girl and a goat on a path going up a hill and around a bend. "It struck me then. The path was the same yellow-ochre I had dug out of the mine! Imagine that. The very hue I was selling as pigment, and here it was on a painting! It made me feel important in a way I had never felt before, and that Roussillon was important too. I had brought something out of the earth, and it was used to make something beautiful. I was part of a creative process. Can you understand?"

"Yes," I said, and with this understanding came respect.

"See how the painting shows the light bouncing against the ochre houses and softening the edges of everything? The light does that here in the south. It makes things quiver."

He gazed lovingly at the painting on the wall, and I did too, and saw what he meant. The sunlight shimmered with life.

"Ah, but the graybeard had a problem," Pascal said. " 'I have to pay my share of the costs to the group,' the painter says. 'Then who will pay the rabbi and the cantor and the grave diggers?' The poor man's voice wavered, I remember. Think of it, Lisette. An old man like me remembering such a thing."

"You have a fine memory."

A rabbi and a cantor. I had seen Jews in the Marais quarter coming out of a large synagogue in rue Pavée, had noticed the fringes of the men's shawls hanging below their coats, and had heard them speaking beneath their broad black hats what might have been Yiddish or Hebrew, but I had never known any Jewish person. I remembered the women in their long dresses with long sleeves; I had smiled at them, wishing I knew just one friendly word to say to them that they would understand.

Pascal continued, "In that same instant, my heart cracked for the man who had made this painting with a substance that we had dug out of the earth right near our village. I would have thought Madame Tanguy's heart would have cracked too, but she was shielding herself from pity by holding a newspaper in front of her face.

"I told him that I wanted to help. He raised one eyebrow and asked if I was a frame maker. I told him I knew wood and had made *panetières,* so I could learn to make frames.

" 'Puh!' he says. 'In a dozen years. That's how long it takes to be admitted to the Guild of Encadreurs. That's the frame makers' guild. I need five frames in a week,' he says, and his head sank down. I asked him if he would be content with simple uncarved molding. He didn't answer. I asked Julien if he knew where I could buy molding and borrow tools.

"From behind her newspaper, Madame Tanguy declares, 'No framer is going to lend tools to an upstart who is not in the guild.'

" 'Then let's borrow one tool from five different people,' I say."

It was amusing, the way Pascal told it, how excited he became.

"The painter raised his head. 'I have a tack hammer.'

" 'Four people then,' I say. 'Tell each one you need it to repair a chair.'

"Then madame lowers her newspaper and names some widow who might still have her husband's miter box and saw. So I ask Julien if I can use the alley behind the shop. The painter nods in quick jerks of his head, but Julien says no, that I must not be seen, so he offers to clear a space in his back room.

"I ask him if he has any glue, and Madame Tanguy snaps, *'Bien sûr,* we have glue. What kind of a shop do you think this is, young man?' She crumpled the newspaper and thumped a jar on the counter. 'Sixty-five centimes. Up front. No negotiation.'

"I smacked the coins onto her open palm, and she dropped them into a drawer and slammed it shut."

"This really happened?" I asked.

"It did, Lisette. It's the very truth, I swear. Now the painter, he has hope beginning to shine in his eyes, so he tells me that wide molding painted white would do, and madame produces a jar of white gesso from a shelf. 'One franc forty.' She slaps the counter, and I count out the coins."

I stared at Pascal in wonder. "How can you remember what people said? Or those prices?"

"When something changes your life, Lisette, you remember everything. Someday you'll see."

"So what happened?"

"Each day the painter shuffled into the shop as though the world would end soon and watched me work. I learned how to miter cleanly, and peg the corners as my uncle and I had done on the *panetières.* By the end of the second week, I had four frames, simple but acceptable. I inserted the four paintings. He called them *The Orchard, A Morning in June, A Garden of Pontoise,* and I can't remember the fourth. He was astonished, Lisette. He had tears in his eyes. Four simple frames, and he was astonished."

"I am the one astonished, that you can recite their names."

" 'The white makes my colors glow,' he says. 'But I left five paintings here. Where's the fifth? The one of Louveciennes?'

" 'Madame is holding it behind the counter,' I say timidly.

"With her hands on her hips, she declares, 'A negotiation. I consider four frames made without charge and on short order worth that one small painting.'

"The painter flinched and cast his eyes at the painting. Finally, he turned to me with resolution and said, 'And so do I, young man.'

"He shook my hand, and I became a frame crafter, a collector, and a friend on the spot."

"And he was Pissarro?"

"The very man. Camille Pissarro."

I clapped my hands for him, the second time since we had arrived, the only appropriate reaction to his tale.

CHAPTER FIVE

PASCAL, PISSARRO, PONTOISE, AND PURPOSE

1937, 1875

AFTER WE WERE IN ROUSSILLON A FEW WEEKS, ANDRÉ WENT to Maurice's house to ask if he knew of any frame shop in Avignon when Pascal came out to the courtyard, where I was shelling peas in the shade of the lean-to. He sat close beside me, shaking a half sheet of paper.

"Almost *boules* time," I said.

"This first. I slept in fits and starts last night, because I was so afraid that I might forget something."

"About what?"

"Pissarro, of course. He told me to come to Pontoise on the Jewish Sabbath. That's where he lived when he was not visiting other painters in Paris. I remember him saying, 'On the Sabbath Julie always reminds me that I must not paint, and because all the colors of the rainbow are in her eyes, I cannot refuse her. Sometimes, though, if the fire in me is burning hot, I must, but I always apologize with a kiss.'"

"That's nice."

"His house clung to a hillside near a stream in the quarter called the Hermitage. He wore a stained, broad-brimmed felt hat and rumpled trousers tucked into tall, mud-caked boots."

I looked at Pascal's own rumpled trousers. "Like the men do around here?"

"Try not to interrupt me, Lisette. I'm sorry, but it makes me forget what I was saying.

"So on that same day he welcomed me with outstretched arms, took me inside, and introduced his wife and children to me, all of them busy and making noise, but amid all that hubbub, Camille wore an expression of absolute contentment. He had an amazing capacity to lift himself out of sadness."

"What do you mean? How?"

"Please. Just listen. That first show of his group failed, and they lost all their investment. He only sold one painting for some pitiful price. The press cut them all to shreds. I thought he might give up, but no. He was working with fierce energy for the second show, as if some great success had spurred him on."

"Did you bring him a frame?"

"Yes, I did, made according to a note he had sent to Julien. In between calls on pigment customers, I had made half a dozen frames over a year's time and had begun to carve the moldings with simple leaves or arabesques at the corners. I had taught myself how to design a curve loosely so that I could carve it more easily, how to make a smooth, shallow groove with a U-gouge, how to prevent the V-gouge from digging too deeply by pressing down and forward on its handle instead of tapping with the mallet. I brought him the last of them, my most complex, with arabesques all around.

"He *admired* it, Lisette, and said that I had progressed rapidly. Can you understand what that meant to me?"

I did understand it, and it revealed him to me in a new way. I saw the humility in this man whom I would have loved to have had as a father.

"So Camille says to me, he says, without bitterness, as though it were the lot of all painters, 'I haven't a sou, but you can choose a painting from this row for yourself.'

"Just think of that, Lisette. He let *me* choose. He went back outside, and I was left to look at the paintings. Sowers, plowmen, hay wagons, haystacks, barges on the Oise, the hillside of culti-vated land behind the Hermitage, a town square on market day. It was agony to choose."

"I should think so," I remarked. I tried to plant these subjects in my mind so that when we went back to Paris I might be able to pick out a Pissarro painting in a gallery, but I was afraid my memory wasn't as good as Pascal's.

"Later Camille asked what I thought of them, and he chuckled like a bashful boy, this grown man with a long, untrimmed beard. He was starving for a mite of praise from somebody outside his group of painters. The dear unwanteds, he called them.

" 'What about praise from an ochre miner?' I asked him. 'What's that worth?'

" 'From a pigment salesman with a good eye for color? Plenty,' he said. I'll never forget that. I only claimed an eye for the seventeen hues we made from ochre. I think I told him that his colors were in harmony, and that his little dabs that didn't mean anything up close looked like the real thing from a distance. I felt like a fool talking like that. All I wanted to do was to look at more paintings. He stood like a carved hunk of wood, waiting for me to say more. I could feel him suffering there, waiting, so I said something like this: 'You know, the painting you gave me, of the yellow-ochre path? It makes me notice the range of ochres in all paintings. They make me think I'm doing something good selling those pigments. And the world you paint is one I know. It's not just beautiful. It's true. To the countryside. The light.' That seemed to please him. I wanted to please him, Lisette."

"I'm sure you did please him."

"I was overwhelmed by so many paintings and told him so.

"He let out a kind of snort and said he had fifteen hundred once. When he went back to Louveciennes after the Prussian war, he dis-covered that Prussian soldiers had been living in his house. They used his frames as firewood and made pathways of his paintings so they wouldn't muddy their boots. Imagine that, Lisette. They kept their horses indoors in winter and slept upstairs. They used his studio to butcher sheep and his paintings as aprons. He had to dig out from the floor a thick layer of dung and dried blood that covered more paintings. Twenty years' work, and he was able to save only forty canvases." Burning with outrage, Pascal bellowed, "The barbarians!"

I flinched and dropped a pea pod on the ground.

"That painting of the girl and the goat?" I asked. "You said it was done in Louveciennes?"

Pascal nodded.

"Then it must have been one of the forty."

The stark realization of its narrow escape made it more valuable in my eyes, made me want to be in Paris all the more in order to search out all the other Pissarro paintings of Louveciennes.

Pascal passed a moment in reflection before continuing.

"Camille just stood there, this big man, watching me sputter, needing me to sputter, me, a laborer who knew nothing but what I loved. Do you understand, Lisette? He was heroic to keep on going. Unaccountably heroic. For years afterward, dozens of women wore the canvases of his looted paintings as aprons while doing their laundry along the Seine."

"What a pretty sight that must have been, all of them lined up along the bank, wearing his paintings."

"You don't understand! It was a crime! They had *stolen* them! And *they* glared at *him* when he returned to Louveciennes because he had spent the Prussian war safely painting in England."

Maybe they had lost their sons or husbands, I thought, but that justification didn't satisfy me. I could only imagine one day having the chance to tell the rich gallery visitors in Paris this story. I wanted them to feel the outrage and injury Pascal and I felt. In that moment, I was beginning to glimpse my purpose here.

I finished shelling the peas and stood up to take them inside.

"Sit down. There's more I have to say."

I overlooked his rudeness. It was only his passion to be sure someone heard his story. "There's more?"

"He told me about a fine painter in his group who encouraged everyone else. Frédéric Bazille was his name. Idealistic but stubborn, Camille told me. The army wouldn't admit him because he refused to shave his beard, so he joined the Zouaves, which had no such regulation. They were engaged in the fiercest fighting. He was killed in Beaune-la-Rolande, an inconsequential battle. 'We grieved for the loss of that good man,' Camille said, 'so what sense does it make to mourn the loss of paint on cloth?' "

To think of the great paintings that might have been, Pissarro's and this man Bazille's, was enough to make *me* grieve. Pascal might have collected a painting by Bazille, and I would be able to see it hanging here with the others.

"Camille took me outside to see the view from his house. What he told me was important, so I wrote it down."

Pascal read from his paper slowly, contemplating each thought. "He said, 'When a man finds a place he loves, he can endure the unspeakable. Pontoise was designed especially for me. The random pattern of cultivated fields and wild patches, the orchards that have given their pears to generations, the rich smell of this earth, the windmills and water wheels and smokestacks, the stone houses all a-kilter, even the pigeons dumping on the tile roofs—everything here moves me. I belong here as much as that stream by my house which runs into the Oise and then to the Seine and on to the sea. Everything is connected here. That stream quenched the thirst of Romans, even of Celts before them. When I paint it, they are a part of me. When I walk this land, there is a painting waiting for me around every bend. Isn't there a hunger in every human being to find a place in the world that gives to him so richly that he wants to honor it by giving back something of worth?' "

Pascal stopped speaking and folded his paper. I wanted to tell him that I agreed with Pissarro, but I would be referring to Paris, and saying so might hurt his feelings.

"So I want to give something back to Roussillon," he said.

I nodded my understanding. What was true for him about Roussillon didn't make it true for me. But the principle, that I could embrace.

"And now I'm going to tell you about the perfect gift Camille gave me. In his studio I took another look at a group of paintings of a sprawling factory with several smokestacks that dominated the plain directly across from the Hermitage, the quarter in Pontoise where he lived after he left Louveciennes. Those paintings didn't have any relationship to me.

"'How about this?' Camille asked, and pulled from the back of the stack a small painting of a factory built of stone. 'It's the Arneuil paint factory in Pontoise,' he said.

"Then I recognized it! I had sold ochre pigments there! 'That's the painting I want!' I said.

"Come back inside, Lisette, and really look at it with me."

He had given this painting a space by itself between the two south windows. He stood transfixed in front of it, and for some time, we were not in the house. He was there, in front of the factory.

Nondescript was what I thought of it, a word Sister Marie Pierre had taught me. The painting showed a blocklike building with a peaked roof, taller than the nearby houses set against a hillside of trees. The creamy yellow stone of the smokestack and factory caught the light and made the whole scene mellow. That was all I could see in it.

"I like the color of the building."

"*Jaune vapeur*, we called it. Inside that building, at long lines of tables, dozens of workers turned raw pigments into paint and filled the tubes Tanguy sold to Pissarro, Cézanne, Van Gogh, Gauguin, and others—the hues *we made* in the furnaces of the Usine Mathieu, our factory right here in Roussillon, as well as those made from other substances. Red roots of the *garance* plant cultivated here in the Vaucluse, sap from Turkish trees, powders of blue stones from Siberian and Afghani riverbanks, dried blood of South American beetles that fed on cactus—all the colors of the world on their way to become paintings. I saw it, those colors.

"In the meadow, there, in front of the factory, see, Lisette? The tallest man? I imagine that it's me calling upon the purchasing agent." He lowered his chin, as though a little embarrassed to reveal this.

Right then I understood why Pascal had chosen that painting. Despite its ordinariness, it spoke to him of his purpose, his participation in the world of art, the link in the chain from mine to majesty, and therefore it merited being hung alone.

I looked around the *salle* at his seven paintings. Was there any one that spoke to me of my purpose? What was my purpose anyway? It had to be something greater than shelling peas. But today, and in the days to come, it was to absorb all that Pascal was telling me so that I might impress Monsieur Laforgue. Beyond that, I couldn't see.

"Someday, Lisette, the world will love the *jaune vapeur* on that building."

"He's famous now, this Monsieur Pissarro, *n'est-ce pas?*"

"By the time Camille was an old man, his paintings sold well for high prices. I could never buy one then. He had a framer from the guild carve intricate frames and cover them with real gold leaf. He was far beyond what I could make or trade for."

"So you treasure them all the more?"

"No, Lisette!" he bellowed. "Not because they're valuable. I treasured each one the day I acquired it, for what it meant to me."

"Oh."

"That isolated paint factory makes my heart swell even today. Every miner I ever knew, every sore back, every day they never saw the sun, every choking breath, and every tongue caked with ochre dust—Maurice, Aimé Bonhomme, my father, and I swinging our pickaxes in rhythm all day long—all of that is in this painting. And it's in the painting of the girl walking up the ochre path with her goat. And the history of Roussillon is in this one of the tile roofs of the Hermitage in Pontoise. Those roofs are stained red-orange from Roussillon pigments. And the red ground and the row of bushes aflame—that's Roussillon red-ochre. That may not mean anything to you now, but if you had lived here all your life and had seen those miners come home filthy and exhausted, it would."

I THOUGHT HE HAD finished talking for the day until I heard him murmur, *"Red Roofs, Corner of a Village, Winter."* Then *"Le Verger, Côtes Saint-Denis à Pontoise,"* as if one title wasn't enough. "Six roofs, *ocre rouge.* Five chimneys, *jaune nankin clair.* Six fields on the hillside behind—*vert foncé,* green so rich and dark it must have been spinach growing there; *ocre de Ru,* pale, like wheat; *ocre rouge; vert de chou,* the light green of a cabbage; rose earth; and the duller olive green, *vert Véronèse.*"

He found another sheet of paper, sat down at the small desk, and wrote down the colors.

"Why are the names of colors so important?" I asked.

"Because God conceived of those colors, and we mined the ochres that *made* them! Because there is holiness in color. It's the queen of art." His voice exploded with exasperation. "Because I don't want to forget when . . . when I go on."

Oh my, what I had caused him to think.

We were quiet awhile, until I asked, "How many frames did you have to trade for *Red Roofs?*"

His head sank slowly until he was looking at his lap. "The number didn't matter."

The effort it had taken to make me understand had exhausted him, and he rose and grasped the railing to pull himself upstairs to bed.

But I *was* understanding, at least a little. I remembered how much importance color held for Sister Marie Pierre. Once she sent

me across place de la Concorde on some errand, and when I returned she asked me what was the color of the hollows of the hiero-
glyphics carved into the Egyptian obelisk.

"I don't know. Gray!"

"Don't just tell me gray. Gray is a noncolor. Strictly speaking,
the Impressionists never used it." She motioned with her arm that I
should go back out.

Fuming, I grabbed my coat and walked the distance again. When
I got back, I reported, "Green-gray on the south side, yellow-gray
on the west side, violet-gray on the north side, and blue-gray on the
east side." Then she was pleased, but I remember having taken secret delight in including the word *gray* in each color.

ANDRÉ CAME IN THE door with his lips turned down at the corners
and his eyes downcast as well.

"What? No frame shop in Avignon?"

"He doesn't know of any. Maybe I can get some furniture repair
work." He took a weary breath. "I've been to the post office." He
held out an envelope, but he seemed painfully reluctant to let go
of it.

"Who could it be from? Maxime!"

He had already opened it. I yanked it out of the envelope,
skipped the salutation, and read:

> *I hope you are well and enjoying the warm south. Without
> you here, I have been in a definite slump until early this week
> when I sold a painting in Galerie Laforgue. It was a dancing
> harlequin with a sad face by André Derain. Monsieur La-
> forgue had been away for a few days, and when I told him
> the news, he was elated. So elated that he took on a woman
> as an apprentice gallery attendant, I regret to say. That threw
> me back into a slump again. To celebrate the sale, he took me
> to the Théâtre des Champs-Élysées to see Josephine Baker*

dance wearing only a skirt made of bananas, but after having seen it before, I thought it had grown stale. I'm sure it was due to my mood. I had hoped he would hold off hiring anyone until you came back. She may not last long. She's haughty, overbearing, and opinionated, though she does have a good eye. I'm dreadfully sorry, Lisette.

I have hope for Pascal's swift recovery and for your quick return.

Your friend, Maxime

André put his arm around my shoulders. "I'm sorry, too."

CHAPTER SIX

ANDRÉ'S GIFT

1937

F OR DAYS, I COULD HEAR ANDRÉ SAWING, POUNDING, AND sanding in our courtyard, working until dark. He had told me not to come out there. He had even closed the shutters so I couldn't look out the south windows. Even so, the aromatic scent of freshly cut pine told me what he was doing, and it wasn't making a frame. Still feeling ashamed for creating trouble, yet full of pride in his grandson's resourcefulness, Pascal knew too.

"André loves you," Pascal said.

"I know." Never for a moment did André let me feel unloved or taken for granted.

"We want so much for you to be happy here."

"I know that too." I arranged a plate of apricots and peaches on the table in front of him, but I felt compelled to offer him something more.

"When I was seventeen and still living with the Daughters of Saint-Vincent-de-Paul, a nun found a position for me in a fine *pâtisserie*. On that first day I was supremely happy learning the names of the pastries and smelling almond, vanilla, and cinnamon, but she told me two things that morning that I will never forget. 'No matter where life takes you,' she said, 'the place where you stand at any moment is holy ground. Love hard and love wide and love long, and you will find the goodness in it.'"

"She's a wise woman. Camille would have agreed."

AFTER MORE THAN A WEEK, André invited us out to the courtyard. There it stood near the edge of the cliff, just what I had suspected but hadn't dared to say in order not to spoil his joy in surprising me. An outhouse, complete with a peaked roof. The door, facing over the cliff, had a window and shutters, like a little cottage. André stood back proudly and gestured for me to open the door. Inside was a wide smooth bench attached to the side walls at about knee height, and a smoothly finished square wooden toilet seat, contoured with rounded corners and dovetailed joints, varnished. And square.

"I'm sorry I couldn't make an oval."

"André! It's beautiful. It's like a frame!"

"Well done, André," Pascal said.

André had hung a sprig of dried lavender under the roof beam for the unveiling. How thoughtful, this husband of mine.

"Go in, go in," André urged. "Just pretend."

I stepped in. Sticky tears of sap seeped out from the freshly milled pine, my tears of gratitude made solid. Then I looked down. The pit he had dug wasn't very deep.

André closed the door and said, "Turn around. Sit down."

He opened the shutters. Laid out before me was a valley of the Vaucluse, our *département* in Provence, cut by canals, dirt roads, and rows of cypress trees, France's fertile Garden of Eden. There were vineyards and orchards on hillsides, and vegetable plots and rows of lavender in the valley. Beyond, the mountains of the Luberon. A grand panorama.

"It's like a painting in a frame."

I stepped out. "But what do you do with . . . ?"

"Dig it out. Or I'll dig a trench, and we'll use a bucket to wash it down the cliff once in a while."

"That is what we *Roussillonnais* do," Pascal admitted.

And do the *Roussillonnais* go outdoors to their outhouses during the monstrous thing called the mistral, or in the rain? Or at night? It wasn't perfect. It would never be perfect here, but André had done what he could, and I loved him for it.

"One more thing." Grinning, André reached around the corner and presented me with a square board with a raised edge, the corners bisquited the way he joined them for his frames, a little larger than the seat and as smoothly sanded and varnished. He turned it over and set it on the seat like the lid of a box. "*Voilà!* A cover."

"Carved!"

"A fleur-de-lis, for my Lise."

"Oh, André! How good of you. It's exquisite." He had carved away the wood around the fleur-de-lis so that the bloom was rounded and raised above it.

I laughed. "I never thought I would ever say I loved a toilet, but this one, André, I do love."

"No one else in Roussillon has an outhouse as *haut bourgeois* as this," Pascal said. "You could start a business here."

"Ah, how the mighty have fallen," I said. "From making frames for the painters of Paris to framing village derrières." I gave André a sympathetic look.

"Let's go to the *épicerie* before it closes. I want to buy a new roll of toilet paper."

We all set off. How straight I stood at the counter announcing proudly, "One plump roll of toilet paper, *s'il vous plaît*." It felt marvelous to make the proprietor wonder why we were all grinning. A moment later, I blurted, "For our fine new outhouse."

"Ah! *Oui! Certainement!*" He pointed to one roll after another on the shelf, then held them up and turned them for my inspection as though they were works of art. We left the store laughing.

As we approached the café on the way home, I said, "Let's celebrate with a pastis. Maybe we'll find Maurice there." I pulled André along toward the door. Pascal looked alarmed.

I parted the hanging beads and peeked in. There were no small round marble tables with black wrought iron bases like those in the cafés in Paris, only rustic wooden squares. There was no mirror behind the bar. And though the café was full, there was not a single woman. But there was music playing from a radio, Suzy Solidor's deep voice singing a tango—the sound of Paris.

"Lisette, we had better not," Pascal said.

Several men stood quietly at the bar. Others sat at the tables having lively conversations, drinking the rosé produced here or the milky pastis in tall slim glasses. Group by group, I realized, they were scowling at us. André tugged at my elbow, and I stepped away from the door. He turned me toward home.

"Men only," said Pascal. "Women don't go to the café."

"Ever?"

"On rare nights with their husbands when Monsieur Voisin shows a movie, or in the afternoon to refill a wine bottle for supper."

"Is there some law?"

"Tradition."

"Well, it's provincial. Primitive!" I cried in the most disgusted tone I could utter. All my earlier elation vanished.

André looked stricken. "I'm sorry, Lisette. That's the way it is here."

CHAPTER SEVEN

PASCAL'S LIST

1937, 1885

I WOKE UP VIOLENTLY SCRATCHING A SPIDER BITE ON MY ANKLE.
"Don't scratch. It will only make it worse," André murmured.

Five minutes later I was sitting up and digging at it again. I shook out the sheets and quilt to try to find the culprit and pulverize it in retribution, but no luck. That black beastie was sly and would live to bite again.

It was a Monday, so André was going in Maurice's bus to scour Avignon again for any carved furniture repair work he could do at home. Except for a few rainy Mondays, he had been going every week throughout the summer, convinced that he would find something.

Pascal had kept to his bed the day before, but he came downstairs when we heard Maurice call, *"Adieu, mes chers amis!"*

I opened the door wide. "Adieu, Maurice." I giggled self-consciously at what seemed so strange coming out of my mouth.

Pascal said, "Come in. André has something to show you."

"Do you like our village, madame?"

"It's very quaint."

"*Oui. C'est la Provence profonde.*"

I was amused. He had adapted the expression *la France pro-fonde,* which referred to rural central France as the soul of the nation, to his own province, naming Roussillon as its soul and center.

They all went out to the courtyard, and I followed, not wanting to miss the lift of Maurice's exuberant eyebrows.

"*Merveilleux!*" he cried.

Pascal gave him a little push. "Look inside."

"*Oh là là!* Such a thing in Roussillon. A window too! A room with a view! And the symbol of France."

"With my Lise's symbol," André said.

"Provence will have the last laugh over Paris. A stream of people will come to see. But madame my wife. *Non, non, non.*" He shook his head, his hands, his jowls. "We must not tell Louise."

In this gossipy village, she would find out sooner or later.

He held up a chubby index finger. "Me, I must christen it, *non?* It is a long ride to Avignon. Ha-ha. As we say in Provence, madame, I had better change the water of the olives." Nimbly, he stepped inside and pulled the door closed. "*Quel trône!* Fit for a king."

Pascal chuckled. "A throne. He called it a throne, André. The pope in Avignon would have been jealous."

Outside once again, Maurice let out a long, breathy "Ah."

Laughing, Maurice and André started downhill to the bus stop, smugly whistling.

I EMBARKED ON A thorough housecleaning to get rid of any nests or hiding places for wicked little creatures. I swept up mouse droppings and grit from the last mistral. I carted buckets of water from the faucet in place de la Mairie and set to work scrubbing the red tile floor. On my hands and knees, I discovered a black widow spider's thick web and her white egg sack within it on the underside of the kneading table. Furious, I chased the ugly little devil around the edge of the floor until I had smashed her flat, thinking of the she-devil with a good eye who had taken my position at Galerie Laforgue.

I stood up in victory and found Pascal writing what appeared to be a list with annotations. With his brows knitted together in concentration, he worked on it for an hour, using both sides of a second sheet, while I worked my way around the floor of the *salle*. Finally he sat back and let his arms flop to his sides, exhausted. He exhausted? What about me?

"There. Today I shall tell you about Paul Cézanne."

"Maybe later." I squeezed cloudy gray water out of a rag.

"But it has to be now, while it's in my mind." The paper trembled in his hand. "Please, Lisette, sit down and listen."

"I can listen while I do this."

"You have to be still so I can think out my memories. All I am is my memories. You'll learn that about yourself someday."

I surrendered, only too happy to sit for a spell. I just wished the settee were more comfortable.

"I met Paul Cézanne in Julien Tanguy's art supply shop. Julien was convinced that Cézanne would introduce something new in art. His shop was the only place in Paris exhibiting him. He told me that Cézanne needed cheering up because he doubted himself. At that, I recall Madame Tanguy saying something snide, like 'With good reason.'"

Pascal turned to look at the Cézanne still life. He was squinting, so I stood to take it off the wall and propped it on a chair closer to him. The painting left a rectangular outline of dirt on the wall where it had hung. In fact, the whole wall alongside the stairs that once had been whitewashed was now yellowish, stained by tobacco and woodsmoke. Pascal might have praised the color as pale yellow-ochre, but to me it was dingy and depressing. It was a disgrace to hang a beautiful painting on a grimy wall. I would have to clean the whole expanse. Since I was still standing, I dipped my rag in a fresh bucket of soapy water and raised it to the wall.

Meanwhile, Pascal kept talking. "Cézanne came into the shop

wearing a cape, and underneath it he was carrying this very painting. Take a minute to look at those pretty apples in that white compote dish, and the oranges spilling out of that tilted plate, and that one lone pear on the table."

When he said "one lone pear," I stopped scrubbing, and in my mind's eye I saw the single pear in the Madonna and Child painting in the chapel of Saint-Vincent-de-Paul. It was just below the babe's chubby toes, which looked like a row of corn. The golden skin of the pear made a lovely contrast with the Virgin's deep blue cloak, and I thought how remarkable it was that a person's memory could call forth such details from days gone by.

Pascal looked up from his paper. "That blue patterned cloth is an *indienne,* made here in Provence with cotton grown here and indigo dyes. Everyone here has olive pots dipped in green glaze like that, made in Aubagne, east of Marseille. But it was the *compotier,* that shallow bowl on a pedestal, that brought tears to my eyes in Tanguy's shop. Are you listening, Lisette?"

"Yes," I said, my mind still in the chapel. "So why did it make you weep?"

"My mother had a compote just like that, which she had bought on a rare trip to Marseille. She was proud of it because it was more refined than the rustic terra-cotta vessels from Aubagne called *terres vernissées,* with only their upper portions glazed. In season, she filled it with fruit. When I was a boy, I knocked it off the table and it broke into pieces. She never got another one."

"I'm so sorry," I said, my rag dripping water down my still upraised arm. "Tell me about meeting Cézanne."

"Ah, Cézanne. A saint of a painter." He consulted his list to shift his memory back to what he had started telling me.

"When Julien introduced us, Cézanne didn't raise his head to look at me. He only said in a heavy Provençal accent, 'I won't offer my hand. I haven't washed in a week,' but when I answered, '*Eh, bieng'* in an equally strong Provençal accent and extended my hand, he lifted his chin and gave me his.

"Then, looking at the painting, Julien cried, *'Magnifique.'*

" 'No, it is definitely not *magnifique,'* madame interjected. 'A pear can't stand up at that angle. That's ridiculous. And apples and oranges aren't ripe at the same time. France doesn't even grow oranges.' She flung out her arm dismissively. 'And they definitely can't stay in place on that crazy, tipped plate.'

" 'Ignore her,' Julien said. 'Leave the painting here for me to love until someone buys it.'

" 'And you'll hope no one will,' says madame. 'Meanwhile he won't pay what he owes us.'

" 'The apples, so smooth. I want to caress one,' Julien said.

" *'Non!'* declared Cézanne. 'What do you think I want to hear— that it is real, that you want to hold it, take a bite out of it, or that it is beautiful because the passage of colors in it from green to yellow to red makes it unique in that pyramid of apples?'

"I could not be silent. 'That I want to take a bite,' I blurted, 'because it *is* real.' But Cézanne shook his head.

" *'Non.* I paint to paint, not to depict. See with your eyes, man, not with your mind.'

" 'What if I see with my memory?' I say. 'That painting means more to me than any apple. It means my mother and her compote that I broke. And it means Provence, the *indienne,* and the green *terre vernissée.* The colors of the apples and oranges mean Roussillon, where I come from. I used to mine those ochres.' "

" *'Eh, bieng.* Then you understand color. It remains to be seen whether you understand form.'

" 'I want to buy it,' I burst out.

" *'Non.* You are too quick. You have to study it until you forget about your mother and her *compotier.* See it as an ellipse. The foreground edge is straighter, and the background edge is more arched. Can you see that? It's contrary to perspective vision, but that gives it character.'

" 'You're a fool, Paul,' says madame. 'Don't give him a lesson. Sell it this instant so you can pay your debts.'

"'Let it hang here awhile, Julien, and you, monsieur, come in and look at it from time to time. I'll come back in a month. If you have learned anything and still want it, then—'

"'I *will* want it, but I can only pay in frames, you understand. Do you need any frames?'

"'Frames? A painter always needs frames.'"

Pascal straightened his shoulders as if that was all.

"That's a good story, Pascal," I said.

"I'm not finished." He motioned to me to sit down.

"In a minute." I headed to the courtyard to get a ladder, wondering whether what he had told me was just a delusion of an old man, a real experience, or something in between.

Irritated that he didn't have my full attention, Pascal talked louder when I returned. "The next time I saw Paul Cézanne, I told him that his painting made me think that the apples and oranges knew each others' positions, that they fit together comfortably, each tilted its own way, like boulders in the Calavon River when it's dry, and that their colors were all friends—red streaks on the yellow apples, yellow streaks on green apples, the chartreuse of new spring leaves in our vineyards, and the orange of a Roussillon rock.

"'Don't think of vineyards or rocks,' he says. 'See the parallel slanting brushstrokes. Notice how each piece of fruit displays its colors in visible steps.'

"'In streaks?'

"'Yes, if you want to call them streaks.'

"That satisfied him, so he let me have it for eight large carved frames. Madame Tanguy sold me two bottles of gilt so the frames could look reasonably like the expensive ones with real gold leaf, only she charged me double because she made me pay for her instruction in how to apply it. In the end, everybody was happy except Julien, who pouted when I took the painting away. And that's how it started, my second friendship with a painter."

"That's nice."

"*Nice!* Is that all you can say? That it's *nice*? Just imagine, Lisette, what it was like to be in his presence! A man who painted to live, and lived to paint. They were the same to him. He thought only of painting, loved only painting. There was not a minute of the day that he did not respond to the world as a painter. He was obsessed, the poor man, and that separated him from normal life. He complained that he was never understood, yet he said that his progress was at least some consolation for being misunderstood by fools."

With that I went back to my scrubbing, knowing that I did not live to scrub. Or did I?

Out of breath at the end of the day, I rehung the still life on the clean white wall. It looked all the more splendid. The colors were richer. The highlights sparkled. Pascal stood up in acknowledgment of what I had done and turned in a circle, mournfully surveying the other stained walls. His arm waved vaguely to them.

"Yes, I will. But not today."

I carried the buckets outside. The instant I flung the dirty water over the cliff, a thought burst cleanly into my mind. This I could do for Monsieur Laforgue someday. I could wash the walls of his gallery. She-devil would be too haughty to do it. I could even wash walls for other galleries. Their paintings would look more brilliant, and I would be the cause of it, just like a framer sets off paintings. I could have gallery clients across Paris! Even the Louvre. And the Louvre had kilometers of walls. Floors, too. I could study the paintings as I cleaned. I clanked the wash buckets together in ecstasy.

I would write to Maxime. I would write to Monsieur Laforgue. I would write to *the Louvre*!

CHAPTER EIGHT

AN EARFUL
FROM CÉZANNE

1937, 1897

ANDRÉ HAD COME HOME FROM AVIGNON WITH A SUPPLY
of hardwood and an order for two frames from an antiquar-
ian shop selling Roman maps of Provence. He started working immediately. Pascal spent the morning writing at his little desk. From
time to time, he pressed his fist against his forehead as if to squeeze
out a memory. Their absorption in their work gave me time to write
to the Louvre.

I had to think out carefully what I would say—that I wanted to
serve the Louvre by cleaning walls and floors to make the paintings
even more beautiful, that I wanted to dust the frames and the sculptures, that I didn't care how humble the work would be, that I just
wanted to be surrounded by art. It seemed to me that Pascal was
not dying and we could return to Paris soon, so I wrote that I
couldn't begin quite yet but that I would come to inquire the very
day I returned to Paris.

My letter probably sounded naïve, but it was from my heart.
Before I could change my mind, I went to the post office and mailed
it. If the Louvre rejected me, I would write to Monsieur Laforgue
myself. When he saw how hard I worked, he would advance me
above stiff-necked Madame Snob. Someday.

—

BACK HOME IN THE courtyard, I watched André practice drawing acanthus leaves on the plywood board he had set across two sawhorses.

"Pascal told me why he sent you that desperate letter. It was so he could tell us everything about the painters he knew while he can still remember them," I said.

"No. So he could tell *you*. He has already told me. Let him talk. He's an old man."

"Oh, I do. His stories fascinate me."

André fell silent as he scribbled out some measurements and determined how many leaves there would be on each side.

"Be patient with him. His love for those paintings runs deep. They've been his life. The paintings, and me, and now you too. It's hard to let your life dissolve and your love amount to nothing. He wants it to live on, to show that he mattered, that Roussillon mattered, and still matters."

"I understand that now."

He lodged his pencil behind his ear. "Those paintings will be ours someday. It would behoove you to learn about them."

"I want to. And other paintings too."

I knew enough not to distract him while he measured and positioned the molding in his miter box. Carefully, he inserted his saw and drew it back, establishing the cut.

When the piece was released, I said, "I wrote a letter to the Louvre today."

He gave me a look of complete perplexity.

"You see how Pascal's still life looks so good now that I've washed the wall behind it? I'm going to wash all the walls, so all his paintings will shine. I want to do that in the Louvre." I knew that the next thing I would say would sound silly, but I had to tell him anyway. "So I wrote a letter asking for a job washing walls."

"Lisette! You mean you're going to leave Pascal and me and go off on some fool's errand to be a *washerwoman*?"

"Not now. Someday, when we're living in Paris again."

"Oh, my naïve darling." He set down the piece of molding and put his arms around me.

"Why do you think Pascal is so intent on telling me his experiences with painters?" I responded. "It's because being a participant in art meant so much to him. I want that just as much."

"But not as a *scrub*woman!"

"How else? I can't paint. I can't go to university. I have no qualifications, no money. But what I *can* do is to be a frame duster or a washer of walls in the Louvre."

"Don't think so lowly of yourself. A gallery assistant, someday. Maybe not at Galerie Laforgue. But no, oh, no. Tear up the letter. Or give it to me. Let me burn it." He held the back of my head and kissed my forehead. "We've got to be patient, Lise. We'll help each other be patient."

"I already mailed it," I said against his chest.

He grasped my shoulders and pushed me back to look at my face. "Truly?"

I nodded.

"Go back and get it. Tell the young woman in the post office that it was a mistake." One corner of his mouth lifted. "I want to read what my humble darling wrote. *Then* I'll burn it. Go now."

I did leave, dutifully, but I lingered in the bakery, chatting with Odette. She knew everything about everyone, and she shared recipes with every housewife in town, concocted herbal remedies, even helped to deliver babies. I liked her easy manner, the way she mothered the whole village.

Between Odette and her daughter, Sandrine, the post office clerk, nothing slipped by unnoticed. Sandrine announced with good cheer, "The *poste* was just picked up, and your letter is on its way. My, my," she said, her hand patting her heart. "To think you have important business with the Louvre!" She handed me a letter. "The driver left this for you."

It was from Maxime. I hurried home to read it aloud to André. Maybe Monsieur Laforgue had fired that woman.

19 SEPTEMBER 1937

Dear André and Lisette,

Mother and I were finally able to get tickets to the Exposition Universelle. We stood in a crowd from all nations staring at the pompous, propagandistic architecture and sculpture of dictatorships—Germany and the Soviet Union facing each other with a snarl in stone. Seeing it, Maman held my arm and shuddered.

Thirty works by Picasso were exhibited in the Spanish pavilion. They made me think your grandfather's study of women's faces might be his. Guard it well. It may be worth a fortune someday. Picasso's most monumental and disturbing work was the central mural, Guernica, a Cubist jumble of anguished bodies in tortured positions and a screaming horse, the whole chaotic scene commemorating the Basque town destroyed by German bombers in April. The painting was shortsightedly dismissed by the press as the dream of a madman. As for me, I can't get it out of my mind.

We both felt more comfortable in the Finnish pavilion, surrounded by trees and made entirely of wood, with undulating ceilings and curved walls. You would have appreciated the craftsmanship, André. When night descended, the Eiffel Tower and the banks of the Seine were lit gorgeously, as though strung with diamonds. I wish you could have seen that.

I miss you both and want you back in Paris soon.

Your best friend,
Maxime

The letter took me from the depths of foreboding to a vision of glorious splendor.

"No word about Monsieur Laforgue," I said.

THE NEXT DAY WHILE ANDRÉ was working in the courtyard, I asked Pascal to tell me more about Paul Cézanne. That pleased him, and he took out his pages.

"I haven't told you about visiting him in his hometown, Aix-en-Provence, south of here. Julien and I hadn't seen him since I had acquired that landscape of his, so I went there to set Julien's mind at rest. I asked after him in galleries, in art supply stores, in cafés along cours Mirabeau, the shady main avenue lined with mansions. You must get André to take you there."

"He'll tell me he has to work. You tell him."

"I stopped to watch a *boules* game and asked the players if they knew him. It was baffling. No one had heard of him—one of the finest painters in all of France. Had he no friends in his own town?

"Finally, I went to the Hôtel de Ville. A clerk of town records gave me an address, and there I saw him trudging home, hunch-shouldered under a slouch hat, looking like a tramp. He was carrying a game bag with the neck of a green bottle poking out and his oversized paint box, with an easel and a painting strapped to his back. His face was sunburnt and his beard was smeared with paint. He recognized me, Lisette. Imagine that."

Pascal picked out his pages from the desk. "This isn't exact. It's just what I remember. I told him I had come to ask if he needed any more frames, but mostly to see his paintings.

" 'My paintings? Humph. I am only a beginner,' he muttered.

"I told him not to degrade himself, that I had gone to his big exhibition three times, and that I wanted to see his paintings so I could remember them.

" 'It is no great thing to remember paintings,' he said. 'Look at nature instead. It's fresh every day. Think of its author. You do not get that in a painting. But we try. We try. Look over there, at the space between that tree and us. The air. The atmosphere. You can feel it, smell it, even taste it. But how the devil do you paint atmosphere? It's a mixture of air and water, light and shade, constantly changing. I have to chase it.'

" 'Now, that tree is easier. It's solid. A cylinder. And the foliage above it, a half sphere. The road, a trapezoid. That bush, a cone. See? The shadows of the divine create those shapes. But be careful. After all, art is a religion.'

" 'The same thing as soul?' I asked.

"He answered, 'You might say that. Or that it is created with soul. How you *appreciate* a thing is soul. Appreciate those vibrations of light in reds and yellows. Blues, too. You can't feel the air without blues. If you're living in the grace of God, you should be able to express it. I'm still working it out. I'm never satisfied. I'm afraid I won't live long enough to paint with confidence. Do you know, monsieur, what it feels like to be called a fraud? The torment never goes away. And that makes life terrifying.'

" 'A fraud? Never!' I told him. 'You're a master.'

"He turned to me at his doorway, and his eyes were moist and deep. 'Am I?' he asked. He let a moment pass as though he was trying to figure me out. Then he invited me in.

"It was a grim, cluttered old house. The studio had high ceilings and tall windows. I seem to remember a potbellied stove. Along a shelf there were white *compotiers* like my mother's, straw-wrapped wine bottles, a candlestick, gray jugs, pitchers, and the green glazed *toupin* that's in my painting."

"What's a *toupin?*"

"An olive jar. He called it moral pottery. He thought by painting it, he was honoring the rustic crafts of Provence. He said that a canvas and a marble block are luxury items, but the craftsman who gives an artistic touch to a simple piece of pottery or a basket, or a *panetière,* or wooden utensils, or pine furniture brings art to the people. Think of that, Lisette, the next time you sit on that pine bench over there."

"Or on André's toilet seat."

"He told me about the poet Frédéric Mistral's Félibrige movement to restore and honor Provençal crafts and traditions and language, and he gave me a copy of *Letters from My Mill,* by Alphonse Daudet, a true son of Provence. You should read it.

"All the while, he couldn't stand still. One after another, he pulled out unframed landscapes done around Aix showing a pattern of vineyards and orchards and pale *ocre de Ru* wheat fields alternating with green rectangles, often with Montagne Sainte-Victoire in the background, thrusting up like a pyramid. 'My rock of a thousand challenges,' he called it. 'The queen of mountains.' He said its roots dig down beneath civilization. He even called it his Mount Sinai.

"There were also paintings of *pigeonniers,* those round towers for roosting pigeons."

Pascal consulted his notes. " 'Look! Look here,' Cézanne says. 'This *pigeonnier* is Provence, man and nature in harmony. Paris dealers don't understand. They insult me. Why shouldn't I paint what is important here? Pigeon droppings are used as fertilizer. What a thing to paint, they say, but from pigeon shit come apples, pears, grapes, the delectable fruits and wines of Provence. And who doesn't love a good *salmis,* all its juices and herbs of the countryside mixing in a delicious pigeon ragout, eh? *Pigeonniers* are far more important in Provence than decrepit castles. *Cabanons* are too.'

"He showed me some paintings with stark, narrow cabins made of stone, one room stacked on one room. You've seen them isolated in fields and pastures. Farmers and shepherds use them from time to time. 'Who will give us back our *cabanons,*' he says, 'when the big farms move in and tear them down for another two rows of apple trees?'

"I was afraid he was working himself into a fit of rage, so I tried to calm him. 'Eh, bieng, you paint them to preserve them.'

"'It's something I can do,' he says. 'Frédéric Mistral can compose a poem about *cigales*. Daudet can write a story of his windmill. I can paint *cabanons* and *pigeonniers* and *toupins*. I want to die painting them. To die painting. Do you understand? I do nothing but work, but the evidence, *la réalisation*, I don't see it. I go to mass, I go to vespers, but I don't see it.'

"His voice turned sad. He pulled out paintings of blocklike ochre rocks and cut cliffs of a quarry, one after another.

"'The Bibémus quarry near here,' he says. 'I painted it from the upper story of a *cabanon* I rented. Without it being right there in a field, I would not have been able to get this view. But dealers don't like quarries. They aren't pretty like the Impressionists' picnics. They don't understand their importance.'

"'But Julien Tanguy understood?'

"'The only one. He saw what I did, that I painted the earth's structure manipulated by man, yet all in harmony.'

"And with that I asked how many frames I should make for the quarry painting with Montagne Sainte-Victoire in the background."

Pascal gazed at it steadily, his chest heaving, as though he were a quarryman resting from swinging a pickax. Perhaps he was drawing from the painting the substance of his soul. I envied that, finding a painting that could depict one's own soul.

"Think of the shame of it, Lisette. That town below his studio, it knew *nothing* of how he struggled, day after day, working in a frenzy, draining himself with the effort to honor Provence. They didn't even know he was there! A native son! There's more to tell about him, but I feel *fatigué*. Tomorrow. Can you wait until tomorrow?"

"Yes, I can wait."

He asked me to prepare *daube* for him on Saturday. His voice was pleading, almost like the whine of a child. I had to ask him what it was.

"A traditional Provençal dish, sort of a beef ragout simmered with red wine. It has orange peel and tomato and carrots and those little round onions. Pick some rosemary for it. Cézanne would have eaten it on a Saturday too."

In a few moments, his eyes closed, his head dipped to his chest, and he snored lightly. To the soft rhythm of his exhaustion, I went out to the courtyard, where André was sharpening his large U-gouge.

"I'm not sorry we came here," I said softly. "He's giving me something I couldn't get anywhere else. His memories of two great artists."

"So are you beginning to feel privileged?" André asked.

"I am. If we three were living in Paris, I would be working, and in our free time there would always be something else to do. But here in quiet Roussillon with these empty afternoons, there is time for me to sit and listen."

André set down his tools and enfolded me for a long, swaying moment before he whispered, "So now we know why we came."

CHAPTER NINE

A GOOD LIFE

1938–39

I T HAD BEEN A MILD WINTER, WITH ONLY TWO MISTRALS. IF they were the fiercest they could be, I ceased to worry, and, after March, the month of contrasts, I enjoyed the coming of spring and the potent aroma of thyme on the hillside below our courtyard. Pascal came inside one April afternoon, the shoulder of his arm that held his pouch of *boules* sagging, his chin thrust forward. He was inhaling hoarse, congested breaths through his mouth.

"This is the worst day of my life," he growled.

"Oh, *non, non, non*. Don't say that. I'm sure—" I began.

"I'll say what I want to say."

He started up the stairs to his room, hung on to the railing a few moments, his thin chest heaving, then carefully set the *boules* sack on the second step and turned back. He made it to the dining table, slumped onto a chair, and swept his arm across the oilcloth as if sweeping away some bad experience.

I sat down next to him. "Do you want to tell me about it?"

Slowly he raised his head and looked at me.

"The color of your cheeks is like a Cézanne peach."

I laid my hand on his arm.

"What's that garlic for?" he asked.

"*Daube.*"

"Wrong time. It's an early winter dish. Wait until November."

"All right, but that's a long time from now."

I turned away so he might not read my reason—that I was making it now as a precaution. Instead, I should have recognized that Pascal's complaint revealed his will to live.

He regarded his trembling hands.

"Not a single *boule.* I couldn't fire or point where I wanted to. They called me names. Even Aimé did. I bent down to point and my knees gave way. I sank to the ground and Aimé had to help me up."

By now Pascal went to play *boules* only once a week. Even though he was *fatigué*—a worsened state than *peu fatigué,* but still not *très fatigué*—that was not enough to keep him home entirely. Ashamed, diminished, perhaps even fearful, he covered his face with his hands, as if the whole world had come crashing down on him without mercy.

"Wasn't there anything good about the day?"

It took him a while to think of something. "Only one thing. Aimé stopped calling me names after he helped me up."

His childlike thinking in the face of end-of-life concerns produced in me a warm sensation of mothering.

"They chased him. Did I tell you?"

"Chased Aimé?"

"Chased Cézanne. A gang threw stones at him, and at his painting. They called him an imbecile and other wicked names."

"No, that couldn't be."

"How do you know? You weren't there. I saw it."

Getting up to crush the garlic cloves, I let him rage. I would use tomatoes, onions, and green olives instead of orange rind and anchovies, and white wine instead of red, and I would call it *boeuf à l'Arlésienne* instead of *daube.*

"Such a noble man," Pascal murmured. "He devoted his life to art, and what did he get for it? Scorn, dissatisfaction, exhaustion."

Points of light appeared on his wet lashes, and then full round tears spilled onto his lower lids. I walked over to the doorway to the courtyard and motioned to André to come inside. He brushed sawdust off his clothes, took one look at Pascal, and sat down next to his grandfather. He laid his head on Pascal's shoulder and reminded him of how he, Pascal, had once made a small wooden boat and rigged it with a handkerchief sail and a tow string for André to sail in the pond of the Palais du Luxembourg in Paris.

"I remember." Pascal sucked in a long, rattling breath. "You were still in short pants. You fell and skinned your knee and let go of the string. I waded into the pond to retrieve it."

"Wearing your Sunday trousers."

"Oh, life." A sigh erupted from some deep, private place. "I came back to Roussillon because I wanted to feel young again with my good friends, and now I feel old. How does it happen, André?"

I held my breath, waiting, wondering, while André searched for the words. "Little by little."

THE SPRING AND SUMMER of 1938 slipped quietly into autumn, the diminishing season, when the *cigales* stopped their scratchy mating calls, laid their eggs underground, and died. Farmers left their fields fallow. Black figs disappeared from the market stalls and were replaced with Marseille figs, which Pascal called "the pope's balls," chuckling at my shock. Three-day rains sent Pascal and André to the café earlier than usual, where they grumbled over their *apéritifs*. They came home talking of men's things, hunts for *sanglier*, the wild boar of the Monts de Vaucluse, while this woman's appreciation of petals had to wait for half a year.

There were trying days, heavy days, turbulent days. Pascal's habits began to irritate me. He slurped his *grand café* and swished it around his mouth and let the bowl slam down on the table, splashing the oilcloth. Morsels of food clung to his mustache. It was unpleasant to pick them off, so I offered to trim his mustache. That brought on a fit of crying. I hadn't meant to embarrass him.

He was constantly clearing his throat in a guttural way, saying, "I have to tell you . . . ," then demanding that I stop moving even when what he wanted to relate to me flitted away like a moth.

Apparently he overcame his humiliation about not being able to fire or point because he began going to the *boules* terrain again, but I suspected it was only to watch. I noticed that Monsieur Voisin, the café owner, had moved a chair with arms next to the players' bench so Pascal could push himself up from it. After the first sign of cool weather, I insisted that he wear his winter overcoat. He fussed at me, saying that I was overdressing him, as if he were Saint George going out to slay a dragon, but he eventually relented.

Once after he went to the café to play *belote,* he came home grumbling, holding on to the bent arm of a man I didn't recognize. André greeted him as though they were acquainted and introduced him as Bernard Blanc, the *garde champêtre,* constable of the commune, which consisted of the village and its surrounding farms, orchards, and pastures. André invited him inside.

"I found Pascal teetering in place de la Mairie, so I thought I had better help him home," the constable told us.

"Thank you. That's very kind of you," André said.

Irritated, and maybe even ashamed, Pascal extricated himself from the constable's grasp, collapsed onto a chair, and said, "Now that you're here, young man, you might as well take a look at the paintings."

He did so, standing in front of each one, so tall he tilted his head down to look at them, not saying anything while André and Pascal watched him.

"A fine collection. Are they by well-known painters?"

"By *famous* painters!" Pascal bellowed. "Pissarro and Cézanne!"

The constable nodded, as if he knew the names, but something told me he didn't. After a few minutes, André saw him to the door and stepped outside with him, thanking him again.

—

ANDRÉ AND MAURICE MOVED Pascal's bed downstairs because Pascal complained that his sitting bones ached when he sat on the bare wood chairs. I worried on the days when he slept long hours, his breathing like pebbles pouring out of a jar, his mouth open, his head at an angle, drool darkening his shirt. With André working in the courtyard or going back and forth to Avignon, who would urge Pascal to eat if I weren't here? Who would bathe and shave him, rub his feet, put cool cloths on his forehead when he was feverish, sit with him and listen endlessly? It was right that I was here. This was now holy ground.

Once he risked his balance and lunged across the room, teetering toward me.

"You won't go back to Paris before . . ."

"No, Pascal. We'll be with you."

"You will be happy again in Paris."

"I am happy now, with you."

"How old am I?"

"When were you born?"

"In 1852."

"Then you're eighty-six."

"Eighty-six," he said with wonder. "Who would have thought I would live so long?"

"And still be handsome."

"How old are you?"

"Twenty-one. Twenty-two in November."

"I want to ask you something, *minette*."

"Anything you want."

A bashful look came over his face and he stroked my cheek. "Will you call me Papa?"

"Yes, Papa. I'm happy to call you Papa." Descending softly, the word sounded both strange and right. I couldn't remember ever saying it before, certainly never to the ghostly father who'd left me at the orphanage like a sack of grain, then went to some far-off country and died there, my mother too.

—

WE KNEW WINTER HAD come when the silence of the countryside was pierced by the reports of hunters' rifles and the raucous barking of dogs. Woodsmoke from the burning of the vines and the oily scent of olives being pressed rose to our hilltop perch. Ice crystals formed on the moss of the village washbasin. That suggested that a harder winter than the last one lay ahead. More mistrals. Colder ones.

Pascal normally had a throw-open-the-windows-in-winter attitude, but now he complained that it was as cold in the house as it had been in the mine. He fell asleep breathing cold air, woke up choking, and struggled to say through stiff blue lips that the mine had collapsed on him. Contradicting him would make him angry or feel foolish. "How terrible! *Grâce à Dieu,* you weren't killed," I said, letting him have his imagined moment of triumphant survival.

He drifted into a reverie, naming the hues made from the ochres of the Usine Mathieu, the pigment factory on the outskirts of Roussillon. "*Rouge pompéi, fleur de guesde, cuir de Russie.* I sold them all in Paris. *Jaune nankin, prune de monsieur, désir amoureux.*"

I told him I liked hearing the names.

"Maurice was much younger, so he had to wait some years before he could work. Because he could pickax right-handed and left-handed, he was the miner of progress, like a captain, pickaxing at the farthest point of our gallery. The rest of us chiseled and scraped and dug out the ore from the walls. Fifteen meters high, those passages. We made them arch perfectly so they didn't need wooden beams, and when you looked down the gallery line, each arch appeared smaller than the one closer. It looked like a cathedral, Lisette, and we *made* it. Even the life of a miner is worth living when you recognize beauty."

He had called the passageways galleries. "Then the mine was a showcase of your work," I said.

He nodded, pleased with me. "There were bats in those galleries. Scared the piss out of us when they streaked by our heads." He chuckled at the memory, but that lasted only a minute. His expression darkened. "Some of the mines are shutting down now. You can't tell me they aren't. You don't see as many men coming home wearing clothes caked with ochre. That can't mean anything good."

ONE MORNING PASCAL THUDDED down his coffee bowl and pushed himself upright. "I'm going to the ochre quarries. The colors glow at this hour."

"No, Papa. The cliffs are too dangerous."

"Don't tell me what to do. And don't follow me."

I burst out crying.

"You are too sensitive." He slammed the door behind himself.

André was in Avignon, repairing the massive, elaborately-tooled dining table in the Palais des Papes, and would return with the first two of the twenty-four carved chairs to mend and restore the carving at home, an important commission. He had ridden Maurice's bus and wouldn't be back until the next day. I fretted about Pascal's impulsive departure, then threw on my coat and went after him.

He could be anywhere along the lane—in the café, at the *terrain de boules,* inside the *boulangerie,* talking to Odette and René, who often gave him a warm slice of olive bread. I hurried downhill, poking my nose into places where I might find him. The quarries were beyond the lower end of the village, somewhere in the ochre canyons. I went uphill first, past the cemetery to the entrance to the canyons, then down into them a short way. I understood why he wanted to see them at this time. They did glow golden ochre, orange, and the red of paprika. If he went too far, it would be hard to find him, and he would have trouble climbing back.

I slipped on the places still wet from the recent rain, and stained my shoes with orange mud. Frightened, I called his name. He was nowhere. I needed the help of Constable Blanc, so I turned back to ask for him at the *mairie,* the town hall.

Passing alongside the graveyard, I had a hunch and peered between oleander bushes, then entered through the iron gate by a tall, lone cypress, which cast a gray, shroudlike shadow across the closest tomb. Wind whistled through the tops of pines and rustled the leaves in the olive orchard above and behind the tombs. Every *Roussillonnais* family knew their place of rest. Alongside a small oleander whipped by the wind, the Roux family vault lay in full sunlight. With both palms on the stone slab to support himself, Pascal was leaning forward, breathing hard.

I approached cautiously. His shoes were not filmed over with ochre dust or orange mud. He either had been afraid to venture down or had gotten distracted.

"You shouldn't have followed me," he said, sensing my presence, still looking at the tomb, "but I knew you would."

"I was worried, Papa. I'm not strong enough to help you get up if you fall."

"You can't control everything, Lisette. There is a time to let things be."

He patted the stone tomb and chuckled. "I'm not really going to be in this box. Instead, I'm going to follow Cézanne wherever he goes and carry his easel and canvas and paints, so he can paint unencumbered the glories of heaven. So vast, so infinite that making a frame around them is impossible. The other side has beautiful colors that we can't imagine on this side. Cézanne said so. Oh, happy days ahead."

FATIGUÉ PASSED INTO *TRÈS FATIGUÉ,* and it was hard to get Pascal out of bed to go to the outhouse. I tended to him where he lay, using a bedpan.

"Such love you show me. Like a daughter's. It will make the end easier." He let out a quavering sigh. "But there's more to tell. About Cézanne especially. Can you find my list?"

When I brought it to him, he said, *"Eh, bieng,"* in the Provençal accent he used when he spoke about Cézanne. "The painting called *The Card Players.* I haven't told you about that. Two *Provençaux* playing *belote* at a small table with a bottle of wine between them. Maybe that was the prize for the winner. I liked the game, but I never seemed to pluck the right cards from the stack, so I wasn't any good at it."

Maurice came that afternoon to bring us honey from his hives. "Here. This will make you feel better. My bees are descendants of those buzzing around the rosemary in the garden of the pope's palace in Avignon."

"Ah, holy bees. Imagine that." Pascal chuckled.

Maurice pulled a chair up to the bed to play a hand of *belote.* Their teasing about who would win and who had won the last game rolled gently, soft-voiced and mellow.

"Did I ever tell you? I posed for one of Cézanne's card players. The one with a chamois hat like mine." Pascal reached for my hand as I set a bowl of almonds on the bed, and I saw that the month-old bruise on the back of his hand had turned yellow-green.

He grabbed my wrist. "You do believe me, don't you?"

"Yes, Papa."

"Eh, Lisette, such a good woman."

PASCAL DIDN'T COMPLAIN WHEN he felt nausea or pain. He simply said, "Bring me the third Pissarro" or "I want to see the still life," and I knew he wished to lose himself in a painting. I suspected that his absorbed study, his searching for something in each painting he had not noticed before, allowed him to rise above discomfort. I would have to hold the painting up for him, frame and all, at the foot of his bed while he pored over the scene until my arms ached.

When I held up Pissarro's red roofs, the largest painting, Pascal murmured, "Such a pretty orchard. You know, those globs of paint protruding from the canvas, they catch light on their upper edges and create small shadows beneath them. That's not an accident, Lisette. That's genius."

Even in this he was teaching me to notice details. But beyond that, he was saying goodbye to each of the paintings.

After long thought, he said, "With Pissarro, I had looked for a story in his paintings. The girl with the goat, where was she going? Why was she alone? But with Cézanne, there was no story in the panorama or in the fruit. You see, the apples and oranges were important in themselves. I had to learn to regard them as products of the painter's way of seeing. I made myself refuse to imagine which of the card players would win the game. The act of their playing was enough."

He squirmed in bed with agitation, a frustrated attempt to get out of bed on his own.

"If I could kneel in adoration, I would. You kneel for me, Lisette. Get André."

I went to the courtyard. "You had better come in."

When André entered, Pascal said, "Kneel in front of Cézanne's fruit. I'll give you the words to say."

André and I glanced at each other, sharing the strangeness of the command. He knelt. I knelt. He took my hand.

"Ah, yes. Now say, 'We will, with all our hearts, love these paintings as we love each other.'"

André's expression showed that he was amused by Pascal's ceremony, a vow so unnecessary. Despite that, solemnly, humoring his grandfather, he began and I joined in. "We will, with all our hearts . . ."

Papa's waxen face shone with joy. "There. Now they are yours. Hélène would be happy if she knew." After a few moments he added, "Maybe she does."

Unable to speak, André kissed him on his bald spot.

"One thing I have to ask you, André. Will you repair the kneelers in the church before you go back to Paris? Hélène often gets splinters from them."

I mouthed the question *Who is Hélène?* to André, thinking she might have been his wife. André merely said solemnly, "Yes, I promise."

He went back to the courtyard. Through the window I saw that he didn't take up a mallet or chisel or even a pencil for quite a while.

After a brooding hour, Pascal murmured, "I failed today, Lisette. Something that should have been first on my list. I haven't shown you any love today. I have only loved the paintings and my memories. I have ordered you around. I'm sorry."

"That's all right, Papa. I know you love me. Tell me more about Cézanne."

"Did I tell you that I went back to Aix again? I had saved some money and for once in my life I wanted to buy a painting outright, legitimately, with francs. I wanted to do something good for Cézanne. I knew which one it would be. *The Card Players.* I wanted to ask him to explain what made a painting great.

"When I arrived, all his paintings were gone. His housekeeper was cleaning. She told me I was too late. He had died two weeks earlier. Apparently he was painting Montagne Sainte-Victoire again and had gotten caught in a rainstorm. He collapsed on the roadside, and the driver of a laundry cart found him. A week later, he died."

Pascal shook his head mournfully. "I asked her where *The Card Players* went. To the dealer Vollard, like all the others, she said."

Papa reached out a thin-skinned arm to me and wiggled his fingers, asking for mine. "Let that be a lesson to you, Lisette. Do the important things first."

THAT EVENING, WHILE PASCAL lay in a stupor watching me, and André was at the café for the men's *apéritif* hour, the stillness in the house made me reflective. I took a sheet of André's stiff paper and wrote at the top, *Lisette's List of Hungers and Vows*.

What *was* most important?

1. Love Pascal as a father.
2. Go to Paris, find Cézanne's *Card Players*.
3. Do something good for a painter.
4. Learn what makes a painting great.

Looking up at the Pissarro, I noticed the blueness of the girl's dress, so lovely alongside the white goat.

5. Make a blue dress, the blue of the Mediterranean Sea on a summer day with no clouds.

After that, a period of dull waiting set in, and André and I held on to each other more tightly at night. I asked him, "What are the most important qualities a person should have to live a good life?"

"Love and courage."

I knew I felt love and was richly loved, but did I have courage? Was being a witness to the ebbing of Pascal's life a means of developing courage for something else to come?

THERE WERE NERVOUS STIRRINGS in the local paper, *Le Petit Provençal,* after German troops took Czechoslovakia. We didn't tell Pascal, but he probably read it in the newspaper in the café. Every letter from Maxime reported actions against degenerate art. We kept that news to ourselves as well. In one letter Maxime wrote:

My dearest friends,

I can only take a few minutes to write. Do you in the south know that the art of the Louvre is even now being sealed in cases to be hidden? One by one the galleries are systemati-

cally being emptied. I volunteered to help pack. It's cold and dreary in the long galleries without my old friends hanging in their usual places. We work quickly and are bewildered and exhausted. Our dry voices echo against blank walls. We sleep only three hours a night. This will be the only chance in a lifetime to spend a night in the Louvre. Soon there will be more NO ADMITTANCE *signs than paintings.*

The Entartete Kunst, that "Degenerate Art" exhibit last year when people shouted epithets at the paintings, that was only a beginning. It recently leaked out to the volunteers here that 16,000 contemporary paintings have been purged from German museums to be auctioned in Lucerne. I fear for France.

I need to get back to packing. The Comédie-Française lorries are waiting like dark maws for crates to be loaded. Take good care of each other.

Maxime

Whatever monster lurked on the horizon, André hoped it would hold back its claws until Pascal had gone. Pascal knew that the German army had marched into Austria and had taken it last spring, and it plunged him into a state of despondency. From then on, for a whole year, we didn't mention anything to him about the world beyond Roussillon. Better that he pass in peace.

One May morning in 1939, after I had known and loved Pascal for two years, André and I sat on both sides of him while he struggled to get his tongue to work. "Give my *boules* to Maurice. Remind him that at one time, I could make him bite the dust." His mouth twitched in a slight smile. After a long period of waiting for his next breath, he murmured, "A good life. Take care of each other. And let the paintings care for you."

It seemed like the passing of time halted for a moment while the larks made their mournful song. Poised in perfect peace between past and future, which blended into an eternal now, he added, "But some, I think, belong in Roussillon."

Then, with a soft, contented breath, he slipped through and traveled on.

BOOK II

CHAPTER TEN

MAXIME'S
LETTER

1939

A N OUTING ALL BY MYSELF! WITH MORE COINS IN MY DRAW-string bag than I ever had on market day in Roussillon, I approached place du Pasquier, where people boarded Maurice Chevet's bus for the short trip to the Saturday market in Apt, the larger town to the east. Behind his funny-looking bus, Maurice hauled a wagon for engine parts, petrol cans, furniture, rabbits in cages, anything a person would want to transport.

We had been grieving over Pascal, and André had hoped that a trip on my own to a large market would lift my spirits. He had been paid for repairing the enormous carved dining table in the Palais des Papes in Avignon and was still working on the twenty-four matching chairs, a profitable project that kept us in Roussillon. For the first time since we had come here, he felt free with money, so I was bursting with anticipation.

OUTSIDE HIS BUS, MAURICE SAID, "Adieu, Lisette," with the enthusiasm of a long absent friend. "You go to buy pastis today?"

"You guess wrongly, monsieur."

"Then a new dress for madame? A pair of espadrilles?"

"A cotton tablecloth." I wanted to replace the discolored oil-cloth, cracked and torn from age where it bent over the edge of the table.

"*Eh, bieng.* A Provençal tablecloth! Go to all the stalls before you buy."

In the bus, Aimé Bonhomme, Pascal's *boules* partner and the *secrétaire de la mairie,* lifted his bowler hat off the seat beside him and beckoned to me. I took his invitation. He and Mayor Pinatel, who was sitting behind him, agreed with a jolly laugh that they had official business in Apt, but it was Saturday, so I didn't believe them. I suspected that they just wanted to get out of Roussillon for a day. It was more believable that Monsieurs Cachin and Voisin had busi-ness there—stocking the store and the café.

"We're going to buy corks," chirped Mimi, the little daughter of Mélanie Vernet, the vintner's wife. "Lots of corks."

The bus rattled down the winding road, swaying around the curves, everyone knowing instinctively when to brace themselves. In anxious voices, they speculated whether Hitler would stop with Po-land or whether France would be next. To change the subject, I asked Monsieur Bonhomme how long Apt had held a weekly mar-ket.

"Oh, just short of eight hundred years."

"You're teasing me, monsieur."

"Oh, no, madame. The Romans built the arcades where the ta-bles are set up. Crusaders provisioned themselves there. Feudal lords, purchasing agents of Provençal counts, papal underlings when Avignon was the center of the church, they all went to Apt to buy or trade or just socialize."

We passed vegetable fields along the nearly dry Calavon River, and trellised green beans on the low hills. One abandoned hilltop village had a newer village at its base, as though it had cheerfully slipped down its hill intact.

All the residents of Apt and the surrounding villages seemed to be out and about—petits bourgeois in suits and leather shoes, la-

borers in blue smocks, and women in flowered cotton dresses. Mélanie, a little older than I was, fell into step with me and told me to
stay with her. I found that she was adept at elbowing her way
through the crowds in front of fruit and vegetable stands and tables
of herbs and spices, olive oil and vinegar, and cheese. Everything
here was probably locally produced.

"The trick is to buy early and quickly for items with a set price,
slowly for items you can bargain over," Mélanie advised.

At a table where wooden utensils, string bags, lamp oil, and
household goods were sold, I caught the sweet aroma of some handmade lavender soaps. They were without wrappers but stamped
with L'OCCITANE, a curious name I wasn't familiar with. Mélanie
bought two gunnysacks of corks. The vendor drew a face on one
cork and gave it to Mimi.

After leaving the sacks in Maurice's bus, Mélanie led me down a
side street where table after colorful table displayed cloths. Oh,
such colors, with prints of sunflowers, lavender, grapes, olives,
wheat, even *cigales*. Pretending her cork was a little doll, Mimi
danced it across the fabrics.

"Which one shall I buy, Mimi?"

"This one. No. This one. This one with the grapes, like Papa's
vines."

We discussed the merits of each, agonizing with delight over
which one to choose. Finally I made a decision, and Mimi agreed.
Yellow sunflowers, something we didn't have in Paris. With Mélanie's shopping recommendations, I had money left over. "Spend it
all," she advised. "You don't know when you'll get more." So I
bought a straw sunhat with Mimi's approval, a pair of red espadrilles, and an issue of *Modes et Travaux*, which had sewing projects. There was nothing like a day of shopping to turn two women
and a little girl into fast friends.

Excited to show André my purchases, I burst into the house,
spread the cloth, and stood back to look. With a jolt, I saw only
empty walls. No paintings. No frames. Confusion descended on

me. André came in from the courtyard, and I demanded to know what he had done with them.

He pulled a chair back from the table. "Sit down, Lisette."

"You didn't sell them, did you?"

"No. I would never do that. I hid them."

"Where? Why?"

"They're not safe here. Many people in the village have seen them. Pascal talked about them to everyone. I can't fault him. It was innocent exuberance that made him want to share them, but these aren't innocent times. People will need food and many other things. The black market will be rampant. Need and suffering can turn a person. Friends have secret friends who may be black market dealers. Art can be traded for items no longer available. Poof! The paintings will become untraceable. I can't trust anyone."

"Even me? You can't trust your wife?"

"I trust you, but it's better that you don't know. An inadvertent glance at a hiding place might reveal it."

Pained by his secrecy, I scanned the empty walls and struggled not to cry.

It wasn't just that he was keeping the hiding place a secret from me. It was a darker ache—that *he* was a secret to me. He had secret thoughts, secret plans. No matter what he told me, there were things unsaid. Maybe he had sold them. Maybe they had been stolen and he was just appeasing me by pretending they were hidden. Was it wise for him not to tell me? To have made his plans without consulting me?

He handed me a letter from Maxime.

27 AUGUST 1939

Comrade,

Read this twice, then burn it. Hide your paintings. There are more than rumors here. Métro stations are being fitted out as

air raid shelters. If the Germans penetrate France, God for-
bid, all of France's art is endangered—the paintings still in
museums and those in private hands as well. Every single
museum in Paris closed its doors today. The art market here
is in chaos. Every day the workers in the Louvre hear of cun-
ning plans for quick sales to Germans and to anyone buying
to save important paintings from destruction. At that auction
in Lucerne, Monsieur Laforgue bid to save a Van Gogh self-
portrait and Picasso's Absinthe Drinker *but was outbid on*
both. There was a frenzy of bidding for Matisses, Braques,
Klees taken straight from Germany's own museums, with
proceeds to the Nazi Party.

This past spring one thousand oil paintings and nearly
four thousand watercolors and drawings deemed of no inter-
national value or considered objectionable by the Reich
Chamber of Culture were burned by the Berlin Fire Depart-
ment to "purify" the art world. It's horrifying. If any paint-
ings are in line with Hitler's aims, sycophants drooling over
prestige positions steal them to give to Hitler, buying favor
with art. Either way, the art is lost to its owners.

If the Germans take Paris, nothing is safe. Hide your
paintings, André, and hide them well. Tell no one.

People here fear the worst. We must enlist together or get
conscripted separately. Come to Paris. Better that we fight
shoulder to shoulder to save our country's treasures, our pat-
rimony, our cities, our identity, and our freedom—in short,
to save France.

Give a kiss to jolie Lisette for me. Come soon.

Maxime

"Oh, André!"

Sudden dryness stopped my mouth. I handed the letter back to
him. He read it one more time, lifted the circular lid of the cooking

stove, and fed it to the flames. Seeing the edges curl and turn Maxime's handwriting to ash, I could only imagine what André and Maxime would see, what they would have to do.

We read the Paris newspaper clipping Maxime had enclosed about Kristallnacht, the night ten months earlier of brutal attacks on Jewish synagogues and businesses throughout Germany and parts of Austria. An estimated thirty thousand German and Austrian Jews were rounded up and sent to camps.

That evening, we ate our dinner silently, shocked, watching each other raise fork to mouth. Every second of silence thickened my fear. Something was shifting. The sundering of our parallel thinking pierced the closeness of our lives, and in the tiny opening, acute sadness poured in. I said with my eyes what I could not say with words: *Don't go.*

He touched my shoulder as he stood up, lingering a moment, his hand resting there, before he put on his cap. I stood too and reached for my shawl.

"No, Lisette. Stay here," he said with softness in his voice, and left for the café.

Every evening since Hitler had taken Czechoslovakia, he had been going to the café in order to listen to the radio and talk with the men of the village about the likelihood of the German army penetrating France. Could he not understand that I wanted to hear it for myself?

I tried to recall Maxime's letter—all those paintings turning into an ash heap, the art world of France and of my dreams shattered, hope shriveled. Thank God Pascal didn't know. I washed the dishes and went to bed, chilled to the bone on this hot summer night.

THE NEXT DAY, SUNDAY, we went about our work quietly. I searched André's face at supper before he left to go to the café, saw only worry written there, and went to bed alone. I awoke when André's shoes dropped heavily onto the floor. Under the sheet he pulled me toward him, his breath smelling of beer as he said, "De Gaulle declared war today."

It was the third of September, a date impossible to forget now. He cupped my breast, but he didn't fondle me as he did most nights before our lovemaking. We lay still, our hearts too heavy for playfulness. My mind tumbled with questions. When he felt me tremble, he held me tighter. Tomorrow's dawn would bring a new reality. Then we would talk about what to do.

IT WASN'T LIGHT THAT awakened me. It was the sharp rasp of André's saw going through wood that made me shudder. The tapping of a mallet, then the sanding went on for two weeks, so intent was he on finishing a large, waist-high cabinet, a gift to me, while the glue was setting on each pair of palace chairs. I had seen in his drawings that the carving on the double cabinet doors would be an *A* and an *L* with their upright strokes leaning against each other; all around them he would carve a circle of fleurs-de-lis. He intended the cabinet to be for dishes, so they wouldn't be exposed on shelves when the mistrals blew dust through the house. He was going to position it beneath the place where Cézanne's still life of fruit had hung, next to the stairs. Once the war was over, the cabinet and the painting would look magnificent together.

Surely we should have been doing something other than this feverish work, and we did, savoring delicate, tense moments together, our arms around each other's waists as we watched the sun sink behind the windmill on the promontory beyond the ravine, cherishing each other in every way, stroking each other's favorite places, unable to love enough to last the duration. I prepared his favorite dish, *cassoulet béarnais,* a casserole made with mutton, pork, andouille sausages, and white beans. I bought *pain fougasse,* a flat olive loaf, which he loved, and I asked René to make some *palmiers,* André's favorite pastry. We fed morsels to each other just as we had done in Paris when he called me his perfect lily. And of course, we slept in each other's arms.

He was right about one thing. My eyes naturally went to possible hiding places—beneath the mattresses, under the beds, behind the headboards and dressers in both bedrooms, in the root cellar. He had puttied the holes where the paintings had hung so expertly that no one could tell a nail had been there. I had to believe that he had hidden the paintings with equal care.

I watched with an aching heart as he made his methodical preparations. He took down the wide plywood boards he used as work surfaces, folded up his sawhorses, laid out his tools on a shelf in the lean-to, covered them with canvas, and weighted the canvas with rocks. He bought firewood at the communal woodpile and stacked it neatly against the house. At our Thursday market, he bought a huge sack of rice and another of dried white beans, four long sausages, six tins of sardines, a large tin of coffee, a sack of sugar, another sack of flour, a salt cake, and olive oil. He shook the almonds from our tree, and I gathered them. He left all our money from the Palais des Papes job in the green ceramic olive jar. Only one thing remained to be done—to repair the kneelers in the church, his promise to Pascal. Now he vowed that it would be his first task when he came home.

It was when he packed his satchel that I couldn't stand to be silent.

"Can't I go to Paris with you? I'll find a way to live. As a seamstress of army uniforms, or back at the *pâtisserie*."

"You think there will be sugar for pastries? Be realistic."

But even with the windows along les Champs-Élysées boarded up, the streets dark, cafés closed, statues cocooned within mounds of sandbags, there would still be the Seine. I could sit on my favorite iron bench in the square of Vert-Galant at the point of Île de la Cité and watch the fisherman too old to be in the army. The chestnuts would soon be dropping, the leaves of the plane trees crunching under my feet, and the faucets would still be running.

Despite my longings, I knew that when he said, "No, *chérie*. It's safer for you here," he was right. Paris was the capital, after all, and so it would be vulnerable.

He would leave the next Monday, a week after his twenty-sixth birthday, and would ride Maurice's bus to Avignon. I counted down the days, then the hours. There was no crowd shouting "On to Berlin!" at the bus stop, only Constable Blanc standing off to the side. André approached him to speak to him privately, then came back to embrace me. He kissed me one more time and said, "It won't be long, and I'll be home. Then we can live in Paris. I promise."

I stood between him and the bus, a foolish barrier between war and peace, until Maurice climbed up behind the steering wheel. André and I were left on the ground while the people in the bus watched us through the windows, knowing. Maurice started up the sputtering engine, which rattled my heart to pieces. André had to grasp my shoulders and move me aside in order to get on.

Gray exhaust snarled out at me, and I stood motionless, looking at André's form as he made his way through the bus, his neck and jaw and left ear already shadowy to me.

Watching until the bus turned downhill, I felt an arm rest heavily on my shoulder. It was the *garde champêtre,* Bernard Blanc, who had brought Pascal home once.

"Worrying won't help him. You have to help yourself now," he said.

I wrenched my shoulder free and hurried home and knelt in front of André's cabinet, trying to calm myself, trying to pray, tracing with my fingertips the *A* and the *L* leaning against each other.

CHAPTER ELEVEN

THE RADIO
AND THE CAFÉ

1940

I TRIED TO BE HOPEFUL AS I WALKED TO THE POST OFFICE. Maybe this time there would be a letter from André. I thought again of the last thing he had said to me. *It won't be long, and I'll be home. Then we can live in Paris. I promise.*

I filled my mind with that vision, that he would come home from the war and I would be delirious with happiness. We would make joyous love, and I would conceive a child. We would sell this drafty house, and I would give birth in Paris, and our child would learn all the lessons well at *école élémentaire,* and if she was a girl, she would wear flowered dresses in summer like Mélanie's Mimi, and if he was a boy, he would wear short gray pants and show his dimpled knees. As André rowed in the upper lake of the Bois de Boulogne, our perfect child would trail a delicate hand in the water, and all that would be lovely, but we would never be quite as we had been because André hadn't trusted me.

THEN, THE HAPPY SIGHT: Odette's daughter, Sandrine, the post office clerk, balancing a letter on her palm. "*Voilà!* From your husband," she said with great respect.

At home, I opened it carefully.

17 JANUARY 1940

Dearest Lisette,

Maxime and I managed to get in the same platoon. It's comforting to have a friend here, wherever here is. All I know is that our train passed vast cemeteries from the Great War—this presumably is the petite one—with crosses laid out in rows like stone vineyards. I wonder if my father is sleeping there. I must finish the work he began.

To that end, we've been fitted out with scratchy uniforms, boots, kit bags, and rifles. We're learning how to march, fall lizardlike onto our bellies, squirm along like worms, and shoot. I'm better at squirming. Maxime is better at shooting but worse at marching. My first sight of blood was his bloody blisters, thanks to his stiff, tight boots. Next we're going to learn how to operate machine guns.

This turning of art lovers and craftsmen into killers doesn't sit well with me. It's against our natures, but being here in this atmosphere, a person can't help but get caught up in the importance and necessity of it. In a month, we're supposed to be hardened soldiers—ha!—and will go to the front, somewhere, to repel the Germans. In the interim, all I want to do is to repel mice. I suppose my rifle isn't the appropriate instrument.

I miss you terribly, and think of you in every quiet minute we're not being yelled at.

> *Forever, my love, I am yours,*
> *André*

Anxiety shaped itself into a piteous memory I couldn't shake. The horror and sadness I had experienced as a little girl seeing a man leaning on a single crutch with half a body slid uninvited into my mind. No left arm, no left leg, no left ear. Left eye sunken, half-closed. His face sewn together in a lumpy purple seam below the left eye and across the jaw. "Dry him off and bring me someone who has half a chance," I now imagined the surgeon saying. But he did survive. This soldier from the Great War had done one more courageous thing. He had come to see his son, who lived where I was living, in a home for unclaimed children. I felt only awe for his bravery.

If André came home in a similar condition, I was certain I would still pour out my love for him from a bottomless well.

No letters came while he was on the move. Then this:

6 MARCH 1940

Mon petit trésor,

I pray that you are warm and well. I can say that at least the latter is true for me.

En route to our position, we had our first view of the Maginot Line of concrete fortifications and wicked-looking tank obstacles. We are not told how far they stretch, but rumor has it that in one form or another there are emplacements from Switzerland to Luxembourg. We hear that some units are connected by underground passageways and even a rail line and telephones, with comfortable living quarters.

Nothing so grand for us here. Max and I learned how to make a bunker of wood and cement to shelter a big gun. We made a splendid trench for ourselves, connecting one bunker to another. With the woods behind us, we get afternoon shade, which we dread this time of year. The humane thing would be that by international law, all winter wars would be called off. Last week the ice in our canteens never thawed. I can't tell you where, but from the ridge behind our trench home, we have a grand view of a beautiful frozen river a short distance away, German ice and French ice indistinguishable.

As new recruits, we have been scattered among the reservists. Max and I hope that means that they know what to do in a moment of truth and we can just follow their lead. Simple, right?

Nothing new here in this phony war. That's what our lieutenant calls it in disgust, he who wants it to start so we'll all be heroes and he will be decorated. Other than that, he never talks about the reasons for war.

The days pass, empty and interminable, and the enemy hasn't poked their noses in our business. Busy elsewhere, I suppose. We huddle around a makeshift stove and speculate until all we do is repeat each other's words, like crows. Any day now, we expect, they will try to cross the river and get at us. This waiting sets our nerves on edge at every sound. We hear rumbles and trucks and tanks and, in our sardonic moments, alpenhorns and bassoons and Dudelsacks. Max swore he heard sleigh bells.

Some fellows brag about how many Boches they're going to kill. I stay away from them. It's that silent one with the vacant eyes I worry about. Waiting and wondering whether we'll distinguish ourselves or turn coward and run preys on everyone's mind. Our lieutenant boasts about a quick victory. I wish we had more men and more artillery. To my mind, we're spread too thin—just like the beans in our bean soup. I wouldn't mind having some thick goulash, even if it's Prussian.

The waiting isn't the worst thing. Missing you is the worst thing. Imagine that I'm holding you tonight. I'll do the same.

> *With a full heart,*
> *André*

Despite his levity, I worried that the man with the vacant eyes might be André himself. Or Maxime.

THE WAITING WAS HARD on me too. I hated not being able to do anything other than send him letters. If I could just discover where the paintings were, take a peek at them, and leave them there, I would feel closer to him again. I would touch the stones or boards or plants or earth he had touched.

But where to start?

The bell tower, ostensibly to see the view. Father Marc gave me the key, and I searched on every landing, in every crevice, to no avail. Sandrine let me look around the post office, in case a letter from André had been put in the wrong cubbyhole. While there, I peeked behind doors and in large cabinets. I asked Aimé if I could look in the *salle des fêtes* for a lost scarf. Could André have hidden the paintings in the café? He went there every night. I asked outright if I could watch Madame Voisin prepare *fricassée de poulet*. "No," Monsieur Voisin said crossly, turning his back to me while he did something behind the bar.

"Would you permit me just to look in your kitchen?"

"Certainly not!" He whirled around. "There's nothing here that would interest you."

"There might be, monsieur. I just thought—"

"Don't think. You'll be better off that way."

And that was that, for the present.

ANDRÉ'S THIRD LETTER HAD no date, which was disconcerting because I couldn't tell how long it had taken to reach me.

Dearest Lisette,

I hope that the wood I banked alongside the house has lasted the winter. You should be receiving my army pay warrants by

*the time the Palais des Papes money runs out. Then you'll
have enough to buy from the communal woodpile, and to eat
as well as rationing allows.*

*This waiting is deeply frustrating, and the incessant drill-
ing and marching is a bore. The ice on the river has broken
up into fanciful icebergs. Max drew the scene on his canteen
with a piece of charcoal. After that, he did a good likeness of
me on mine. Now everyone in our platoon wants a portrait
on their canteen. Some of the men pose with exaggerated
dignity, while our overzealous lieutenant bares his teeth and
puts on an expression like an angry bulldog. Interesting, the
personalities in our platoon.*

*Our armored tanks are big and heavy but slow, only
twenty-five kilometers an hour. It remains to be seen how
they will fare when they face the Panzer II.*

*I have rethought my decision not to tell you where I hid
the paintings. I didn't tell you because I thought your innocence would protect you, but it might be just the opposite. If,
God forbid, the Germans take France and if it's known to
them that we have paintings and some German officer comes
to the house to seize them before I get home, you could come
to harm for not telling him where they are. I would never forgive myself for that. What I mean is, if there is any trouble,
give up the paintings. They are not worth bringing injury to
yourself, my darling. They are under the big woodpile.*

*Keep safe, my love. I am expecting to be showered with
your kisses the moment I see you.*

> *With love and infinite devotion,*
> *Your André*

I was both relieved to know where he had hidden them—what
an odd hiding place—and worried that behind his change of heart,
he had some doubt that he would come home.

—

WINTER HERE HAD ENDED with a three-day mistral, and a vivid spring sunset that faded to reveal a full moon rising. The hills below the village were just becoming fragrant with flowering wild arugula. Plump Odette Gulini, old enough to be my mother and wise in the ways of the country, told me I could use the leaves in a salad, so we went to gather them. It would be a pleasant diversion from thinking about the war.

On the way, she pointed out her favorite wildflower, aphyllanthes, which had six narrow lavender petals with a purple stripe down each. I picked one and threaded it through her hair. Looking at her, I couldn't be sure, but I thought she had moved her beauty mark from her right cheek to her left. When I questioned her, she said, "We think our son, Michel, is somewhere near the Belgian border. He's left-handed. I cannot betray him."

That seemed as reasonable as anything else these days.

We found primroses in a clearing in the woods. Pascal would have called the pale yellow of their petals *jaune vapeur*. The thought coming so unbidden made me miss him.

Suddenly in my pathway I saw the lacerated body of a rabbit, the ears and feet still intact, the breast torn and bloody, the casualty of an attack by a hawk. I grew quiet.

Back in the village, our arms laden with arugula and primroses, we stopped on the road in front of Odette's house. She gave me a kind look and turned my collar down, a maternal gesture.

"You seem particularly quiet today. Is it because of the news?" she asked, gently introducing the only subject of importance.

"What news?"

"Germany invaded Luxembourg, Belgium, and the Netherlands the day before yesterday."

The shock of it made me shudder. "Three countries in one day? How did you find out?"

"René went to the café and heard the news. The men were arguing about who would be next, and when."

"Did he say more?"

"I suspect there was more to say, but he didn't tell me."

Hating not being able to hear the news directly, all the news, I went home in a daze and flung the arugula into the sink, spilling my primroses too. If I were living in Paris, I could go into any café, day or night, alone if I wanted to, and have *un petit crème,* enjoy its frothy milk and listen to the news on the radio, or a musical program, but oh no. Not here in this hinterland.

That evening at *apéritif* time, I put on a high-necked white blouse and my maroon suit, conservative enough for Roussillon but stylish enough to say *This suit came from Paris, and so did this woman.* Nobody needed to know I had bought it at a secondhand shop across the street from the synagogue in the Marais district. Brushing my hair in front of the mirror above the dresser, I had a thought. André was right-handed. I twisted the point of my eyebrow pencil on my right cheekbone.

I marched downhill to the café and paused to square my shoulders before parting the beads that hung like a curtain separating me from the world.

The proprietor, Monsieur Voisin, was ranting about something to anyone who would listen. "It's not my fault if you're going to be cold in here this winter. Mayor Pinatel took all the wood that was left in the communal woodpile."

Just the word gave me a start. Was that the woodpile André meant, or did he mean our own, in our courtyard? I listened more attentively.

"That's hard to believe," said Constable Blanc, standing a head above every other man at the bar. "He could afford to pay his own wood gatherer."

"Don't tell me!" said Monsieur Voisin. "I saw him with my own eyes, the bourgeois poser. He never comes here. Thinks he's too good to socialize with farmers, even though his father was a farmer just like yours."

That seemed like exaggerated bluster to me. My chin held high, looking directly ahead, I took a few steps in. All those hunched old men straightened up in their chairs, as if accosted by an enemy. Silence descended around me. I walked boldly to a table near the radio and sat down, in an effort to get as close as I could to where the fighting was happening in the north, one quavering radio wave linking me to one beating heart. No. Two hearts.

Some of the men ignored me and turned back to the bar while others stole squinty-eyed glances at me. Maurice acknowledged me with a small nod, but distress carved tight little wrinkles around his eyes. Most of the others, including Monsieur Voisin, glared at me outright, as though trying to make me feel guilty for breaking some time-honored rule. I had intended to order a *café crème,* but Monsieur Voisin did not approach me to take my order.

Eventually the BBC news came on in French, scratchy because of German interference. It was true. German paratroopers had landed from planes in Holland, while the Wehrmacht had crossed the frontiers of Luxembourg and Belgium and were moving into the forest of the Ardennes. Norway, too, had already been invaded. After so much waiting, such speed astonished me. The news was brief but devastating, and was followed by Maurice Chevalier in an old recording of the romantic song "Valentine," in English. Mustering as much grace as possible, I stood to go and felt Monsieur Voisin's cold eyes push me from behind as I departed.

THE NEXT EVENING, I went again. It was a bit easier. Maurice bought a glass of the local rosé for me. Most of the men gave him scornful looks. The BBC opened its news bulletin with the first four notes of Beethoven's Fifth Symphony. Maurice said it was the signal in Morse code for the letter *V,* London's symbol for victory.

The news was worse than the night before. Selfishly, disregarding my friends, I felt its import aimed precisely at me. Nevertheless, the BBC played "La Marseillaise." With a stone in my throat, I was the first to stand. Some of the men didn't budge at first—reluctant to follow the lead of a woman, I supposed—but eventually everyone in the room was standing.

AFTER THE MORNING RUSH for baguettes at the *boulangerie*, I beckoned to Odette and we walked to place du Pasquier, empty this time of day. I told her what I had heard the night before that René hadn't told her. The Maginot Line had proved to be folly. The Wehrmacht troops and big panzer tanks had swung wide, north of the northernmost Maginot fort, and had crossed the Ardennes in sixty hours. The next day, a terrifying all-day bombardment by German dive-bombers had hurtled down on the sparse French infantry defending the frontier along the Meuse River between the northern end of the Maginot Line and the city of Sedan. I feared that it was the river André had described. My voice cracked when I told her this last horrifying report, and it was some minutes before I could say any more.

"It's not fair that René didn't tell you everything."

"He must have had his reasons. Protecting me, I suppose, on account of Michel. I wonder whether Mélanie Vernet knows. Her brother is in the army."

"Come with me tonight. I'll ask her to come too. We don't deserve to sit out this war ignorantly."

"But my husband. Mélanie's husband—"

"They'll just have to get used to it. These are not normal times."

AS WE HAD EXPECTED, we three women coming into the café together angered the men.

"Now see what you did, Maurice?" a farmer said. "You'll have all of the wives of Roussillon here before long, and then who will

cook our dinners?" He walked out in a huff, and two others followed.

The BBC reported fierce fighting over the next week as the Wehrmacht, with its panzers, made a rapid and methodical push across
France and reached La Manche, what the British announcer called
the English Channel, pinning tens of thousands of the British Ex-
peditionary Force, together with French and Belgian soldiers, on
the beaches and harbor of Dunkerque. Meanwhile, two more
women whose sons or husbands or brothers were in the army
pushed east, into the café. By the end of May, the Allied escape at
Dunkerque was under way and the allied women of Roussillon
were occupying the café, beauty marks on their cheekbones for sol-
idarity, right or left depending on their men at war.

Our table of five women celebrated with beating hearts and
moist eyes the inestimable bravery of humanity. We pooled our
money and bought bottles of wine for the men's tables, in honor of
the crews of hundreds of British destroyers, ferries, merchant ma-
rine vessels, private fishing boats, pleasure craft, and lifeboats who,
day after day, under air and artillery attack, rescued hundreds of
thousands of exhausted Allied soldiers off the beaches and quays at
Dunkerque, while the French rear guard fought the advancing German infantry and forestalled catastrophe.

Could André and Maxime be among them, pushed all the way
across France and through the waves to a fishing boat? Or were
they . . . I refused to imagine anything else.

Sandrine was in a stupor, worried about her brother, Michel.
"Hold up your glass," I whispered to her. "He's one of the lucky
ones. I can feel it."

With my glass aloft, I announced to all, "I hope you know that
drinking this wine means you accept that women are not going to
retreat. We will not go back to the way it was in this café before the
war."

"You, madame, and your highfaluting Paris ways are an offense to my steady customers. You're not wanted here. Can't you see that?"

"And you, monsieur, are an offense to our men in uniform fighting for justice and *freedom*." That sounded rude. I added in a softer voice, "We should all be fighting for that together."

"Now you have twice as many customers," Odette said merrily. "That should make you happy."

"But your husbands are buying fewer drinks because you are here spying on them from across the room," Monsieur Voisin muttered.

Odette's cheerfulness was short-lived. Three nights later, we heard the tragic news that on the ninth day of the evacuation, after holding off German troops for four critical days and sacrificing their own escape, the French rear guard was captured and forced to surrender. Even with the playing of "God Save the King" and "La Marseillaise" after the broadcast, the news of tens of thousands of our countrymen taken prisoner cast gloom over everyone.

THE NUMBER OF WOMEN coming to the café increased to eight who had relatives in the fighting, plus two more who didn't. We found comfort in sitting close together. The men speculated, argued, cursed as though they were at a *boules* tournament. The women didn't speak during the BBC news reports, trying to make out the sense despite the transmission crackling like electrocuted moths too close to a lightbulb. We heard the voice of Winston Churchill calling the evacuation a miracle, yet cautioning his nation with the ominous statement, "We must be very careful not to assign to this deliverance the attributes of a victory. Wars are not won by evacuations." That sent me further into the depths.

The broadcasts repeated themselves, drumming home the despair by describing the refugees' movement southward. The exodus started in Belgium and collected thousands more in Paris. Bedraggled families gripped by panic carried carpetbags and valises, rolled bundles, pet canaries and cats in cages, china, silver chests in wheelbarrows or piled onto bicycles or on their backs, and they shed heavy loads along the roads, beside dead farm animals. That was the chaos that André hadn't wanted me to experience.

On 14 June, a male voice quavering with emotion announced that German troops had entered the capital. Paris had been declared an open city, which saved its architecture and monuments and many lives, but had sacrificed its liberty. The French government had abandoned the city to set up operations in Bordeaux. A German victory parade marched under the Arc de Triomphe and down the Champs-Élysées. My spirit was crushed by the stomp of jackboots.

In the café, we women grabbed each other's arms, hid our faces in each other's breasts. The men looked positively wounded. It was inconceivable, the speed of this defeat—hardly more than a month of fighting. Maurice's face contorted in anguish. *"Quelle catastrophe,"* he muttered, and then gave in to weeping.

As if the news weren't enough, Rina Ketty sang over the airwaves yet another time that slow, heart-wrenching song of longing and desire and endurance, "J'Attendrai," promising to wait for her man. The effect of its anticipated refrain was hypnotic.

The next week revealed more startling events. Prime Minister Paul Reynaud resigned under pressure from Marshal Pétain, the highest-ranking military officer, who installed himself as premier of a new French government that would seek an armistice with Germany. "The shame of it," René murmured in disgust.

With a mix of misery and courage, Roussillon managed to get through the next day. The café was crowded and noisy, with all the notables there—Mayor Pinatel, *Secrétaire de la Mairie* Aimé Bonhomme, Constable Blanc, and the town notary, Monsieur Rivet. Everyone quieted to hear the BBC broadcast a speech by General Charles de Gaulle, the minister of war, in which he defied Pétain's willingness to surrender.

"France has lost a battle, but she has not lost the war," he declared in a strong voice. "Nothing is lost because this war is a world war now. One day the forces of the free world will crush the enemy. France will recover her liberty and her grandeur. This is my aim. My only aim. Therefore, I call upon every French person to unite with me in action, in sacrifice, and in hope. Let us all strive to save her. *Vive la France!*"

I clung to the spirit he exhibited.

Nevertheless, four days later the scratchy voice of that English radio announcer revealed the terms of the armistice. France was to be divided into an Occupied Zone in the north and west, giving Germany access to all industries and ports, and an Unoccupied Zone in the middle and south, leaving its wine and olive oil and sunflowers to us, to be governed by Pétain in Vichy. As if the loss of life and liberty weren't enough, Hitler rubbed our noses in defeat by staging the signing of the armistice in the Forest of Compiègne, in the very same railway carriage in which Germany had been forced to surrender in 1918.

The radio clicked off. A hush settled over everyone like a leaden fog, like creeping poison gas. Monsieur Voisin motioned to the door, a signal that everyone should go home. With a hand raised against proffered coins, he refused payment. Wives and husbands sought each other's eyes and shuffled out into the evening in pairs. The constable asked if I would like him to walk me home. Sick with anguish for France, for André, for Maxime, I shook my head no and plodded home alone on heavy feet.

CHAPTER TWELVE

THE MISTRAL AND
THE MAYOR

1940

A LATE MISTRAL RACED DOWN FROM THE ALPS AND TORE through the Rhône Valley like a banshee, clawing its way below doors, howling down the chimney, blowing ash from the stove over everything, whistling against the window sashes like a bomb-bearing fighter plane, wrenching loose a pair of shutters, breaking their latches, banging them against the house like a battery of explosions, assaulting my nerves with the suspicion that the mistral had not yet launched its full virulence, that these winds were the mere pacings of a caged hyena.

I had no choice. After three days of being a prisoner in my own house, I needed bread, but I needed a letter from André more. Every week without one widened the crack in my hope. Hearing that letters from the front were taking longer to get here after the armistice, I recited the litany I had been telling myself:

Of course he was safe. Of course he had been in some peaceful place, loading ammunition on trucks or filling out papers. Always in war, papers had to be written out, didn't they? He had such beautiful handwriting, with flourishes on his g's and y's. Documents. Lists of tanks, machine guns, ammunition, vehicles. Lists of medicine, splints, bandages. Lists of names. The missing. The wounded. The dead.

I wrapped my head in a woolen scarf and opened the door. The wind yanked it out of my hand. I fought it closed just as a gust tore free some coral oleander blossoms and cast them tumbling down the hill. How prettily they sailed, like butterflies freed from a jar. One flung itself onto a man's pant leg right beyond my door and refused to be set free despite the agitated leg shaking of Mayor Pinatel.

Flanked on the right by Monsieur Aimé Bonhomme, the secretary of the *mairie,* and on the left by Constable Blanc and the notary, Monsieur Rivet, the mayor, cleared his throat and said, in the flat tone of dispensing dully with a routine business matter, "Adieu, madame. May we have a word with you?" Yet I detected an edge of strain. Seized with an instant's paralysis, I shook myself into action and managed, with the constable's help, to control the door and get us inside.

"I come on a sad errand."

I felt a spear enter my heart.

Head lowered in solemn ceremony, Monsieur Pinatel held out a letter. I stared at the seal of the Ministry of War and my name, Madame Lisette Irène Noëlle Roux. All four of them had known before I did.

I took the letter with a trembling hand, trying to be careful with it, knowing it was something I should save, inadvertently tearing the envelope. The words on the page squirmed like poisoned worms.

Chère Madame,

We regret to inform you that Lieutenant François Pinaud, commander of the 147th Fortress Infantry Regiment, in which your husband, Private André Honoré Roux, served,

has reported to General Charles Huntziger, commander of
the Second Army, that Private Roux was killed in action on
the afternoon of 13 May 1940, while defending the French
border along the Meuse River south of Sedan. Lieutenant
Pinaud has requested that this notice carry the following re-
mark: Private Roux was a fine soldier and fought valiantly
against the onslaught of the German forces to preserve the
liberty of France. It would do us great honor if you would
accept our sincere condolences.

Holding the letter away as if it were an evil thing, I groped behind myself for the arm of the settee and sank down onto its edge.

Monsieur Pinatel could not meet my eyes. "I'm sorry, madame."

Wooden. He struck me as wooden, with a wooden tongue.

"André was a fine man," said Monsieur Bonhomme. "All of us
will remember him so. He is the first from our village."

What right did he have to claim André, as though he were a permanent resident?

Monsieur Rivet said, "As notary here, I will draw up the deed of
the house in your name."

Officious functionary, hiding behind a task. How could he imagine I would be thinking of that now?

I could not believe that this was happening. It was someone else
sitting here in a daze, half-hearing, half-breathing, declaring im-
petuously that there had been a mistake.

Monsieur Bonhomme took my hand and held it between his
thick palms. "No words can express how deeply grieved I am. I will
do everything within my power to help you. Please, call me Aimé."

After Aimé's comment, Constable Blanc could find nothing to
say other than what the mayor had said. "I'm sorry, madame." But
unlike the mayor, he had the courtesy or the courage to look at me
directly. His face was pinched with what I took to be genuine sympathy.

I, also, found no speakable words. It was all I could do to stand upright again and watch them fumble their way out the doorway into the angry wind and then to push the door closed against their *sad errand*.

I HEARD MYSELF HOWL, louder than the mistral, the ugly sound ricocheting off the walls, hammering the truth. I was that banshee, half-crazed, ferocious, with rage in my chest so fierce I thought I would die.

"André! Couldn't you have helped yourself? Couldn't you have stayed out of danger? Couldn't you have been more careful?" Foolish questions: it was war.

"And God. What kind of a God are you? You could have prevented this. You could have led him to a safe place. But you didn't. You didn't."

Blinded by tears, I stumbled upstairs in a stupor, threw myself onto his side of the bed, and held his pillow hard against my chest. I sobbed my throat raw, imagining André's last moments, the raging battle, his disbelief that he'd been hit, his desperate call for help, his struggle to stay alive, the loneliness of dying. Was Maxime with him? Could André speak? Could he see the sky? Did he suffer long?

Horrible pictures battered at me until, exhausted, I felt sleep mercifully take me. I woke to a shutter banging like gunshot, and reality. Light pierced the narrow space between the shutters, bringing the recognition that a new day had dawned, a day that proclaimed that I was a war widow at twenty-three. It took mental effort to acknowledge that; it took physical effort to get out of bed and go downstairs, famished. No bread in the *panetière;* the walk to the bakery had been aborted. The need to live kept grinding convulsively.

Catching sight of the bare walls took me by surprise. There was that to deal with—the missing paintings. But what did paintings matter when I had lost the man I loved?

I paced around the *salle* weeping, railing at the war, the Germans, depravity, duty, patriotism. How could I think of anything other than André? My mind cried his name continually. The claustrophobia of four blank walls pressed in on me. I went outside to André's workshop. The wind had taken no notice of the magnitude of this day. With neither sympathy nor respect, it had blown the canvas off his tools, which lay neatly on the shelf—small and large V-gouges and U-gouges, narrow and wide chisels, concave and convex chisels, small and large mallets, sharpening stones, files, rulers, hammers, clamps, miter box—the tools that had bought Pascal the paintings, had built my new crockery cabinet, and had provided our bread. I picked them up one by one to touch what André had touched, hoping that they had been burnished by his soul. Sharp, every one of them, and cold as death.

I imagined his hand grasping the narrow U-chisel, his long index finger pressing it down along the wood to release a perfectly curled ribbon, but I could not make my eyes travel up his arm to see his face. We had used those ribbons and shavings as kindling. Would that I had kept just one.

Back inside, I spotted his woolen cap hanging on the peg by the door. I buried my face in it to get the smell of him, then held it in my palm upside down, trying to remember where he had come from when he hung it there the last time. I was dumbfounded. I could not bring it to mind.

Carrying the cap around the room like a sacred relic, I brought it into the light of the window and found a hair in the inner band. I plucked it off. Something of him, alive once. I sucked it between my lips and swallowed it, choking, forcing it down.

CHAPTER THIRTEEN

LAMENTATIONS

1940

THE SOLE OF MY LEFT SHOE SPLIT FROM THE UPPER, FLAP-
ping and breaking away more as I ascended the stairs to the
church for my own *sad errand*.

The *abbé* Autrand, Father Marc, suggested a Low Mass for the
standard offering of eight hundred francs. My good intentions were
shattered. I emptied out of my drawstring bag sixty francs. It would
not have mattered to André at all if he didn't have a funeral mass.
It was for me, an attempt to acknowledge God, that I offered a
fourth of the money he had put into the olive jar.

Father Marc stared down at the coins in my palm a moment
longer than necessary.

"If the government sends me some compensation, I'll bring you
something more."

"This will be sufficient since there will be no interment."

IT FELL TO THE mayor's wife to tell a few key people discreetly.
From the moment Madame Pinatel told the first person, I pictured
the news flying through the village on bat wings, each person flit-
ting through the lanes in order to be the teller rather than the told.

Maurice and Louise, his wife, burst through the doorway without knocking. I fell into his soft bosom, and he held me there, crooning lamentations as Louise rubbed my back in circles.

"Do you know how he died?" he asked.

"Maurice! What a thing to ask."

"It's all right to ask, Louise. No, I don't know. I probably never will."

I showed them the letter. Louise wept openly, Maurice silently, biting his lip. Seeing them so broken up brought on a new wave of my own tears. They both showered me with comfort, commendations of André, and generous assurances of their support.

Maurice's thick eyebrows struggled to reach each other over the bridge of his nose. "I will be devastated if this means that we'll lose you, our *gaie Parisienne,*" he said. His pout, normally put on for humor, was genuine. "Can you find some reason to stay?"

"Yes. For a time." I glanced around the room at the barren walls. "The paintings."

Louise followed my gaze. "The paintings!"

Maurice turned in a circle, his feet splayed outward. "Where are they?"

"André hid them."

"Don't you go looking for them until we win this war and every German is routed out," said Maurice. "They might find them and confiscate them. Leave them hidden."

"Win? We've already lost."

"Only the battle. Not the war. De Gaulle's words."

To my surprise, an elfin smile stole across his face. "Better for us—the paintings hidden," he said. "It will keep you here longer. Besides, Roussillon is safer than Paris."

I knew he was right—about the paintings and about Roussillon. "I have to go to Apt tomorrow, Maurice. My shoe broke," I told him.

"The sitting-in will be tomorrow, Saturday," Louise said. "Maurice will take you today."

"A special trip, when petrol is so scarce?"

"We'll go now," Louise declared. "I know a good shoe shop."

Ridiculous, a broken shoe, when it was my heart that had shattered. A splintered sole was nothing compared to a splintered soul.

"Once Pascal told me that when something changes your life, you remember every detail. Does that mean I'm going to remember this pitiful old shoe?"

"Let's hope not. Instead, let's hope you remember the love we feel for you," Louise said, and with that, we set off for Apt.

THE NEXT MORNING, LOOKING DOWN at my new shoes, I tried to settle the tumult of emotions enough to receive people at the sitting-in. Custom here dictated that on the day before the funeral mass, every *Roussillonnais* stopped his work for an hour to view the body in the house where the deceased person lived, but in the event that there was no body, only a government document to put on the table, what then? Odette said some people might come anyway.

She sat with me all afternoon, a solid presence I leaned on as though she were my mother, while she altered a black dress of her own to fit me. I felt uncomfortable about letting her. What if she would need it later for herself?

"When I married André, I saw no heartbreak on the horizon, no longing for what I didn't have, no end to our happiness. Now I see no end to sadness."

She stitched silently for a while. "There will come a time when your life will be full again, and you will look back on this as though it happened to someone else."

"I can't imagine ever feeling that way. I can't imagine living without gloom."

"A moment here, a moment there, even just mildly pleasant moments, and you will stitch them together into a pleasant life."

A deep stillness descended over both of us, over her conviction and my fragility.

"Before anyone arrives," she said, "I have to tell you, even at the risk of making you sadder. I can't keep it in. Our Michel is alive."

"Alive!" The word struck the air like a gong. I hugged her. How could I do otherwise? "That's wonderful!"

"We received a letter earlier this week. I wanted to shout it to the village, but that would not be kind to others who haven't heard from their sons, so we have kept it to ourselves."

"Where is he? Do you know?"

"In southwest England, at a recovery camp. He was rescued at Dunkerque. He and his friend buried themselves in sand up to their heads for protection from bombers strafing the beach while they waited for their call to enter the sea. He described long columns of men wading far out in choppy water at night. Imagine, Lisette. They had fought through three weeks of retreat, had gone without sleep and without food and water, but as they came to the beach, they kept their ranks and obeyed commands. There was no jostling for a place in the queue. Apparently, it was all orderly and calm. He waited in freezing, chest-high water for hours, until he was pulled aboard a fishing boat and ferried to a ship."

"And his friend too?"

Odette pinched her bottom lip between her teeth. "When he turned around in the sea to find him, he was gone."

My mind shifted to André's friend. Maxime. What of him? Gloom set in again.

SOON, ODETTE'S DAUGHTER, SANDRINE, whose brother, Michel, would come home someday, and Madame Pinatel, the mayor's wife, came to pay their respects. Then Mélanie brought two jars of canned cherries from their trees and a bag of raisins. Aloys Biron, the butcher, brought a large salami. Most unexpectedly, Madame Bonnelly, a stout woman with thick arms whom I had never met, brought a *gratin d'aubergines,* an eggplant-and-tomato pie garnished with bread crumbs.

"Keep up your strength, dear," she said.

The smithy, Henri Mitan, came to the door still wearing his ash-smeared apron, fumbling with his wool cap. The index finger on his left hand was only a stub, purple and puckered at the tip.

"I-I just want you to know, he luh-luh-loved making that . . ." He swallowed as though he had a peach pit in his throat, and the rest of the sentence burst out in a flood of sputtered syllables. "That outhouse for you, madame. He wanted the hinges just so."

"Would you like to see it?"

"I wuh-wuh-would be honored, madame." He bowed to me, or maybe his back was permanently bent from years of work at his anvil.

I opened the courtyard door, and he went to take a look. After quite a few minutes, he came back, struggling to get the words out. "A g-good carpenter, and a good man. *Merci. Merci,* madame."

He noticed the broken window latch on the table. "Will you allow me to make you new ones and put them on the shutters?"

He asked the question without a flaw.

"I would be grateful, monsieur."

He bowed again as he backed out the door.

His manner amused us. We shared a brief lightness. Maybe this was one of those moments, one tiny stitch. Kindness can speak when words cannot.

I realized that even inside the simplest exterior, there was drama and tragedy and courage. André had never mentioned Henri's stammer, nor his finger. Perhaps a village rather than a city was the right place to discover a laborer's humanity, and a husband's grace.

THE NEXT DAY, SUNDAY, the villagers gathered outside our house for the processional to the church. *My house,* I supposed I should call it now. Ownership meant ties to this place, yet through the leaden atmosphere I could not see any future other than the gray of solitude and the sudden bursts of orange when grief flamed.

Odette and Louise sat inside the house with me. Later Mélanie came in wearing a tiny pillbox hat, small enough to show off the new permanent wave Louise had given her.

The *garde champêtre,* Bernard Blanc, was the first man to arrive, befitting his position as constable of the commune, I supposed. In tall black boots, such as an army officer might wear, and a well-tailored black jacket, he took up a post at the side of the room and stood erect and formal, shoulders squared, chin pulled in, as if to give the event some military dignity.

Aimé Bonhomme and Mayor Pinatel arrived together soon after.

"Pascal's paintings!" Aimé said in alarm, looking at the walls and then turning to me.

"The paintings, madame. Where are they?" Monsieur Pinatel demanded.

With the eyes of the three men upon me, I was able to lie without hesitation. "I do not know."

Aimé drew his eyebrows together in genuine concern; the mayor's eyes darted around the room, his back stiffening; the constable, cool and dignified, fastened his eyes on me and didn't look at the walls. They stood like a tribunal, with Constable Blanc, the tallest, in the middle.

Father Marc entered, wearing his funeral cape, and invited us to follow him to the church, downhill from the house. Between mournful peals of the church bell, I heard the old men shuffling out of the café. The solemn tolling disturbed me, so different from the jubilant ringing on Christmas Eve, so slow that I thought the bell ringer had fallen asleep, as slow as Pascal's last intermittent breaths, a year earlier; but then came the peal again. As we approached the church, I felt the vibration stronger in my chest. Its doleful knelling sounded an unnecessary announcement: Your life will be different from this day forward.

What was I to do with it now, my one not-so-precious life?

My new shoes clapped against the church steps, embarrassing me. They had straw uppers that wouldn't last and wooden soles that, regretfully, would. All leather had been appropriated for the war effort.

Standing next to Father Marc at the church door, I imagined that people saw me as a figure of the outside world portending sorrow for Roussillon. Everyone passed with downcast eyes, all the men except the constable, who looked at me as though there were words on the tip of his tongue that he held back, all the women except Louise, who raised her chin minutely, encouragement that I should do the same. They had all come to mourn something more than André, the first *Roussillonnais* to fall to German guns. They were here in recognition that the war had touched their village. My own sorrow spilled over to the wives, mothers, and sisters who would come to know the same sorrow as mine.

Other than the white daisies from Mélanie's porch laid across the cotton-and-lace altar cloth, the interior of the church and its larger-than-life crucifix gave me little comfort. Exaggerated spikes pierced Jesus's hands and feet, and his imploring expression, as if asking, "My God, why hast Thou forsaken me?," was more pitiful than inspiring. Nevertheless, my heart burned at the agony of his abandonment and suffering, and my eyes flooded for him, for me, for the sickened world.

The rickety kneelers were in a wretched state, worn raw and splintery. Never having been in the church, André would not have thought to repair them, had it not been Pascal's last request. Now how long would Roussillon have to wait?

For André to go from creating carved frames for magnificent paintings by well-known Parisian artists to repairing decoratively tooled chairs in the dining hall of the Palais des Papes in Avignon and then to refurbishing the kneelers in this little provincial church might seem like a heartless downward spiral, but André had not looked at it that way. On the surface, he might have seen it as a promise to the man who had loved and raised him, but I knew it went deeper. He would have found satisfaction in doing good in the village of his ancestors.

A plaster Jeanne d'Arc stood forlorn in a corner, lost in her armor, holding a stanchion from which hung a fleur-de-lys flag, the effect deplorable compared to her glorious mounted statue in gold on rue de Rivoli, opposite the Louvre. Oh, for even a whisper of the voices she had heard clear as a clarion call, to give me guidance.

How was I to manage?

Father Marc recited from Lamentations, " 'The joy of our heart is ceased; our dance is turned into mourning,' " as an introduction to his prayers for André's soul. At the mention of André's name, tears flooded my eyes. If only I didn't hear *André, André, André* echoing from all sides, I might be able to pretend it was just a regular mass on any old Sunday. It was all a wash of words anyway, only one statement of which I could grasp—that trials bring humans closer to God.

Then Father Marc launched into a patriotic oration. "Let us not forget that the people of Roussillon have been blessed. In the Great War of our fathers, no bombs dropped on our village. There were no explosions here. No cries. No houses toppled. No ranks of German soldiers marching up rue de la Poste. Let us pray that God will spare Roussillon again—"

"Amen," I heard Constable Blanc say behind me.

"And further, that He will guide us in our prayers for our French prisoners of war. Daily, hourly, let us pray that Allied troops will be victorious over the forces of evil and, though the situation seems grim today, that they will eliminate them from our beloved fatherland.

"We *Roussillonnais* have struggled and united before—against locusts and blight, flood and drought—and we will unite again against human locusts, putting aside all of our petty resentments in order to love our neighbors as ourselves, as our Lord Jesus commanded."

I wondered—Did Father Marc not consider Germany to be our neighbor?

It would have taken only the breath of God to blow that lethal German projectile off its course, or to prevent that evil plane from emerging from the smoke-filled sky, or whatever it was that had killed the man I loved. What part of the field was He succoring the instant André was hit? Was God so absorbed in protecting some German noblewoman's son whose head was filled with melodies yet to be written, the next Beethoven composing his own "Ode to Joy," that He forgot the common man whose simple joy was to make picture frames? Or was it that even God could do nothing to deflect the wave of hatred, the hunger to hurt? Sister Marie Pierre would chastise me for thinking that. Hot shame for doubting rose up in my throat.

It was over at last, and the processional moved downhill to the war monument on avenue de la Burlière. Names and dates were inscribed on a stone monolith: 1870, 1871, 1914, 1915, 1916, 1917, 1918. Léon LaPaille, François Estève, Paul Jouval, and two dozen more who had left wives, children, mothers behind; vineyards and orchards untended; fields unplanted; projects unfinished. Maybe one of them had also intended to repair the kneelers.

Mélanie handed me a wreath of pruned grapevines that she had soaked and curved into a circle and decorated with acorns and lavender. It was a loving gesture. I leaned it against the pedestal. Father Marc said a benediction, and all of Roussillon joined the chorus of "Amen" for this man who was not their native son.

Maurice was so choked up he could not speak. Odette held my one hand, Louise the other. Aimé Bonhomme said to me in a fatherly way, "I'm sorry it had to be you. It was wrong to be you. It should have been one of us."

Perhaps he understood how alone I was feeling in a place I had not chosen. Perhaps the priest and the constable did also. Certainly Maurice and the women did. Nevertheless, inadvertently, Aimé's sentiment made me feel like an outsider, *un autre*. A stranger. I would be watched. People would gossip about how I carried my bereavement. However kindly he meant his awkward little speech that expressed kindness but no logic that I could see, it separated me from this village, which I had been trying, for André's sake, to love.

AT HOME, REELING IN A FOG of excruciating sadness, I added an incomprehensible sixth item to my List of Hungers and Vows:

6. Learn how to live alone.

CHAPTER FOURTEEN

PATRON SAINTS

1940

O N MY WAY HOME FROM THE BAKERY, I READ DE GAULLE'S
speech, which was posted on the coral stucco wall of the *mairie*.
As the leader of the Free French, operating in London, he was resis-
tant to German victory, while Pétain's government in Vichy accom-
modated German rule. I appreciated the hopefulness of the speech
but was afraid the day would come when some German officer would
rip it right off the building and plant some Nazi slogan there instead.

Alongside de Gaulle's speech, a new placard had been mounted:
NATIONAL REVOLUTION—WORK, FAMILY, FATHERLAND. MARSHAL PÉ-
TAIN. Apparently Mayor Pinatel was adopting a neutral position.

Since it was September, there was also a handwritten announcement of the Fête Votive de la Saint Michel, the patron saint
of Roussillon, on 29 September, only a few days away. Saint Michel
meant nothing to me; he had done nothing to protect André, grandson of a *Roussillonnais*. Instead, de Gaulle's appeal rang in my ears:
*Unite with me in action, in sacrifice, and in hope. Let us all strive to
save her.* But what could I do, one lone woman in an isolated village?

I marched straight into Louise's hairdressing salon. I had seen
her scribbled note in the window the day before: *Hair clippings collected for the making of inner soles.*

"Cut it all off," I told her.

"But you have such beautiful long hair, the color of dark choco-late."

"All the more for inner soles. The *Résistance* fighters need good boots. Give me a short bob."

She braided my hair and cut it at the nape of my neck in a hank—it looked like a snake—then shaped what was left.

"No one will recognize you at the fête. You are going, aren't you?" Louise said, trimming scissors aloft in one hand, comb in the other, waiting for my answer.

André and I had enjoyed the *fête votive* weekends of parades, games, *boules* tournaments, music, dances, and fireworks, and we had even gone once to the *fête votive* of the nearby village of Gordes, but I was afraid my going to the fête now might appear unseemly, as if I were seeking gaiety and recreation. If I were really honest, however, I would have to admit that I didn't want to be so intoxicated with mourning that I couldn't have a few hours of re-spite from my dark thoughts.

"Maurice will pout if you don't come."

"What's to celebrate now, after the surrender? The crowd will probably be pretty sparse."

"That's exactly why you should give it your support."

I had been so unbearably lonely, rattling around in that empty house, that I said, "All right. I'll go to some of it."

THE MORNINGS OF THE FÊTE, there would only be the *pétanque* and *boules* tournaments. They didn't interest me. Since a votive meant an offering or act performed in accordance with a vow, I preferred to stay home and make my own votive. It would have to do with André. I added to my List of Hungers and Vows:

7.   Find André's grave and the spot where he died.

Would I fall apart if I saw either one? Despite my qualms, I let it remain and wrote another vow:

8. Forgive André.

The heaviness of forgiveness descended the moment after I wrote the words. He could have postponed going until he was conscripted. Maybe then he would not have had to fight at all, but oh no, off he had gone with Maxime.

Yet holding a grudge against the man I loved felt terribly wrong. It was entirely against my conscience and would only compound my grief. I would have to forgive him anew each day, in a surge of love, perhaps even begrudgingly at times, until I forgot what I'd needed to forgive him for. At the moment, I could not imagine that day ever coming, though I resolved to try.

WITH THAT HOPE, I went downhill to the church and arrived in time for the processional. It began with a choir of ten giggling girls positioned on the church steps singing the Litany of the Saints. Father Marc led the processional, and behind him an acolyte carried a huge wooden image of Saint Michel, so top-heavy that he lost his balance going downhill on the uneven cobblestones and almost fell, to the gasps of the girls following him.

I was sure the girls had been told to walk solemnly, but the littlest one, Mélanie's daughter, Mimi, wearing a yellow dress and a single sock, couldn't restrain herself and skipped down the road out of line. Could that teetering statue deliver me from the depths of despair? No, but seeing Mimi frolicking along like a ray of sunshine did, for a moment. If I could follow Odette's advice, I would string such moments together into a new life.

As soon as the processional reached place du Pasquier, where the statue would be erected, the girls ran to the schoolyard to watch the boys' wrestling matches and to play the bottle game, the three jumps, and the strangle-cat. Crank-handled Victrolas at every food booth issued forth a tangle of melodies, each defiant voice singing loudly to prove that the *Provençaux* had not lost their joie de vivre just because the north was occupied.

People came from farms and vineyards, from Apt, Gordes, Saint-Saturnin-lès-Apt, and Bonnieux. Their odd dressing amused me. Wooden clogs with a suit. A bowler hat with a workman's smock. A peasant's straw hat with a jacket and wrinkled, shapeless trousers. Dresses in old styles and plain fabrics. Even so, I recognized a dignity in their unpretentiousness.

Merrymakers greeted those they hadn't seen for a few weeks with the same exuberance they showed for those they hadn't seen for years. Yet their gaiety seemed forced, and they soon fell into quiet conversations beneath the plane trees or strolled up to the cemetery to visit their departed.

The advertised symphony concert was performed by a guest orchestra from Apt consisting of nine instruments. I had hoped for the Brandenburg concertos, but hoped in vain. No Bach. No Handel. No Beethoven. Only French composers. Debussy, yes. "Clair de Lune." Berlioz, yes. The ball scene from *Symphonie Fantastique,* very popular in Paris. And Bizet's *Carmen*—the sensual "Habanera," the moving and dreamy pastoral of the smugglers' trip into the Pyrénées, and the "Toreador's Song." Even though the sound was thin, I loved hearing the melodies, and the finale, "La Marseillaise," made me proud to be French.

Tambourines signaled that the dance was about to begin. Maurice and Louise scooped me up from behind into the *salle des fêtes,* Louise admiring the new hairstyle she had created for me.

"You can't escape, Lisette. Louise agreed to share me with you for the polka and the waltz. Imagine, a man as round-bellied as I dancing with two beautiful ladies. Even Maurice Chevalier would be jealous!"

Maurice's knightly bow was charming, but I declined. He

pouted, of course, though I knew he understood. I actually enjoyed watching him waltz with Louise. He was surprisingly light on his feet.

Constable Blanc approached me, holding out his hand, palm up.

"You can't escape, Lisette," he said, echoing Maurice, but there was a sharper edge to his voice.

"No, thank you. I prefer watching."

He continued to hold out his hand. Was that politeness or insistence? Shouldn't he have known why I didn't want to dance? Did I have to spell it out for him? A grieving widow does not dance. I turned away, and he did a quick about-face and disappeared into the whirling crowd.

I watched the polka and the gavotte from the sidelines for the rest of the evening, not unhappy that I wasn't dancing. I was honoring André and remembering how smoothly we used to dance together, and that felt right.

Under other circumstances, I would have enjoyed the farandole, a Provençal dance that started with everyone holding hands and skipping in a circle, giving a little kick and stomp on every fourth skip. The leader called for *le serpent,* and a line broke off and made tight, snakelike turns around the *salle. L'escargot* was announced next, and the line made a spiral in ever-decreasing circles.

Mélanie called out to me when she passed, "You look like Kiki now." I smiled back. I hadn't realized that people this far south would know Kiki de Montparnasse—an artist's model, cabaret singer, actress, and painter. I had idolized her, so Mélanie's comment pleased me.

No fireworks lit the evening sky as they had done the year before. It would have been too much like the explosives of war. There was no bonfire either. A waste of wood. There was only a tray of candles that Father Marc supplied. Slowly the crowd dispersed. People lingered under the trees of the square saying lengthy good nights as though they wouldn't see each other for a year, when in actuality, they would gather again the next day for the morning *boules* tournament, the parade of the Apt bugle corps, and the afternoon dance. Since there was no moon and there were no streetlights, not even gaslights in Roussillon, Maurice insisted on walking me home, five houses past his.

He bowed at my doorway, and I went in and lit a gas lamp. Shock ripped through me. The house had been ransacked—chairs upturned, the yellow sunflower tablecloth in a heap on the floor. André's cabinet had been moved away from the wall, its doors flung open and the contents scattered. Dishes lay broken on the tile floor. I called out to Maurice. He came back, took one look, and ran off downhill in his funny gallop to get the constable. Before he returned, Constable Blanc arrived.

"Just doing my nightly rounds when I heard you call and saw your door ajar. Is everything all right, madame?"

"No!" I opened the door wider for him to survey the *salle*.

He shook his head, which made his thickly pomaded hair gleam in the lamplight.

"Did you see anyone leave?" he asked.

"No."

"There were many here today from beyond Roussillon."

"But why my house?"

"Do you have anything hidden here that someone would want?"

I knew he meant the paintings, so why didn't he say so? He had seen them. André's first reason for not telling me the location of the paintings flashed through my mind. I could look at Constable Blanc dead in the eye and say, "No. Nothing," because it was true.

"Do you mind if I look upstairs?"

We both went up and found that the bedding and mattresses had been pulled off the beds in both rooms, the armoire and bed moved away from the wall in my bedroom, clothes dumped on the floor, the chest of drawers at an angle in Pascal's room. The constable put the mattresses back on the beds and moved the furniture into place. Downstairs, he walked André's cabinet back against the wall.

"Thank you, Constable."

"Call me Bernard, please. Be sure to report anything missing."

"To you or to the mayor?"

"To me, of course. I am the arm of the law."

"All right."

"Be on your watch for strangers. Germans, I mean. They aren't likely to be in uniform. They are scouting out spoils and resources. Listen carefully in the streets. They may be speaking French, but not like we do. Whoever ransacked your house has friends, and they know more than we think they do." He moved two steps closer to me. I tensed, and he noticed. "Those paintings aren't worth endangering yourself. Give them up if you need to."

The comment about the paintings' worth struck me as harsh, but the similarity of his words to André's last letter startled me.

"Take care what side of the bread you butter, madame. Think ahead. Take care of yourself. Good night." He ducked out through the doorway.

I checked the olive jar. My money was still in it. Then it wasn't money the thief wanted.

In a few minutes Maurice returned, fretful that he hadn't found the constable.

"Who wants my paintings?"

"I don't know, but someone definitely does." He put his arms around me in an avuncular way. "Your dishes may be broken, but you will not be."

I STAYED AWAY FROM the fête the next day, unable to free my mind from the violation of an intruder in my house. The ransacking justified the hiding of the paintings. Passing between the windows where the painting of the little factory of pale yellow stone had hung, I felt a pang. That painting had meant so much to Pascal. Then I turned to the opposite wall, where there had been four paintings, *Red Roofs, Corner of a Village, Winter,* the largest, was near the center of the wall. He often called it *Le Verger, Côtes Saint-*

Denis à Pontoise, which made it seem like this painting had four names. He had said that the roofs were red-ochre, the branches where light hit them a dark golden yellow that was surely made from ochre—he would have said the proper name for them—and the ground, the color of pumpkins. I turned in a circle, trying to bring to mind each of the paintings, wondering which one had been André's favorite. Regret pricked my conscience. I had never asked him.

Above André's cabinet, Cézanne's still life had hung. André had said it was the perfect spot for it. Maybe that had been his favorite painting. He loved apples. I moved a white bowl of three apples, two early pears, and one Spanish orange from the table to André's cabinet. The dark red of Cézanne's top apple was a self-assertive red, full of boldness in assuming its imperial position. André would have liked my mimicry of the painting. In placing the fruit on his cabinet, I had performed an act of resistance against the intruder; more important, I had performed an act of love for André.

In Cézanne's painting, were there three apples? Four? Three oranges? Or were they peaches? My memory of them was already fading, just as the memory of André eating his last apple was fading. Was he standing in the courtyard rolling his shoulders after bending over the last of the popes' chairs? Had he said anything when he finished, knowing that with the last chair, our time together was growing shorter? I could not remember. I hated it that I could not remember. I understood now Pascal's desperation to tell someone, me, so that his memories would not be lost forever. I had to hold on, to cherish every word André had said to me, every smile. I had not cherished enough. I had been too self-absorbed. It was excruciating not to know everything he had said to me our last week, our last day.

LOUISE HAD INVITED ME to a gathering of friends to take place the evening after the second day of the fête. She called it a *veillée.* I was grateful. I had spent too many hours alone in that house.

Besides André and Maxime, I'd had only a few friends in Paris—Sister Marie Pierre, of course, and Jeannette, the other counter girl at the *pâtisserie*. Jeanne d'Arc I had called her, because she claimed that she heard voices and that she had Gypsy blood. Whenever Maxime came in to buy a pastry, she leaned over the counter to show her breasts and flirted outrageously. He may have flirted back, but he always gave the pastry to me. That threw her into a temper, and with rough words, naughty gestures, and the evil eye, she would shoo him out of the shop. Maxime and I always laughed at those episodes later. What I would give for a day with her now!

Here in Roussillon, I had more friends than I'd had in Paris. Three other families were already at the Chevets' house when I arrived—Émile and Mélanie Vernet, who had a vineyard, and their darling Mimi; Henri Mitan, the blacksmith, and his wife, who must have developed infinite patience with his stuttering; and the Gulinis, Odette and her Italian husband, René, their daughter, Sandrine, and Sandrine's husband, Louis Silvestre, whose uneven gait and shortened leg had kept him out of the war. Louise must have run out of real coffee, because she served the *faux café* made of hickory nuts, and everyone followed Mélanie's lead and took just one cube of sugar instead of the usual two, sugar being rationed now. Maurice offered a small glass of marc to the men, who drank it straight, sipping a few drops now and then to make it last the evening.

"There will be two events tonight," Louise announced. "I'm in charge of the first, the chestnuts. Maurice is in charge of the second."

She lay two chestnuts for each person in a pan so old that there were holes in the bottom and roasted them in the fireplace while Émile opened a bottle of his rosé.

"Are we going to have a dessert?" Mimi blurted.

"Shh, no, Mimi. You mustn't ask," Mélanie said.

"I'm sorry, Mimi," Louise said. "We must provide our sweetness by acts of kindness, not by sugary confections."

"My turn," Maurice said quickly. "Come with me, Mimi." His face, speckled with red sting marks from his beekeeping, wore the mischievous grin of a boy at play.

He waddled out the back door, holding Mimi's hand. When they came back inside, Mimi was leading a small goat on a rope.

"Mimi and I think you should have a little goat, don't we, Mimi?"

Mimi led it right to me. "You have to take it, madame. See? She likes you."

"A goat! You're being silly, Maurice."

He looked momentarily wounded, but he would not be swayed. "She's a pretty thing, don't you think? She gives more than a liter at every milking. Louise and I don't need another goat. You do."

"Maurice, I'm a *Parisienne*! I don't know the first thing about keeping a goat. Or milking one."

I remembered how at the orphanage, every third day, a goatherd had brought half a dozen goats. I had hopped with glee the moment I heard their bells in our courtyard. Their stuttering goaty noises charmed me. Sister Marie Pierre would hand me a pail, demanding to know what they sounded like, and I had to tell her in words, not by imitation. The goatherd would milk a goat while I held the pail steady beneath it until it was full. Sometimes I was brave enough to pet the smallest goat, the one without horns.

"Milking is easy. I will instruct you." Maurice's eyes sparkled. "Just squeeze the teats to the rhythm of 'La Marseillaise.' Gently, so you don't hurt her."

"*Allons enfants* (squeeze a teat) *de la* (squeeze the other teat) *Patrie* (squeeze), *le jour de gloire* (squeeze) *est arrivé* (squeeze)."

Soon we were all singing robustly *"Aux armes, citoyens!"* and squeezing imaginary teats. By the spirited refrain of *"Marchons* (squeeze), *marchons,"* we were all standing, and then we collapsed in laughter.

"But what will I do with all that milk?"

"You can make cheese," Odette said. "Nice soft chèvre."

"It will be too much cheese for one person." I felt a sting of sadness when I said "one person."

"You can sell me some," René Gulini quickly said. "I will invent a pastry to put it in. A large round brioche with chèvre inside and apricots on top."

"Or apples!" I said.

She was a white goat with black ears and a black tail and only nubs for horns. I petted her, and she looked up at me with liquid eyes that said, *Take me.* What leapt into my mind was Pissarro's painting of the girl and her goat on the ochre path. I supposed it was a silly notion, but I suddenly felt that if I had a goat of my own, it would bring me closer to finding that painting.

"*Bien.* I accept. *Merci.*"

I decided then and there that I would add another item to my list:

9.   Learn how to live in a painting.

"She has to have a name," Mimi said.

"A name. Hmm."

I thought of the goats we children had named at the orphanage. Jeanne d'Arc. Marie Antoinette. Empress Joséphine. Madame du Barry.

"I know!" I exclaimed. "Geneviève! The patron saint of Paris! She became a saint because she led the prayers that stopped Attila's Huns from conquering the city."

For an instant, the frivolity was dampened, but I pressed on. "Later, when a different band of warriors did conquer Paris, Geneviève convinced them to release their prisoners. Her statue is in the Jardin du Luxembourg."

I placed my hand on the goat's head and declared, "I baptize you Sainte Geneviève."

CHAPTER FIFTEEN

THE SECRET
OF GORDES

1941

I LAY IN BED, AWAKENED BY MY OWN WEEPING AND BY THE slant of milky light passing between the shutters, conscious, as always, of missing him, of knowing he would not experience this new day. Why get up? Before, it had been to listen to news in the café at the other end of the day. Now a more urgent answer came in the small, bleating voice from the courtyard. Geneviève wanted milking.

I threw on some clothes and washed the pail I'd found in the shed "Oh, you poor girl, thinking I had forgotten you." I squeezed her teats and sang "La Marseillaise," which lifted my spirits. We went down the hill outside the courtyard to find grass and thistles. "Look here. Oh, this looks good. *Miam, miam.*"

Having an animal was a responsibility. I couldn't think only of myself, couldn't indulge in late, self-pitying mornings in bed. The January chill had set in, so I cut and gathered grass to store for her as she munched.

"Now you'll be happy until I get back."

"*Baa,*" she said, which I took to mean "*Merci,* madame."

Some mornings I had to congratulate myself just for functioning. This morning was one of them. I took account: I'd gotten up.

I'd washed and dressed myself. I'd opened the shutters. I'd made my bed. I'd milked Geneviève. I'd gone to the *boulangerie* to see Odette—oh yes, for bread too. Now I heated water for hickory nut coffee, a milky substitute. I went through the steps, just as if André had sat down to sip his *grand café* from his grandmother's bowl. I licked its edge where his lips had been.

Dressed in clean clothes, I boarded Maurice's bus for the surprise he had promised me when he had walked me home from their *veillée*. As we descended into patchy veils of fog below Roussillon, Maurice told me to keep secret what we did and whom we saw. That only made me more curious, and I said, "Fog is the right atmosphere for clandestine activities."

"Truer than you think. If we're stopped by Mayor Pinatel, or anybody else, say that I'm taking you to visit Pascal's sister."

"He didn't have a sister."

"All the better. He won't find out any information."

Shortly after the narrow road to that circle of ancient stone huts he called bories, Maurice turned right, up the switchbacks to Gordes, and parked the bus just below the village. We walked up more than a hundred uneven stone steps and passed along the back of the château and the apse end of the church, then took a crooked route down the opposite side of the village, where the narrow streets seemed to descend forever, sometimes so steeply that flat stones had been placed at intervals down the middle of the incline to make steps, while the sides had been cobbled into two ramps to accommodate wheels. Not a soul was about. I turned my ankle and grabbed hold of Maurice. For the rest of the way, he held on to my upper arm to steady me.

A spring trickled gaily through strings of chartreuse moss and fed a stone washing basin. Maurice said it had been used by a tannery for the once active shoemaking trade of Gordes. In this quiet quarter of houses, I peeked in windows discreetly, trying to see through lace curtains whether there were cushions on the settees.

Curiously, a three-story building had no door onto the street.

We turned in at a narrow, rock-strewn alley that led to a courtyard behind it. The stone lintel bore the name of a girls' school.

"So you think I ought to go to school?" I whispered.

"In a way, you will, but it hasn't functioned as a school for a long time." He pulled the cord on the school bell.

A beautiful woman with dark hair cut as short as mine looked out an upper window. I caught a glimpse of a white lace collar against a violet dress.

"Ah, Maurice! You brought her!" she said. "One moment."

"You told her about me?" I whispered.

I heard the rattle of keys and latches as she let us in. "He is working upstairs."

I knew at once why Maurice had brought me here. Paintings! Hanging, leaning, stacked everywhere. Bizarre, fantastical images in strong colors. Nothing like I had ever seen.

Maurice pushed me up the stairs. An artist was painting in a studio. A real artist!

He introduced the couple as Marc and Bella Chagall. "This is my friend Lisette, whom I told you about. She will keep your presence here a secret."

Why was that necessary, I wondered.

Unruly tufts of curly brown hair, silver at his temples, cascaded around the man's large ears. He was a small man wearing suspenders and a collarless shirt. More than any other feature, his eyes attracted me, blue as precious stones from a faraway land, almond-shaped and wide-set. There was a similarity in their angular faces such as older couples attain, but they weren't at all old.

"Maurice told us that you're interested in art," Madame Chagall said.

"My husband's grandfather . . ." I stopped. "Yes, I am." I turned to Maurice. "How did you come to know each other?"

"He rode my bus to Avignon to buy art supplies. Of course."

"Now I give him a list and he buys what I need and delivers it."

Monsieur Chagall spoke French with a foreign accent I couldn't identify.

"A true chevalier of the roads," I said.

"But this chevalier must tend to another sort of delivery, so I'll come back in an hour or so to take you home."

He pointed to a large painting lying on the floor in which a green-faced fiddler was playing a violin on a snow-covered rooftop, his knees bent outward, one foot in midair, dancing. As Maurice passed it, he did a little jig with his knees bent outward too.

Madame laughed. "You have an animated friend."

"As jolly as that fiddler," I said absently while the painting held my gaze. "Nothing is as it should be."

"Yet everything is as it must be," monsieur said.

"But these three little men are no taller than the fiddler's knee."

He tipped his head in gentle forbearance. "You're being rational. Throw rationality out the window when you come here. Bella, instruct her. Then we'll talk."

Monsieur turned to the unfinished painting on his easel. On his palette, he worked paint into his brush and swirled a wide path of crimson onto the canvas. I gasped. What was he going to do with *that*? I couldn't stay to watch because madame was waiting to take me upstairs.

"Since you live in a village," she said, "I'll show you his paintings from our village of Vitebsk in Russia."

"Russia!"

In a classroom without furniture, dozens of paintings lay on the floor, with only narrow spaces between them.

"He doesn't sell them?"

"Oh, yes. He does. But he paints so many, working day and night, that they accumulate. He likes to be surrounded by them."

One captured my interest instantly. In it, a milkmaid was stretching far forward on her stool to milk a cow whose legs were also stretched impossibly forward. A violin rested on the cow's back leg.

Of course. Why not? Doesn't every cow own a violin? Beyond a fence, the same cow was upside down, with another violin. The girl leaned forward, and her breasts hung down at the same angle as the cow's teats did. I couldn't say that I understood it, but it delighted me.

The paintings weren't detailed or realistic. The figures were childlike, soft-edged, done in a naïve style, innocent and lovable. In one painting, two goats walked toward each other on a narrow plank over a chasm, heads down. An impasse. Which one would give way?

I laughed. "These are delightfully droll. They couldn't be memories. They have to be fantasy."

"They could have been dreams or Russian legends or Jewish stories or children's folktales. He experienced them so intensely that they are still a part of him."

The painter's disregard for the relative sizes of things was humorous, but one in this vein suggested something to me. A large recumbent rooster enfolded in his wings a small woman, as though keeping her safe from a village aflame behind them. It reversed the order of humans caring for domestic animals, and it made me glimpse that Maurice and Louise had known that Geneviève would help me through dark times in more ways than by giving milk.

One painting had a haunting quality. A giant man in a black overcoat with a bulging sack slung over his shoulder was suspended in the sky diagonally over a snow-covered village and a large building that resembled the synagogue I had seen in the Marais quarter.

"Tell me about this one."

"In our Jewish upbringing, the Yiddish idiom 'goes over the houses' represents a beggar; it means a message from God could come in the form of a beggar."

"Is the message good or bad?"

"Good. Oh, so good. What you see as a stiff old beggar worn by years of deprivation and sadness is not all there is to see. It isn't his

misery or exhaustion or loneliness that touches me in those paintings. It's the spiritual force that keeps him aloft despite all gravity—
that's what I find moving."

She was so gracious that I dared to ask her, "Is that part of Jewish belief? Keeping aloft despite forces that pull you down?"

"Part of Jewish history, I would say." She reflected for a moment
and then ventured a question of her own. "Do you know about
Kristallnacht?" Her voice fell as she spoke.

"Yes. We read a newspaper clipping. We were shocked and
sorry."

The worry in her voice made me worry too, for how the war
might affect them. I understood now why they were here in this remote place, and why Maurice delivered monsieur's painting supplies from Avignon. I wondered if other Jewish artists were hiding
in the rural south.

Despite our solemnness, I was hungry to grasp more of her husband's artistic whimsy. Madame directed me to look at a large
painting she called *I and the Village,* in which a man's green profile
faced a cow's head almost nose to nose. From the man's eyeball to
the cow's eyeball ran a fine thread, connecting them. It had to be
the thread of love, I decided.

Laid over the cow's jaw was a tiny woman milking a cow her
size, and in the background, a peasant with a scythe over his shoulder was walking toward an upside-down woman. Behind them was
a row of houses, some also upside down.

"Separate moments," I said.

"But a single vision."

"Why are some things upside down?"

Apparently she sensed that this wasn't criticism, only inquiry,
because she tried to explain. "There is a contradiction to every
statement, the questioning of belief, and often the shattering of
everything we hold to be certain."

So I glimpsed that the upside-down woman and houses represented contradictions, the rooster cradling a woman questioned the belief of size and the capacity to protect and comfort, and the man in the sky shattered the certainty of gravity.

"Then he has a reason for everything."

"I can't say that for sure. Sometimes he baffles even me."

When we went back to the big studio, we saw that her husband had progressed on the painting. The crimson swirl had grown larger, more rounded, puffy as a cloud, upon which a buoyant bride and groom embraced, the man's hand drawing his lover's head against his shoulder. Above them a huge rosebush loaded with white roses took up the width of the painting. If that curved spread of crimson was in fact a cloud, logically it should be above them and the rosebush at their feet. Likewise, the cloud should be white and the roses red. I hadn't completely thrown rationality out the window. I sensed that the artist was playing with the viewer. The figures were suspended over a village, and cherubic heads were nestled between diminutive wings tumbling in the sky. A floating man was playing a violin, and a goat rested on folded legs.

"Your paintings sing, monsieur. Or maybe I should say they make me want to sing."

"Even better!"

"You look right through reality in order to reveal something strange and wondrous and, if I might say so, childlike. Have you always wanted to be an artist? From childhood, I mean?"

"That word, *artist,* did not exist in my village, so I dreamt of being a singer, then a fiddler, which was more acceptable in my culture, then a dancer, and a poet."

"May I ask—why are there roses in the sky?"

"Because they are not on the ground." The smile that crept over his face wrapped me up in him like an uncle would wrap a child in a warm blanket.

"Why is that cloud red?"

"It's my cloud. I can paint it whatever color I want."

"Why are there angels tumbling?"

"Because I needed something to fill the space."

"I don't believe you. They are there to bless the couple."

"If that suits you, fine."

"You don't just paint what you see in front of you, like other painters."

"No, I paint what I see inside me."

"Did you dream this couple?"

His amused expression slid into a wistfulness. "Maybe. Or maybe I remembered them. Or maybe Bella and I *are* the couple."

"Memory makes everything beautiful," I said.

"Indeed. It erases the ordinary and gives us the extraordinary, the essence of our experience."

"They're not scenes. They're . . ." I moved my hands as though I were collecting things, drawing them toward me. "Collections of holy sparks."

His arms flew up and his fingers burst apart. "Yes. Yes! That's it! Assemblages of inner images that possess me."

"Like those goats? Do goats possess you?"

"Yes, they do. There were goats in our Russian shtetl."

I chuckled. "You must have liked them. They're in a lot of paintings."

"I do, and the cows and the chickens and roosters."

"Maurice gave me a goat. I named her Sainte Geneviève, after the patron saint of Paris. I'm a *Parisienne,* even if you can't tell."

"Oh, but I can, in the elegant way you speak. A *Parisienne* with a Provençal goat."

"My goat, oh, how I love her. She seems to know by how I touch her whether I am sad or happy. When I'm gloomy, she comes up to me and pushes her body against my leg. I think she's trying to comfort me, like that big rooster holding the woman in his wings."

"Then you understand the language of animals *and* the language of art."

"Maybe I'm beginning to. When I milk my goat, I sing 'La Marseillaise.'" I stifled a laugh at myself, for telling him this, but *he* didn't laugh. "She likes that. She's a patriot." He nodded thought-fully, as though recognizing something serious.

"Do you like Provence?" I asked.

"I love it. The wheat at harvest time reminds me of home. And I love the grapevines marching across hills in streams of green, and the light. Oh, the light. When I came to Paris, I thought that was light—ha!—until we came here."

"Is that the reason you came to Paris, the light?"

"That, and to learn the language of art. After hundreds of years in Rome, in Toledo, in Amsterdam, Art settled in Paris. I knew I would feel the comradeship of other painters there. I wanted to bring my homeland to them. I haven't really left Vitebsk. I haven't painted one single painting that didn't breathe its spirit."

"To you, does Provence also have a spirit?"

"Oh, yes. I feel it when I go out in the early evening to smell the richness of the fields and to listen to the delicate resonance of the Angelus bell after it stops ringing." His dreaminess lasted for only a few moments, and then his expression darkened. "I would be con-tent to live here permanently," he murmured.

I knew enough now not to ask him why they couldn't.

WHEN MAURICE CAME TO get me, Monsieur Chagall wished him good health.

"Get home *safely*, God willing," madame said.

In the bus, I spilled out all I had seen. "They are kind, gracious people. They said I could come again."

"I will take you as long as I can get gasoline."

"They're hiding, aren't they."

"Yes, but you must not tell anyone."

"I won't. I'll just hold them between my wings."

—

IN MY OUTHOUSE, I opened the shutters to see the landscape of the Vaucluse. What did Monsieur Chagall see that I could not? The vineyards and oaks, bare of leaf in winter, held little beauty, but one night the temperature dropped below freezing and left a glaze on the leaves still hanging on the passionflower vine. In the morning, they looked like pieces of emerald stained glass, like those in Sainte-Chapelle on Île de la Cité. At that very moment, a breeze made them tinkle. It would have been nice to share that moment of loveliness with Madame.

Now, walking back across the courtyard, I caught sight of Mont Ventoux peeking over the smaller mountains. Its white chalky sheen looked as though it were lovingly painted with quicksilver.

If Monsieur Chagall could teach me to see beauty here in dull winter, I would have to visit him again.

CHAPTER SIXTEEN

LOVE

1941

O N A SATURDAY MORNING I HEARD A KNOCK ON THE DOOR
and opened it to Constable Blanc with his pomaded hair
swept up into a wave. Who could afford pomade in these times?

"I'm just making my rounds and thought I would check in on
you. Is everything all right?"

"Yes."

"Have you had any more disturbances?"

"No. None."

"May I come in?"

"I was just going out."

"A shame you cut your hair. You had beautiful long hair. Like a
sea siren."

"De Gaulle called upon every French person to unite with him in
action and in sacrifice. Hair clippings are being collected for inner
soles."

"You're unhappy, I know."

Stating the obvious. What was his business here anyway?

"I know what you need to be happy."

"No, I don't believe you do."

"Yes, I definitely do. Love."

If I had not been raised by the Daughters of Saint-Vincent-de-Paul, I would have spit in his face for his impertinence.

"In the meantime, you have other needs. Sugar, coffee, meat. I can get them for you. More than your ration coupons can provide. What would you like?"

What was this other side of him? Was he making a sincere offer? He had always been pleasant to me, except for that moment at the dance. Now again he was presumptuous, but maybe beneath it, he was just being kind to a widow in need.

Monsieur Chagall's painting of a rooster cradling a woman in the burning village blazed across my mind. Not a rooster; but a hen would give me a steady supply of eggs.

"A chicken. A hen," I blurted. "And some rennet tablets."

"What's rennet?"

"Never mind. Forget it." I shouldn't have asked for anything when I couldn't really trust his motives. "I don't need anything. I have to go."

I closed the door in his face and went upstairs to put on my old flannel coat.

Louise and I were going to take Maurice's bus to the Apt market. She had promised to show me how to make chèvre, the cheese from goat's milk. We needed two things—a starter culture, which she could give me from the buttermilk she made, and rennet, which she didn't have. It was a solidifying agent, she said. It would make the milk curdle.

In Apt, we scoured all the food booths at the market for rennet in powdered or tablet form, as well as the *épiceries* on the side streets, to no avail. One vendor told us to go to a shop behind the filling station. The door was closed, with a sign saying, PLUS D'ESSENCE. No more gasoline. We knocked just as a *gendarme* approached and nailed a poster to the wall. It depicted a frightened boy sitting behind an empty bowl. The menacing black hand of a skeleton was reaching for the bowl. The words on the poster read, LE MARCHÉ NOIR EST UN CRIME. We had just knocked on the door of the black market! Wide-eyed, we took one look at each other and scurried away.

When I arrived home, there was a package wrapped in newspaper sitting in the pot of lavender by the front door—a plucked and gutted chicken. I laughed at the constable's mistaken notion until I remembered his insinuations.

A whole chicken. There was something dark and secretive in that. Rationing permitted only large families to purchase a whole chicken. I didn't think he had a large family, but even if he didn't, how could he give away food? If he was unmarried, what connections did he have, that he could so quickly obtain a whole chicken? May my hands fall off, I thought, if I put that foul-gotten fowl in a cook pot!

That there was a chicken sitting in a pool of guilt on my sink counter was, at least in part, my own fault. I had asked for it, but I had failed to say a live chicken. Had he taken a risk to get it? Should I be grateful or wary? Was he showing off or had his act been motivated by genuine concern? Should I be suspicious or impressed by his quick willingness to commit a crime for my benefit, he, an officer of the law? Certainly, his character was now called into question.

Could the misbegotten chicken possibly be traced to me? How could I dispose of it safely? There was only one way. This was no time to waste even a misbegotten and misguided gift. It tasted delicious, with mushrooms, onions, celery, carrots, and lemon juice.

LOUISE WOULD NOT BE DEFEATED. The next day she took me to the *boucherie,* and we waited at the end of the long queue of women holding their ration books to get the meat legally allotted to them based on the size of their families. Could guilt be read in my eyes? Louise asked the frazzled butcher, Monsieur Aloys Biron, if he had any lining membrane of the fourth stomach of a calf.

"What in the world . . . ," I said.

Monsieur Biron chuckled his relief. "Since you are at the end of the queue, it's a good thing you want something undesirable."

"It's worth a try," Louise said. "My mother used it before there were rennet tablets."

With that, I entered a realm no *Parisienne* would think to investigate.

WE CHOPPED THE STOMACH lining very fine and pounded it to a mushy pulp. I was impressed when it did curdle the milk in Louise's cheesecloth sack, which I had hung from the *panetière,* and I ran five houses downhill to tell her. She told me how to use the whey that dripped out to make ricotta cheese. Geneviève produced two liters of milk a day, so, using two days' worth of milk, I was able to make a substantial amount of both types of cheese.

IT HAD BECOME COMMON to see strangers on the street, refugees from the north. I tried to listen discreetly in the bakery and grocery to detect any German accent in their spoken French, as Bernard had cautioned me to do. Louise and I saw a woman dressed in men's tweed trousers and boots accompanied by a woman in a Scottish tam whose monocle kept falling out of her eye socket. It was hard not to giggle.

"*Résistants,*" Louise whispered. "The one in trousers is a British novelist. She smokes a pipe. Maurice saw her do it. The other operates a mobile radio communication with England. There's a playwright too. Beckett is his name. Irish. Maurice knows him."

"How?"

"Certain deliveries."

The code words for Maurice's clandestine activities.

—

FOR THE FIRST TIME since we came to Roussillon, I saw people entering and leaving the windmill on the promontory. Curious about what was inside a mill, and how people could live in one, I walked around the high road to get to it, carrying some of my new batch of cheese. The mother was grateful and gave me a few centimes.

Four children hovered around the central works of the windmill.

"How are you managing?" I asked.

"We're scraping by. The oldest boy is good at trapping birds, and Constable Blanc brings us stew meat from time to time. Imagine. He uses his own ration tickets. He has delivered food to other refugees too."

Walking home, further perplexed by that man, I doubted that it was his ration tickets that he used.

A FEW DAYS LATER, I wrapped the larger portion of cheese in one of André's handkerchiefs and took it to the Chagalls. At last I was doing something on my list. They were touched by the gift and remarked that they could not remember the last time they had eaten fresh chèvre. They marveled at its smoothness. Their gratitude was a gift back to me.

Bella looked so radiant that I asked Marc—they had both said that I should use their first names—if he had ever painted her.

He gazed at her with the softness of deep love. "I'll never stop painting her. Show her, Bella."

Leading me up the stairs, she said, "I'll show you the first one he painted of me. I didn't know him well at that time. What a strange bird he was. Introverted, dreamy, eccentric, his hair growing every which way, like an untended garden. I thought his arms and legs had been attached haphazardly because they jutted out at odd angles. But in him was a burning intensity, like a small sun, which fascinated me, and his drollery and spurts of playfulness could change in an instant to lightning intelligence.

"I gathered wildflowers for his birthday, stole candies from my mother's kitchen, and took my flowered and paisley scarves to decorate the little room he rented by the river. I surprised him by coming there. 'Do not move. Stay just as you are,' he commanded, with what I can only call hot urgency."

She stopped at a closed door to pantomine her story.

"He put a fresh canvas on his easel, snatched up brushes, and flung himself at it so passionately that the easel shook. Dabs of red, blue, white, and black flew through the air and swept me up with them. Up and up. I looked down and he was standing on tiptoe on one foot. He lifted me off the ground, leapt up himself, and glided with me up to the ceiling."

Bella flung open the door, and there it was—a painting of both of them soaring upward on a diagonal, his neck swooping back on his supple body so that they were nose to nose, airborne in the little room.

"He whispered a song, and I could see the song in his eyes. We flew out the window as easy as could be, dancing through space hand in hand. I saw at once that he had painted my ecstasy."

She became quiet and reflective. "Life was new after that."

"Love made visible," I murmured.

"You have to understand that for the Hasid—our village had a Hasidic community—"

"Pardon me, Bella, but I don't know what a Hasid is."

"Oh, of course. It's a member of a Jewish sect that emphasizes mysticism, strict rituals, religious zeal, and joy. In fact, spontaneous joy and love are just as important to them as law or ritual. It was not uncommon to see a Hasid explode with happiness and dance in the street or climb onto a roof and play his violin for the moon. Hasids think it's possible to commune with God through music and dance."

That explained Marc's fiddler dancing on the roof. I asked if there were more paintings of the two of them.

The pointed corners of her dainty mouth curved. "He will be so pleased when I tell him that you asked."

She showed me one she called *The Promenade*. In a meadow with Vitebsk behind them, Marc, dressed in a black suit, stood on tiptoe, his face a broad, toothy smile. One arm was raised, and pivoting on that uplifted hand, Bella, in a long violet dress with a violet ribbon in her hair, had leapt up high above him and was fluttering horizontally, like a banner in the breeze.

"Pure exuberance!" I murmured.

"The October Revolution had just happened, and for Jews, it meant liberation, the end of humiliations and restrictions. It simply sent me skyward."

"It's more than that. It's a love painting. Your two hands are connected in your happiness, and his lips are the same violet color as your dress."

She gave me the kindest, warmest look I could imagine. "Listen to you, *bashenka*. You're learning how to read a painting."

She showed me another—Bella as a bride, Marc nestled behind her as they rode on the back of an enormous chicken. A dark blue Eiffel Tower stretched skyward behind them, with diminutive Paris buildings huddled under its arch. A little man wearing a cap was reading a floating book above a cow whose body had become a violin. Angels flew around them, and a tiny Vitebsk, like a distant memory, was crowded in a bottom corner.

"It's a picture of your leave-taking from Russia, isn't it?"

"You might call it that, yes. I can show you only one more, because last time you were here, Marc was disappointed that I had taken you away for so long."

When she uncovered it, my breath escaped in a long, trailing sigh. Whereas the others showed exuberant, shout-it-to-the-sky love, this was quiet, private, exquisitely loving, an intimate portrait of an embrace. Marc's half-open mouth pressed against her shoulder, his eyes nearly closed, his forehead against the side of her cheek. He looked as though he felt himself in heaven; and in a lace collar and a dark dress, her deep eyes open, her small, three-pointed mouth closed, Bella was loving the moment. All was gratitude, all surrender.

I surrendered to the enchantment of this painting as well. I only wished that Marc had painted André and me in such a state of perfect love.

Downstairs, I stammered my appreciation. He asked me how I had come to love art. I told him of the Madonna and Child in the orphanage chapel, of the many paintings André and I saw on our gallery walks; and I explained how Pascal had acquired his collection, who the painters were, and how much he loved them.

"They are very important painters. How many did he have?"

"Three of each, plus a study of heads with one woman's face all stretched taut and disarranged with one eye higher than the other. His son bought it cheaply from a concierge. I don't know who painted it."

"That could be either Modigliani or Picasso. What you have is a progression. Cézanne learned from Pissarro, and Picasso learned from Cézanne. A very important collection. Maybe you'll let me see them."

"I would if I could. They're hidden now. I don't know when I can recover them."

The next part was hard to say, but I explained it all. Except for telling Pascal at the cemetery, this was the first time I'd had to tell anyone about André's death. My world was so small in Roussillon that everyone knew. Marc and Bella instantly enfolded me in their arms, murmuring words of comfort.

Marc drew back, looked at me seriously, and gave my shoulders a little shake. "You must retrieve those paintings. They are too important to the world."

"To the world? I had only considered them important to me!"

"Think larger, Lisette. Promise us that when the time is right, you will dedicate yourself to retrieving them."

"I have already promised myself."

In the kitchen, Bella cored an apple, cut it crosswise and arranged the discs in a circle, overlapping them slightly, like the petals of a flower around a dollop of the soft cheese. I wished I had cut an apple like that for André. Having no coffee, we drank hot water. The atmosphere was so homey that I asked what I had been burning to know.

"Were you ever acquainted with a young art dealer in Paris named Maxime Legrand? He worked at the Galerie Laforgue."

Marc thought for a moment and shook his head. "A friend of yours?"

"My husband's longtime friend. He was in my husband's platoon. I don't know if . . ."

Instantly they shared the same impulse, to lay their hands on my wrists.

I WAS FULL TO bursting on the way home. In careful handwriting, I added one more line to my List of Hungers and Vows.

10. Try not to be envious.

THAT EVENING, I SAT at the table staring at my empty walls. Perhaps it was a higher art to invent a painting by assembling elements from one's heart, like Marc did, rather than painting what one actually saw. I wasn't sure. I had to think about it.

If I were to create a painting of my own, what would it contain? Like Marc, I could put anything I wanted in it. In my mind's eye, I saw a couple, André and me, floating close together between the girders of the Eiffel Tower, held aloft by his open umbrella; a short-haired lady drifting alone in a rowboat without oars in a lake of the Bois de Boulogne; a row of small beds, one of them upside down; the sewn-together man resting his one hand on his son's shoulder; a nun whose starched white headdress wings waved to me; a calendar with 13 May 1940 completely blackened; a narrow outhouse with a window and shutters; a white goat in profile wearing André's wool cap and shedding a blue tear.

CHAPTER SEVENTEEN

THE MARTYR, THE GOAT, AND THE CHICKEN

1941

GLORIOUS SPRING HAD DECKED THE ORCHARDS WITH PINK and white apricot, plum, and cherry blossoms—enough to give a woman hope, if she hadn't lost someone already. I could hardly reconcile myself to the thought that André wasn't here to enjoy their fragrances.

The hillsides on the way to Gordes were deep yellow with broom—beautiful, until I remembered the edict from Vichy that broom, wild or cultivated, was to be appropriated for the making of fabric. But tractors for the harvest sat in the fields, unused because of the gasoline shortage. All farm work had to be done with horse and plow.

In the spirit of getting by, Maurice told me, his bus would be inoperable while the engine was rebuilt to run on gasogene, a fuel extracted from smoldering wood chips. This would be his last trip before the work of installing the apparatus would begin. In the same spirit of making do, I told him that by selling Geneviève's cheese to René, I had been able to buy a live chicken already laying from a farmer at the Thursday market. I felt uncomfortable about it, since the chicken was worth more than what I had paid him, but I was happy to bring eggs as well as cheese to the Chagalls.

Maurice dropped me at the outskirts of Gordes, so he could go about his business quickly. I gathered that it was for the *Résistance,* maybe to collect some dropped ammunition. He was, after all, a patriot, a true *chevalier de Provence,* delivering ducks and ladies in distress and grenades.

That left me to discover alone the trunks and packing cases on the ground floor of the school. Bella's lips were tight with resolve when she explained apologetically, "We've been advised."

It took a moment for me to comprehend what she didn't say.

"We saw the treatment of Jews in Poland half a dozen years ago. It was unspeakable then, and we suspect it's worse now."

"But here, in France?"

"Yes. Paris is not immune to a bully. Come upstairs."

My fear for their safety suddenly loomed large. "Where will you go?"

"Come see Marc."

It was a measure of his nature to welcome me in such a situation as warmly as he had done on my previous visits. He asked after Geneviève, remembering her name, and I told him about the chicken and presented him with eight eggs.

He opened the box and admired their soft color. "Like *café crème.* A shame to crack them open. Have you named your hen?"

"Not yet."

"All animals who serve us deserve a name."

"What is the Russian word for hen?"

He chuckled. "*Kooritzah.* Same as for chicken."

"*Kooritzah?*"

"*Kooritzah.*"

"From this moment, her name is Kooritzah. She will remind me of the chicken that bore the two of you on her back in Paris."

"May she support you as well."

He had been working on a painting he called *The Martyr.* Against the background of a village aflame, a man wearing a Russian cap and partially covered by a fringed cloth was tied to a stake.

I felt outrage at that. When I questioned Bella about what the cloth was, she explained that it was a Jewish prayer shawl. Now I recalled seeing similar shawls hanging below men's coats in the Marais district. Although the figure's skin had turned yellow, his face was strangely peaceful. Below him, a suppliant woman leaned against his leg. The figures made me think of Christ and Mary Magdalene. Around him a crimson creature, half cow, half man, and a frightened chicken were tumbling in the sky. A soldier was ransacking a house, throwing chairs out an upper window, while a bearded Jew appeared to be reading verses from an open book and a fiddler was playing out his sorrow.

Beyond Marc's innocent, childlike paintings of village life, here was what his art could do—mirror the blast of barbarity now happening in Europe. A painting such as this, seen by enough people, could get them to feel my outrage. It could get people to act, to resist, to march willingly to war, as André had done. With this single painting, I realized that art wasn't just about love and beauty. It could also be a strong political force.

Marc had stopped working to talk to me, but I motioned to his brush. "Continue." Watching would put me in the very heart of the art world, seeing an important painting in the making.

He laid down a worm of deep blue on his palette, flattened it into a circle, and worked black into it from the edges. "The most important aspect of a composition can be accentuated by the brightest color, or by the strongest value contrast," he said.

With that, he painted two diagonal blue-black stripes on the figure's white prayer shawl, using the flat of his brush. Then with the same pigment, he painted narrow straps on the man's arms, using the edge of the brush.

"There is delight at the edge as well as at the end of a brush. Now there is no question that he is a Jew. And if you outline something, that draws attention to it." He outlined the man-cow in the same hue.

"Are you suggesting that chaos and cruelty affect man and beast alike?"

"Oh-ho, aren't you a quick study!"

He wiped the brush dry and touched it lightly to the roofs of the houses. As if by magic, the painting was coming together. Although it depicted conflict and cruelty, all of its elements were in harmony. He stepped away from his easel and asked if I had retrieved my paintings.

"No. It's still not safe to have them in my house."

He looked straight at me. "You're right, but you must never give them up."

I nodded. Vow number eleven would be *Retrieve the paintings.* Why hadn't I put that on my list earlier? Only because it was so obvious that it didn't require being written.

It was a privilege to help Bella lay some canvases in a crate and to wrap the portrait of lovers in a sheet. "I will never forget the tenderness of this one," I told her.

"I postponed packing it in case you came again."

"Thank you." I couldn't say that I needed this vision of love to offset the evidences of hatred in Marc's martyrdom painting, but perhaps she understood that.

"May I ask you something? If I find the paintings and return to Paris, my deepest yearning is to be a part of the art world in some way. I was hoping for a position in a gallery, but I have no education. Do you know any kindly gallery owner who might take me on as an apprentice, just on the strength of my longing?"

"I'll ask Marc. Maybe he can write to someone."

"I know it was impulsive, but I offered myself as a washerwoman in the Louvre."

"Lisette! That's much too humble for you."

"No, it isn't. I would be happy doing that. Maybe you know a painter whose studio I could clean."

She smiled. "I'll ask Marc that too."

They were preoccupied, so I didn't stay long. At the door, I asked the question that had been distressing me: "Will you be safe?"

"If we act quickly," Marc said. "Good health and long life, *lapushka*."

"It's Russian. It means something affectionate, soft as a kitten's paw—something like 'darling.'"

"I'll come again before you leave."

An embrace, and I stepped outside, feeling anxious for their safety. I hurried on in the spring drizzle to the place Maurice had left me, trying to hold on to those two words, *kooritzah* and *lapushka*.

THE MEN IN THE CAFÉ had begrudgingly become accustomed to women coming in at the *apéritif* hour. I had stopped going during the cold weather of January and February, but Odette and I resumed our visits in April. A Vichy broadcast blamed the defeat of France on American bars, the English weekend, Russian choirs, Argentine tangos. "Absurd," "ridiculous," "shameful" were the muttered reactions. More serious was the proclamation that all previous French culture was decadent and only Aryan culture was pure. It was hideous to hear that said by a French announcer.

Would this mean that if my paintings were found by someone other than me, they could be turned over to the Germans to be destroyed? That made me anxious to retrieve them, but where else could I put them? For a moment, I was glad André had hidden them so well. No one would think to look in a woodpile. But what if they found Marc's whole life's work before he could get it out of France? The Germans would certainly burn every one of his paintings as degenerate. And what if they found Marc and Bella?

Soon after that, we heard the announcement that Pétain's government had established a Department for Jewish Affairs, which had made the anti-Jewish laws already in place more strict and added new ones. Now I was all the more anxious to get to Gordes again. I went to Henri's forge to see how the conversion of Maurice's bus was coming along. I found Maurice sawing wood into small cubes while Henri welded a platform onto the front of the bus for a canister as large as a trash can to sit on. "It's a fi-fi-firebox," Henri explained. "Th-th-the wood is p-put in here, and the f-f-fumes come out the bottom into a fi-filter, and then th-through a pipe to the engine." It was good of him to make the effort to explain it to me—apparently it was that important to him—but if he stopped work to explain the workings of the gasogene device to everyone who asked, the bus would never be ready.

It had been nearly three weeks. I couldn't wait any longer. Pascal had gone to Aix to buy *The Card Players* too late. I didn't want to make a similar mistake. I made a batch of cheese, collected eggs, and set out on foot for the nine-kilometer journey. This time, it wasn't to see the paintings. It was to see Marc and Bella.

ALTHOUGH THE MORNING WAS CLEAR, by the time I got to Gordes, two and a half hours later, the sky in the distance was turning the color of plums, and the heavy air bore the acrid odor of approaching rain. Birds cried out in single syllables their complaints about the wetness to come. I picked up almond blossoms that had blown off their branches to give to Bella, their creamy white petals cupping yellow centers that sprouted pink filaments—as beautiful as any cultivated orchid in a Paris florist's shop.

I rang the bell, but neither of them leaned out an upper window. The latch wasn't locked, so I opened the door a crack. *"Bonjour, madame! Bonjour, monsieur!"* No response. I entered. A wail escaped me. I *was* too late. I went through the empty classrooms, stupefied and crying out my worry. Wondering how they had escaped, I prayed that they were safe. I tried to remember the paintings I had seen in each room. The same fear of forgetting that had anguished Pascal anguished me as well. I understood the depth of his grief when he found that Cézanne had died. Like Pascal, I had waited too long before I asked what made a painting great. I scattered the petals on the floor where the portrait of the lovers had been.

I knocked on a neighbor's door, and an old woman answered. I identified myself as Lisette Roux from Roussillon and gestured to the school building.

"Gone. They stayed with me the night before they left."

"Are they safe?"

"How can we know? Someone in an American car came to get them at four o'clock in the morning. Their crates and trunks had been picked up the week before."

"An American car? Were they going to America?"

"I presume so, if they could make it there."

A ridiculous image popped into my mind—an American car motoring across the Atlantic Ocean. Then a grimmer image followed it—Marc and Bella wading far out into the sea at night, to be picked up by a fishing boat and taken to a ship, as at Dunkerque, Marc looking over his shoulder every couple of minutes to see that Bella was still there. I shuddered.

"Monsieur left a painting for you," the woman said.

"He did?"

She went into another room and brought it out. "It was wet when he gave it to me, but it's dry now."

Instantly, my throat became tight as a thread. It was a painting of a dark-haired woman looking out an open window while embracing a chicken against her chest. With the other hand she drew a goat to her side. The lines indicating the chicken's beak and the goat's mouth curved upward slightly, as though smiling. The woman wore the same expression as the animals did. The feeling the painting evoked in me was the opposite of what I had felt looking at *The Martyr*. Here, in the south of France, a human being and animals were safe, but apparently the Chagalls were not.

On the horizontal muntin of the window in the painting, a tiny man was dancing, his right leg dangling behind him. Although he was offering her a bouquet of flowers, the woman seemed not to notice him; she was content enough to be holding the animals. Through the lower windowpane, houses of a distant village stepped up a snowy slope. Was it Vitebsk? Gordes? Roussillon? Was the woman Bella or me? Was the man Marc or André? A crescent moon, or maybe it was a slim fish, hung in the rosy sky. I was tantalized by the ambiguity. The image blurred as I recognized Marc and Bella's love for me.

The painting appeared to be opaque watercolor and colored chalk on paper mounted on cardboard. It was slightly broader than my shoulders, taller than it was wide. I could carry it easily, but not the cheese and eggs too. I gave them to the woman and thanked her for taking care of Marc and Bella on their last night.

"They were very solemn when they left. They loved it here."

I stepped outside into damp air, and the woman called after me, "Wait! I almost forgot. They also left this for you."

She waved a piece of paper bearing a Parisian address and the scribbled words *a friend*. I pocketed it and hurried up the roughly cobbled hill, through the village, and down the other side to the road to Roussillon. If it rained before I got home, the painting would be ruined. I had to find a place to hide it along the way.

I ran down the switchbacks and the long incline below Gordes, the wind flapping the painting away from me; I had to hold it close to my body to keep it from sailing off. I should have asked the old woman to keep it for me until better weather, but I had been too excited to have it. Thunder rolled above mighty Mont Ventoux, to the north.

Out of breath, I reached the flat road to the village of bories, the thick, beehive-shaped stone huts built by ancient people. Pascal had told me that every slab of stone must have been chosen carefully and overlapped at an angle so that water would be shed on the outside and no rain could penetrate within. Perfect, but I didn't want to use any borie close to the road.

The sky darkened to charcoal, and the rain began, with pinpoint drops on my cheeks, sparse, delicate, polite, then gathering comrades, splattering my face, trickling down my neck, intent on ruining my treasure. I took off my jacket and wrapped it around the painting.

A crack of thunder startled me, and I ran wildly, away from the main road, along a high rock wall encircling the village of bories, until I found an opening. I spotted a hut in good repair, the opening hidden by nettles, through which no one in his right mind would go. I shouldered my way through the thicket and entered. The rain was falling in ropes now, but not a drop seeped inside the hut. A recess in the back wall could have been an oven. To be doubly safe, I set the painting on edge in it, so I could wall it in with some of the stone slabs that lay around outside, which meant I had to wedge my way through the nettles twice for each slab. Their leaves tormented my skin, and hefting the rough stones bloodied my hands. Finally, I finished the double wall. The painting was surely safe now.

But were Bella and Marc? Were they out in this storm, crossing the Pyrénées on foot? Were they hiding in some leaky barn?

A nasty night was advancing, and I knew I couldn't stay there much longer. Already the temperature had dropped, already puddles were growing outside, already the paper in my skirt pocket had become damp. By the time I arrived home, it would be sodden and unreadable. I memorized the address, 182 rue de Vaugirard, saying it a dozen times, then tucked it between my breasts, buttoned my jacket, and set out into swift rain that seemed in a hurry to drench me.

CHAPTER EIGHTEEN

NEW LIFE

1941

MORE THAN TWO HOURS LATER, SOAKED TO THE SKIN and shivering, I hurried through the village, still repeating the address to myself. Luckily, the rain hadn't stopped falling, so all the shutters were closed and there were no women's sewing coteries gossiping in the streets.

The next day the azure sky was marbled with wispy swan's-down clouds. I set out dry grass from the barrel for Geneviève and potato peelings for Kooritzah. In the outhouse with the shutters open, I pretended to be the woman in Marc's painting. The window he had painted was in a narrow peaked building no wider than the proportions of the outhouse. How could he have known?

I could hardly believe that I, Lisette Irène Noëlle Roux, raised in an orphanage, a twenty-four-year-old widow with little money, possessed a painting of my own, painted expressly for me, with love in every brushstroke.

I stepped outside for a wider, grander view. The yellow honeysuckle André had planted near the outhouse to offset the smell was blooming. Beyond the rosemary bushes marking the edge of the courtyard, deep pink monkey orchids grew wild on the downhill slope. The stone windmill, Moulin du Sablon, perched on a windy promontory, had lost its vanes but it was still imposing.

In the clarity after the rain, the valley appeared as a living version of Cézanne's landscape, at least as I remembered it. The terrain was divided into distinct shapes, each in a different hue—the striped chartreuse green of the vineyards, the solid, darker green of vegetable plots, the golden grass of wheat fields, the sprays of pink cherry and white apple blossoms, the cultivated fields of sunflowers, their faces turned to the sun. Exquisite.

André had framed the landscape in the outhouse window perfectly to show the best of the view. Might that mean that the Cézanne landscape was his favorite painting? Thinking so allowed me to feel our thoughts connect.

Beyond the valley, the Petit Luberon rose to the west in foothills of deep green cedar forests, a mere prelude to the Grand Luberon, to the east, where eroded white limestone cliffs thrust upward. If I could arc the path of my vision over the mountains, I could see the Durance River flowing swiftly this morning, and a Cézanne quilt of colors that spread over the land all the way to the blue of the Mediterranean. I breathed in spring as a drowning man rising to the surface of the sea gulps air, and exhaled new life.

An unseen bird issued a soft, repetitious *whoo-whoo-whoo.* Whether it was an owl, which Pascal had called a *bubo bubo,* or a mourning dove, I didn't know. Was its plaintive cooing urging me toward wisdom or perpetual sorrow? "Whoo-whoo," I sang along with it, softly at first, then robustly, the Provençal way. Geneviève came to my side and joined in with her *baa-baa.* Putting my arm around her neck started Kooritzah fussing and fluttering her jealousy, throwing herself against my leg until I cradled her too.

"Such a silly chicken you are. Don't you know I love you too? *J'ai deux amours,* the song goes. I have two loves. Do you understand now, mademoiselle? Don't forget it."

—

DAYS LATER, A LEADEN TRUTH landed when I happened to glance at the calendar on the desk. It was May 13, the day of André's death a year earlier. How had I gotten through the twelve months? One day of hollow sadness at a time. I had cried in every room in the house, sometimes in great gasping sobs, other times like a quiet rain at night. Sometimes a memory crept into my mind like a sly serpent. Other times a thought exploded like a grenade, as it did when I opened a government envelope and found the first check marked "War Widow's Pension." More than once, tears had fallen into my milky hickory coffee. My onion soup was flavored with my own salt.

Spring was suddenly mocking me. Nevertheless, the day cried out for some recognition, for me to do something to acknowledge it. I looked at the view of the Luberon Valley and thought of Cézanne's landscape painting, which I felt sure André would have wanted me to have. He knew that beauty gave comfort, that there was solace in the play of colors against one another, and upliftment of spirit in the grace of an arabesque curve.

Meanwhile, I had pressing needs. My government compensation for André's death was pitifully small because I had no children. I added an item to my list,

12. Learn how to be self-sufficient,

and went in search of Maurice. I found him at Henri Mitan's forge, working on the top-heavy gasogene converter, which was now sitting above a smaller canister on the platform attached to the front of the bus.

"What a crazy, unwieldy contraption that is!"

"What do you mean? She is beautiful, this girl." He stroked the side of the firebox lovingly and then patted the filter box below it.

"I need work," I said.

"Then hand me that wrench."

"I mean work that pays."

He suggested I pick cherries for Émile Vernet in June and mulberry leaves for Mélanie's silkworms anytime. During the *vendange,* the time of gathering grapes in the fall, I could work in Madame Bonnelly's vineyard.

"Her husband is a prisoner of war. She promised work to a Parisian refugee for the *vendange,* but I'll wager she could use more help than one picker."

"Fine. I'll do those things in season, but it's spring now, time to plant a vegetable garden."

"Oh! Our pretty *Parisienne* is becoming a *Provençale.*"

"A widow has to live, Maurice."

"All right then, Madame Jardinière. Usually you can get seeds at Cachin's grocery or at the market in Apt. But now?" He raised his shoulders and lifted his greasy palms. "That's doubtful."

"What does it matter?" I said. "You're not going to Apt or anywhere for a while. We're stuck here on this hill."

I took him aside, out of earshot of the old men working on equally old vehicles, and told him that the Chagalls had escaped and that Marc had left a painting for me. Maurice asked where it was, and I told him precisely. It wasn't wise to have only one person know the location.

"Just keep it there. Roussillon is changing. Strangers live here now. You can't trust anyone anymore."

I went directly to Jérôme Cachin's *épicerie* to ask if he had any seeds for growing vegetables. No, he didn't.

"I'll ask the constable of the commune if he knows of any farmer's wife selling them from their last crop," he offered.

"No. no. Please don't do that."

He shrugged. "It's no trouble, madame."

I was trapped by need and said no more.

"Are you enjoying the toilet paper?"

"Immensely."

—

THREE DAYS LATER, BERNARD BLANC was at my door, instantly thrusting his foot forward onto the doorsill. His ostentatious boots were an offense to me, and probably to the farmers of Roussillon as well. He brandished a handful of envelopes and read the penciled words on each one in a voice that scraped like sandpaper. "Onions, carrots, beets, cauliflower, green beans, tomatoes, lettuce, celery." Shaking each envelope to taunt me with the rattle of seeds, he kept checking my expression for a covetous reaction. I refused to respond.

"You see now what I can do for you?"

"I can manage on my own."

"How long would it have taken you to walk the countryside asking at each farm? I know the farms, the crops, the farmers' wives, and I have a lorry."

A pause while he looked me over head to foot.

"You would be back in Paris now if it weren't for the paintings, wouldn't you?" His tone had softened.

I was annoyed that Roussillon was so small that everyone knew everyone else's business.

"You must be lonely living here, a pretty woman like you alone, especially in the long evenings." Now his arrogance slid into a leer. "What do you think about?"

"I am not lonely."

"I venture to say you would like some company."

"No. I prefer solitude."

He guffawed at my lie. "Maybe someday you will change your mind. Maybe you will come around to wanting a new life, a better life than a widow's stale grief."

He grabbed me around the waist and pulled me to him so that our bodies pressed against each other, shoulders to knees. I pushed back with all my strength, and he let go, except for my hand, which he held so tightly I couldn't pull it away. He turned it palm up, placed the envelopes in it, and firmly closed my fingers over them.

"I'm glad to see that you wisely wish to follow Pétain's doctrine that tilling the land is patriotic. The only thing more patriotic is that he urges us to use our bodies more than our minds. Children, Lisette. Sons to join the Legion. It would be a new life for you. I am a patient man. Up to a point."

Hubris oozed from him like seeping oil.

"Did you like the chicken?"

Despite the unsavory origin of that savory chicken, his civility in the face of his inconsistent kindness, this time in providing seeds, forced me against my conscience to say yes.

He straightened his shoulders, removed his foot from the sill, nodded, and left, smug in his perception of victory.

He was a fool to think he could win me by force, by intimidation, or by gifts. I turned from the door, my thoughts swinging from anger to mild annoyance to grudging gratitude for the seeds.

I went down into the root cellar to look for garden tools. They lay on top of a spread of burlap sacks. From the edge I had seen only lengths of wood, so I hadn't taken apart the pile. Now I did. I shrieked. Pascal's frames! I dropped to my knees. No paintings, just empty frames, one inside the other, and disassembled stretchers.

"Oh, André, why didn't you keep the paintings in the frames? It would have been so much easier. Why did you make me go through this agony?"

My vow to forgive him shriveled. No. My grief was not stale. It erupted fresh and toothed every night. I stayed on my knees, unable to move from this spot, staring at the frames and burlap that he had handled. I rubbed the scratchy, rank-smelling cloth against my cheek.

Maybe there was a reason for this framing of frames, the smaller ones placed inside the largest one. Maybe telling me that the paintings were under the woodpile was a ruse, not to trick me but to mislead anyone I told. Maybe beneath the frames . . .

I found a shovel and dug in the hard earth without making much progress. Surely he would not have buried them too deeply. I unearthed the whole area. Nothing. If the paintings had been wrapped against dampness or placed between boards, this would have been a good hiding place, far safer than the large communal woodpile at place de l'Abbé Avon. In truth, they could be under either one. I lifted off all the frames and stretchers, not in order to bring the paintings into the house, just to be assured that they were there.

Nothing. Not a single canvas.

Light waned in the courtyard. All I had to show for myself was a filthy dress, mud-caked shoes, broken fingernails, and utter disappointment. Tomorrow, I promised myself, I would dig a garden, which would at least be digging with a purpose.

I FOUND THAT TURNING earth for a garden wasn't any easier than digging in the cellar. The ground hadn't been broken up since Pascal's parents had cultivated it. After a week of hard labor and a good long rain, I planted the seeds in rows and commanded, "Grow your roots! *Poussez! Poussez!* Push through the earth and stand up for yourselves!"

Louise told me that Geneviève's dung would make good fertilizer. Now when I milked her, I chanted, "Poop, Geneviève, poop!"

Cherry picking was hard work too, but the occasional plundered cherry revived me—satin-smooth on my tongue, the dark purple meat sun-warmed, sweet, and juicy. I liked thinking of the people of Roussillon having this rare pleasure, until Émile said that all cherries grown in Provence had been requisitioned by the Vichy government to grace German officers' tables. After hearing that, I ate my fill of them when Émile wasn't looking.

By August, I had gathered my first harvest from the ladies of my garden: Thomassine and her sisters, the tomato plants, whose small green marbles had swollen into plump red hearts; Claudine and her row of amply endowed sisters, the cauliflowers, billowing like white thunderclouds; Céleste and her siblings, tall and stately, trying to befriend the sky by stretching their pale green stalks and leafy crowns; Lutèce and her court, standing erect like queens unfurling their ruffled green robes; Beatrice and her friends, who kept their secrets below the surface in purple balls with root tails; Caroline and her maidens, so shy they grew their orange roots downward while shaking their green frizz in the joy of clean air; Bérénice and her cousins, who hung their pendulous green tubes until they were ready for a *salade niçoise;* Ondine and her next of kin, who could spice up my *daube* with pungency, even shedding their brown paperlike dresses, and then, peeled and peeled and peeled, they would give themselves completely to me until there would be nothing left of them. Oh, the glory of growth! All day I thought my thanks for the plenitude of my garden. Begrudgingly, I recognized Bernard as having been the source of it.

In November, I flung a rope around the lower branches of the almond tree and yanked on it sharply to shake loose the nuts, then hauled a burlap sack of them to Jérôme Cachin to sell in his *épice-rie.* A week later I dragged them home. No one had bought any. Nuts were a luxury. I might as well give them away.

I had thought it would be easier to be bereaved in Paris, where there were diversions, where I could order soup in a café and not be stared at. Now, without André, would the city be enough? Might I long for my patch of garden and the daily rhythm of milking Geneviève? Would I miss Kooritzah's proud clucking when she laid an egg? Would I miss Odette and Louise and Maurice?

The approach of winter of 1941 came upon us with a vengeance, one mistral after another. Although I dragged my mattress downstairs to sleep by the stove, I still could not keep the house warm. André's woodpile was shrinking, so I limited myself to three sticks a night, then two, then one, just enough to steam vegetables. When my own woodpile was gone, there would be the frames.

No. I refused.

But there was something I could sacrifice. It might bring in a little money. The thought grieved me. It was so final, a severing. They had been Pascal's before André had used them. I tried to ignore it, but the thought beat at my temples. All right then, I would do it, but André's hammer I would save to rehang the paintings, and the mallet to split the almonds.

This was the second time I had visited the cemetery since Pascal had died. The first wrenching time was when I had come to tell Pascal that his grandson had been killed. This time would not be as hard. I knelt and placed my palms on the Roux tomb.

"Hello, Papa. I am still here. I miss you dreadfully, and André too. The two most important people to me, and you're both beyond my reach. I would gladly give up all the paintings to have one of you back for a day.

"I met a painter in Gordes. I did something nice for him and his wife—brought them chèvre and eggs." In a whisper, I said, "He *gave* me a painting. I thought you would like to know.

"I've come to ask your forgiveness. This winter promises to be exceptionally cold. I've tried to provide everything for myself, but I have to buy wood or I'll freeze. Do you remember the furniture re-pair shop in Avignon where André worked? When Maurice finally gets the parts he needs to allow his bus to run on gasogene, he could take me there. Maybe the man . . ." I didn't even want to voice the words. "I know they were yours. André sharpened them before he left, out of respect for you, I think. You'll forgive me, won't you? I love you, Papa. Never forget that.

"You told me to let the paintings care for me. I have a fine vege-table garden now just like Louise has, and a goat, like the girl had in the Pissarro painting, so I am doing what you said. I'm living in at least this painting. It's a new life for me. In spite of my Paris dream, I seem to be growing roots here."

CHAPTER NINETEEN

SHAME

1941–43

Louise and Odette and I sat in our coats, enjoying a new kind of coffee made from sweetbriar while we waited in place de la Mairie for the five o'clock news, both from Radio Vichy, which came through too loud, and the BBC, which was scratchy with interference. We had been occupying the same table in the café most nights to hear the events of the world.

That night, December 8, both reports announced a surprise attack by Japanese bombers on a harbor in Hawaii the day before, damaging eight United States Navy battleships. We were stupefied. On the other side of the globe, Hawaii seemed exotic to us.

"Is this the same war?" Odette remarked.

"This will surely bring the Americans into it," Louise said.

And in a few days, it did. Our hopes lifted.

Just before Christmas, Constable Blanc knocked on my door and announced that he had a truckload of wood for me and a wheelbarrow.

"I know you've been cold. You can't tell me otherwise. These are the last of the split logs and bundles of kindling from the community woodpile."

He was already unloading them into the wheelbarrow.

"How do you know I don't have a big stack of firewood in the courtyard?"

"I can see it from the promontory across the ravine."

"You make it too much your business to know my business."

"Do you want me to drive off without leaving you a stick? I will. Just say the word, Lisette."

"Madame Roux."

"Lisette."

Without my telling him, he wheeled the load around the corner to my side gate. How did he know there was a gate there? It was overgrown with passionflower and honeysuckle vines. He stacked the wood where André had stacked it, loaded the wheelbarrow four more times, brushed off his pant legs, and wiped off his boots with a folded white handkerchief.

I admitted my gratitude only to myself, feeling it shameful for me to accept such a generous gift.

"Christmas is only a week away. You wouldn't like to spend it alone, now, would you? I can bring a nice roast capon. More than enough for just the two of us."

"No, thank you, Constable. I already have plans."

"I have a little gift for you that you will love. Something you can't get here."

"That's kind of you, but please keep it. I have no gift to give in return."

"Oh yes you do, if only you knew."

He grasped my shoulders and forced his kiss upon my clenched lips, which I'm sure injured his pride more than gave him pleasure because he let me push him away, and then he left.

Late on Christmas Eve, when I came home from Louise and Maurice's house, I found his gift wrapped in newspaper in my lavender pot. Leaving it there was crafty of him. It prevented me from refusing it. Silk stockings! Unbelievable. He certainly had connections.

In the wrapping there was a note.

Chère Lisette,

The time will come when you will see what I can do for you. My patience is wearing as thin as these stockings.

Joyeux Noël,
Bernard

I lit the stove with a precious piece of kindling and watched the precious silk shrink from the precious flame and burn itself out.

A YEAR CREPT BY on bare hands and knees. Geneviève was giving less milk, so Louise bred her with her buck. Months later, Geneviève's belly and teats grew large and her udder firm. One morning I came out to see two baby goats suckling hungrily. When they were large enough, after three months, I gave them to Louise and Maurice. One by one Louise roasted them, *chevreau provençal* style, with garlic and herbs. Toughening myself, I ate two hearty meals at their house. I was becoming reconciled to the ways of the country.

Bernard brought me more seeds. I called him by his first name in my mind now, but I would never be so informal as to say that to his face. He was polite, so I gave him carrots from my root cellar. The vegetable garden and Bernard's delivery of wood saved me from dire want, and my friends saved me from unbearable loneliness.

The Allies invaded North Africa in November 1942. That seemed close enough to mean something good to us. Unfortunately, it also meant that now the south of France was an occupied territory. German soldiers were garrisoned in Apt and elsewhere, and long lines of German tanks on transport trucks and armaments lorries rumbled through the countryside, heading south. A couple of times, they exploded, thanks to the *Résistance*.

Now, every time I passed under the Gothic arch separating the upper village from the lower village, I looked down, shuddering, so I wouldn't see the huge red-and-black flag with its ugly swastika hanging against the stone of the arch. Coming home, I had to pass another one on the opposite side of the arch. We had learned on the radio that it was called *die Blutfahne,* "blood flag." What depravity had made up such a name? Our arch was no Arc de Triomphe, but it was the only striking architectural feature in Roussillon. To have it desecrated with that reminder of our shameful national defeat was an outrage aimed at crushing our spirit.

One afternoon after the new year, as Odette and I sat in front of the café, a German patrol marched up the incline, escorted by Constable Blanc in his tall black boots, just like theirs. They stopped at the *mairie,* to our right. On the broad steps, the constable introduced the officer to Mayor Pinatel. We watched, horrified, while they both stood by, helpless, as the officer ripped de Gaulle's speech off the wall and, after a torrent of angry words, ordered a trooper to replace it with a poster of Marshal Pétain.

We turned away from the soldiers goose-stepping their arrogance through place de la Mairie, just to humiliate us. The instant they passed, Louise darted out from her salon, spied de Gaulle's speech in the street, where it lay crumpled and torn, snatched it up, and hurried back inside. I was astounded at her bravery.

"It's one thing for smirking soldiers to march down the Champs-Élysées for a big show, but to come here to our unimportant village and do the same is ridiculous," I said.

"Then why?" Odette asked.

"Just to be bullies," I said, but privately, I had dark misgivings. They must have had a reason. My mind turned on what it might be. Monsieur Beckett? The two British women? Maurice and Aimé? The paintings?

"Do you think Bernard escorted them willingly?" she asked.

"No. He was forced. Did you see his face? He wasn't proud. He was embarrassed." Whatever else I thought of him, of that I had no doubt.

THAT EVENING, JUST BEFORE DUSK, as I was about to ladle out my vegetable soup, there was a knock on my door—loud, rapid, insistent. I froze. It came again. What if it was Maurice telling me that Louise had fallen and needed help? No, Maurice would come right in. I stood just inside the door and heard gruff voices. I opened it to the German officer with the peaked hat who had led the patrol. Next to him on one side stood the soldier who had posted Marshal Pétain's photo on the wall of the *mairie,* and on the other, Bernard. My throat went suddenly dry. The Germans burst into the room, and Bernard followed more slowly, with a shamefaced look similar to the one he had worn when he'd escorted the patrol.

"Sit, please, madame," the officer said in harshly accented French.

The soldier pulled out a chair from the table and set it in the middle of the room. Feeling weak in the knees, I sat down. The three stood around me in a semicircle, Bernard farther away than the others.

The officer wore a small firearm in a holster and a snugly fitting gray-green jacket. Oddly, I wondered what Pascal would have called the color, or what ugly name I would invent for it when this was over. Moldy olive? The large brass buckle on his belt bore the inscription GOTT MIT UNS. I guessed its meaning. What a lie. God certainly was not with *them.*

The blond soldier, with his trouser legs tucked inside his boots, had a tubelike black rubber stick attached to his belt by a loop. I couldn't help but stare at it.

The officer stood before me with his feet wide apart and drew out from his breast pocket a little black book. He thumbed through the pages.

"Madame Lisette Roux, I presume."

"How is it that you know my name?"

"Just answer the questions. Are you or are you not Madame Lisette Roux?"

"I am."

I glanced at Bernard for some clue or some support. "Look at me," the officer ordered. "Only at me."

I did, and noticed his oily skin shining in the lamplight.

"The German state is extremely cultured and values music and art. You would agree?"

"I wouldn't know."

He scowled. "We are given to understand that you own some French paintings, which, by right of victory, belong to Germany. Is that true?"

I turned away and sought a cue from Bernard.

"Look at me only!" the officer shouted. "The answer," he resumed softly, "is in your heart, madame, not on his face. Is it true that you own some paintings?"

"How do you know this?"

I shot a look at Bernard. He had betrayed me, the bastard.

"You need not glare at him. Herr Constable did not tell us."

"Then how did you know?"

"I take that to mean that you do own some paintings." He paused. "Say it."

I felt my underarms grow moist. I was silent for some minutes, resisting his trickery.

"If I may advise you, madame," the trooper said, "it is not wise to keep *Herr Leutnant* waiting." He moved his hand to the top of his stiff rubber bludgeon.

So he spoke French too.

"Yes, I own some."

"How many?"

"Three."

Herr Leutnant consulted his book. He raised an eyebrow and

pursed his lips. "Perhaps my aide can help you remember the number accurately."

The aide slid his rubber stick slowly out of the loop, watching
me watch it come out, and smacked it hard against his palm, which
instantly turned pink.

"Seven."

"*Merci,*" the lieutenant said, smug and cool. "And now you can
tell us where they are."

"I don't know."

The lieutenant's slap came instantly and burned my cheek. Bernard flinched and took a step forward, as if to protect me from
another.

"It's best not to intervene, Herr Constable." The lieutenant
cleared his throat. "Would you like to amend that, madame?"

The trooper approached me with his bludgeon raised, and the
lieutenant stopped him with a slight gesture of his open palm. "We
are not cruel. Her face is beautiful. It would be a shame. . . . Give
her time."

This was the moment André had prepared me for, and Bernard
had as well. The sting on my cheek continued to burn. I touched it
with my trembling hand to try to cool it. Bernard wet a dish towel
with water from a pitcher, and the lieutenant let him hand it to me.
It seemed a reminder of his advice the night of the ransacking: *Take
care of yourself. Give the paintings up if you need to*. I struggled
not to cry. I would not give them tears.

Herr Leutnant raised his face and sniffed. He turned around and
noticed my pot of vegetable soup simmering. He dipped in the
ladle, blew on it, and slurped the broth. May God let him burn his
tongue, I said to myself.

"Ah, the French cuisine, so delicate and savory." He ladled out a
bowlful, pulled out a chair, and sat at the table facing me. Waiting
for it to cool, he put his feet, in their muddy boots, on a chair to the
side and drummed his fingers on the table. When he began spooning the soup into his mouth, I fumed at his sense of entitlement and

was outraged again, remembering what the Prussian soldiers had done to Pissarro's home in Louveciennes.

"Not bad, madame. What do you call it?"

"Pistou à la provençale." I exploded my *p*'s at him as if they were bullets.

"Pistou à la provençale," he repeated, gently mocking me.

He lit a cigarette.

"If you refuse to tell me, I will be forced to tell my captain, who has a ravaging hunger for art, and a rough way about him."

To give up the paintings just because of a short-lived pain seemed faithless. But how much pain would that bludgeon cause? And what disfigurement? What would André have me do? Let them go. His letter said so. I tried to reconcile myself to that—the loss of Cézanne's still life, of the girl with the goat on the ochre path, of the Provençal landscape. My heart was breaking.

"Ah, we see that she is resolute." He nodded to his aide, who lunged toward me with his bludgeon raised.

"The woodpile. A community woodpile." My throat was raw for no physical reason.

"I am glad that you understand our position. My captain will be happy to receive them." He put out his cigarette in the bowl half full of soup and stood up. "Take us there."

I sat rooted to the chair. The trooper grabbed me under one arm and yanked me upright. I walked toward the stairs, and the trooper quickly positioned himself in front of them. "May I get my coat?"

"Let her," I heard behind me, Bernard's voice. I turned just in time to see the lieutenant assent.

I made the walk to the woodpile last as long as I could, thinking of the red roofs of Pontoise, the quarry in front of Montagne Sainte-Victoire, the girl with the goat, absurdly asking her for forgiveness, asking Pascal as well.

It was nearly dark when I stopped in front of the neatly stacked wood and saw that the enclosure was three-quarters full. The lieutenant held a light, and the trooper went to work lifting off the wood. Bernard stood next to me without helping. Curiously, that was some small comfort. The officer could have ordered him to help. I sensed a silent power struggle. After quite a while, the trooper removed the last of the wood and the kindling and lifted a large piece of canvas.

There were no paintings, not a single one! Only the blank canvas André must have used to cover them.

Disoriented and disbelieving, I staggered forward to get a better look, and gasped. "They're gone!"

The lieutenant shined his battery torch right in my eyes, blinding me. Tears came suddenly.

"Who else did you tell?"

"No one."

The lieutenant kicked the kindling. "She doesn't know," he grumbled. Disgusted, he jerked the light toward his aide as a sign to leave.

"We will be in Apt, in case you *remember* another place where they might be found. If they are ever traced back to you, I assure you that you'll be sorry. Good night, madame."

The three went off downhill, leaving me there and leaving the wood scattered. The paintings were lost. I was lost. I turned toward home, stumbling in the dark to Maurice and Louise's house instead of my own farther up the hill. I told them through sputtering sobs what had happened, and they insisted that I sleep there that night.

SANDRINE STOPPED ME IN the street on a Sunday morning not long afterward and told me she had a piece of mail from Germany that had been waiting for me for several weeks.

"Germany! I'll get it right now."

"We're closed. It's Sunday. You'll have to wait."

Impossible. The hours crept torturously. I paced. I shook. I couldn't sleep. I dared not hope. I could not keep from hoping.

Early Monday morning, she handed me the envelope. Maxime's handwriting! He was alive! That was enough for the moment. I held it unopened against my chest as I hastened home.

It contained one piece of paper, with his letter written in pencil on both sides.

14 MARCH 1943

Dearest Lisette,

I am alive. I am a prisoner in Stalag VI-J, some place called S.A. Lager Fichtenhein in Krefeld, which I ascertain from other prisoners is close to the border with the Netherlands. The shame of being a prisoner, when I think of how André died, fighting right next to me, has prevented me from writing to you. I've been afraid that you would not like to hear from the living, only the dead. But I cannot bear to cause you any anguish, not knowing whether or not I am alive. And, just as true, I cannot bear not knowing how you are faring.

I am completely broken by André's death. No words can express the sorrow I feel for you. I will have to rely on deeds, if I am ever released and have strength enough to see you—if you will agree to that. I think of you and André every day, a hundred times a day. Sometimes I weep, but that does no good for the other prisoners in my barracks, so I try to control myself.

I am forced to work in a coal mine for ten hours a day, living two months at a time in a mining camp, with two weeks off for recovery back at Stalag VI-J. In winter I never see daylight, and the cold, damp floor seeps through my worn boot soles. I hate my grimy body, hate myself, in fact. I think of Pascal working in the ochre mine, but he was working for beauty. I am haunted by the thought that every piece of coal

*I dig may fuel the trains that bring more prisoners. The thing
we most fear is not to be healthy enough to work. If we can't
work, they don't feed us. I am managing, though.*

*We are given one sheet of paper, an envelope, a pencil,
and a stamp once a week at the permanent barracks to write
a letter. There is no provision for letter writing at the mining
camp, but all week at the permanent camp, I frame my sentences to my mother and memorize them because we only
have fifteen minutes to write. So she won't worry, I wrote to
her that I was going to skip a week in order to write to you.*

*To the extent that I am able to pray, I pray for you, and I
pray for André. Do I dare to hope that you will pray for me?*

Affectueusement,
Max

Alive! Thank God! I wept great tears of rejoicing tinged with
sadness. Prison. Deprivation. What had he been forced to do to be
alive today? Avoid offending his captors? Show that he was likable
so they wouldn't shoot him for some inadvertent glance or for not
being able to work fast enough? Lick a guard's tall black boots? My
imagination went wild. Sleep in mud? Eat ants? What shame had
they put him through? Swallowing his own urine? After my encounter with *Herr Leutnant,* I hated to imagine worse bullying.

How would André have managed under such treatment if their
fates had been reversed? Would he have had the strength to endure?
I hated to think of that too.

I read the letter again, hungering to know how to help Maxime.
I took out my list and added, in handwriting jittery with joy,

13. Do something good for Maxime.

CHAPTER TWENTY

AN ENDING AND
A BEGINNING

1943–45

I FELT A WILD NEED TO FLY OVER ROUSSILLON, LIKE BELLA DID in Vitebsk, and shout, "Maxime is alive! My good friend is alive!" But there were five *Roussillonnais* whose sons had died, and over a dozen in prisoner of war camps. Their names were posted on the wall of the *mairie* just below PRIVATE ANDRÉ HONORÉ ROUX.

Nevertheless, containing my joy was impossible. I had to tell someone. I invited Maurice and Louise to come to my house after dinner for sweetbriar coffee, knowing that they could just as well drink that ersatz concoction at their own house. I made a paste of pulverized almonds and acorns and mixed it with some of Geneviève's milk, a Kooritzah egg, and Maurice's honey as a sweetener to make a pudding, using a lemon to curdle the milk. It didn't solidify and was more like lumpy soup, but Maurice said, "Such a delight!" He licked his lips like a little boy, held up his plump index finger, and concluded, "It's approachable, leaves a pleasant nutty flavor as an aftertaste, and has a personality all its own."

With that, I spilled my happy news.

They both hugged me instantly. *"C'est bieng!"* Maurice cried. Louise said more softly, *"Grâce à Dieu."*

"When I have some yarn ready, can you show me how to knit socks? I want to send him some warm socks."

Maurice immediately pulled up his pant legs and kicked out his short calves. "Look! She made these for me before the war, and they still walk well." He stood up and walked in a circle, showing them off. "Best socks in Roussillon."

I laughed, realizing that I hadn't done so in longer than I could remember.

"But certainly those aren't the best shoes in Roussillon," I said. He had tied the soles onto the uppers with twine and used twine for shoelaces as well. "Wait a minute." I went upstairs and came back with an armful of shoes. André's were too narrow, but the one pair of Pascal's fit.

"It will be an honor to fill the shoes of the best *boules* player in the commune. Or at least the man who thought he was the best." He stood up, pushed out his chest, took the starting position, bent his knees, and pantomimed firing a *boule,* running a few steps and pointing where it knocked another imaginary *boule* out of the way, then raised both arms in victory. "See? I have winner's shoes. Now *I* will always be the winner." A big grin puffed out his round cheeks, and he spread his arms wide. "You and me, we can both be happy today."

ALIVE! I COULDN'T STOP saying the word as I unraveled another row of stitches in André's freshly washed wool pullover. I wanted to be alone and at home when I committed this act of desecration. It seemed so much an ending, an unraveling of our life together, until nothing would be left. Yet as I pulled the unruly brown yarn stitch by stitch, I felt quite sure André would want me to do this. The smell of damp yarn stretched between two ladderback chairs was comforting and cozy, and I hoped each sock would carry those feelings to Maxime.

Meanwhile, my mind was flooded with questions. Had Maxime been wounded? Was he in good health? Was he well-nourished?

Was he in good spirits or in despair? Could he sleep soundly? Did he have any moments of peace? Had his natural affability hardened and become bitter? Would he ever regain his pure love of life?

I wrote from my heart without censure.

21 APRIL 1943

Dear, dear Maxime,

Thank God you are alive! Imagine the depth and height of my joy at receiving your letter after three years of agony, not knowing. Think of that joy, and never think of shame. Max, understand this—there is no dishonor in being a prisoner or in surviving when another is killed. The outcome of events is not given to our doing. Do not carry the weight of that thought. It does no good. It is false guilt.

I hate that you have to work in a coal mine. I fear for your health. Please remember with me our beautiful times, you in your immaculate shirts, maroon cravats, sharply creased trousers, and white spats, the picture of health sitting at the Closerie de Lilas, talking about new art. I long for such a day. It will happen again. Receiving your letter has convinced me.

Pascal's paintings were not in the woodpile where André wrote that he had hidden them. Did he tell you any other place? I am committed to the core of my being to their recovery. That keeps me in Roussillon. There are some good people here. I am getting by.

What a relief it is to know you are alive. Hang on to that life with all your strength. A good end will come. I will write again, and some beautiful day, I will welcome you here with all my heart. Only endure.

Affectueusement,
Lisette

—

I PICKED GRAPES IN the fall for Madame Bonnelly, a robust middle-aged woman with thick hands and arms as strong as a man's. She picked two rows to my one and filled the cone-shaped basket on her back in a matter of minutes. When I saw her carrying crates of grapes on both hips, I felt for her, trying to keep the vineyard going without her husband. She had only one hired refugee to help her, Monsieur Beckett, whom she called Samuel in a motherly way. He spoke French with an Irish accent, placing the stress on the wrong syllables. Maurice and Aimé Bonhomme and this foreigner often met under an oak tree at the edge of the vineyard and talked quietly. Sometimes, after a plane passed overhead, Monsieur Beckett ran out of the vineyard and the three of them drove off together in Maurice's bus. I imagined it was to collect dropped ammunition.

One day, while we were eating our lunch under the oak tree, I mentioned to Monsieur Beckett that since he needed to pass as a Provençal, he ought to pronounce *bien* as *bieng,* and *vin* as *ving, pain* as *paing,* and *raisin* as *raising.* "Add a *g. Ang, ang,* at the end," I said. "It needs to be nasal. And pronounce the final *e* on words as another syllable. *Je par-le. Le, le* at the end. Make it bounce. Speak it with more energy, more urgency. Decorate the words. Make them robust. Sing them." And so he practiced.

"When I first came here six years ago," I told him, "I thought their speech sounded ugly. Now I find it amusing.

"And another thing. Your shoes. Anybody can tell by your shoes that you are from Paris. Tomorrow I'll bring you my husband's outdoor work boots. They're scuffed and worn enough to look Provençal."

"Won't he need them?"

"No" was all I said, but he gathered the truth.

After some moments of quiet, he asked in a near whisper, "Do you have a strong stomach and a stout heart?"

"Yes," I said, with some doubt, remembering with shame how I'd broken under the threat of that bludgeon.

He reached into the pocket of his shirt and showed me two pages from *Défense de la France,* a newspaper of the *Résistance.* "As far as I know, these are the first photos of Nazi barbarism in the camps," he said.

Shock after sickening shock drove into my chest until, mercifully, the photos of skeletal men blurred before me.

"Who are these people?"

"Mostly Jews."

"Are they in prisoner of war camps?"

"No. Extermination camps." He paused while I took in the meaning of the word. "Few people know of the mass atrocities, or believe that they have happened."

"I believe now."

"Besides preserving our liberty and way of life, whether or not your husband was aware of it, this was one reason he fought." He pointed to a photo. "And why we are still fighting, covertly. Why we are doing more than just waiting under this tree for God to deliver us."

Then André had been protecting us from *that,* preventing *that* from happening here. I saw at once the nobility in his act and felt proud. He had accepted his place in the bigger picture without the reluctance I had felt.

Monsieur Beckett folded the pages and put them back in his shirt pocket, and I went back to picking grapes, unable to see what I was doing, my hands shaking with relief that Marc and Bella had gone away, although I might never find out if they had reached safety. If they had known that this was happening, and that they had to flee for their lives, what a bighearted man Marc was to have taken the time to paint a picture for me when danger loomed, and what a caring woman Bella was to get that address of a friend in Paris who might be able to help me one day.

How many thousands, maybe even hundreds of thousands were

suffering, hopelessly dying at this very hour? Out of a black sky that night, the sad old moon shone down on the cruelty of humans. What must he have been thinking? What must God have been thinking? How deeply disappointed He must have been.

WHAT COULD I DO? I remembered de Gaulle's speech, which Louise had rescued and posted in the window of her hair salon. *I call upon every French person to unite with me in action, in sacrifice, and in hope.* With all leather going to Vichy and from there to Germany, there were people other than Maurice walking around in tattered shoes. After giving Monsieur Beckett André's work boots, I still had three pairs of his shoes. I saved one to wear while working in the garden when it was muddy and for cleaning the outhouse and took the others and two leather belts to the *mairie.* Alone in the office, Aimé Bonhomme welcomed me warmly and asked how I was doing.

I told him I was getting by, then asked, "Would you see that a refugee or a farmer in need gets these shoes and belts?"

"That's very kind of you."

I thought for a moment. "If you suggest this gently to other widows, we could establish a giveaway box here."

"A fine idea."

"I can help with that. I mean, I would like to. It doesn't have to be only widows who contribute, or only shoes and belts. I can get started knocking on doors right now."

I whirled around to go out the door and ran smack into Mayor Pinatel coming in from the square. I apologized but he didn't, even though he had stepped on my foot; nor did he even greet me. He just peered at me slantwise and shuffled the papers in his hands. "Did you ever find Pascal's paintings?" he asked gruffly.

It was prying, not compassion, that colored his tone, so it irritated me. "That's my business, monsieur, not yours." I slipped out the door, wondering if it had been he who had told the German officer about my paintings.

IN CONTRAST, I APPRECIATED Madame Bonnelly's kindness and down-to-earth company. In the evenings, Samuel and I stayed to help her write the labels identifying the wine as the vintage of 1943. Would it ever be known as a war vintage? Samuel felt sure that it would. I asked him what he did later in the evenings, because Madame Bonnelly went to bed early.

"I'm writing a play about waiting."

"Just about waiting? That doesn't sound very interesting."

"About waiting and about cruelty."

That made me think of the camps, so I asked Madame Bonnelly for the name of her husband's prisoner of war camp, hoping it was Maxime's, Stalag VI-J.

"First it was XII-A, Limburg, a horrible transit camp. Now it's XII-F, which was moved from Saarburg to Forbach, where he is now. It's better. He works in a factory."

"Better than digging coal in an underground mine."

"When he's back here tending the vines he loves, I'll be so happy I won't be able to take my eyes off him."

I admired her spirit. Working alongside her every day, by the end of the *vendange*, I knew her well enough to ask if André had hidden anything there. No, she said, not unless he had done it before her husband left.

I wondered whether there would come a time when I could go house to house through the whole commune, asking that question. It wasn't wise to do that yet.

NOW I WENT TO the post office every day and came home to tell the sad no-news to Geneviève, and to receive her compassionate bleat in reply. Often I stood with her looking out over the valley, resting my hand on her neck while trying to resolve the knotty question of loyalty. I bore my sorrow for André so deeply that I doubted I would ever get over it completely, yet I longed for a letter from Maxime.

Finally, in November, he wrote.

Chère Lisette,

The socks, oh, the socks. If I were a poet, I would write an ode to the socks knit by Lisette's lovely fingers. Thank you from the bottom of my heart and the soles of my feet.

To combat boredom, I have taken to counting things. It is my morose entertainment. One hundred and twenty days of waiting in the phony war, one day of fighting, six days in a cattle train, twenty-one days in that hellhole, Stalag XII-A, the transit camp in Limburg, and one thousand two hundred fifty-one days so far as a prisoner fighting a private war. How many days more?

Six horizontal bars in the miners' cage descending eight levels. Three dead of exhaustion in the mine. I take stock of myself: Ten working fingers, ten dirty toes. Two ringing ears. A stretcher-bearer here says a man has twenty-four ribs. I can see fourteen of mine easily.

One hundred twenty men in my barrack. Twenty barracks in this camp. Twenty-four hundred men using two rows of trenches as latrines. Bunks three tiers high. One stove in the center. When the man closest to it died and prisoners were ordered to drag him out, other prisoners took to fighting violently over his bunk. We are hardly human.

For the sake of my life, remind me of Paris.

Bien affectueusement,
Max

Oh, dear God, dear God. I closed my eyes and felt a responsibility, no, a yearning to knit together his wounded soul. I was sure André would have wanted me to help him.

6 DECEMBER 1943

Cher Maxime,

In the spirit of your counting, here is Paris. Twelve streets radiate out from place de l'Étoile like spokes of a wheel surrounding the Arc de Triomphe. Thirteen streets cross the Champs-Élysées from there through les Tuileries to place du Carrousel. If you count each bridge separately from Pont d'Austerlitz to Pont de l'Alma, there are twenty-one, I think. You can see if I'm right when you return. Try to name them now. Eight connect Île de la Cité with the banks, and one small one connects the two islands. Pont Neuf has five arches on the southern span and seven on the northern span. Do you know the number of grotesque stone heads on the sides? Sister Marie Pierre made me count and describe them. There are over 380. Can you believe that? Six columns stand before the Panthéon. How many on La Madeleine? Are they Doric, Ionic, or Corinthian? Sister Marie Pierre would have demanded to know.

How many portraits of Suzy Solidor are in La Vie Parisienne? Do you remember that we counted them once, before the cabaret show began? Thirty-three, I think. My favorite is Raoul Dufy's because of the strong blues. How many steps from place Saint-Pierre up to Sacré-Coeur? My guess is eighty. How many wagons in the Funiculaire de Montmartre? How many galleries in the Louvre? You ought to know this last thing precisely.

Which is the greater distance—the depth you go down in the mine or the height we can go up in the Eiffel Tower when

you get back? We will count all of these things. You can be
sure of that!

Reading this, he would have to sense that I ached for Paris nearly
as much as he did. Ached to be there, but also ached for her, for her
safety, her well-being, her suffering citizens fated to suffer more before this war was over.

It was silly, this counting, but it might occupy his mind for a few
minutes with pleasant memories. It was only a substitute for what
I wanted to say.

However, the most important things can't be counted,
Max. I'm thinking of the feel of spring in the air when they
set out the tulips in the Jardin du Luxembourg. The bright
colors of the marzipan fruit in the windows of confiseries.
The cheerful melody of the organ grinder's music box at
place du Tertre, and the squeals of small children when his
white-headed monkey takes their coins. The taste of roasted
chestnuts sold on street corners in the fall, and the warmth
of the paper cones in your hands. The slightly dank but not
unpleasant smell of the Seine on foggy mornings. The exhila-
ration of being up in the Eiffel Tower after a rain. The sheen
on the cobblestones, and on wet rooftops of Haussmann
buildings with wrought iron balconies.

I experienced again, as I was writing, the shivery thrill of being
on the topmost platform, André on one side, Maxime on the other,
and the adoring look in their eyes when my hair blew free.

Stop counting days, Max. Keep a list in your mind of things
you want to do after your release, and we shall do them all.

> *Bien affectueusement,*
> *Lisette*

I couldn't bear to tell him that the German authorities had burned more "degenerate" paintings in Paris this year; nor did I mention *Herr Leutnant* and my relief that he had not found mine. I sent Maxime my rationed amount of canned sausages and a small tin of pâté. For Christmas, I saved my meat ration coupons in order to buy him a canned *terrine de canard,* plus another of *lapin,* sure that he would appreciate the taste of duck and rabbit, even in small quantities. He certainly wouldn't get pâtés in a prison camp! In the same package I sent him André's wool scarf and leather gloves. And at Midnight Mass, I lit two candles, one out of gratitude and one out of sorrow, and the flames made my falling tears glisten and sizzle.

THANKFULLY, HIS NEXT LETTER was less despairing.

4 MARCH 1944

Chère Lisette,

Thank you for the lifesaving reminders of Paris, and the life-saving food as well. The scarf and gloves I recognize to have been André's. For you to have parted with them shows a generous heart, which I hope can heal as time passes. They are helping me through the winter.

The Red Cross delivered Christmas packets here. I had missed the last two deliveries because I was at the mining camp. I had my first taste of sardines in a year. Eight in the tin, shared with my ration mate. To celebrate, I decorated my mess tin with a yellow dandelion blossom. It looked like the sun I so rarely see. Van Gogh would have liked it.

An Englishman in another barrack made a sign and posted it in three languages by the latrine: DON'T THROW CIG-ARETTES INTO THE LATRINE AS IT MAKES THEM ALMOST UN-SMOKEABLE. *It made me chuckle. I have asked my mother for*

English and Italian language textbooks, whichever she can get.

A couple of the young Brownshirts, storm troopers who run the camp, are humane fellows. I have had some halting conversations with the guard of my barrack about his home in Cologne and mine in Paris. Two spectacular cathedrals, we decided. Anyone who loves a cathedral cannot wholly serve evil. I traded twenty Red Cross cigarettes with him for seven sheets of paper and a new pencil. I am imagining your paintings from what André told me in order to draw them. If they are decent, and if I can save them, I will give them to you.

It would be interesting to look up this fellow in ten years to see how he's thinking. I am hopeful, at times.

Très bien affectueusement,
Max

THE EVENTS OF 1944 seemed to speed up. Our hearts beat faster and our love for France quickened as we anticipated an Allied invasion. We stayed in the café most days so as not to miss any shred of news from the BBC. Odette, my staunch café partner, and I held hands, held our breaths, and prayed. Then, at last, came the announcement from Vichy, reported by the German state radio at seven in the morning: D-Day had begun. The Allies had landed but would be swiftly annihilated, the announcer crowed. We waited more than two hours for a special BBC news bulletin confirming the landing on the beaches of Normandy. Despite inestimable loss of life, the Allies were moving inland. At noon, Churchill reported that all was going according to plan.

We hugged each other in gratitude, and all day, with watery eyes, I could think of nothing but those brave men and the dying they did on our beaches.

Not much work got accomplished in the next several days, with so many people traipsing in and out of the café, asking for news. On the evening of 28 June we learned that American troops had liberated Cherbourg the day before. A cheer went up in the café. Monsieur Voisin couldn't stop smiling, even at me. We felt the end wouldn't be long now.

Bernard came in and ordered a bottle of champagne and two glasses. He strode over to my table and poured a glass for me.

"I didn't think there was a bottle of champagne left in all of the Vaucluse," I said and pushed the glass away, not wanting to encourage him.

"I need to tell you two things," he said in a near whisper. "I was under pressure to escort that German patrol and was commanded to bring that lieutenant to your home. I didn't tell them about the paintings. They knew already."

"How?"

"I don't like to say. The way they treated you made me want to beat both of them to a pulp. Thank God you relented."

I supposed that I believed him.

The next day I wrote to Maxime in case he didn't know of the liberation of Cherbourg, ending the letter with *Surely the Allies will recapture Paris soon,* and hoped the letter would not be censored.

ON 15 AUGUST, an evening sultry with humidity, we learned that Allied amphibious troops and paratroopers had landed on the beaches of Provence as they had done in Normandy, and that they were fighting in the streets of Marseille as well. Dear Provence, dear Provence. If only Cézanne knew of the efforts to save her.

When I told Geneviève that night, she bleated some words of jubilation, a whole sentence, in fact. I'm sure it was "This is the age of courage."

—

A FEW DAYS LATER, Bernard came to my door and said with authority and urgency, "Don't go anywhere near Gordes, with or without Maurice. It's a hotbed of the *Résistance* in the village as well as in the *maquis* terrain, the scrub woods below Mont Ventoux where *maquisards* hide out in between their forays against German troop movements. They attacked a German patrol near Gordes. I expect there will be some retaliation. There was a reprisal at Saint-Saturnin-lès-Apt for some *Résistance* activity there. Villagers were rounded up and shot in the main square. So stay at home, I beg of you."

"How do you know all of this?"

"It's my job. I'm the *garde champêtre*."

This time he was all business and left without lingering.

THE NEXT DAY, a distant explosion blasted the air and was quickly followed by more. I ducked instinctively at each one. Between blasts I heard Geneviève bleating urgently, so I stepped outside and was rocked back on my heels by the impact of the explosions. She ran to me. Kooritzah, cowering in her coop, jumped crazily when she saw me.

"Some chicken you are. Stop flapping so I can hold you."

I carried her inside and smoothed her feathers, with Geneviève close beside me. "It's all right. It's far away."

But it wasn't all right. Bombardments continued throughout the night. I went to the outhouse under an orange sky thick with smoke. The acrid smell made me choke. Gordes was burning just as Marc and Bella's Russian village had burned. The lives. Oh, the lives.

In the morning, ashes black as the swastika blanketed the courtyard. Kooritzah did not lay an egg. Geneviève followed me around and butted me. Maurice came by, told me to stay at home, and left quickly.

The next day, the people of Gordes were ordered into their houses and were shot if they didn't move fast enough. Then cannons set up on the Bel-Air rock let loose a mighty barrage of explosions. About twenty houses were destroyed, and the people in them as well. The castle was dynamited, and five people were taken away as prisoners. Maurice heard it all from Aimé Bonhomme, who heard it from a resident of Gordes who had managed to escape to Roussillon.

The domestic alternated with the tragic. Kooritzah stopped laying altogether. Knowing I could not bring myself to eat her, Louise told me that I should give her away for food. That hit me hard. Kooritzah had become a friend. Sadly, I did as Louise directed, and pictured Maurice enjoying Louise's *fricassée Arlésienne* with onions, garlic, eggplant, and white wine.

The *Roussillonnais* remained nervous. Although Maurice had the gasogene conversion now, he drove only to Apt, which was overrun with German soldiers garrisoned there. With Louise's help, I chose a new hen and named her Kooritzah Deux, not knowing the Russian word for two.

In disbelief, we stumbled upon a market table piled high with yarn that had somehow been shipped to Apt in a relief package from Switzerland. We bought all of it, and quickly handed it out to the women of Roussillon who Louise knew could knit. By working feverishly night and day, we were able to send two cartons of socks to the Croix Rouge in Paris to be delivered to prisoner of war camps in France.

On 19 August, the BBC reported that the French *Résistance* had attacked the German garrison in Paris. Maurice reached for his wine tumbler to raise a toast and knocked it over. Louise called him clumsy, and Mélanie shushed her, straining to hear.

On 25 August, just ten days after the landings in Provence, the BBC triumphantly announced the Liberation of Paris. We were delirious with joy. Our City of Light would sparkle again. I hoped with all the hope in my heart that Maxime knew. Back home, on her knees, Geneviève prayed with me for the release of prisoners, as Sainte Geneviève had done fourteen centuries earlier.

But that was not the end of the war. Fighting continued in the south and in the German-held Atlantic seaports. All the terrain east of Paris—Alsace, Lorraine, and the Rhine—had to be recaptured, and the German offensive in Belgium had to be put down. The BBC called that the Battle of the Bulge, and the miserable fighting in the snow lasted for more than a month. Every week, the Allies pushed on toward Germany, and on 29 April 1945, the United States Army liberated a prison camp called Dachau. The next day, we heard later, Adolf Hitler committed suicide. The day after that, Aimé discovered that Mayor and Madame Pinatel had fled in the night.

For a week, the disbelief, the tension, the excitement, the relief crackled the air. By universal agreement of a crowd in place de la Mairie, Aimé Bonhomme was declared the new mayor. He and Maurice and Monsieur Beckett had a sense that a big announcement would come soon. Louise, Mélanie, and I did not stray far from the café those days, but Odette was running back and forth between the café and her daughter's house, checking to see if Sandrine was in labor yet.

Louise and I were sitting in place de la Mairie when Monsieur Voisin cranked up the volume on the radio at the same moment that Aimé leapt down the steps of the *mairie* and shouted through a homemade megaphone, "The war is over! France has been liberated! *Europe* has been liberated! Today, the eighth of May 1945, is and ever shall be Victory in Europe Day! Victory in Europe Day! Victory in Europe Day!"

People burst out of their houses with their arms raised, beating on pots and pans, crying out, *"Grâce à Dieu! Grâce à Dieu!"* through streams of tears. Samuel Beckett ran into the square shouting, "Right has prevailed!" Surrounded by a delirious, cheering crowd, he grabbed my hand and we followed Aimé through the village just to hear him shout again and again, "The war has ended! The war has ended!" and watch him tear down the swastika flags on the Gothic arch. A young boy who would remember his act for the rest of his life touched a lit match to them. Known enemies hugged and kissed and danced in the streets. Women tossed packets of sugar they had been hoarding, and men poured the last of their marc for refugees.

Maurice drove through the village sounding the horn on his bus and shouting, "It's over! It's over!" He scrambled out and hugged Louise, kissed her loudly and swung her around, and then me, bending me backward and kissing me on both cheeks, right and left and right and left, laughing and whirling me around so that my feet lifted off the ground, until I squealed and laughed and squealed again.

Odette came running into the street shouting, "It's a boy! They've named him Théo Charles Franklin Silvestre. De Gaulle and Roosevelt will live in Roussillon! Théo's life will begin in peace!"

The first sounds the babe must have heard were shouts of joy and the church bell ringing with all its wild might, as if to welcome him. The bells from Gordes and Apt and Saint-Saturnin-lès-Apt and Bonnieux answered ours in wild jubilation.

The constable was nowhere to be seen.

BOOK III

CHAPTER TWENTY-ONE

THE UNSPEAKABLE

1945

I RECEIVED A LETTER, BUT IT WAS MERE TRICKERY SINCE IT WAS my own to Maxime, now bearing the stamp RETURNED UNDE-LIVERABLE. It sent me into a panic. What was the meaning behind UNDELIVERABLE? I couldn't help but think the unthinkable. An accident in the mine. Or some revengeful atrocity in the last days of the war. I wrote a hasty letter of inquiry to Monsieur le Chef d'État-Major de l'Armée begging him for information. Sandrine searched through a postal directory for an address.

Contrary to my own anxiety, the general mood in Roussillon was buoyant, as people stood on cliff edges watching long lines of defeated German troops trudging east in the valley below. Some gun-happy *Résistance maquisards* took potshots at them from the woods below the cliffs, injuring a few, which I thought was unconscionable when I heard about it in the café. Apparently a single unarmed Frenchman thought so too. He was reported to have stepped forward between the line of unarmed retreating soldiers and the armed *maquisards* and ordered them to desist. At least that was what they said in the café. Most people speculated that it had been Aimé Bonhomme, but he denied it. I thought it must have been Samuel Beckett.

Despite the end of the war, I could not shake the gloom gener-
ated by the return of my letter. I made a batch of chèvre and took
it to Madame Bonnelly, whom I found carrying a wooden crate of
filled wine bottles on her ample hip as if it were a feather pillow. I
showed her the envelope.

"Puh! Don't let that scare you, *minette.*" She pulled out from a
stack of papers an envelope of her own, with the same stamp, and
slapped it against her palm. That ruled out an accident in the mine.

"I imagine the camps are in chaos," she said. "They probably
closed some of them and moved their prisoners just ahead of the
Allied advance. Don't worry your pretty head under that Parisian
haircut. It will all get resolved."

Her explanation washed me clean of fear.

She crooked her index finger around the neck of a bottle to lift
it out of the crate. "Take this with you. To celebrate the peace. And
if my husband does not come home before the *vendange,* come pick
for me again."

So I WAITED, AND went to the post office every day and held baby
Théo in my arms while Sandrine sorted letters. I often saw stout,
stouthearted Madame Bonnelly there, who came for the same reason. "Any news?" she always asked, and when I shook my head, she
would say with amazing cheer, as though someone had poured steel
down her backbone, "Any day now."

Finally that day came, and I read,

4 JUNE 1945

Chère Lisette,

*Please forgive me for letting such a long time pass without
writing to you. Stalag VI-J was closed at the end of 1944,
and we were held at another camp for weeks or months.*

Obeying your wishes, I did not count them. There was no arrangement for writing letters there.

Now I am in Paris, our beloved Paris. Elle existe encore! Can you imagine my flood of emotions when I stepped out of the train and saw her with my own eyes? I was processed for readmission at Gare d'Orsay, where a portrait of Charles de Gaulle welcomed us, along with young women handing out French bread rolls. Just think—I was housed for repatriation and recuperation at Hôtel Lutetia. Those elegant salons defaced with swastikas and Nazi slogans on the walls soured my happiness but did not destroy it. I was free!

I was only one among thousands of prisoners housed there, some of them dazed, pitiful shells of men who had survived camps worse than mine. The repatriation bureau did what they could for us, but since my condition was not considered critical, I was released quickly. Now I am staying at my mother's house, where she is filling me with more food than my shrunken stomach can accommodate, doting on me, and fluttering around like a nervous sparrow. She cannot grasp that I am stupefied by the vast difference between her beautiful apartment and the barracks. I miss my prison mates terrifically and wonder where they are living.

I will come to see you when I am able. Please don't worry if it isn't soon.

> *Très bien affectueusement,*
> *Max*

I showed the letter to Louise and Maurice, and when Madame Bonnelly told me her husband was home, I showed her too. She gave me a rib-cracking hug. "See? I told you so."

During the next months, fourteen other prisoners of war came back to Roussillon. Mayor Bonhomme posted a notice on the *mai-*

rie when each one arrived, so I was very busy milking Geneviève twice a day, making chèvre as well as ricotta from the whey, using lemon to curdle it, and delivering it to Madame Bonnelly and fourteen other homes as "welcome home" gifts. What a joy that was!

IN NOVEMBER, A SOFT knock at the door sounded like a child's knock. I felt no fear. Maybe it was Mimi. I opened the door to a skeletal stranger, still as a statue.

Maxime.

Sudden weakness made me sway. I took in his presence in electric silence. Neither of us was able to utter a word. For the moment, just his breathing sufficed. Our mutual restraint rendered us motionless, tumbling me with relief and joy.

"Come inside."

"I wasn't sure that you would want to associate with a prisoner of war. France needs heroes, not specters of defeat." The voice I recognized, but his tone was apologetic.

"Every man who fought is a hero, Maxime."

He stepped across the threshold. "Even those who fought for only a day?"

"You fought for five years."

He pursed his lips at that. I must have touched a nerve.

Behind the closed door we fell into each other's arms, and held on and on, our beating hearts pressing hard against each other's, breathy sounds escaping from our lips, wetting each other's faces with our tears.

"Let me look at you," he murmured, and we drew back.

Then, in a soft voice, "You are beautiful, Lisette."

The former full contours of his face had shrunken to reveal jutting bones thinly covered by yellowish skin, the tendons in his neck protruding as though an inner layer of flesh had dissolved. His eyes, now deeply set, as if trying to retreat from what he had witnessed, carried the prison camp in them.

"So are you. Beautiful."

"Short hair. Chic. Like Kiki. I like it."

With Max standing in the center of the room, the house, which had been so empty for five years, sprang to life. How ill-prepared I was to offer him comfort with only a wooden settee and ladderback chairs. Quickly I brought downstairs all the quilts and bed pillows and spread them out for him to sit wherever he wanted. Jittery with joy, I prepared a *café crème,* such as it was, an omelette with chèvre, boiled carrots, and bread. He watched my every move.

"The cream and cheese are from my goat, Geneviève. Patron saint and protectress of Paris."

He smiled at this, and I saw that one of his front teeth was chipped to a point and two others next to it were missing. Despite that, his smile gave me hope for his well-being.

We stumbled over our commonplace words—*I'm happy to see you; I'm happy you're home*—silly, safe understatements. While he ate, so slowly, it was enough just to absorb each other's being.

With equal slowness, our fingers stole across the space between us on the table, a hairsbreadth apart for an age before we felt the tender tickle of each other's skin. The knobs of his knuckles rose like mountain peaks. A nasty mauve scar on the back of his hand had been stitched together inexpertly. I let my index finger graze over it. Without flinching, he offered it to me as evidence of something.

I ventured a question. "How did you lose your teeth? Do you mind talking about it?"

"I didn't do it falling down a flight of marble stairs at the Lutetia, that's for sure."

"I'm guessing something a far sight worse."

"The camp was run by storm troopers who brutalized the weaker prisoners. Day after day they found ways to satisfy their hunger to hurt. It enraged me to see one of them kick and beat a sick man for not being able to stand. The prisoner had vomited, and the guard made him lap it up like a dog. That was one cruelty too many. I cursed him and shouted for him to leave the sick man alone, in compliance with the Geneva Conventions, which we had learned about in our training. He struck me in the mouth with his rifle butt."

He told it without rancor, a mere fact of life. I would try to do the same when I would tell him about my encounter with the Germans.

"I know it's not pleasant to look at. There's a long delay to see dentists in Paris. I couldn't wait until then to see you."

"That's what I mean about being a hero! You stood up for a comrade, unarmed. The missing teeth are evidence of your courageous resistance."

"Or a mark of my stupidity."

"No. Maxime. Please don't think that way."

When he finished eating, he said, "I've come to tell you about André. You have a right to know."

"Tell me only what you are able to."

At that encouragement, he could not bring up speech from his throat. He took a deep, faltering breath and looked away from me, as though reconstructing the scene of battle, as he had probably done a hundred times.

"We were stretched thin north of the Maginot Line of cement defenses, with only four anti-tank placements to the kilometer where there should have been ten. And only one anti-aircraft battery in the whole area."

How strange and alien to hear him speak of military matters.

"From our position up there on the Marfée Heights, we had a splendid view of the beautiful Meuse River, which sparkled in the morning sun."

Relief! That was a glimpse of the Maxime I knew.

"Early one morning, it was the thirteenth of May, waves of German dive-bombers—Stukas, they're called—began screaming toward us, hundreds of them, Lisette. The sky was peppered with them hurtling down, shrieking their sirens above the engine noise, and shattering our nerves. Whenever a rain of bombs fell, we flattened ourselves in the bottom of the trench, amazed when they landed even a kilometer away and we still felt the impact through the earth. Explosions came so close together that there was no time in between. Blasts hammered at us all day. Seconds after each one hit, we marveled that we were still breathing but were certain the next one would be the end of us.

"Nothing had prepared us for the fury of this assault. Some of the men in our platoon were already running to the rear. One man was crying. We were all dazed, cowering against our earth embankment, or recklessly rising above it to let loose a round of machine-gun fire at a diving plane, or even just to aim rifle fire at the pilot, hungry to see one black swastika plunge nose-first into the ground." Then, in a softer tone, he said, "For better or for worse, in those hours we were transformed from our former selves.

"André and I kept a constant watch for each other, asking with gestures toward the sky why our planes weren't there defending us. Being undefended from the air made us all half-crazed. It was our first glimpse of defeat.

"As soon as the aerial pounding lessened, the German troops were on the move, launching rubber dinghies into the river. We had good results firing on them, but a few got across, and their loads of men attached a makeshift floating bridge to our bank so their armored personnel carriers could come across. They emptied out their infantry, giving us more targets than we could handle."

It appalled me to hear him speak of human beings as *targets,* and of killing as *good results.*

"One by one, their explosives took out seven sod bunkers to the left of us, with the explosions coming our way. Then, just as we had dreaded, a line of panzers appeared, German tanks carrying small mounted cannons. Apparently they had crossed to the north out of sight and were heading toward us along a ridge, and another line was coming from the south. Their shells blasted across great distances, leaving gaping pits."

He choked up, and it took him several minutes before he continued. "They were coming at us from all directions, behind us too, close enough to lob grenades. I could hardly believe what I saw when the sod bunker to the right of us exploded, a direct hit, spewing out metal and propelling bodies into the air. Another shell tore into the end of our own trench, sending sharp metal fragments flying into flesh. Our friends . . ."

He stopped and shook his head vehemently, as though trying to obliterate a memory. Neither of us dared to move while he gathered the strength to continue.

"I came here fully intending to tell you everything."

"I can wait."

Some long moments passed. Looking only at the floor in front of him, he resumed, "I was firing our squadron's machine gun, which was mounted on a tripod, so I had to raise my head to keep the barrel level over the sandbags, and André was feeding it ammunition and could stay low in the trench. We had been trading off positions because one was more dangerous. It was futile, but we fought on anyway. A grenade landed right next to him, the side opposite from me."

Max's voice tightened to a high pitch. "His body shielded mine."

I let him weep silently until he gasped back his voice enough to say, "Sharp metal fragments riddled . . ."

He held out his scarred hand. A fit of coughing racked his chest. I brought him a glass of water.

"The lieutenant waved a white flag, and eventually the explosions stopped. I spit out dirt. 'Hold on,' I said to André. 'It's over. Hold on.'

"He was trying to say something. I could make out 'Lisette . . . Lisette . . .'"

A hot current coursed through me.

"He . . . I . . ." Maxime's face contorted, and again he couldn't speak for some time.

"Everybody laid down their weapons and was forced at gunpoint to walk away, into an open field, and lie flat on the ground in rows. I had to leave André lying sprawled, so I gestured to a guard for permission to go back to him. He nodded and came with me, his rifle drawn on me the whole time. I laid André right and searched in his clothes for anything the guard would let me remove. I allowed our blood to mingle."

Maxime laid in my hand a worn, folded scrap of paper, brown with dried blood, containing a single line:

Dearest Lisette, my own true love, my life

"This is enough for today," I murmured.

WE CLIMBED THE STAIRS, and I showed Maxime to Pascal's bedroom. When he was finally breathing the rhythm of sleep, I went into my own room, peopled now with the images from his words.

I woke hearing screams from the next room and rushed to Maxime's side. I grabbed his flailing arms and tried to quiet him.

"Finish," he cried, thrashing in the bed. "Finish . . ." The rest became muffled, with his face in the pillow.

"Wake up, Max. Wake up. It was only a dream. Leave it behind. You're safe. You're with me. Lisette."

Words were inadequate to wash away his visions, so I lifted his hand to my cheek, which set off a trembling through his body. Awake now, he pulled up his legs into a fetal position and moaned.

I stroked his head, his temple. "Shh, Max. It's all right. You can be calm now."

"Calm! I spent five years in hell, burning in fury that I was kept out of the war and couldn't retaliate for his death, and now you expect me to forget it all and be calm?"

Great sputtering sobs issued from his throat, and I was mortified for having said something so shallow. I had relegated his inner battle to a child's nightmare. All I could do was sit on the bed, lean down over him, hold him, and hope that the closeness of my presence would quiet his agony.

Eventually exhaustion allowed him to breathe naturally. I moved away from the bed and brought a chair alongside it to keep watch all night, fighting off a nightmare of my own. The room was filled with blackness such that I could see no limit to it, no end of pain, no respite from sorrow.

I WAS AWAKE TO see the morning star wink its pale light in the predawn gray. Maxime's nightmare must have exhausted him, because he slept late. He finally came downstairs, one hesitant step at a time, humbly, as though he doubted I would want to see him.

"Come. Sit down." I poured him a hot drink. "It's made from the rose hips of sweetbriar. It grows wild around here. Goat's milk is good in it."

A wan smile told me that he appreciated my chatter.

"I am at a loss to explain how terrible I feel about last night. I thought I could control it, but telling you brought it all up."

"Don't berate yourself, Max."

"Was I screaming?"

"Yes."

"Words?"

"Just one that I could make out. *Finish.* You said the rest into the pillow."

"I don't suppose you know what I meant?"

"No."

Maxime leaned toward me, waiting for me to figure it out, willing me with the intensity of his eyes to comprehend it.

"He asked for his quietus, Lisette, his finishing stroke. He said, 'Do it.'"

The rest of André's plea exploded into sudden clarity. *Finish me off.*

"There was no time to reason out right and wrong. The Germans were bearing down on us. That was the moment to do it. I couldn't stand to leave him suffering. The white flag went up. Enemy soldiers ordered us to the surrender area. If I had stayed with him until he died . . . on his own—"

"You would have been killed too."

I MUST HAVE GONE upstairs to be alone, because I found myself lying on my bed in a stupor. Slowly new images emerged, raw, vivid, unspeakable. I wrestled with the question *How could he?* and rose and fell on waves of hurt as on an angry sea. After some time, I broke onto the shore and arrived at the thought I needed: No matter how horrifying, Maxime's deed had made André's end easier. It was an act of love. In that split-second decision, Maxime had begun his soul's dark journey, and for that instantaneous act of love, I ought to be grateful.

I found him downstairs, leaning forward, elbows on his knees, staring at the tile floor. At the sound of my presence, he drew in an agitated breath but would not look up.

"You must hate me. You have every right to hate me."

I sat down in front of him and put my hands around his.

"No, Max. How could I? He would have died anyway. You fulfilled his final wish."

"Do you think being a prisoner was my punishment?"

"We don't get punished for acts of mercy, Max. It was a moment of grace between friends. You sacrificed your peace for his. Thank you."

He did not weep outright. There was no sound, just a tear slowly filling each eye and tumbling. After some minutes he raised his head.

"I wish it had been me."

CHAPTER TWENTY-TWO

PROMENADE

1945

LATER THAT MORNING, WHILE RIPPING MORSELS OFF A BA-guette, we began haltingly to speak of other things. Only then did Maxime notice the bare walls.

"You never found the paintings?"

"No. Just the frames in the root cellar."

His knit brow told me he was thinking something out.

"If I had not told André to hide them, you would still have them."

"Don't do that to yourself. They would have been stolen. In fact, they were."

Then I told him about the encounter with *Herr Leutnant*.

"There was only a blank piece of canvas, which he must have used to cover them. We have our own woodpile in the courtyard. I used up all the wood he had piled up. There was nothing beneath it either."

"How about under the ground beneath it?"

"It's worth a look, but then why was his canvas at the communal woodpile?"

Without an answer to that, we went outside, and I said to Geneviève, "This is my friend Maxime, from Paris, your city." I told

Max, "Maurice, the bus driver, and Louise, his wife, gave her to me. When I'm sad she leans against my leg to comfort me. And this is Kooritzah Deux. She's Russian and likes to be carried around."

"Of course. Russian chickens are like that." He indulged me with a wry smile. "I see that rural life has beguiled you."

I arched an eyebrow at that, and he chuckled. I went down to the root cellar and got the shovel, then went back out to the courtyard and started to dig.

"Let me," he said. "I'm used to digging. I don't want you to get dirty."

"Dirty! I am a countrywoman now."

Gently, he took the shovel out of my hands. "You'll always be a *Parisienne* to me."

We traded off digging but found nothing.

I slumped onto the bench in the lean-to. "It would have been so simple if they were here, so wonderful to see them again with you, to have you put them back into their frames and hang them."

"It's been a long time since life has been simple for either of us."

I SUGGESTED THAT HE rest and then we would take a short promenade around the village. There was nothing else to do here, and only the horrible things to speak of again. We stayed in the upper village at first, stopping to sit on benches in the shade, and climbed up to the Castrum, the high plateau at the north end of the village, which was a camp and lookout of Roman soldiers in former times. I didn't tell him that. We could see the Monts de Vaucluse to the north and, beyond them, the white limestone sliver of Mont Ventoux. I explained that it was where the mistral came from.

We descended through the Gothic arch to place de la Mairie and sat awhile at an outdoor table in front of the café. I told him about being the first woman to enter the café at *apéritif* hour and how that had spread to other women.

"See? A *Parisienne* through and through."

As I described to him the people I knew, a surprising pleasure warmed me. I told him about the giveaway box and going house to house with a wheelbarrow, asking for donations for the refugees and farmers. I explained how doing that had made me feel part of the community, André's ancestral home.

I suppose it wasn't so strange that taking a walk with Maxime made me think of the many walks André and I had taken in Paris. It was a warm feeling, not comparing, only enjoying. Just as in the city, where we would often stop to have a pastry, here Maxime and I went into the *boulangerie* in the lower village. I introduced him, and Odette smiled at him so genuinely that I knew she accepted him as my good friend. He bought a *pain au chocolat* for me, and we shared it while sitting in place du Pasquier, facing the valley.

"Do you remember in Paris when I worked at the *pâtisserie* and you often came in to buy a pastry and then gave it to me?"

"And that made that other counter girl so mad." Maxime laughed softly at the memory. It was heartening to hear him laugh. I may have been mistaken, but I thought I recognized yearning in his eyes. The war had no power to dissolve their beautiful blue. Blue as the Mediterranean on a summer day, I surmised. I could swim in those eyes.

I felt embarrassed for looking at them longer than was proper, so I quickly said, "This is the Roussillon version of our Paris promenades. Oh! How could I have forgotten to tell you! There's a painting called *The Promenade* by Marc Chagall."

"I've seen it. He exhibited it in Paris."

"I've seen it too, Max! *Here.* Well, near here. In it, Marc is standing in front of his village of Vitebsk and Bella is floating horizontally, supported on his arm."

"As though she had taken a flying leap."

"It was just after a revolution in Russia, and they were jubilant about their new freedom. She was so elated that she couldn't stay on the ground."

"How do you know this?"

"She told me."

"Impossible! They were living in Paris."

"Yes, but they came here to hide in a hilltop village nearby, and I used to visit them and take them eggs and cheese. The bus driver Maurice bought art supplies for Marc in Avignon and introduced me to them in their home."

"Is this your imagination? You've always had a good imagination. All your outlandish tales of what the nuns at the orphanage whispered to each other at night. And now a compassionate goat and a cuddly Russian chicken and you talking with Bella Chagall. You must have just seen the painting in Paris and dreamt this."

"It's the truth, Max. I can prove it."

"Oh, you can, can you?"

With that, I knew he was teasing me.

"Yes, because he *gave* me a painting."

Maxime puffed air out of his mouth. "Truly?"

"I've hidden it, but if it's still there, you can see it."

"And if it isn't, you expect me to believe you?"

"Yes, Max. I do. On the strength of our friendship, I do. It was safer to keep it hidden. My house was ransacked. But I suppose it's safe to get it now. We can go there tomorrow, when you've rested some more."

I made him take my arm and we climbed home slowly, a different way than we had come down. I wanted him to see that Roussillon wasn't just a one-street village. We went up a narrow avenue where I knew the broad-leafed ivy growing against the houses had turned the lane Roussillon red, orange, and bronze, but their harmonious, warm colors did not hide the peeling ochre stucco made from local sand covering the gray building stone, which showed sadly in places.

At place de l'Abbé Avon, Maxime suddenly stopped. I thought he was out of breath, so I looked for a place for him to sit.

"Look!" he said. "A huge woodpile!"

"That's the one. But they weren't there." In a near whisper, I went on, "It's so exposed. Why would he hide them here?"

"Maybe because it's such an unexpected place."

I considered the idea. "The pile gets depleted every winter, and in the summer a forester gathers and chops wood and piles it up again. People put coins in that tin can to pay for their wood. André hid the paintings at the end of summer, when we received your letter."

Maxime looked at the roof over the woodpile. "It's not very weatherproof."

Trying to appear casual, we noticed the edges of two large plywood boards serving as a platform, one directly on top of the other, with the firewood for the coming winter stacked more than two meters high above them. I hadn't seen that there were two boards when I had been with *Herr Leutnant* in the dark. Maxime and I looked at each other. Despite my new hope, I scowled my puzzlement. Maxime shrugged his shoulders. We walked on.

In a low voice he said, "You say the paintings are removed from the frames?"

"Yes."

"And off the stretchers?"

"I can't be sure. There are some sticks in the root cellar that look like stretchers."

He strode uphill with renewed energy. In the cellar, he confirmed that the sticks under the burlap bags were stretchers.

"How can we remove all the wood without making a mess in the street and without people questioning us?" I asked. "Every wife we've just passed has seen a strange man with me, and the rest of the village wives will have heard it secondhand at the *boulangerie* in the morning. They'll be watching."

"Do you have a battery torch?"

"No, but there's a lantern hanging under the lean-to."

"Then we could work at night."

"Unload all that wood, remove the paintings from between the boards, pile it back up again exactly as it was, and sweep the street so people wouldn't wonder? All in one night? Impossible."

"You're right," he said. "It's better to work at the end of winter, when the pile is depleted."

I hated to think of the wait it would entail.

"Why do you think he didn't hide them on our property?"

"Maybe to separate them from you for your safety."

AFTER AN EARLY DINNER and Madame Bonnelly's wine, Maxime grew quiet as we prepared to go upstairs. At the landing I said, "Promise me you won't have a nightmare tonight."

With a wry smile revealing the absurdity of such a request, he said, "I promise."

His response to what I had intended as lightness, a little joke, I took to be an affirmation that he would not be controlled by the past.

"Before the war I saw a painting by Picasso called *The Weeping Woman*," he said. "It depicted the raw grief and horror of a woman of Guernica, the Basque town bombarded by the Luftwaffe."

"I know what happened there. You don't have to describe it."

"All of the woman's features were disordered, deranged with pain, in lurid colors. Tears burst out of her eyes like white bullets. It made me imagine you the moment you learned of André's death. I have nightmares about that."

"You shouldn't. I don't."

He held me with his eyes. "You weren't the one to end his life."

Awkwardly, I touched his cheek. "Neither were you."

He responded by touching my cheek in the same way. We turned and went into our separate bedrooms.

I hugged my pillow, hungering to fulfill my latest vow. *Do something good for Maxime.*

CHAPTER TWENTY-THREE

GIFTS FROM
CHAGALL

1945

"EVERY STEP IS ONE STEP CLOSER TO MY PAINTING," I SAID to encourage Maxime on the long walk to the bories the next day. I buttoned my jacket and breathed in the woodsmoke from the burning of the vines after the *vendange*.

Not long after we set out, we heard the sharp, sudden report of a rifle. Maxime's shoulders jerked, and he whirled around in alarm.

"It's only the hunters. There are wild boars in the foothills. They hunt them with hounds."

"Men are primitives."

A little while later, with the wind blowing our way, we heard the calls of the hunting horns.

"I like the way they sound," I told Maxime, "so strong and urgent. There's a lot about Provence I like, but there's one big thing I hate."

"Winter?"

"It's that I'm so horribly isolated. I can only go to Gordes, Avignon, and Apt in Maurice's bus. That leaves out Aix and Arles and Marseille, where there are probably art galleries."

The high-pitched trill of a starling made us stop to listen.

"You would not hear that in Montparnasse."

"True, but I would hear art talk. Oh, how I long for that."

"We're walking through a painting right now, Lisette. Just look around us. Coming back on the train from Germany and seeing the north so damaged, I thought that the beauty of rural France was only in children's books now, but that isn't so. This place is untouched."

"You're seeing it at its worst." The trees were dropping their leaves, vegetable plots had not a tinge of green, and the lavender fields, cut at the end of summer, were only dry scruffy mounds. I had wanted the countryside to look its best for him. "I wish you could see it in June. Lavender washes the air with perfume then, and the grapevines are decked with new chartreuse leaves. Will you come back in June?"

"Maybe."

That wasn't a promise, but at least he didn't rule it out.

Approaching the Bonnellys' large farmhouse, which the people here called a *mas*, I told him that I had picked grapes in their vineyard for the *vendange* when Monsieur Bonnelly was a prisoner. "Two seasons I did it. It was hard work, but I would do it again. It made me feel that I contributed to the community. People have been good to me here. Madame Bonnelly bolstered my hopes when I didn't hear from you."

"I'm grateful to her, then. Are people here so good to you that you might forsake Paris forever?"

"No. Not forever. Just until I find the paintings."

We stopped to rest in Madame Bonnelly's outdoor kitchen under an arbor. She gave Maxime one of her hearty handshakes and a glass of wine. Bursting with garrulous talk, she ended her typically Provençal discourse on the weather with "Wouldn't you like to stay for the midday meal?"

"*Merci, non,*" I answered. "We are on a promenade. I have packed a picnic."

She offered us two apples, but when Maxime smiled his thanks with missing teeth, she grabbed them back and gave us two ripe pears and a bunch of grapes instead.

Half an hour down the road, I ran ahead of him to the fence post that had the sickle stuck in its top. "Look! Amazing. It's been here as long as I have lived in Roussillon, just waiting for some farmer to remember where he left it. Nobody bothers it. You know, Roussillon teases a person. Just when I'm feeling bored and isolated and deprived, it gives me something that pleases me."

An instant frown clouded Maxime's face.

"This sickle, for example. We need it. Can you get it out?"

"You want to destroy this wayside curiosity?"

"We'll put it back."

"In the same fence post?" He freed it and built a circle of rocks around its base so we could locate the same place on the return trip.

As we approached the village of bories, I explained what they were and how ingeniously they were constructed.

"It's in that one, the one behind the nettle bush."

"You certainly didn't pick one that had a welcome sign."

"Wasn't that the point?"

He began hacking at the nettles with the sickle, and I carefully pulled them away from the borie.

"Is it safe in there? The roof won't fall in on us?"

"These huts have been here for centuries."

"They remind me of gun emplacements."

"Don't think of that." I stepped in and turned around to face him. "Button up. It's cool in here."

He ducked and came inside. "So where is this painting of yours? I don't see it framed and hanging on the wall."

"It's not framed at all. It's behind this panel of slabs."

I started to lift them off, and he worked beside me. I put my face right up next to the opening we made and peeked down into the large niche.

"It's there! I see the edge!"

"Careful. Don't pull it out yet."

Excited, I lifted off another slab and it slipped, pinching my finger between it and the one below it. Maxime removed the rest of the slabs, lifted out the painting, and took it outside into the light.

"Ah, yes. This *is* a Chagall. A sweet-faced goat. He is partial to goats almost as much as cows. The village through the window in the snow must be his."

"Vitebsk," I said.

"The woman is you, the way he saw you."

"Really? I thought it was Bella. What makes you think it's me?"

"Because you tip your head to the right like this woman is doing, like you're doing right now. And your mouth stretches more to the left than the right, like hers. It's definitely you."

That made me so excited I had to fan myself with my hand.

"And the goat and the chicken. He knew about them. He was the one who named Kooritzah Kooritzah." I giggled. "I like saying her name."

"I hate to tell you. That isn't a hen. It's a rooster."

I looked at it objectively. "Oh, I guess you're right. I don't care. Maybe he just put those red things there to fill a space. He does that. He told me so. To me it's a chicken. He didn't know about the outhouse with the window, and there we are, the three of us looking out the outhouse window. My family."

"Don't assume too much. It's just a house that fits the space, just like that little man with a bouquet standing on the muntin fits the windowpane."

"He's dancing," I said, delighted. "I think it must be Marc giving me flowers."

"Flowers and snow. That's just like him to put incongruous things together in one picture."

"To him they are related," I protested, "even though we don't understand the connection. They are images from his dreamworld, so they can be simultaneous. But why did he have to make my hand so big?"

"Maybe because you were generous to them. He is speaking his gratitude with his brush."

I looked at the size of my own hand in comparison and noticed that I had a blood blister.

"Keep away from the painting. Let me carry it when we go."

He put his palm under my hand. "Your blood is beautiful. Like a ruby popping out of your skin." He looked at it awhile, then shook his head. "No. Blood is never beautiful."

"Imagine how they lived here," I said quickly to divert his thinking. I spread out the tablecloth and unwrapped the picnic of bread and chèvre and hard-boiled eggs and Madame Bonnelly's pears.

"If they had language, what do you think they talked about?" I asked.

"The seasons?"

"The stars and the moon, too, I think."

"The sound of wind," he said. "That might have suggested a sound that became a word. How else but by using words would Madame know when Monsieur Borieman was going to come home and want dinner?"

"Not just flat words," I said. "She needed forceful language to tell him that she was sick and tired of eating rodents. Rodent *à la forestière*, rodent *à la vinaigrette*, rodent *à la bordelaise*, rodent *bourguignon*."

"*Mignon de* rodent *à la Maxim's*."

"'Be a man! Hunt me a boar!' Madame Borieman would demand. 'I'm dying to prepare *sanglier chasseur aux herbes de Provence*, hunter-style with mushrooms, shallots, and white wine.'"

"With a disc of truffle on top. Followed by a digestif."

"Of pomegranate liqueur."

We laughed together, and it felt whole.

"They weren't so primitive that they didn't feel hungers beyond food," I ventured.

"Do you actually think that?"

"I certainly do. Hungers are part of being human. The yearning to satisfy their hungers is what led them to words. Just like it does with us."

"You are a deeper thinker than when I knew you in Paris."

"Maybe it comes from living alone and having hungers myself."

ON THE WAY BACK, Max carried the painting and the sickle, and I held the remains of our picnic. The flat countryside was easy going, but I knew he dreaded the uphill climb.

Just after Maxime jammed the sickle into the fence post, a small lorry pulled up beside us and came to a stop. Bernard Blanc rolled down the window on our side of the road.

"Wouldn't you prefer to ride?"

"No, thank you, Constable. We're on a stroll."

He glared at Maxime. "It's too cool for a stroll. Get in."

"No, Constable. It's a lovely afternoon. We prefer to walk. I want to show my friend the countryside."

He ground his gears and roared off, spitting out gravel and raising dust in our faces.

"Who is the hotheaded grouch?" Maxime asked.

"Nobody important."

AT HOME, MAXIME CRIED, "*Oh là là!* Look here!"

On the back of the painting Marc had written, *May it be a blessing to you, Marc Chagall*.

"You have a treasure here."

"Why? Will he be famous?"

"He *has* been famous, for two decades."

"I'm just glad to have it here and to know he painted it for me. And that it looks happy. The last time I saw him, he was painting chaos and cruelty."

"There's a place for that too in art." Maxime propped the painting up on a chair.

"We have to hang it." Standing in the center of the room holding André's jar of stretcher tacks, I considered each wall. "Here. Right over André's cabinet, so I can look at it while I eat."

That done, Maxime said, "Now tell me about his other paintings."

"He puts things together that don't exist together in real life. Like a giant chicken and the Eiffel Tower. And he disregards the true sizes of things in relation to each other. That baffled me at first. So did a woman standing on her head. Houses and animals are sometimes upside down too. He doesn't pay attention to the law of gravity. But that's what I love in his work. All those creatures flying around, as though gravity weren't a law at all."

"His vision obeys higher laws. That's his spirituality. Most good art has some spiritual dimension."

"Is that what makes a painting great?"

"That's just a start. A great painting has to be more than spiritual, certainly more than a piece of religious art. Let's see. It has to be more than original, too, like Chagall's work is. More than a good likeness, more than a beautiful subject painted in pleasing colors, more than an intriguing composition, more than an interesting application of paint."

"What more?"

"Well, let me think." He looked up at the ceiling, as if to find the answer written there. Then he spoke slowly, one word at a time. "A great painting encourages us to feel some connection with a truth."

"You're talking riddles."

"No, no. Great art—painting, sculpture, and architecture—gives us something very rich. It allows us to experience times, places, emotions, that we might not otherwise encounter. It invites us to ponder some item—a piece of fruit or a violin in the sky or a marble figure or a cathedral—until its qualities teach us something, or enrich us, or inspire us. This is difficult to express. It's capable of grabbing a person"—he clenched his fist—"and holding him in a trancelike state of union with the subject until he sees who he is or who we are as human beings more clearly."

"A painting can do that?"

"Individually it can, and collectively too, I believe. Not that a viewer necessarily sees himself as similar to a figure in a painting, or that he adopts the painter's vision of the world. But being completely absorbed by the piece of art, he becomes minutely different than he was before, less limited to his previous, narrower self, and this equips him to live a better life and to avoid getting swallowed by the world's chaos."

"Give me an example."

"Take architecture. That German prison guard must have had such a trancelike experience in his cathedral in Cologne, just as I have had many times in Notre Dame. We each love those buildings, their qualities of solidity, soaring power, intricacy, harmony, light, the feeling you have when you stand in them of being enfolded in the arms of God. Because we both wanted to experience each other's cathedral, our longing for those qualities allowed us to transcend enmity. For that moment we were brothers. It's infinite and powerful, what art can do."

Maxime shook his head and blew out a puff of air. "I haven't expounded on art like this since I left the gallery."

It was more than art that he was speaking about. I glimpsed in that moment that prison walls could not confine him. In reaching out to the German guard, he had seen that beyond the walls, the world was made not merely of stone and wood, material things, but of the meaning of things, of their spirit. This was talk that could heal. I could hardly contain my joy.

"I often saw Pascal stand for an hour in front of one of the paintings. Their ochre colors made him aware of his life purpose— bringing ochre out of Roussillon's mines to Paris for painters to make great paintings. It made him proud to do that humble thing."

"See how it showed him himself?"

I wondered again which of Pascal's paintings had been André's favorite.

"Have you ever been transfixed by a painting until it told you—?"

"A truth about myself? Many times," Maxime said.

"Think of one."

After a reflective moment, he said, "Now that you bring Chagall to mind, I remember a Chagall painting of two standing figures, full frame. The woman was upside down, and one of the man's legs was wrapped around her to steady her, while his arms enclosed her legs and the hem of her skirt. They were intertwined. Their lives were intertwined." He paused. "They needed each other for support."

His questioning eyes asked if I had grasped what had landed so artlessly in our laps. Neither of us moved so much as a little finger, in order to prolong the moment.

Eventually, perhaps out of embarrassment for a truth laid bare, he was the first to speak.

"Chagall picks up a paintbrush and out from the tip of it fly beautiful memories, and freedom, and love."

"Tell me a beautiful memory. Let it fly out of you."

He was silent. Was it so hard for him?

"Are you searching for one, or are you choosing?"

"Choosing. Ah, this. The three of us in the Closerie de Lilas in the spring. A flower seller came by our table selling violets. André bought a nosegay and pinned it onto your dress."

His voice cracked, and my throat seemed filled with petals.

"You were radiant. He adored you, Lisette. Never forget that."

"As much as Marc adores Bella?"

"At least that much."

LATER HE SAID, "You know, I felt almost well talking about Chagall and what great art does."

"Then he has given you a gift also. And because he has, he has given to me doubly."

Maxime raised his shoulders so that his neck was lost between them. It seemed an unintentional gesture of gathering courage to express a thought.

"I was thinking just now that I might be ready soon to speak to Monsieur Laforgue. I would like to help him rebuild his gallery and his business."

I laid my hand on his arm. "Yes, Maxime. Do that."

An afterthought: if things fell in my favor, there might still be a place for me there.

CHAPTER TWENTY-FOUR

SAUSAGES

1945

I COULDN'T POSTPONE IT ANY LONGER. NOW, BEFORE THE first snowfall, it was time. I put on the one pair of André's shoes I had saved, hiked my skirt up above my knees and tied it with twine, wrapped his biggest handkerchief over my nose, and stepped out into the courtyard.

I had been preparing for winter with a light step, gathering grass for Geneviève on dry days and saving vegetable scraps for Kooritzah in a pile the snow would soon cover. Now all that was left was the most distasteful task. I went to work shoveling out the shallow pit in the outhouse, using the hoe to push the waste down the cliff as far as the hoe handle would permit. I gagged and spat and my eyes watered, but I persisted. After every second shovelful I put my nose in the honeysuckle that André had planted alongside the outhouse, hoping for a whiff of last summer's blossoms. In honeysuckle talk, it said that he was still with me.

I wanted everything to be nice for Maxime when he came again. Like Bella had said about her first visit to Marc's cottage, life was new after Maxime's first visit here. I felt a stronger impulse to recover the paintings—not just for me or for André's sake, but for Maxime, so that the paintings would help him escape his memories. Two of my vows—*Retrieve the paintings* and *Do something good for Maxime*—had become one.

When the woodpile was nearly depleted, I would write to him, he would come, and together we would collect the last of the wood, put some coins in the tin can, and lift up the top platform. There they would be, a hidden gallery that had eluded the Germans. Oh, what a pleasure to think about that while I was shoveling and gagging and trying not to breathe.

Just then Geneviève uttered an urgent *baa*. "What's the matter, *lapushka*?" Concentrating on not spilling each shovelful until I could dump it over the cliff, I added, "You don't like the smell?"

She bleated again, and I looked up. Bernard was standing just inside the gate with his hands behind his back.

"*Bon Dieu!*" I snapped in exasperation.

"My, my. What have we here? A *Parisienne* disguised as a peasant. Filth and stink and all. Utterly charming in her getup, if I might say so, showing off her pretty knees. Such odd shoes for a dainty foot. You have a fine white handkerchief, but where are your silk stockings?"

I yanked off the kerchief, soiling it. "I did not invite you here. You have no right—"

"Ah, ah, ah." Uttered staccato, like drumbeats. "Not so. As *garde champêtre*, I do have the right to pass through anyone's property, for the welfare of the commune. And right now I'm checking on the welfare of my good friend Lisette."

"Madame Roux."

I resumed shoveling and didn't look at him.

"A shame that a pretty woman like you has to do the basest work in the world."

I ground my teeth at that.

"Look what I have for you today."

He brought his arm forward to dangle a string of sausages, and swung them back and forth.

"How long since you've eaten *andouille Prussienne*? Have you forgotten what it tastes like?"

He had a point. I couldn't remember the last time I had eaten more than a morsel of horse meat. Just meal after meal of chèvre and eggs and vegetables. But now, with winter coming, there would not be lettuce or celery or tomatoes, only my root vegetables in the cellar.

All those sausages swinging at once, not divided as they would be if he had bought them with ration tickets. It was the black market still operating right there before my eyes, tempting me.

"Why don't you come visit me at my house? You could eat a fat, juicy sausage every night."

His chuckle told me he intended the innuendo.

"Crassness will not win me, Constable, nor will your gifts, your authority, or your shiny boots. I do not want any more of your gifts with assumptions attached."

"I suspect that your war widow's pension does not go far with food prices the way they are now. Why can't you accept a gift as a kindness?"

"Because there is no kindness in your voice."

"A man can't help how his voice sounds."

"Yes, he can!"

He took a few steps toward me and kept swinging the sausages. I kept shoveling.

"You haven't told me. Did you like the stockings? I haven't seen you wear them. I dream of seeing those dark seams down the backs of your shapely legs."

"That's your own foolish fault." I pushed in the shovel with my foot and hurled its contents over the cliff. "You will never see them. I burned them."

"How ungrateful of you. After all I've done for you. You're stubborn as that goat of yours. You persist in being morose, and I know why. You're still grieving over losing a few paintings, and you're taking it out on the world."

"I'm still grieving over losing my *husband*."

"You surprise me, Lisette."

"Madame Roux."

"I wouldn't call promenading in the country with a strange man in broad daylight grieving. More like frolicking."

"He isn't a stranger. If you must know, he was my husband's closest friend. *They* fought in the war together. They did not stay home and watch."

"Except for his sunken eyes and his missing teeth, he wouldn't be a bad-looking fellow to frolic with, if he had a little meat on his bones."

That was too much. I jabbed the shovel into the pit and drew it out wet and heaping, lunged toward him, and flung it at him. He backed away, but not fast enough. He stood there stunned for a moment, looking at the splatter on his polished boots and pant legs, his jaw dropping.

"You'll be sorry for that."

"Get out of here!"

He had his own flinging to do. In spite of our mutual anger, together, for an instant, we watched that string of precious sausages arc through the air and over the cliff before he turned and left.

I took pleasure in imagining his humiliation as he walked home through the village with shit on his precious boots.

A WEEK LATER, I found a surprise in my lavender pot—a bar of lavender soap stamped with L'OCCITANE, as I'd seen in the Apt market, and wrapped in paper with a few handwritten words: *You might find this useful for the kind of work you do.*

Exasperated again, I held the soap to my nose. It smelled divine. For all his bluster, he apparently had the capacity to forgive.

CHAPTER TWENTY-FIVE

THE WOODPILE
AND THE LIST

1946

I N MARCH I CUT MY OLD GATHERED PEASANT SKIRT INTO TWO equal halves to make a curtain, then tacked it up above both sides of the window in Pascal's bedroom, for Maxime's arrival the next day. I had already washed the sheets at the faucet in place de la Mairie; the stone half-bowl there had a ridged inner curve that served as a washboard. Then I'd washed André's best shirts to give to Maxime. They were about the same size, medium chest, although Maxime was a little shorter.

On the way home with my wet laundry, I couldn't help peering in the direction of the woodpile. Because I had seen André's blank canvas that night with the Germans, I was sure the paintings would be under the top piece of plywood. Soon they would be in the house, and Maxime and I would put them in their frames and hang them in their rightful places. What a grand celebration we would have, the two of us surrounded by paintings.

The morning of his arrival, I fashioned a small wreath of dried lavender I had saved from the summer. Where to hang it? Over the base of the stairs? No. Somewhere in Pascal's bedroom. That way, Maxime would know it was meant expressly for him. Its fragrance was faint, so he would more likely catch its scent if I hung it above the headboard. It looked lovely there. All was ready.

As an afterthought, I began to empty out the top drawer of Pascal's dresser for Maxime to use. I sorted the contents to take usable items to the giveaway center in the *salle des fêtes*. At the bottom of a tangle of cravats, I found two yellowed pieces of paper written in Pascal's hand and sat down to read them.

"They're driven, both of them," Madame Fiquet, Cézanne's *compagne,* said.

"They're madmen, both of them," Madame Pissarro said. "That's what the critics say."

"And you agree?" I asked.

"One critic wrote, 'Seen close up, his landscapes are incomprehensible and awful. Seen from afar, they are awful and incomprehensible.'"

"That's snide," I said. "Camille doesn't deserve that injustice, but I am untrained and don't know how to trust my feelings."

How could Pascal have remembered such a conversation and his reactions? Of course, he might have written this down a long time ago, maybe shortly after hearing it. His handwriting here was much steadier than it was in his more recent notes.

"Will they paint the same thing today?"

"Most likely," Madame Pissarro said.

"But their paintings will turn out differently," Madame Fiquet said with an air of boredom.

Madame Pissarro nodded. "Camille dabs."

"Paul smears," Madame Fiquet said.

"Camille touches."

"Paul presses."

"Camille is light."

"Paul is dark."

"Camille mixes colors on his palette."

"Paul doesn't mix. He buys."

"Camille is fussy, if you ask me."

"Paul is simple, if you ask me."

Amusing, this passage. Like a duet.

"They are good friends anyway?"

"The best of friends," Madame Pissarro said.

"Paul says he has learned heaps from Camille," Madame Fiquet said. "He idolizes him, calls him the great Pissarro, my master. They all look to Camille. He sustains them all."

"That may be, but Camille is so obsessed that he makes me crazy. One more painting, one more. We have hundreds that have not sold, yet he is forever looking for something new to paint. This will show them, he says, and his face shines with such hope that out of love I have to keep silent and let him go on."

"Paul gazes at something outdoors until I think he's in a trance, and then paints in a frenzy. More often than not, when he finishes, he leaves the painting there, right in the weeds or leaning against a rock, and comes home in a daze without it. It's exasperating."

"Camille would never do that. He's desperate to sell every canvas, and well he should be with a family to feed."

"Paul is either in that trance or he's fidgety or he's pacing. He's terribly moody. Bad weather makes him agitated. Only good painting calms him. He goes to bed early and wakes up in the night to examine what he painted that day. If it pleases him, he wakes me up, excited to share it with me. Then, as an apology for having awakened me, he lures me to play a game of checkers."

"You do agree that they're both great painters, don't you?"

"Time will tell," Madame Fiquet said.

"Be honest, Hortense. You know they will both become famous someday. We cannot have suffered in vain. We go without so the world will have them. That's our lot."

"True enough, but if I were married to Camille, I would tell him to stop fooling around with landscapes. He should paint portraits. At least you get paid for those."

"And if I were married to Paul," Madame Pissarro said, "I would tell him to stop painting that same mountain again and again. People are bored with it. He should paint fruit. People like fruit."

"Can't you say something good about them?"

"Yes, I can." Madame Fiquet thought awhile. "Paul's paintings have a timeless grandeur that makes me contemplate life."

"And Camille's have a radiance of color that lifts my spirit," Madame Pissarro said.

"We accept their obsessions because we love them."

Oh, those dear, long-suffering women. I wondered if this conversation might be valuable. Probably not. Who would care that an old man, an untrained pigment salesman, jotted down a conversation that must have happened fifty years earlier? It might not even be true. Still, I saved it as a curiosity to show Maxime.

MAXIME ARRIVED IN THE AFTERNOON, lost in his beaver-collared overcoat. With hardly a greeting he practically shouted, "He took me back! Monsieur Laforgue!"

"Teeth! You have teeth now."

He grinned, showing them off.

"*Mon Dieu,* what a handsome man you are!"

He blushed like a boy.

A flood of words poured out. "He said I could work whenever I am able to, but he can't pay me as much as he did in the past. His gallery was looted, and now his paintings are scattered God knows where in the tangle of corrupt dealers. It infuriates me that the Nazis called stolen art *Biens sans maîtres,* 'goods without owners.' Monsieur Laforgue said that Pétain called them 'artworks collected for safekeeping.' It's despicable."

Still holding his valise, he continued, "He isn't a major dealer of priceless treasures, but he is honest and fair. I was offered a better-paying position with a disreputable dealer who bought looted art at cut-rate prices and sold it quickly at a hefty profit. I told him no. 'Plunder pirates,' Monsieur Laforgue calls them. It will take a decade for him to rebuild his stock."

"Slow down, Max. Take a breath. Sit," I told him. Say hello, I thought.

"He intends to reopen by selling his private collection, which he hid in a meat locker of the *boucherie* below his apartment. It's a huge personal sacrifice."

"What about the woman apprentice?"

"He chose to rehire me over her."

My hope sprang up.

"I am to assist in the search for the lost paintings."

"And here too, Maxime. For my lost paintings," I said urgently.

"Yes. Here too."

At last he seemed to notice me.

"We'll do it tonight. I wouldn't think of letting you be anxious another day."

Finally. A softer voice, a direct look, an embrace—our second, more natural than the first, when he had arrived at my door unannounced four months earlier.

"Do you have a wheelbarrow for the wood?"

"Yes, and an oil lantern."

"Too cumbersome. I brought a battery torch."

I prepared my standard meal for him, omelette with chèvre, beets and carrots from the root cellar, and a tin of sardines I had been saving.

"I wish I had something better to give you, but it's winter."

"I can tell. The house is cold."

"I'll put more than a few sticks in the stove when we come back. Keep your coat on."

JUST AFTER TWILIGHT, we went to the woodpile and loaded what little wood was left into the wheelbarrow. I was so excited that I dropped the coins on the ground instead of into the slot in the tin can. They rolled downhill, bouncing on the cobbles, and I had to scramble after them in my clackety wooden-soled shoes.

We checked uphill and down. No one was around. People went home early in winter. Only a few seconds and I would see my gallery. I clapped with tight fists and lifted off the canvas. Maxime tipped up the top sheet of plywood.

Nothing was there!

Again, I couldn't believe my eyes. I shined the light in the far recesses. Not a single painting. Maxime tipped up the bottom sheet of plywood. Only the dirt of the ground was visible in the circle of yellow light. He lay the bottom sheet of plywood down and was about to lay down the top one.

"Wait!"

Along the forward edge I noticed some pencil marks. I shined the light there and recognized them as André's patterns, which he often penciled out on the plywood that rested on his sawhorses, the preliminary step in his carving. I dropped to my knees and ran my fingers over his beautiful arabesques, acanthus leaves, and fleurs-de-lis. My throat filled with sawdust. It took a few moments before I could say, "This board was André's. He hid the paintings here. But they're gone, Max. They're gone."

I lowered my forehead onto an arabesque and wept, not just for me and the lost paintings but for André and Pascal. Max waited, his hand on my shoulder, before he laid down the plywood and helped me up. He replaced most of the firewood and lifted the handles of the wheelbarrow full of wood. "Let's go home."

ONCE WE WERE INSIDE, he said in a defeated tone, "Even a big war will have small-scale pillage. Your paintings will surface, but I'm afraid not in our lifetimes."

Losing all sense of propriety, I flung myself at his chest, pounded my fists on his bony shoulders, and cried, "No! Why do you have to be so . . . so absolute? You will help Monsieur Laforgue, but what about me?"

He peeled me away from him. "If I help him, he will be more amenable to me when I remind him of you."

That was some consolation.

"In Paris, we search documents, sales records of auction houses, the Caisse des Dépôts et Consignations, the Bureau des Biens et Intérêts Privés, banks that may hold paintings as collateral for loans, even pawnshops. And we look through the remaining works in the Jeu de Paume, where that scoundrel Rosenberg showed them off to Göring. It's all coming to light now. There are ways. But here, we have nothing to go on."

"That's not true, Maxime."

"What then?"

I was caught up short with nothing to offer.

"Granted, things are different here, but it's not impossible."

I strode over to the writing desk in exasperation, took a pencil and my list out of the drawer, slapped it on the dining table, and crossed out the word *Retrieve* in number eleven. I wrote *Find* above it, so that it read *Find the paintings,* and added the words *in MY lifetime.* I wrote with such force that my pencil probably gouged the letters into the wooden table beneath the tablecloth. There. That was a vow I could not forget.

"What's that?" Maxime asked.

I hesitated. "Just a list I've been keeping."

"About what?"

"It's a list of promises to myself. I call it Lisette's List of Hungers and Vows."

"May I see it?"

"Oh, no." I held it to my chest. "It's just for me. Something I do. I learned it from Pascal. It's not important to anyone else."

"To me, it would be. If it reveals something about you that I wouldn't know in any other way, then it's very important. I won't make judgments."

I read over the list silently in order to consider each item and what Maxime might think of it.

1. Love Pascal as a father.
2. Go to Paris, find Cézanne's *Card Players*.
3. Do something good for a painter.
4. Learn what makes a painting great.
5. Make a blue dress, the blue of the Mediterranean Sea
on a summer day with no clouds.

I started to cross out number five. It seemed inconsequential now. Maxime put his hand on my wrist to stop me. "Don't change it for my sake."

6. Learn how to live alone.
7. Find André's grave and the spot where he died.
8. Forgive André.
9. Learn how to live in a painting.
10. Try not to be envious.
11. Find the paintings in MY lifetime.

12. Learn how to be self-sufficient.
13. Do something good for Maxime.

He turned his hand over, palm up. "Please?"

I could not deny him. If I were honest with myself, I would have to admit that I wanted him to know me better, but I could never bring myself to speak these things. I slid the paper—the gossamer fragility of a new intimacy—across the table, clasped my hands together in front of my mouth, and held my breath. He read slowly—thinking about each item, it seemed. The muscles of my shoulders relaxed. I realized that laying bare my soul was not as hard as Maxime laying bare what had happened in the trench.

"Maybe I can help you with number two, Cézanne's *Card Players*."

"I would like to discover it myself."

He read on. "You did something good for a painter. You brought him food. Something every painter needs."

"I wish I could have done more."

"What makes a painting great? *Oh là là*. Every dealer and every painter has a slightly different answer."

"You have already helped me with that one."

He smiled at something, maybe the dress.

He didn't comment on either of the items having to do with André. Certainly the situation with the paintings was not what André had anticipated. I was proud of his willingness to go to war. Neither required any forgiveness. I could cross off that item.

"Living *in* a painting? Hmm. Pure Lisette."

I felt myself blush.

"Who are you envious of?" he asked gently.

"Bella and Marc Chagall. They have such a perfect, complete love, sharing everything with each other, thinking each other's thoughts. I can't imagine them having any secrets from each other. And he painted that love in exuberant fantasies and in tender, private moments. It seemed so rich, their love."

"Don't call it envy. You don't wish them not to have that ideal love. Call it longing. Call it grieving. Call it hoping. Call it waiting. Any of these, but not envy."

With embarrassment I admitted, "I haven't done most of the things on that list."

"You *have* done something good for me."

"Socks don't count for much."

"I didn't mean the socks."

CHAPTER TWENTY-SIX

LAPUSHKA

1946

I N THE MORNING, THE COURTYARD WAS BLANKETED WITH POW-
dery snow. On it, bright winter sunshine sparkled in flecks of
light. The long shadow of the outhouse stretched toward the west
in the palest lavender blue. Pascal would have noticed that, his eye
trained by Pissarro.

"Look, Maxime. How beautiful. I hate to spoil it with my footprints, but—"

"You don't have to." He swept me up in his arms and I lost touch
with the earth as he carried me, laughing and making spumes of
breath-clouds, and set me down at the outhouse door.

"I would have flown you here, like a Chagall painting, if I were
capable of it."

Despite the cold, we stood outside for a few moments after I
came out, to enjoy the view. All the rough edges of fence posts and
rooftops were softened, and the round cap of the windmill across
the ravine looked like a mound of whipped cream, but it wouldn't
last. Some roofs already showed surprise patches of red tiles where
the weightless snow had blown off. Bare grapevines threaded the
hills in dark lines.

"The vines are like ranks of thin men in the prison yard holding out their arms to each other," Maxime said.

"You have to train yourself not to think those thoughts. Look at the beauty of the land instead. Look at the foothills of the Luberons. Don't they look like the humps of white elephants praying on their knees?"

He smiled at me. "If you think so."

The change of seasons reflected the timelessness of the land, which had endured whatever storms or armies had passed over it. A black-and-white magpie landed on our fence rail. His white shoulder feathers lifted in a breeze.

"A Monet painting," Maxime said, so softly that the quiet lying over the valley and over us was not disturbed. "It's peaceful here. I'm glad you were here during the war years."

We waited until the magpie warbled, which made us laugh because it sounded like a puppy whining. When it flew off, Maxime swept me up again, and I felt Bella's exuberance in being freed from gravity. He was careful to walk backward, stepping in his own footprints, as he carried me to the house.

I had just started milking Geneviève when the exultant clucking of Kooritzah Deux announced that she had just laid an egg.

"That's chicken language for 'Pick it up.' Go inside her coop and find it before it freezes."

The instant Maxime bent down and entered, Kooritzah let loose a fury of squawking and wing flapping at the stranger in her domain.

"*Vite! Vite! Vite!*" I said. "It's under her."

He mustered his courage and snatched it from beneath her. "I've got it!" he shouted, cupping it in his hands.

"Bravo, you city boy. *Eh bien, lapushka! Merci.*"

"What does that mean, *lapushka*?"

Feeling myself blush, I said, "Something like 'darling.' It's Russian."

—

GLAD TO BE INSIDE, I laid the pages Pascal had written in front of Maxime at the table. "It's Pascal's handwriting. I found them in one of his drawers yesterday."

As he read, silently at first, then punctuated with murmurs of interest, I went to work making cheese. "This will be ready for you to take home with you."

"Lisette, this is priceless! Is it true? Did this conversation happen?"

"I don't think he could have made up such detail."

"Monsieur Laforgue should see this. Do you mind if I take it to him?"

"I was hoping to do that myself someday."

"You're right. You should be the one."

I served him *un petit noir* made with real coffee and laid a round loaf of René's *pain d'épeautre* on the table, explaining that it was a traditional bread made with primitive wheat grown near Sault, a village to the north.

"You've learned a lot about this region."

"I should think so. It has been nine years."

He broke apart the loaf and tore off big morsels and ate them one after another. I was sure Provençal bread would make him hearty again.

He stopped eating long enough to concede that there might be ways to find the paintings in rural Provence that he didn't know about.

"Is there anyone here you trust who might help you?"

"Yes. Maurice. The bus driver. And 'madame his wife,' Louise. My best friends."

"Let's go see them."

—

WHEN WE ARRIVED AT the Chevets' house, Maurice welcomed Maxime robustly, pounding him on the back, and Louise insisted that we join them for cream of potato soup, boiled beets, and red rice from the Camargue. In a rush of words I spilled out why we had gone to the woodpile and what we had discovered there.

"I'm certain André put the paintings there. Why else would his boards be there but to make a double platform to keep the paintings flat and dry?"

"A pretty poor hiding place, if you ask me," Maurice said.

"It does have a roof," Louise responded.

"That's irrelevant now," Maxime said. "Who could have found them? The wood gatherer?"

"Not likely. He has the round eyes of a goby," Maurice said.

"What's a goby?" Maxime asked.

"A useless little fish in our rivers here. Not worth the hook to catch him," Maurice said. "A simpleton."

"Could they be in someone's house?" Maxime asked.

Maurice blew a puff of air. "Nobody would hang them in their house. This is a small village, monsieur. We have all been in each other's houses. No house is private. Everyone knows the paintings belonged to Pascal."

"It is possible that he hid some under the woodpile and others elsewhere?" Louise ventured.

"Where? Where is a likely place?" Maxime asked.

"If it were Pascal and not his grandson, I would say in the Bruoux Mines," Maurice said.

"That still could be André's hiding place," Louise said.

"Or someone else's who found them in the woodpile and hid them again until they could be sold outside Roussillon," Maxime said.

That seemed more likely. "Who?" I asked.

"Who has contacts outside Roussillon?" Maxime asked.

"The mayor, Aimé Bonhomme, but he is honorable. He would

never do anything underhanded. The whole village respects him," Maurice said.

"We were trusting of Monsieur Pinatel when he was mayor," Louise said, "but his fleeing on the night Hitler committed suicide has cast suspicion on him. He has contacts outside Roussillon."

"Then I suppose it might have been him," I remarked. "Monsieur Voisin complained early in the war that Monsieur Pinatel had taken all the wood, down to the platform, but I had thought he was just exaggerating. He could have lifted the top plywood and have taken the paintings *anywhere*," I wailed.

"No," Louise said. "I can't picture him creeping around at night to steal them."

"But I *can* picture him telling that German lieutenant," I said.

I thought of one other person who had contacts outside the village, and I was surprised Louise didn't mention him. The words "you'll be sorry" echoed in my mind. Bernard was enough of an enigma that he might be the one.

I was about to say so when Maxime launched a speculation. "Let's assume, for the moment, that they were stolen with selfish intent. You probably know that Hitler, Göring, and other high-level Nazis amassed huge collections of art that were found in salt mines, particularly Altaussee, in Austria."

"We heard. We're not that isolated here." Maurice sounded peeved. "There is a radio in the café."

"Surely the mayor would have had knowledge of that. So he might have hidden Lisette's paintings in a mine near here until such time that he could sell them to a German officer or government official, who would then ingratiate himself with a gift of art to someone of higher position. The paintings could have traveled up the ranks. Paris is buzzing with such stories."

"Pascal's paintings in German hands!" I cried.

That possibility silenced the four of us. Privately I thought how devastated André would have been.

A few minutes later, Maxime said, "It would have to be some-one not very knowledgeable about art—"

"No one here is knowledgeable about art," I muttered.

"—because Lisette's paintings would have been considered too modern, what the German chief of culture, Goebbels, called degen-erate art. So if the thief intended them as a gift to a German cul-tural officer, he would have made a mistake."

"Can we at least look in the mine?"

"There are many mines. The earth under the commune is rid-dled with passageways," Maurice said.

"It's not smart to go into a mine you don't know, Lisette," Max-ime warned. "I would have to go with you."

"Puh! You don't know them either."

"The closest mine stopped its operations when the war started. Only a small exploitation of one area has begun again," Maurice said. "We can't go where they are working, but we can explore other areas in it."

"How do you know where?" Maxime asked.

Maurice pantomimed wielding a pickax at imaginary walls to his right and his left. He tapped his chest. "Ambidextrous. You are, my good man, looking at a miner of progress, the forward-most miner of Team Three at the Bruoux Mines. Aimé Bonhomme worked directly behind me. Being a left-hander, which was rare, he was paid more than right-handers. Miners of progress were paid by the distance we picked in a day. One meter was a good day."

Louise waved her hand as though she were sweeping away a fly. "All right, all right, Maurice. They don't need to know that. You will have to excuse him, Maxime. The miners of Roussillon are proud men."

"I know the portion of the mine excavated by 1920, but not after that," Maurice said.

"Would there be safe places to hide paintings there?" I asked.

"Some. There are wall niches we axed out for statues of Sainte

Barbara, patron saint of miners. A couple of the miners were talented at carving them. Paintings could be hidden behind the statues. The question is whether I can remember where they are. It's been twenty-five years. I won't go in without thinking it out."

"You shouldn't go in there in winter anyway," Louise said. "Lisette would freeze. Wait till summer."

"In the meantime, I'll work on a map."

Another wait lay ahead.

IN THE MIDDLE OF the night, I heard Maxime yell, "The timber! Get out!" I ran into his bedroom and found him in the throes of a nightmare, gasping and choking and thrashing around in his bed. I grabbed his arms to bring them to his sides.

"You're here in Roussillon. You're not in a mine. It was a bad dream, but you're all right now. I'm here."

He turned away from me and covered his head and drew up his knees. I sat on the edge of the bed and threw my arm over him until his shuddering stopped.

THE NEXT MORNING I poured Maxime's *petit noir* into a small cup as if we were in Paris, rather than into a bowl, which was the Provençal way.

"It's enough that I go with Maurice," I said. "You don't have to."

"I can't let you do that. I've got to be there."

"No, Max. I'm not going to put you through that. There's no sense in fueling more nightmares."

He shrank at the reminder and looked so ashamed that I was sorry I had said it.

"This is it, Lisette. This is as good as it gets. I'll never be clear of it. Accept it."

"I don't believe that," I whispered.

He lifted his shoulders in a shrug.

"I might never be whole enough to live without attacks of fear or fury. I even raged at my mother."

"A little at a time, Max. Roussillon has taught me how to wait."

"How long will you stay here?"

"I told you. Until I find the paintings."

"What if they can't be found? What if they're not here?"

It was my turn to shrug. How could I know?

"Can you stand the cold enough for us to take a walk?"

He answered by putting on his coat.

The snow had melted off the cobblestones but had left them wet and slippery. We took the downhill with caution, holding on to each other. In the lower village, we stopped at the bakery to buy two brioches. Maxime pulled out the moist center knob of his and fed it to me. We ate them as we walked toward the end of the village.

"I want to show you something extraordinary, the only thing in Roussillon worth visiting."

"You are worth visiting. I didn't come to see any sights. I'm not a tourist."

"This sight you'll never forget. People who hope for tourists call it the Sentier des Ocres."

We passed the cemetery, walked along a ridge edged with pines, and descended a little way into a bowl or basin with its high walls grooved and striped in all the shades of ochre.

"Originally, the walls were scooped out by centuries of mistrals, which exposed the ochres, and then miners went at them with their pickaxes. Pascal said they are sixty meters high."

Pinnacles and cliffs surrounded us. The red-orange glowed in the morning light, and deep green pines shaded patches of snow.

"It's as though waves of color swirled against the canyon walls and then froze," Maxime said. "Someone should paint this."

"Apparently, it is even more magnificent farther on, but the paths are treacherous when they're wet. We can come back in the summer and bake in the heat reflected off the walls."

"I wouldn't mind some of that heat now."

We both shivered at once and turned toward home. What I had to tell him weighed heavily on my mind as we trudged uphill. I resolved to tell him later, after we had onion soup and felt warmer.

Stalling, I took a long time selecting the onions in the root cellar. Back in the house, I sliced them very thin, then sautéed them, poured in water, and dropped in three beef bouillon cubes. I cut three slices of baguette at an angle, floated them on top of three bowls of the soup, then grated some ricotta over them. After kindling a fire in the firebox, I set the three servings in the oven to toast.

"Why three?" he asked.

"You're going to have two of them."

Then I sat down to watch him eat.

"I have something to tell you," I said softly.

He waved his spoon aloft. "Tell on, *lapushka*."

That nearly dissolved my resolution.

"Remember when we were coming back from the borie?" I began. "A lorry stopped and the driver offered us a ride."

"Yes. He glared at me suspiciously."

"The *garde champêtre*, Bernard Blanc. An arrogant fellow they call the constable. He's extremely moody, veering from kindness to aggressiveness. Without my asking, he gave me things I needed during the war. A stewing chicken, seeds to start the garden, wood. He implied that in accepting them, I owed him something. Some feminine favor. Twice he grabbed me in a forced embrace."

He stopped eating. Broth spilled from his spoon.

"Max, please understand. I gave him no indication that I was interested in him. In fact, I have been rude."

"How?"

"I closed the door in his face once. Another time, he came right into the courtyard, entering by the side gate while I was shoveling out the outhouse. He taunted me by swinging a string of sausages and saying something crude, trying to tempt me into going to his house, where he would provide a sausage every night. When he said

I was frolicking with you instead of grieving over André, I couldn't bear it, and I dug the shovel into the outhouse pit and drew out a big pile and flung it at him."

Maxime laughed, a buoyant, guilt-freeing laugh that exploded and filled the room. "Served him right."

"Then he flung the string of sausages over the cliff and threatened me. Seeing that string of sausages sail through the air was actually droll."

"That's something Chagall would have put in a painting," Maxime said. "He has fish and chickens in the sky. Why not sausages?"

Chuckling, Maxime went upstairs and returned wearing a wry look. "After hearing how he tried to win you over with gifts, I hesitate to give this to you, but I brought it, so here it is."

He placed on the table a small box, only about eight centimeters square, with gold letters spelling À LA MÈRE DE FAMILLE, the name of the oldest *confiserie* in Paris, on rue du Faubourg Montmartre.

I lifted the lid. "Marzipan! You remembered how I adore them." I held the box's lid to my chest and gazed down at four perfect fruits—an apple, a pear, a cherry, and a peach. "The colors of Roussillon!"

A man who would give a gift of marzipan would surely not have nightmares forever.

CHAPTER TWENTY-SEVEN

OCHRES OF
ALL HUES

1946

SPLENDID SUMMER, AT LAST! I SUSPECTED THAT THE ENTIRE *département* of the Vaucluse was sweetly blooming. The passionflower vine climbing the side fence was covered with delicate, intricate blossoms—the pale green petals spread wide like a sunburst, a circular fringe of violet rays, a yellow center with a red ring within it, from which sprouted chartreuse filaments supporting pockets of pollen. The air in front of Louise's house wafted fragrances of lavender and sweet pea. My almond tree was sprouting nuts as green as new parsley, their velvet casings taunting me to touch them, but if I ate one now, it would be as bitter as vinegar. Provence was teaching me to surrender to the seasons, and to wait with patience.

But when Maxime stepped through my doorway in the middle of August, I didn't wait. I hugged him instantly. I had been patient long enough.

He looked healthier and had put on some weight. His chest was no longer concave, the skin around his eyes not so drawn. Even his wrists were not so thin.

He had come for the exploration of the mine, not to enter it, just to be here in case Maurice and I came home with the paintings.

—

THE BRUOUX MINES, WHERE Maurice and Pascal had worked, were about six kilometers east of Roussillon, near the village of Gargas. Behind some rusty ore carts on rails, a row of mine entrances, tall rounded arches cut into a cliff, loomed ominously. Fifteen meters high, Maurice said. He took great pride in explaining that the width of each passageway—which he called a gallery, claiming that Roussillon did have a gallery after all—was measured by two miners, one right-handed and one left-handed, standing side by side and reaching out their outside arms with their pickaxes. By measuring frequently, they had made all the galleries the same width, which gave the ceiling vaults stability without the need for timbers.

"You mean there's nothing holding up the arches?"

"Just geometry. It's quite safe, and our accuracy made it beautiful. Six generations of miners have worked here. Ochres from this mine have been sent all over the world."

We entered into the cool air of one of the entrances and heard the echo of pigeons warbling and trilling. As we walked the downward slope, it became darker, so we turned on our battery torches. Instantly a flock of bats flew out at us. I screamed and ducked.

"Oh," Maurice laughed. "I forgot to warn you."

"*Merci bien, monsieur le chevalier.* Are there any other creatures in here?"

"Only a fire-breathing dragon, but we tamed him. All the same, stay close behind me."

Where I shined my torch, the walls were what Maurice called deep cadmium yellow and cadmium orange, but farther into the mine, some veins were the color of gold, and other bands were creamy white or maroon. It was all eerily strange and wondrous. I picked up loose rocks, wanting to show Maxime the colors, until I could hold no more.

Peering ahead, I could see the ribs of the arches diminishing in size the way they did in the nave of Notre Dame. In Paris, I knew them to be all the same height, so I assumed these must be also, although the farther ones did appear shorter. Here was a cathedral, excavated for the extraction of ores that made the beautiful paintings of the world. To be *in* the earth instead of *on* it thrilled me.

"Do you think any other woman in Roussillon has ever been here, inside the earth?"

"No. No woman would want to."

No other woman was as motivated as I was.

Sometimes the ground dipped downhill sharply and I lunged forward, which brought my heart into my throat. The sound of water dripping made me uneasy, and some areas were muddy and slippery. Pillars of stone diminished in girth as I looked up, and white stalactites, wet and glistening, diminished in thickness as I followed them down with my eyes. We found a lake of sulfurous-smelling liquid and had to pick our way along its slick edge.

Every so often, a perpendicular gallery stretched to the right and left, and from these, other galleries had been opened parallel to the main gallery. I soon lost all sense of where I was. We walked each side gallery its three hundred meters until we reached the blunt, stepped ends, like giants' stairways of blocks, each step about a meter high. Then, methodically, we returned to the main gallery, crossed it, walked the opposite gallery to its end, and came back.

Occasionally at the crossing of galleries, niches carved into the walls held eroded carvings of Sainte Barbara, which made the space seem even more like a church. In every instance, we looked behind her and removed loose rocks, but we found nothing.

Maurice aimed his light on the map he had drawn and said, "This is as far as I pickaxed, but I see they have penetrated much more. I'd like to keep looking, if you don't mind."

By this time I was tired and cold, but I wanted to go on. Maurice noticed me shivering and gave me his jacket.

"You are a true chevalier after all, not just on the roads but under the roads."

The jacket had pockets, so I could load my pieces of ore into them and pick up more.

He turned the map over and drew as we proceeded.

"How far have we gone?"

"Each cross gallery is three hundred meters apart."

"How deep do you think we are now?"

"Not very deep."

The statues of Sainte Barbara were in better condition as we proceeded through the more recently excavated galleries. At the end of one of them, Maurice shined his light on the top platform, probably eight meters above us, as he had been doing at each gallery's termination. Rocks had been placed side by side to form a neat little wall. The end of no other gallery had such a careful arrangement.

"What is *that* for?" I said.

"I don't know."

He huffed and puffed as he hoisted himself up backward to sit on each step until he got to the top step and could remove the row of rocks.

"Oh! Lisette!" He lifted out a roll of something. "This is either the engineer's map—"

"Or a painting!"

He brought it down carefully, and, taking great care, we unrolled it.

"The still life!" I shouted.

Still life still life still life echoed through the gallery.

"Who would have thought to put it here?" he said, more baffled than inquiring. He rolled it loosely, just as it had been. "The others may be here too. I'll come again another time. This is enough for today."

"No! We found one here. The others may be near. We've got to keep going."

We searched futilely for what seemed like hours, exhausting the tributaries of the main gallery. I was freezing, and Maurice was breathing hard.

He accompanied me home in order to see Maxime's reaction. I called his name just inside the door. No answer. I rushed upstairs. His bed was mussed but empty. Maurice checked in the courtyard. A note lay on the dining table: *Do not worry. I am with Louise.*

We hurried back downhill the distance of five houses and found him calmly spooning *minestra,* Louise's thick Corsican bean and vegetable soup, into his mouth.

"Look!"

Maurice unrolled the painting.

"Cézanne!" I shouted.

"Cézanne," Maxime affirmed with a nod and a broad smile.

Louise hugged me.

Tumbling over my words, I described the interior of the mine, and Maurice described the hiding place.

I laid down the ore samples. "Look at these! Ochres of all hues, in stone and on the fruit in the painting."

Maurice poured pastis for us, and we congratulated ourselves.

"This was not put there by André," Maxime said, a dispirited declaration. "He would have known not to roll the painting. This was rolled painted side inward, which could make the paint buckle. If it had to be rolled at all, he would have rolled the painted side out. Anyone who works with paintings knows that."

That information pointed to a thief.

AT HOME, MAXIME TOOK great care in stretching and cleaning the canvas, and I found the frame that fit it.

"I want it hanging over André's cabinet, where it was before. I want all of them where they were before."

"Then where do you want your Chagall?"

"For now, here, between these two windows."

I tacked it there while Maxime hung the still life over André's cabinet, and then I arranged the ochre rocks on top of the cabinet.

At first, we were quiet, just taking in Cézanne's painting. On its left was a green glazed olive jar of the sort that was in my kitchen and Louise's, and just to the right of the jar, nearly touching it, a plump blue-gray ginger jar encased by willow netting. Farther to the right was a white porcelain compote dish containing apples. Tilted precariously in the foreground on a bunched-up white table-cloth, a small white plate spilled over with oranges. And one yellow pear stood by itself.

"All the colors of Roussillon are swirled onto that fruit," I said. "And the blue cloth with shadings of darker blue is what I imagine the Mediterranean Sea to be like. I love it." The painting blurred in my adoring wet vision. "There were days during the war when I thought I would never be reunited with it."

Maxime's arm stole around my shoulders. "Monsieur Laforgue told me a legend that Cézanne, with typical Provençal impetuous-ness, boasted, 'I will astonish Paris with an apple.'"

"He is astonishing us with five apples."

"You had better value each of them separately. He probably worked on each one for days, meditating over it until he discovered its individuality in order to create its shape on the flat canvas."

"By subtle hue changes," I added, showing off.

Maxime chuckled. "I always knew you were smart."

I lifted my shoulders and grinned.

"Cézanne's conscience was so pure that he never depended upon a prior painting of an apple—his or someone else's. To him, each apple had a unique character—"

"Like people," I blurted.

"True, my unique darling. Cézanne discovered each apple's uniqueness little by little, loving each discovery." He smiled at me, and I knew he meant more than apples. "Then, with effort, he could quiet his passion for each apple and put it to rest in the painted apple forever. He was as devoted to every object he painted as a saint is to his God."

"Did he use five apples for any particular reason?"

"Look at them—four in the dish, and one resting on the four. Squint until your eye straightens the curves and obliterates details. What is its form?"

"A pyramid."

"Good. That's why he used five. He simplified shapes by seeing his subjects in geometric forms. Cones and spheres here. What about that pear?"

I puzzled over that until he suggested, "A small tipped cone on top of a sphere. Why do you think he painted only one pear?"

"For its uniqueness!"

"And because there is a dynamic principle in playing a lot against a little."

I saw that the five apples and three oranges contrasted in importance and weight to the single pear, but what moved me more was the memory of the weight and importance of the Virgin Mary and the Christ Child in contrast to that single pear in front of them in the painting at the orphanage.

"Would you still call this Impressionism? It's not feathery like Pissarro's work."

"We call it Postimpressionism now. It stems from Impressionism, in that the white cloth takes on the colors surrounding it. So does the blue-gray of the jar and the yellow-ochre streak on that apple. But Cézanne didn't let the principles of Impressionism restrict him—in this case, perspective. See how the plate is tipped? It can't be resting on that fluffed-up cloth, yet he positioned it that way intentionally to give us a better view of the oranges. He meant to violate the rules of perspective and gravity. That's his own primitivism, something he didn't borrow from any school or movement. He worked it out himself over a long period of time."

Maxime stepped closer to the painting, and I followed. The

slow, curving gestures of his hand traced the repeating roundness of the plate, the ginger jar, the apples and oranges. I found myself looking at his hand, which would be here for only a matter of days, instead of at the painted plate and jar, which would be with me forever. I noticed that the curve of the scar on his hand was parallel to the curve of the edge of the plate. It almost made me weep. That curve must have been cut the instant the grenade exploded, the moment we lost our André. It traced an arc that bound us together.

As if to himself, Maxime murmured, "We're looking at the work of a genius."

That brought my mind back to the painting, and I said, "I see now that the pear is more yellow on the side of the oranges and greener where the blue cloth is behind it. The colors move into one another with such minute gradations that you can't tell where green stops and yellow begins."

"So natural, as if every dash of color were aware of all the other dashes of color, shoulder to shoulder, like friends in an army."

I felt a scowl pinch my forehead.

"It's not a negative thing, Lisette. A color comes into its own in response to another color, just like soldiers do, like friends, like lovers. Our proximity to each other brings about our wholeness."

He turned to me with an uncomplicated smile that melted my doubt about his well-being. He was winning his victory.

CHAPTER TWENTY-EIGHT

MARZIPAN

1946

AFTER TWO MORE DAYS OF SEARCHING IN THE MINE WITH-
out success, we came to the conclusion that no more paintings were hidden there. Maxime suggested that we stop. I agreed. It
wasn't fair to him to make him stay home alone day after day just
because I knew that if he came with us to the mine entrance, he
would naturally follow us inside it.

Instead, accompanied by Aimé Bonhomme, we searched Mayor
Pinatel's house. It was obvious that he and his wife had left in a
hurry, abandoning so many lovely things. If the mayor had found
the paintings when he'd emptied the woodpile, he must have taken
them with him. Now they could be anywhere, lost forever. I wept
on Maxime's shoulder.

"It's not necessarily the end, *chérie*," Maxime said when we
came home. "It could have been that constable fellow who brought
you wood, so be sure you don't antagonize him. And don't ask him
directly. If indeed he was an opportunist and stumbled upon the
paintings and was going to use them to advance his position with
Vichy or the Germans, thinking that he might be found out might
prompt him to burn them. We have to be cautious. We may even
have to search his house."

"Oh, no, Max. That would be dangerous."

"How badly do you want the paintings? For the sake of France, if not for yourself, they should be in the right hands. See if you can find out if he will ever be away from Roussillon."

Resolutely but with misgivings, I agreed.

I TRIED TO THINK of something lighthearted to do while Maxime was with me. I put a teacup upside down on André's cabinet right under Cézanne's painting, then covered it with a white napkin just as Cézanne had done with a tablecloth. I placed the marzipan fruit on a white saucer and set it at a slight angle, leaning it against the cup. The precious pieces of fruit rolled off. I scrambled to catch them before they fell to the floor. Max laughed, which made me laugh too.

"How did he make his oranges stay in place?" I asked.

"He might have used thick globs of gum arabic, a binding agent in watercolors used to make the pigments adhere to paper."

In Maxime's gift of marzipan, there was a glimmer of the former Max, the prewar Max, the Max who could be frivolous, who enjoyed small things. This was the greater gift.

"There is Paris in these marzipans," I said.

"Can you hear her singing to you?" he asked.

"I've been hearing her for a decade. Can you hear Roussillon sing to *you*?"

"Yes, faintly. The *baa*s are the melody and the clucks are the harmony."

"I have an idea to make the song more robust."

I gathered the pieces of ochre I had placed on the cabinet top and went out into the courtyard. Facing the smooth rosy ochre stucco of the house, which was still damp from last night's rain, I asked, "How do you think those cave artists did it?"

"They spit."

"You don't know that. You weren't there."

Nevertheless, I spit on an ochre rock, rubbed my saliva around on it, and drew it horizontally across the wall. It left a red-ochre line. "I'm painting!"

"A fresco," Maxime said.

I spit again and drew a shorter parallel line under my first line, then joined them with a vertical line at each end.

"Brava. A trapezoid. Cézanne would approve."

"It's more than a trapezoid. Watch this!" I spit again and made a cone protrude at one end, and a smaller cone that angled down from the first one. "It's a head, in case you don't recognize it." Then I drew four very narrow rectangles descending from the body. "What is it?"

"Hmm. If it had horns, it would be a goat."

"It's Geneviève!" I drew two arcs pointing from her head back across her body. "Come here, Geneviève, to approve your portrait."

She approached at my call, took one cursory look, then turned her head away, like an aristocrat of the barnyard, and walked off.

"Maybe she doesn't recognize herself," Maxime said. "Maybe she's looking for her udder."

"Oh, I forgot." Giggling, I drew a half circle under her belly and added teats so she would be proud. I dragged her over to her portrait and held the sides of her head, forcing her to look.

"*Baa. Baa. Bad.*"

Maxime laughed. "Any new style of art is first met with criticism. The cave painters suffered from it, I'm sure. Now you know how the Impressionists felt."

"Watch this!" I spit on a different rock.

"Wouldn't it be easier to dip it in a bowl of water?"

"No. Spit's the thing. It's more authentic. Didn't you know? It's a binding agent."

I reached up high and drew an oval—Kooritzah's body tumbling upside down in the sky, her wings spread wide, her toes splayed, her beak open. "She's squawking the song of Roussillon."

The act of creating was infectious. Maxime picked up a chunk of rock, spit on it, and drew a tall, very narrow rectangle and a wide half sphere at its top.

"A tree!"

"No. *The* tree."

Together we put some almonds in it.

"What else?" I asked.

He looked around and, with much hacking and spitting, drew a tall trapezoid, narrower at its upper reaches, topped by a small half sphere.

I stroked my chin like an old man might do, pondering something. "I hate to sound like an ignorant critic," I said, "but close up it's incomprehensible and awful. Seen from afar, it's awful and incomprehensible."

"I'm not finished," he said. "Be patient."

He added four trapezoids, their narrow ends attached just under the half sphere and radiating out like spokes.

"The windmill! Moulin du Sablon in all its former glory! Oh, Max, it's exquisite!"

"Wait. One more thing." He chuckled as he drew a section of fence with something oval on the top rail. "Monet's magpie. Now our fresco is a Cézanne, a Chagall, and a Monet all in one."

THE NEXT DAY, UNABLE to leave it alone, we added some small touches: a fleur-de-lis flag on the windmill, hooves and eyelashes on Geneviève. Maxime departed in far greater spirits than when I had seen him off after his first visit.

"Paris," he said out the window of Maurice's bus.

"Paris," I echoed.

KNOWING THAT SOMEDAY I would see the Seine again, hear lively talk in the cafés, peer at beautiful displays in shop windows, and listen to accordion music at a *métro* station loosened the grip of isolation and exile I had been feeling and, curiously, allowed me to appreciate my home more.

The daylight lingered; I could enjoy our playful mural of stick figures outside, and Cézanne's still life of fruit in the evenings. The joyfulness and humor of the tipped plate amused me. Maybe it had been wrong to hope that all the paintings lying between the boards would be waiting for me to snatch them up in one fell swoop. Seeing them all at once might have been too much. I might not have paid any attention to the single pear. I had to get reacquainted with each canvas as with an old friend—in unhurried moments, until it was secure in my heart before another would take my attention away.

My gaze went from Cézanne's fruit to Maxime's marzipan fruit. What would prevent me from making my own marzipan? I would have plenty of almond meal come winter. Sugar. Sugar was still expensive. But if I bought small amounts from time to time and drank tea with Maurice's honey instead of using sugar in coffee, by Christmas I would have enough to make marzipan gifts for my friends. And after that, Odette could sell them in the *boulangerie* or Jérôme Cachin in his *épicerie*. And over time, I could earn my rail ticket to Paris.

In the meantime, I would have to find ways to make natural dyes and try them out on white potatoes. During the next several weeks, I roasted my carrots in embers, scraped and mashed the skins, and dried and pulverized the residue. Mixed with a few drops of water, it turned a skinned and boiled white potato a beautiful orange.

I tried acacia blossoms for yellow, but they turned the potato bitter, and I spit it out. I went to Apt and found yellow saffron threads at the spice table. They were expensive, but I bought a minute amount. I needed yellow to blend with orange for a peach.

The leaves of my beets distilled into yellow-green for pears. I boiled my smallest beet root to make a rich reddish purple juice for red grapes. I tried a bee orchid, but it yielded a grayish mauve, suitable only for a mildewed plum. Yellow dandelions produced a pale urine color. But wild heliotrope blossoms made a deep purple, just right for dark grapes.

I remembered from the time I took chèvre to the refugees living in the windmill that there was a pomegranate tree there. I would have to wait until November for the hard fruit to develop seeds and ripen. I felt sure that the juice would make a deep, ruby red for apples.

But how to make the almond paste? One afternoon, I took the four marzipan fruits in the little box to the *boulangerie* and opened it in front of René.

"Have you ever made marzipan?"

"Oh yes. In Italy. Almond paste and sugar."

"What else?"

"A couple of eggs. You'll need some cream of tartar to stabilize the egg whites and give a creamier texture. For my cake frostings, I get it from the sediment produced in the process of making wine. Émile Vernet will give you all you'll ever need. Just a pinch."

"Anything else?"

"Trial and error. And patience."

WITH AS MUCH PATIENCE as I could manage, I watched the soft green almond pods turn hard, their surfaces becoming pocked like cork. Finally November came, time of the almond harvest. As I had done before, I flung a rope around the lower branches and shooed Geneviève away, but she stubbornly refused to move.

"You'll be sorry," I sang out to her, and I remembered Bernard Blanc saying those same words in this very courtyard. I yanked the rope sharply until the nuts rained down on us, which brought an angry *baa* and an unmistakable glower as she scampered away.

Then came the tedious task of setting them on edge one by one on a flat stone and tapping them open with André's mallet. I ate the first one and choked on the skin. I would have to blanch them in boiling water to remove the skins. I burned the shells in the stove to heat the water—the Provençal principle of no waste.

Following René's instructions for almond paste, I pulverized the blanched almonds, heated the sugar slowly, added Émile's substitute for cream of tartar, boiled it for three minutes, put the saucepan in cold water, stirred until it thickened, stirred in my almonds, added egg whites, stirred again for two minutes over low heat, and spooned the mixture onto a board dusted with powdered sugar. It was not hard to knead it into balls, but the taste—! Blah!

I went back to René. "It's tasteless," I said.

"Help it along with some almond extract. Jérôme sells it."

"*Now* you tell me. I've wasted sugar."

Odette looked at me with compassion, smacked a *baguette* on her glass counter, and waved away my coin. I left discouraged, until I thought of trading almonds for almond extract. Monsieur Cachin drove a hard bargain, but I got it.

I used the ruined batch to practice making the shapes and testing all the colors. I made balls, squeezed them at one end for pears, pressed in a crater at the top and bottom for apples, rolled them into an oval for grapes, carved and smoothed a groove for peaches. In a strangely satisfying way, this reminded me of André gouging grooves and carving leaves to decorate frames.

"Look, André," I said out loud. "I carved a peach!"

THE END OF NOVEMBER was harvest time for pomegranates too. I was lucky. There were more on the tree by the windmill than I would need. Feeling like a thief, I twisted three off easily and was working on the fourth when I heard a door bang. I dropped them all and scurried away, sure that I would be chased off with a pitchfork.

No one followed me. I waited awhile, crouching behind an overgrown rosemary bush. The banging happened twice more. I peeked out and saw the door of the windmill swing open of its own accord and slam shut. Of course! Windmills are built where there is wind.

I crept back and gathered my four pomegranates. Thinking that the refugee family might still be living there, I knocked politely and heard nothing. This was an opportunity I couldn't pass up. I propped open the door with rocks so I could see inside. It was clear that people had been living on the ground floor, but there was no evidence of the family's belongings. A barrel had been turned upside down for a table. Empty sardine tins and wine bottles and crows' feet—refuse from their meals—lay scattered. How bizarre it would be to live in a circular room without being able to see across it because of the mechanism and the circular stairway around the central shaft.

I moved every dust-covered thing that would move, tipped the barrel sideways to look beneath it, turned every grain sack inside out, and found nothing but a dead mouse.

I climbed the stairs, through cobwebs, to an octagonal landing. A wheel with ratchets was mounted there, intersecting with a smaller one with spindles. I moved every piece of wood, every tool.

A ladder led up higher. When I stepped on the first rung, it cracked and gave way, but I was able to pull myself up, hand over hand. Just under the rounded roof cap, in a narrow space, I saw that wooden wedges had been stacked neatly. In the dim light, I counted the rows so I could put them back exactly as I'd found them. They had been stacked on what appeared to be a canvas! I brought it down into the light of the doorway.

Pissarro's *La Petite Fabrique*—the paint factory in Pontoise!

What if I were seen leaving with it? *I* wasn't the thief. Why shouldn't I have it? It made no sense to be cautious, but something told me to come back and get it after dark. I put it in a flour sack beneath the upturned barrel and grabbed my pomegranates. It was difficult holding on to four at once, so I lifted my skirt and made a hollow to put them in and hurried away, looking at the uneven ground to avoid tripping, until I saw two freshly shined boots in front of me. I stopped short.

"If you wanted pomegranates, I could have reached more in the tree than you could."

The constable stood in the road with his feet apart, a colossus. Would I never be rid of him? Had he seen me come out of the windmill just now, trespassing?

"Oh! I . . . I . . . just wanted a few." Certainly saying that wouldn't antagonize him.

"Your underskirt is lovely, but I would prefer to see it in a bedchamber rather than in the roadway."

Biting my tongue, I brushed down my skirt, and the pomegranates tumbled. I crouched to gather them, and he did too. Our arms tangled. He pushed me onto my back, then lowered himself onto me, holding me there face-to-face. I struggled to free myself, until his eyes widened, taking on a startled look, and he raised himself, helped me up, and let me go.

"THE DEVIL TAKE THAT MAN!" I cried as soon as I got home, relieved that I hadn't been holding the painting. I stomped upstairs, flung myself onto my bed, and waited for the early darkness—my excitement coming in waves despite the encounter with Bernard. His alarmed expression seemed to indicate that he had shocked himself. I hoped he was even now feeling remorse.

As soon as night fell, I went back to the windmill. In the darker darkness inside, I reached out for the barrel and found the sack beneath it.

On the roadway, I happened to kick something that might have been a pomegranate. I felt around on the ground until I found it, and reached home safely with sack and pomegranate both.

IN THE MORNING, I found another flour sack at my door, filled with seven pomegranates. *Bon Dieu!* When and where would he turn up next?

CHAPTER TWENTY-NINE

FRUITS OF
CHRISTMAS

1946

I TACKED *LA PETITE FABRIQUE* ONTO THE SMALLEST STRETCH-
ers, rinsed it with water as Maxime had done with the still life,
and put it in its small frame. It had hung between the two south
windows where I had tacked Marc's painting. Carefully, I took
down the goat, the chicken, and me and moved it to the edge of the
north wall where four paintings had hung. Positioning it close to
the dining table, I could look at it while I ate.

But before I hung the little Pissarro between the windows, I had
to tell Maurice and Louise! I put it back into the burlap sack, raced
down the street, and rapped on their door. Louise answered. Maurice was on the ledge halfway down the cliff where he kept his beehives.

I shouted to him, "I have something to show you."

He scrambled up. Inside, at their dining table, when I had their
attention, I slowly drew the painting out of the sack.

They were as thrilled as I was and asked a dozen questions.

"You realize what this means, don't you?" Maurice said. "Each
of the paintings is hidden separately."

"Why would anyone do that?"

"As a precaution. If someone came upon a hiding place, by intention or by chance, that person would find only one."

"Then the rest of them could be *anywhere*. It might take me years, unless Mayor Pinatel absconded with them. Then they would be lost forever. But why didn't he take these?"

"You could get lucky, like you were with this one," Louise said, cheerful as always.

"It isn't my favorite painting—just a plain boxy building with a smokestack—but it meant a lot to Pascal. It's a paint factory in Pontoise. He sold ochres there. He must have told you."

Maurice rolled his eyes. "At least a dozen times."

I remembered what Maxime had said about great paintings—that they had the power to command a trancelike state of communion with the image so that the viewer would come to know himself or the world more clearly. Now, looking long and deeply at the painting, I recognized a humbleness in that little factory doing its part to turn earth into beauty. The colors of Cézanne's apples and oranges might have been made right there in that nondescript building.

"There are two more windmills near here," Louise offered.

Maurice added, "Moulin de Ferre, this side of Joucas, and Moulin de l'Auro. It means 'wind from the north' in the Occitan language. It's near Murs."

"Can you take me?"

"Not so fast. We don't have permission to enter."

"Who can give permission? Only the owners?"

"The owners or, in lieu of them, Aimé Bonhomme, but he would be obliged to tell the *garde champêtre,* who has jurisdiction over the commune, so that Bernard won't assume you are trespassing."

Bernard again! "No. Please don't ask. I don't want the constable to know."

"He's the proper person."

"No. He's the most improper person. He might even be the thief, for all we know. And I've been rude to him, so even if he isn't the thief I'm sure he won't want to help me. We'll go without permission. At night."

"You are turning my good intentions of being a chevalier of the roads into the bad intentions of being a trespasser. But the trespassing of the knights-errant on their quests for the Holy Grail was forgiven because their motive was pure."

"The troubadours sang about them coming through Provence, didn't they?" I asked.

Maurice lifted his eyebrows. "Troubadours *originated* here, *ma petite*! From Provençal soil, when the whole southern region of France was called Occitania, all the way to two seas." A grin slid over his face. "Chivalry! Courtly love, my lady! Knights undergoing dark dangers for their chaste lovers! *Oh là là! Quelle aventure!* Get Maxime back here, and we'll go a-roving on a night when there is no moon to reveal us."

"Maurice! Be serious!" Louise commanded. "These are Lisette's paintings at stake. This is not a *game*!"

"She's right, Maurice. It's not," I said, but there was no diverting Maurice's well-intenioned desire to lighten the situation.

"Oh, my lady," he whined, stroking Louise's cheek. "Would you deny me the pleasure of a dangerous pursuit for a noble cause?" Louise pursed her lips in exasperation. "You want me to be chivalrous, don't you?" he asked. He nodded for her and said, "*Òc, òc.*"

"What's *òc òc*?"

"It means 'yes' in the old Occitan language, which developed here into Provençal," Maurice said, "and it has secret powers for finding hidden paintings."

"Ouf," Louise said. "You're impossible."

"*Òc, òc,*" I agreed. "Impossible."

Despite Maurice's insistence on turning the windmill search into a caper, and despite being no closer to finding the other paintings, I clutched the Pissarro to my chest and left the Chevets' house with hope. A few days later I wrote to Maxime.

4 DECEMBER, SAINTE BARBARA'S DAY, 1946

Dear Maxime,

Your drawing of the windmill has brought good luck. I found a painting there! All by myself. It's the small Pissarro called La Petite Fabrique. *It has given me hope. There are two other windmills here that we can search. Please come when it's warmer and the threat of mistrals isn't so great. Windmills are in windy spots. We need to search them without permission, at night.*

I am earning my way to come to Paris, but it's going to take a long time. You can guess how if you like. I am inspired by your gift of marzipan.

Geneviève and Kooritzah Deux miss you terribly and pine for the day when you will return. Not understanding that you are doing the work you should in Paris, Geneviève has become irritable and Kooritzah morose.

Joyeux Noël,
Lisette

After I sealed the letter, I took out my List of Hungers and Vows. Number two, *Go to Paris, find Cézanne's* Card Players, I realized, was a hunger. Number fourteen would be a vow:

Earn my way to Paris.

IN MY QUEST TO make perfect marzipan I took pleasure in thinking of its source. Except for the Spanish oranges, the fruit Cézanne painted had been grown in Provence and bought at a market in

Aix. His paint used the ochres of Provence, and now my marzipan would be colored by the plants of Provence. The almonds were from my tree, growing on Provençal soil. Kooritzah Deux, my Provençal chicken, would provide the eggs. It was all of a piece. With a touch of amazement, I realized how important Provence had become for me. I was, in a truer sense than blood, Pascal's daughter.

I started over, making very small batches so as not to waste the ingredients if they didn't adhere or if the marzipan had no almond taste. I prepared juices, distilled carrot residue, and smeared the dyes onto my practice fruits. The colors came out too dark. I learned about diluting and using tiny amounts. It was an alchemy of nature, and I was fascinated, spending days poring over my precious fruits. The first time I gave a pale yellow peach a touch of ruby pomegranate juice and blended it with strokes of my wet fingertip to look smooth and natural, then used the juice full strength for the groove and the stem's depression, I felt like an artist. More difficult to do were the threadlike red striations on yellow apples. I used a pine needle as an applicator. For pomegranates, I laid down a wash of orange from carrot scrapings and overlaid it here and there with diluted pomegranate juice. Inside the crowns, I used a drop of beet juice. I kept records of my experiments and made arrangements on saucers.

When I had a successful batch, I took an apple and a peach to René and Odette in the *boulangerie.*

"Too lovely to eat," Odette said, and put the peach on a saucer on the counter.

"Then how are you going to know what it tastes like?" René asked. He bit into his apple and rolled the morsel around in his mouth, sucking in his cheeks, nodding his head in approval.

"It could stand a couple more drops of almond extract," he advised.

—

FOR THE HOLIDAY MARKET, the day before Christmas, I had plenty of marzipan fruits to sell, so Maurice let me share the vendor's table where he sold his honey. I placed the candies in rows on a white napkin in a shallow drawer I had removed from the desk and wrote *Twenty centimes each* on a piece of paper, which I folded, then stood up like a tent.

Although it was cold, the square was festive. People wrapped in mufflers were happy to engage in the old traditions. *Chanteurs* strolled by carrying candles and singing the sprightly carol "Il Est Né, le Divin Enfant."

When someone came to the table to purchase honey, Maurice said, "Wouldn't you like to buy some of Lisette's pretty marzipan?" And when someone came to the table to pick out a couple of marzipans, I said, "Wouldn't you like to try some of Maurice's delicious lavender honey?" Because marzipan was one of the thirteen desserts served traditionally at Christmas here, my little fruits sold well.

After so many days of solitude, it was exhilarating to have friendly conversations with the people of the village and countryside. Madame Bonnelly descended upon me out of the stream of people, took my head in her large, crablike hands, kissed me noisily, and bought two of each fruit. Not to be outdone, three women behind her did the same.

Sandrine walked by holding Théo's hand. He was a precocious child who was constantly moving. Spotting my rows of marzipans, he pulled Sandrine toward our table.

"*Maman, Maman,* may I have a candy? May I? May I, *Maman?*"

He was learning to speak with Provençal robustness.

"Just one, so pick carefully," she said.

A scowl of concentration came over his face as he pointed to one after another, politely refraining from touching any of my ten types of fruits. Finally he settled on a red apple and said a perfect sentence. "*S'il vous plaît, madame, je voudrais une pomme.*"

I was so delighted that I was tempted to give him two apples, but I didn't want to undermine Sandrine's rule.

Henri Mitan said, "Ah-ah-all the g-grapes, *s'il vous plaît*."

I was nervous when Bernard came by our table, and prepared myself for some snide remark.

"I don't know which is prettier," he said. I thought he was comparing one fruit to another, as Théo had done, until he picked up a cherry and added, "The cherry or the cherry maker."

"If you touch it, you will have to buy it," I warned.

"The cherry maker, you mean? I already have." He ran his finger down the whole row of seven remaining cherries, touching each one, then letting a five-franc note flutter onto the table. He bit into the one cherry he had taken. "Sweet and succulent," he said, flashing a leering look, and sauntered away.

"He can turn any innocent thing into something lascivious," I muttered to Maurice.

"Bernard, he may seem threatening, but he wouldn't harm a flea," Maurice said. "He takes his role as constable seriously. Still, watch your step with him."

Agitated, I left the table, so that he wouldn't find me there if he came back, and meandered in the other direction, where there were displays of *santons*—*santouns* in Occitan, the sign said—the beguiling small clay or wooden figures of saints and nativity characters outfitted as *Provençaux*. Also depicted were white-kerchiefed women carrying market baskets, *boules* players, fishmongers, shepherds, artists, farmers, even René in a tall white baker's hat, Father Marc in his ecclesiastical mantle, and Mayor Bonhomme wearing the red Provençal sash. One *santon* even looked like me, I thought. I was relieved not to find the clay figure of the constable. That would have soured the day.

At one of the *santon* booths, I found the real Aimé Bonhomme wearing his red sash and approaching me with a man I didn't know. Aimé introduced him as Benoît Saulnier, the miller who owned the olive-pressing windmill called Moulin de Ferre. "He just told me something that would interest you."

The two men stepped away from the crowd, and Monsieur Saulnier greeted me with a certain gravity.

"I haven't worked the mill for years. All the olive pressing has moved to the big automated mills in Apt. There's no use staying in Roussillon any longer. We have just moved to Apt. I was lucky to get a post there in a large modern mill. I was cleaning out my mill, packing up all the things that had accumulated over the years, tools and barrels and crates, when I spotted a curious picture, a child's painting of heads."

I stifled a gasp.

"I didn't recall ever seeing it before when I was operating the mill and thought it was my daughter's. She used to play there on rainy days, but she said it wasn't. It being of no value, I just let it stay there, and we finished packing and left. In Apt I told my wife about it and she wanted to see it, so she sent me back for it." Monsieur Saulnier swallowed, and his Adam's apple moved up and down in his throat. "The painting was gone, madame. Aimé thought you should know. I suppose I should have told him sooner. I'm sorry."

"How long ago was it that you saw it?"

"Two months, I suppose."

"Can you describe it to me?"

"It wasn't pretty. They were women's heads, as far as I could tell. They had pointed chins and narrow faces, and their noses were bent to the side."

"Was the painting damaged?"

"No, madame. It was just the way they were painted. Like a child would do. Their eyes didn't match either."

I looked at Aimé. "It was André's painting. I'm sure of it. Was the windmill locked?"

"No, madame. There being nothing of value in it, I took the lock with me to Apt."

I didn't think I should say who might have painted it. I just thanked him, accepted his apology, and turned back.

There was someone moving the paintings around, or someone else searching for them who had happened on this one before I could. Or perhaps someone had just come upon it by chance and recognized its value. I was furious with myself for not acting more quickly.

A great urgency swelled up in me as I walked home. We had to get into that windmill. Maybe the miller had overlooked the painting or had inadvertently placed something over it. Maybe there were others hidden there.

At home, I put twenty-one francs fifty in the olive jar, wrote *Vow Fourteen, Earn my way to Paris* on the back of my paper sign, and slipped it inside the jar. But what did twenty-one francs fifty count for, when I had lost a Picasso or a Modigliani worth who knew how much?

I went to the Chevets' for a Christmas Eve *veillée*. Everyone greeted me with congratulations for my success at the market. I tried to respond cheerfully, but Louise knew something was wrong. Whispering for me to tell her later, she served the traditional Christmas Eve supper of vegetable broth, baked cod with cauliflower, chard stalks, and celery.

The guests laid out the thirteen desserts for tasting, the number thirteen referring to Jesus and his disciples. Mélanie had brought the four beggars, which represented the four mendicant monastic orders—raisins from their vineyard for the Dominicans, hazelnuts for the Augustines, dried figs for the Franciscans, and almonds for the Carmelites. Then Sandrine laid out dates and dried plums, examples of the foods of the region where the nativity had taken place. Odette brought quince cheese and pear and winter melon slices. René had made cumin-and-fennel-seed biscuits, the flat olive loaf called *pain fougasse,* and *oreillettes,* thin light waffles. The thirteenth dessert was my marzipan.

Mimi sang "Les Anges dans Nos Campagnes," with everyone

joining in on the chorus of *"Gloria, in excelsis Deo."* I yearned to feel the love of the angels of our countryside, as the song said. Before I left, I gave Odette the remaining marzipans for her to sell in the *boulangerie,* hoping that it might start a continuous business.

At Midnight Mass, the older boys of the village, dressed as shepherds, formed a living nativity scene. Théo knelt alongside a cow brought close to the manger to shed its warmth on the Christ Child. Monsieur Rivet, the town notary, Mayor Aimé Bonhomme, and Maurice, with his head wrapped in a dish-towel turban that kept coming undone, took the roles of the three wise men. The most recently born babe in the commune, the child of a former prisoner of war, lay in the straw. How deeply joyous his parents must have been to see him swaddled there in the manger. A line from a *chant de Noël,* "Born that man no more may die," came to mind. I considered that a babe born to freedom was more important than a painting. If it were my child, I would certainly think so. A woman wearing a lace-edged white shawl crossed over her breasts like folded wings stepped alongside the altar and, with the voice of an angel, sang "Gloria in Excelsis" in Occitan. If I hadn't been preoccupied with worry about someone else finding the paintings, her voice would have lifted me off the earth.

After the service, I lit ten candles—for André, Pascal, Maxime, Sister Marie Pierre, Bella, Marc, Pissarro, Cézanne, Modigliani, and Picasso. The flames cast a soft golden glow. But what did lighting a candle mean? I suppose it signified that I was asking God to take care of someone. But if God was all-knowing, I reasoned, He already knew my yearning and didn't require a candle to remind him. Still, I felt a need to say an individual prayer for each of them, an affirmation in my own words. I thought God would appreciate that more than my lighted candles, since He was already the source of light and goodness. Thinking that made me feel that all was well with them. That I could not see them or speak with them was not sufficient evidence that they were not living still.

At home, with my own candle illuminating Cézanne's fruit, I sat very still, thinking of the woman's singing, until I felt peace descend like the brush of an angel's wing. Then I ascended the stairs, humming the comfort of the Gloria and breathing in the frankincense of friendship.

BOOK IV

CHAPTER THIRTY

THE OLIVE
WREATH

1946

Ι WOKE UP ON CHRISTMAS MORNING KNOWING I HAD TO TELL Max about the painting that had been moved. It would be easier in a letter than in person. Still, I postponed writing it and went outside to milk Geneviève. Thinking that she might like a *chant de Noël* instead of "La Marseillaise," I tried "Il Est Né le Divin Enfant," but I sang without spirit, so no milk came. Agitated by my efforts, she butted me in the shoulder, and her horn tore my sleeve.

"Stop it! Now see what you've done? Why can't you be good, Geneviève, like you used to be?"

Over the last several months, she had become cantankerous in other ways too, butting her horns against the door and shredding the wood, knocking down the wire fence around the vegetable garden and chewing lettuce, cabbage, and carrot tops down to the roots. Louise had told me that she had outlived her usefulness and that I should take her to the butcher. It appalled me to hear that, but what did I know about animal husbandry? What I foresaw wasn't a pretty picture.

I stopped trying to milk her and just stroked her neck. I thanked her for the milk, and the milk of companionship, and went back into the house to write the letter—the shorter the better. I recounted what the miller had told me and ended with an urgent plea for Maxime to come as soon as he could get away, since it was evident now that someone had found that painting and could well be looking for the others, perhaps even finding them before I could.

I addressed the letter, stamped it, sealed it, and left it on the desk. It suddenly seemed a shabby thing to do, writing to him rather than waiting to tell him face-to-face. André had said that Maxime had taken a special interest in that painting. In the meantime, I would tell Pascal.

I headed downhill, and in place de la Mairie I sang out *"Joyeux Noël"* to the old men stalwart enough to be sitting outside the café. The air was exceptionally still in the cemetery. As I approached the simple Roux family tomb, I was surprised to see that a roughly made wreath of olive branches and red berries had been placed on it.

"Tell me, Pascal, who laid this wreath? Was it Louise? Maurice? Aimé? Odette?" It was curious. No one had mentioned a word to me. And why wasn't it made of pine branches this season of the year?

"I have some good news," I said, and I told him I had found the still life in the mine and the Pontoise paint factory in the Moulin de Sablon. "I know how you loved that little painting." My throat tightened to a straw. "I have some bad news too. The painting of modern heads that Jules bought was hidden in a windmill, and then someone took it. Now it could be anywhere, and whoever has it could be looking for the other paintings. I'm so sorry to tell you this. I'll keep looking, though."

There was no sense in telling Pascal about the German officer. All I could do was to kneel at Pascal's tomb and sing, "Ah! Quel Grand Mystère." *King of the universe, who gives life back to us by breaking our chains.*

I laid my cheek on the cold stone and knew I would mail the letter the next day, when the post office was open.

All the words of all the *chants de Noël* I'd ever known came to me as I strolled among the sleeping *Roussillonnais* in the graveyard, and I sang them.

At the back of the cemetery, a row of a dozen identical unmarked tombs had been placed very close together against the cliff. I assumed they were unoccupied, because the vertical slabs at the foot of the tombs were leaning askew. One was completely missing. Paintings could be hidden in them!

I bent down but couldn't see to the back of the tomb's dark interior. There was no other way but to crawl inside. Louise's *Vogue* magazines had once contained illustrated designs for couture jumpsuits appropriate for descending into bomb shelters. Not having the luxury of proper apparel, I checked behind me, saw no one, tucked the hem of my skirt into the leg openings of my underpants, and got down on my hands and knees. I crept in as warily as a cat, crunching dry leaves that had blown in. In the dimness, I jammed my knee hard against the rough edge of a raised stone slab. A painting could easily be beneath it. I ran my hands under it all the way to the back of the tomb, touched the cold fur of some small stiff animal, and recoiled, backing out quickly, my skirt sliding up.

"Looking for bones?"

The voice came from above. I yanked down my skirt and looked up the cliff. The constable stood at the edge, peering down at me with his arms crossed. He chuckled softly, amused but not taunting, it seemed to me. *"Joyeaux Noël,"* he said wryly.

I clenched my fists. "Why is it that you always find me at my most compromising moments?"

"My good fortune."

"You've been spying on me."

He gestured to the olive orchard behind him. "My home is in the orchard. I was assessing what pruning needs to be done when I heard someone singing, so I came to the edge to see who it might be. Père Noël gave me a gift—the view of two beautiful legs wiggling out of a tomb. What a pleasant resurrection."

Ouf! He never failed to exasperate me.

"By the way, you're bleeding."

Rivulets of blood trickled from a scrape on my shin. I wiped them away and then didn't know how to wipe the blood off my hand.

"Now you've gotten it dirty. You had better come up and wash it. Besides, you can see in all directions from here, the Vaucluse in all its glory. It's nearly as high as the Castrum."

How could I even consider following him after that encounter with the pomegranates? Yet a flash of alarm had streaked across his face when he had held me on the ground, and he had controlled himself and had helped me up. A man of contrary impulses, he was.

I looked down at my bloody leg.

"There's a pathway to your right, at the corner of the cemetery."

Was my agreeing to go up there what Maxime meant when he'd said I should not offend the constable?

"It's steep and treacherous," he said. "Are you afraid?"

"No!"

"No, you won't come, or no, you're not afraid?"

I hesitated, not quite knowing what I meant.

"A woman brave enough to crawl into tombs ought not to be afraid of heights, or anything else."

That was the last thing I wanted him to think, that I was afraid—of him.

I started up the path and slipped in my wooden-soled shoes. He came down and offered his hand to steady me, telling me where to step.

"This is certainly not the normal way you reach your house."

"I'm not taking you to my house. I'm taking you to see the view."

Was he avoiding having me in his house because I would find the painting of heads there? Or all the paintings still lost? I had to see. With Bernard pulling me, I scrambled up to the top. Now blood was on both of our hands.

"On second thought, you had better come inside so I can wash and bandage you."

"I don't need a bandage, but I should wash it."

I turned away from him and looked out over the stepped red clay rooftops of Roussillon. From this distance, I could not see the bare patches on walls where the rose and salmon and golden-ochre stucco had disintegrated or fallen off. With every window and roof and chimney at a different height, it appeared a storybook village, with an open ironwork cupola on the bell tower constructed so that mistral winds would blow through it.

"It's exhilarating," I said. "Like being up in *la tour Eiffel* or on the platform of Sacré-Coeur. Not that this is like Paris. It's just the thrill of being up high and having a grand view."

Surrounding Roussillon on both sides, bare vineyards and leafless orchards lined the slopes. The vegetable farms in the valley lay fallow now, waiting for spring planting, the soil dark and rich like chocolate. And beyond, the Luberons.

He led me along the periphery of the orchard. In one direction below us, the convoluted ochre canyons spread out from the wide, scooped-out bowl. Red and orange pinnacles and curving passageways had been scoured clean by wind and quarrymen.

"Don't go down there in the summer or when the ground is wet. And never go down alone. If you're interested, let me take you."

Making a wide circuit around his house, we could see, to the north, the Monts de Vaucluse and, beyond the ridges, the white limestone peak of Mont Ventoux. And on the knob of a nearby hill . . . "A windmill!" I cried.

"That's Moulin de Ferre. An olive-pressing mill. No one works it now."

The very mill where someone had put the study of heads and

then another someone had taken it! Bernard had a direct view of it. How could we ever sneak in to see if Monsieur Saulnier had overlooked it?

I ventured a safe question and watched his face. "Does anyone use it or go inside?"

"Only the miller, but I understand he has moved away. It will probaby fall into disrepair." Nothing in Bernard's expression revealed a thing.

The *pigeonniers* and two-story *cabanons* isolated in the fields were also excellent hiding places, but Bernard would be able to see me snooping around the ones on his side of the village hill, and that might antagonize him.

He pointed to the northeast, toward a castle in ruins at the top of Saint-Saturnin-lès-Apt, a medieval village nestled against the forested Plateau de Vaucluse. He explained that *Résistance* workers had hidden their armaments and explosives there and in Gordes, and he recounted the atrocity when a German soldier was killed by a *maquisard*. "In retaliation," he said, "a German platoon, maybe the same one that had come through Roussillon, rounded up villagers and massacred them in the central square."

"Yes, you told me."

He peered down at me as if to assess my reaction. There was something hinging on my knowing that, but I couldn't determine what it was. "Imagine how that *maquisard* must have felt" was all I thought it safe to say.

He ended that topic of conversation by remarking that the oak-covered hills were a prime truffle-hunting region.

After we'd circled his property, he noticed the blood still trickling down my leg. "*S'il vous plaît,*" he said politely. With that, I allowed him to lead me along the pathway to the back door of his house. We entered the large kitchen, where he turned on a faucet in the sink and out came water.

"Running water! How is it that you have running water?"

"A water tank on the roof. A flush toilet too."

"You must be the only one in town."

"Oh, no. Several homes on the hill have plumbing. Mayor Pina-tel's, Monsieur Voisin's home behind the café, the Hôtel de la Poste, and the *bastides*, the large estates in the valley."

He held a cloth under the faucet and crouched down to wipe my leg with it.

"I can do it myself!"

"Where would the pleasure be in that?"

Following Maxime's advice not to offend Bernard, I yielded to his attentions. He had a light touch and took great care to clean off all the blood. Then he ripped a strip off a dish towel and began to wrap it around my shin.

"There. Come into the dining room and sit until we're sure it has stopped bleeding."

A separate dining room! I was too inquisitive not to follow, and I felt safe enough. He had been nothing but a gentleman today.

The walls were bare. Shafts of pale sunlight poured in from four tall windows on the south side and fell across an oak table nearly four meters long. In the center was a white *compotier* of the style Cézanne painted, filled with beautiful ceramic fruit.

"These must be from Marseille," I said. Surely the hand of a wife had selected them. "Is there a Madame Blanc?"

He sat down opposite me at the table. "There was once. She died giving birth to our son. He only lived a matter of hours." He looked away, out the window and across the valley. "This would have been his tenth Christmas."

I glimpsed his double grief of losing two, just at his moment of high anticipation.

"I'm sorry," I said.

How strange to find myself feeling empathy toward this man. He brought his gaze back to me, which made me think he could see that the mention of his loss would naturally make me think of André. Sharing each other's pain, if only for a moment, suddenly felt like a mark of friendship.

"I've been thinking," he said, leaning his forearms on the table. "I've been thinking that maybe we could declare a truce."

This was not the constable I knew. I had to be wary. However, the mystery of the olive wreath was suddenly plain. The olive trees in his orchard had the same leaves as those in the wreath.

"You made that wreath, didn't you?"

"If you would ever come to the cemetery, I thought it might say what I've been unable to." He chewed on his lip. "I've decided to forgive you. In the spirit of the season."

"You? Forgive me?"

"For your act of retaliation with the shovel. I admit to goading you."

Remembering the splash, the desecration of his boots, the astonished fury on his face, I couldn't help but smile.

"I like a passionate woman," he said.

"The sausages made a graceful arc."

"Did you find them?"

"Yes."

"How did you get them?"

"I didn't. I left them for the foxes."

"Ah, of course. No upright woman would consider going after *those* sausages."

He chuckled, and maybe I did too. How curious and unexpected, our mutual amusement, but it felt right, and good.

"I admire you. For adapting to the rough life here."

That Bernard, that *someone,* had noticed gave me some dignity.

He reached behind himself to a cabinet and unfolded a street plan of Paris on the table between us. How foolish I was that a piece of paper could excite me.

"Oh, the Seine," I sighed. "And Île de la Cité."

"Show me where you lived."

I leaned over the map, running my finger from the point of the island downstream along the Left Bank of the Seine as if I were walking the distance, then turning in from the quay at rue du Bac and walking away from the river five blocks to boulevard Saint-Germain.

"Here! Just past the antiques shops. La Maison des Filles de la Charité Saint-Vincent-de-Paul."

"An orphanage?"

"Oh, it was beautiful there. Sister Marie Pierre was so kind to me and taught me hundreds of words. When I was too old for the orphanage, I lived in the workers' chambers. She found a good position for me at Maison Gérard Mulot, a *pâtisserie* and *confiserie* on rue de Seine. Here it is! And I met André here, on the corner of rue de Seine and boulevard Saint-Germain.

"Later, when painters moved to Montparnasse, we moved there for the sake of André's frame-making business. We used to go to the Dingo Bar and Closerie des Lilas and La Rotonde. We often went here"—I pointed—"to the Bobino or the Jockey Club to hear Kiki sing bawdy *canaille* songs full of double entendres. André liked them, but I preferred to hear Edith Piaf at Cabaret Gerny. Oh, how I love 'La Vie en Rose.' I admit, sometimes I do see things through rose-colored glasses. That was something about me that amused André. At the Folies Bergère we watched Josephine Baker perform in *La Revue Nègre,* wearing her skimpy skirt made of real bananas. And we danced the Charleston in the basement of La Coupole on boulevard Montparnasse. We felt cosmopolitan, bohemian, modern, and chic all at once."

My memories had tumbled out in a flood, and Bernard hadn't said a word. I sat back in my chair.

"I'm sorry. I've said too much."

"No, no. It's been a long time since there was any excitement in this house. Any feminine voice at all."

An awkward pause settled over the map between us.

"You look like Kiki with your short haircut."

"You know who she is?"

"You love Paris, don't you?"

"Of course I do."

"Better than Roussillon?"

After a moment's reflection, being careful not to disrespect Bernard, in accordance with Maxime's instruction, I asked, "Do you know Josephine Baker's song '*J'ai deux amours, mon pays et Paris*'? Her country was America. She loved them both. My country*side* is Provence. I could sing, 'I have two loves too, my village and Paris.' Don't make me choose."

"I'm going there this spring, or maybe summer," he said.

Aha! Just the information we needed. But how could I make him be more specific?

"You? To Paris?"

"Why is that so surprising?"

"In April? Or May or June?"

He lifted his shoulders noncommittally. His chest rose and fell with his pronounced breathing, and he reached across the table and grabbed my upper arm with some force.

"I want you to come with me."

I choked in surprise. I had been naked in my longing. The moment suspended possibility between us like a gaudy ornament. No. I would be trapped in a Paris hotel room with the wrong man. And yet I could keep him occupied while Maurice and Maxime searched his house. Would our plan require me to do *that*?

"I . . . No. I couldn't. I can't." I peeled his fingers off my arm and pushed my chair back.

"Don't be so quick to reject a gift."

My list. Vow number two. *Go to Paris, find Cezanne's* Card Players. I had to ignore the tantalizing tension that sped like a filament of light from his too-penetrating eyes to mine.

"Thank you. It's generous of you. You've always been generous to me, but I can't."

"Think about it, Lisette. We could see all the places you love. You don't have to tell me today."

How could I go with Bernard when it was with Maxime that I wanted to see Paris again? I stood up. "I have to leave." I headed for the kitchen door and stopped just outside. How to get down the cliff? I turned back to him, momentarily confused. He directed me around the outside of the house to the front, and a road.

"Think about it," he repeated. An uneven smile streaked across his face. "In between crawling into strange places."

I hurried down the road. Passing the cemetery, I looked back. He was standing at the edge of the cliff watching me as I ran away from the Paris I wanted with all my being, clomping my wooden-soled shoes noisily on the pavement, grabbing for the flapping bandage, looking like a fool.

CHAPTER THIRTY-ONE

PREPARATIONS

1947

On New Year's Day, Geneviève butted me from the rear and knocked me down. I landed in a pile of her poop. "Geneviève!" I shouted. "What's gotten into you? You've become a cranky old woman."

She *baa*ed at my anger and shrank away from me. Even though I had bred her twice, she refused to yield a drop.

What a way to start the new year. Picking myself up from her smelly mess, I couldn't help but smile, remembering the look on Bernard's face. Regardless, I felt myself becoming resigned to Louise's advice, but with this consolation—Geneviève, patron saint of Paris, in a supreme sacrifice, would help to pay my way to her city.

Perhaps for her sake, I put it off. Paris was too cold in January anyway.

The effect of seeing Bernard's map lasted for weeks, making me restless, making me dreamy, making me wary. In the city that inspired romance, where lovers embraced on bridges and in small squares, where the rippling river sang quiet love songs, the very things I adored there might set me off balance, like a spinning top, tipping me toward Maxime and then tilting me away, toward the memory of André.

But when Maxime wrote to me saying he couldn't come to Roussillon because he was hot on the trail of recovering one of Monsieur Laforgue's paintings, he asked me again to come to Paris and offered to pay for my ticket. I wouldn't hear of it, but I *was* torn. Stay here and look for my own missing paintings before the "someone else" found them, or go to Paris and be with Maxime?

Did I need to go? Yes. Someday. On my list, my hunger to go to Paris was accompanied by my vow to see Cézanne's *Card Players*. But was it right to go when I knew Maxime was waiting there to give me happiness, maybe even love? That I didn't know. With my yearnings in a tangle, the recurring question of my loyalty to André surfaced again.

Could a lost love endure when it wasn't fed with new intimacies, new causes for laughter, new secrets shared? Could it remain strong when all one had was memories and the places associated with them? I would not be able to be in Paris without the bittersweet draw toward those spots.

Despite my reservations, I said yes, yes I will, and it felt like the yes I had said spontaneously in the rowboat to André. The distinction between faithfulness and dogged stubbornness was not solid but porous. I would have to go in order to see where I stood.

I THREW MYSELF INTO a flurry of preparations. I had bought no new clothes since I had come to Roussillon, ten years earlier, and the maroon suit I'd worn on my way south had already been from a secondhand shop. Though it had once been selected by some woman in a Parisian boutique, it had not been quite au courant when I'd bought it. Nothing I owned was the least bit similar to anything in Louise's fashion magazines.

Christian Dior's New Look featured curvaceous lines accentuating very thin waists, as well as full skirts, a luxury only for the rich.

Dior had removed shoulder pads from jackets, considering them too reminiscent of military wear. My maroon suit jacket was prewar, so it didn't have the brand of militarism, but it wasn't tight-fitting at the waist. I took it to Odette to see if she could re-fashion it.

"Yes," she said, "but I need to look at designs."

We went together to Louise's salon and pored over her maga-zines. In *Marie Claire,* published in Vichy during the Occupation, Louise found what the fashion editors openly called "widows' patterns"—skirt pieces laid out on deconstructed men's trouser pieces.

"It wouldn't give you the new full look, but at least it would be something fresh," Odette said. "Did you put all of André's trousers in the giveaway box?"

"No. I have two—one for gardening, and one good pair in gray gabardine that he wore when we were married. I couldn't bear . . ." I hesitated. "How would I feel wearing that cloth to go and see Maxime?"

Odette laid her hand on my wrist. "It's been seven years, Li-sette."

"What's the difference between using André's trousers and un-raveling his sweater for Maxime's socks?" Louise asked.

"That was need. This is—well, vanity."

"You're wrong," Louise said. "This is need too. You *need* a gray gabardine skirt to make double use of your maroon jacket."

In the end, I agreed, and I spent the next day taking apart An-dré's wedding trousers and trying to salvage the thread, while sal-vaging the thread of memory as well—that first kiss as a married couple, and those moments of oneness when we said the same thing at the same time and then laughed. One night we had even had the same dream—that we were painters painting each other's portraits. What had prompted those dreams was gone forever, but the delight and closeness we had shared when we'd told each other remained.

As long as I could recall those moments, he was not totally lost to me. Wearing the fabric of his trousers would make it seem as though he were with me, a secret I would have to keep from Maxime.

How wonderful it would be if I had some good news to tell Maxime after the sad news in my last letter. I went to the *mairie* to ask Aimé Bonhomme for permission to look in abandoned houses.

"I was wondering when you would ask," Aimé said from his desk. He stacked up the papers he had been working on, grabbed his vest, and said, "Let's go right now."

There were two abandoned homes on rue des Bourgades, and another empty house below them in an untended olive orchard. He knocked on the door of the first one, which seemed an unnecessary precaution.

"Gypsies sometimes stay in them when they are moving through the countryside," he explained.

We entered cautiously, but we didn't find anything. That is to say, there wasn't a stick of furniture. Everything had been taken or burned for firewood; the house had been picked clean as the chicken bones scattered on the hearth. Aimé went up the creaking stairs alone, testing each step. Nothing.

The second house contained only a broken bed frame and glass from broken windows on the north side, where the shutters hadn't been fastened closed against mistrals. The house in the orchard was the most derelict. Mistrals had blown off some roof tiles, and rainwater had puddled in the upper story. The floorboards were rotten and groaned warnings when we stepped on them.

We spent the rest of the day looking in one sad, tumbledown house after another.

"Why are there so many empty houses?" I asked as we stepped across yet another rotten threshold.

"People get discouraged here. A winter too cold, a spring without rain, two bad harvests in a row, severe storms that beat down crops, vine-destroying insects, silkworm diseases, and they move to Apt or Avignon or Aix to try some other work. Or they leave because they want modern conveniences. Or perhaps miners without children died either as old bachelors or in the war."

"Would Pascal's house become dilapidated if I weren't here?"

"Most likely, unless you sell it. But nobody can buy now. Maybe in a decade. Roussillon could be a beautiful vacation spot if we bring indoor plumbing to the village and re-stucco the houses in all the warm colors of ochre, and make safe pathways and steps with railings in the ochre canyons, and enlarge the Hôtel de la Poste, and open a couple of good restaurants."

"Is that your dream?"

"Yes. And my son's. The houses too derelict to save could be razed, and small inns could be built."

"It would be a perfect setting."

"We think so. Artists and photographers would find plenty of subjects here. We could have concerts in the *salle des fêtes* or in the basin of the Sentier des Ocres and expand our Thursday market to include more crafts—pottery and wooden items and *santons* all year long."

We finished off the day by getting permission from Father Marc to search the church. All I noticed was those splintered kneelers.

Tired and dispirited, I said, "My paintings could be anywhere now if a Gypsy found them in one of those houses."

"If it was a *Roussillonnais* who hid them with the intention of retrieving them, he would know not to put them in an abandoned house that the Gypsies might use."

"But a Gypsy might have found one elsewhere and brought it to the house where he was staying," I said. "Do you think the person who found the painting in Monsieur Saulnier's windmill was a Gypsy?"

"Most likely. But he wouldn't keep it. He would sell it to some farmwife down the road, or in Avignon or Aix. I suggest you look just outside the village in *cabanons* and smaller buildings. Even in unused *pigeonniers.* If anyone challenges you, tell him you have my permission. Circle close to the village. Anything farther, you would have to notify Constable Blanc. Ask Maurice to lend you his bicycle."

"Thank you. I will."

"COME TOMORROW," MAURICE SAID when I asked him. "She will be ready for you tomorrow."

"Why not now? What does a bicycle have to do to get ready?"

"I need to prepare her." He wore that silly grin of his and put his right hand over his breast. "Trust the chevalier of the roads."

It wasn't ready the next day, but two days later he puffed out his chest in two mounds and said, "She is ready for you now. She needed tires, but there is no rubber for tires, so . . ." He wheeled the bicycle out of the shed in his courtyard and made an extravagant bowing gesture to the wheels. *"Voilà!"*

"Corks!"

"Forty-eight corks per wheel. I got them from Mélanie and Émile and strung them together with baling wire like beads on a string. More useful than a pearl necklace."

"Where did you get the wire?"

"From a farmer. A crying shame that here in Roussillon, where ochre is extracted to be used as a thickening agent in making rubber, and with so much ochre still underground, there is no rubber. Look. It works."

Maurice got on the bicycle, his bottom hanging down in two large country loaves, one on each side of the seat, his knees splayed out, and rode it around in a wobbly circle, saying, "See? Just like in the circus." He laughed, his belly jiggling, and pedaled faster, picking up speed, then holding his feet out to the sides away from the pedals, shouting, *"Oh là là! Attention, Lisette!* Here I come!"

His clowning around had been subdued during the war. It was heartening to see it again.

He hit a stone and nearly tipped over, then managed to skid to a stop just in front of me.

"Now you try it. Watch out for stones."

I wobbled just as he had. Every time the twist of the wire ends touched the ground, I felt a bump. The faster I went, the bumpier the ride.

"Perfect, Maurice! I love you for doing this!"

He held the gate open, and out I went, glimpsing Louise with both her hands on her cheeks, then concentrating on the narrow, rutted lane between houses, trying to keep from scraping my shoulder along a stucco wall, turning a successful corner onto rue de la Porte Heureuse, bumping along on the cobblestones, my teeth chattering, biting my tongue, going downhill faster and faster past a blur of red geraniums, steering through the Gothic arch, passing shouts on the *boules* court, down and down through Roussillon, scared to death.

I TOOK ONE-LANE COUNTRY roads lined with cypress wind buffers that marked the edges of farms. Aimé had been right about *cabanons* for another reason too—the thief had hidden two paintings in places that were characteristic of the Vaucluse. Judging from that, others just might be hidden in a *cabanon* or a *pigeonnier*. I stopped and looked in every one. If a *cabanon* was being used from time to time, it often had a rustic table, a single wooden chair, a string bed with a straw mattress, and a cooking pot. The *pigeonniers* smelled foul, and the floors were covered with droppings that would be shoveled out as fertilizer come spring. I couldn't imagine anyone who valued my paintings putting one in such a place. Despite that, I didn't overlook them. The least likely location would probably make the best hiding place.

I was getting farther and farther from the village, and I had taken so many turns between vineyards and wheat fields that I wasn't quite sure how to get back. When I spotted a tall, narrow *cabanon* that was probably right on the border between village and commune, I pedaled toward it. The inside was as rustic as the others, but on the small eating table there was a dusty pickle jar of dried lavender. I took this as a good sign of the sort of man who appreciated beauty, or at least nature.

Upstairs, a straw mattress lay on the floor with a rough woolen blanket spread neatly and tucked in. I lifted both. Nothing.

I pedaled toward home, made a wrong turn, was lost for a while, and had to double back. The light was fading on this short day of winter, and it was dark when I arrived in the village, exhausted, sore, despondent.

But I still had Paris ahead of me.

CHAPTER THIRTY-TWO

PARIS
AFTER ALL

1947

M AURICE WALKED WITH ME TO THE PLATFORM FOR THE train from Avignon to Paris, carrying my carpetbag and valise.

"Louise and I want to make sure you have a fine time," he said, pressing some folded francs into my hand.

"Oh, no, I can't accept this."

"Madame my wife will be upset with me if I bring it back. You don't want her to beat me with her skillet, do you?"

"No, but—"

"Or skin me alive and boil me like a potato?"

"No, but—"

"Or lock me outside in a mistral with only my underlinen on, making me do a polka to keep warm?"

The image of his frontal flesh heaving up and down was too much. I didn't want to hear any details.

"Stop. All right. I'll take it."

"And this too."

He handed me a folded piece of paper containing, I presumed, some more francs, because he had written on it, *Buy something pretty for Louise.*

"A scarf," he said, "or something else you think she will like. To show her that I love her."

"How sweet you are, Maurice." It was an aspect of him I hadn't recognized. So was his precaution to keep the three paintings in his house while I was gone.

On the platform, I stole sideways glances at what the women of Avignon were wearing. Some wore Dior's New Look, but others were still wearing dowdy mid-calf straight skirts and military shoulder pads. I was glad Odette had insisted that the skirt she made from André's trousers come to just below the knee.

"One more thing." Maurice held me by the shoulders and gave me a serious look, no longer playing the jester. "Do not hold back. Let yourself love. One note is not a song. It is only music when it combines with other notes."

I nodded and quickly got on board.

After the train pulled out, I unfolded the francs. One bill was the same one-hundred-franc note with the torn right corner that I had given Louise in payment for my haircut the week before.

Riding through the countryside, I saw, or imagined I saw, a white goat in every farmyard. Maurice had offered to take Geneviève to Apt while I was gone. He hadn't named the place, but I'd known what he meant. The slaughterhouse. I had aquiesced. The day before, I'd made sure she had enough water in her basin. I wanted her to be happy in the courtyard during her last days. Fresh spring grass had come up, along with the dandelions she loved.

We had a good conversation. I thanked her for providing all that milk for cheese, and for being a good companion. She promised with a soft look in her eyes that she wouldn't give Maurice any trouble along the way. I caressed her neck and head, and she leaned up against me and accepted my affection. I think she knew. When I thanked her for providing the means for me to go to Paris, she bleated in a sad sort of way.

I didn't like the idea of using my war widow's bank draft, intended for food and property taxes, for my train ticket, but I would replace that money with what Maurice would get for Geneviève. With that and my small marzipan income, I could check off vow number fourteen on my list: *Earn my way to Paris.* I had earned it by milking Geneviève and selling her cheese, thus saving what I would have spent on seven years' worth of cheese for myself.

MY EVERY MUSCLE TIGHTENED as the train pulled into the Gare de Lyon. I spotted Maxime from the train before he saw me. He held a nosegay of violets and was looking anxiously to the right and left. While he faced the other way, I walked within a meter of him and said, "Might I be the person you're searching for?"

He embraced me instantly, kissed me on both cheeks amid a stream of people hurrying by. Was it my imagination that the kisses contained more feeling and were more tenderly placed than the quick customary greetings between friends?

"You know you are. I've waited too long. *We've* waited too long."

I felt moth wings flutter in my throat, thinking he meant the two of us, but he said, "My mother insists that I bring you home right away." He remembered what was in his hand and pinned the nosegay to my lapel. "These are from her."

"They're lovely, Max, but what is from you?" I ventured.

"Only my heart," he murmured to the violets.

EVEN THE DANK SMELL of grease and soot in the *métro* excited me. I was back in Paris! We took the green line to Les Halles, where we had to walk through the interminable tunnel to Châtelet, which made my wooden soles echo embarrassingly. When we came out at Opéra, Maxime explained that his mother worked as a costumer at the Opéra. I stood a minute to take in the building's ornate façade, the row of entry arches, the slim columns between pilasters, the medallions, and, on the corners of the roof, the gold statues of winged muses. I sighed out my relief in seeing it intact in all its glory.

We walked along boulevard des Capucines, and I practically drooled as we passed café after café. "Oh, can't we just sit and have a *café crème*?" I asked. "I want to watch Paris promenade in front of me."

"Tomorrow," he said, his hand pressing the small of my back. "I promised her I would bring you directly."

Turning left, onto rue Laffitte, gave us an odd view up to *la basilique du* Sacré-Coeur, which looked from here as though it were sitting on top of *l'église* Notre-Dame-de-Lorette. We crossed boulevard Haussmann and turned right at rue Rossini, a narrow street of apartment buildings.

Going up the stairwell to the fourth floor, I was embarrassed again by the clackety-clack of my wooden soles and knew that the sound would be even louder on the way down. The first thing I needed to buy, maybe the only thing I could afford, was a pair of shoes with leather soles.

Madame Legrand met us in the parlor. She held out her arms as she came toward me, balancing on very high heels, and kissed me sweetly on both cheeks. She had dressed for my coming in a white silk blouse with long lapels edged in black and a black skirt, semi-full. Her dark hair, pulled back from her forehead into a dancer's chignon at the base of her long neck; her hands, as creamy as a fresh bar of soap; her cheeks, as luminious as the petal of a sweet pea when light passes through it; her ears, adorned with large pearl studs—everything about her was purely *classique*. Compared to her elegance, I knew I appeared young and flippant with my Kiki cut. Her instant casting away of ceremony, asking me to call her Héloïse, rendered me as butter in her hands.

Maxime carried my bags down the narrow corridor, while Héloïse and I followed. "You will have Maxime's room. He will be on the fifth floor. We haven't had a servant up there since my husband died."

She said it so matter-of-factly, almost casually, that it made me wonder if I could ever refer to André's death in a similar fashion.

The walls of Maxime's room were covered by art prints. I was fascinated by a Cubist print of Sacré-Coeur above a jumble of buildings at unnatural angles in shades of gray. A single peach-colored rose in a crystal vase sat on the dresser. The quilt on his narrow bed was a blue-on-blue paisley.

"The blue of the Mediterranean on a cloudless day in June," I said, "complete with wavelets. At least as I imagine it."

Héloïse murmured, "It's only a matter of time—a matter of time, and you will bathe in that silky water the color of a caress."

I was surprised to hear her utter something so evocative.

She served us *café crèmes* and madeleines, arranged as a daisy on a white china plate. The aroma of vanilla took me back to the days when I'd laid the shell-shaped tea cakes in a shingle pattern below the glass counter at Maison Gérard Mulot.

I admired the beautiful old china cabinet made of highly polished dark wood. André would have been able to identify the wood and appreciate its deep and intricate carving. I tried to examine discreetly the pair of amber crackle-glass sconces above the black marble fireplace. Feeling transported to another world, I sat as delicately as I could on the edge of a tufted sofa upholstered in a tapestry of gold roses against pale green leaves. I didn't want to be seduced by what Héloïse owned, but I had no problem allowing myself to be seduced by who she was.

Héloïse asked me about my trip; Maxime asked about Maurice and Louise. I was hoping he wouldn't ask about Geneviève, but he did. My voice quavered when I explained.

Héloïse deftly changed the subject by announcing that she was taking us to Au Petit Riche, a small bistro at the corner frequented by the backstage crews and the Opéra seamstresses. After the coffee and madeleines, and after Héloïse showed me photographs of Maxime in every year of his life, to his infinite embarrassment, off we went to the bistro. A surprise! There were paintings on the walls of scenes from operas. We ate *tournedos à la Rossini,* small beef tenderloins topped with slices of artichoke hearts covered with *sauce béarnaise* and garnished with a round of butter-fried goose liver. I hadn't eaten anything so rich since I had left Paris.

I asked her about her work at the Opéra, and she replied that she wasn't a *première,* so she designed only for the chorus. I asked if operas had been produced during the war.

"Yes. Wagner's Ring Cycle." She lowered her voice. "To see all the galleries in the theater packed with German uniforms was almost more than I could bear. Was I contributing to saving French culture by keeping the Opéra going, or was I betraying France by producing only operas with Nazi approval? Later we produced Wagner's *Tristan und Isolde.* Backstage, we were secretly thrilled by the *French* soprano singing Isolde.

"That was only monumental self-delusion. Ray Ventura's song should have alerted us. Remember, Max? We thought it funny."

He recited the words: " 'All is well, Madame la Marquise. The horses died, the stables and château were burned, your husband committed suicide, but don't worry. All is well.' "

"They performed it in cabarets," Héloïse said. "A sort of comic *Résistance.* In truth, my friends and I were heartsick at the destruction in Montmartre, even up to the very walls of Sacré-Coeur. Despite that, we had to believe we could resist the occupiers."

"How?"

"In subversive ways." She reflected a moment. "We wore yellow-and-black handkerchiefs in our breast pockets to mock the order for Jews to wear yellow stars. It was the rage among seamstresses."

I began to understand that Paris had been no peaceful haven.

"Countless times," I said, "I wished I had been here rather than in the south. If you don't mind, tell me what it was really like."

"Nightmarish. Puffed-up Prussian military bands marching

down the Champs-Élysées, pounding defeat into our hearts in 4/4 time. Nightmarish, too, the exodus, whole neighborhoods fleeing south, clogging the roads."

"Did you consider going?"

"Not for an instant. Maxime might find his way back. Also, for his sake, I considered it my duty to keep track of the art business. Oh, Lisette, the stream of trucks arriving at the Louvre and the Jeu de Paume to deliver paintings from across France to be sorted, sold, or destroyed, other trucks leaving with paintings to be loaded into freight cars headed for Germany. My sister and I stood helpless and horrified, watching paintings by Klee, Ernst, Picasso, Léger, so many, go up in flames in the garden of the Jeu de Paume. Without its art, Paris, all of France, would never be the same."

"I would have cried on the street."

"We did not allow ourselves that indulgence. We kept our heartache private and held our heads high in flamboyant hats made from absent husbands' or sons' fedoras, in order to give the impression that we were *gaie*. Denied the freedom of words in public, we spoke our resistance with feathers and bows and silk flowers, but behind our doors, we struggled to keep warm and fed. In spite of our awkward wooden-soled gait, we walked proudly past Nazi soldiers in a cloud of French perfume."

How subtle. How indomitable. "You made the streets of Paris into theater."

"Oh, *chérie,* the couturiers performed such miracles of grace and invention despite shortages and rationing, despite restrictions, despite the disappearance of foreign clientele. We gladly complied with government regulations that hemlines be raised to forty-five centimeters above the ground because we held to the belief that every saved meter of fabric might contribute to a quicker victory.

"Meanwhile, interminable ranks of German soldiers goose-stepped down the boulevard, and SS men rounded up vast numbers of Jews, no one knows how many. Our own French police, under German orders, grabbed young men coming out of *métro* stations for forced work across the border. Our grand hotels, the Crillon, the Majestic, the Lutetia, were taken over by the Nazis. But on Liberation Day, we were actually willing to see the Majestic burn to the ground if it took that to drive out the Nazis hiding there.

"Then came the reactionary executions of collaborators and black marketeers and *miliciens* who had tortured *résistants.* Nine thousand quick executions."

"That's hard to believe, or to stomach."

"We were inebriated with liberty in those days, and that sudden freedom was the seedbed for extremism. The shaving of women's heads for their *collaboration horizontale,* sleeping with the enemy, exposed their shame, but people had private shames as well." She waved her hand as if at gnats. "Enough of this. Let me tell you what we're going to do tomorrow."

"Unfortunately, I have to work tomorrow," Maxime said. "Monsieur Laforgue wants me to meet with someone who may have a lead about finding a painting."

"So I'm going to take you to Galeries Lafayette. Imagine! Christian Dior is designing ready-to-wear, and selling it there. The endless restrictions on numbers of buttons, pockets, skirt lengths, and the bans on double-breasted jackets, embroidery, and lace are— poof! Gone! By this time tomorrow, you will be dressed anew. It will be my pleasure to give you an ensemble."

"Oh, my goodness! You hardly know me."

"Oh, yes I do. Maxime tells me everything."

"That's very kind of you. Beyond kindness."

"The day after tomorrow," Maxime said with anticipatory buoyancy, "you and I will promenade the Seine, and I will introduce you to Monsieur Laforgue, and we will go to the Jeu de Paume, to see if—"

"If we can find Cézanne's *Card Players*!"

"Precisely."

—

MAXIME LINGERED AT THE doorway to my bedroom that evening. "I haven't been this happy for years," he said. He kissed me lightly, barely touching my lips, and drew my head against his shoulder. We stood in that embrace until I was sure it wasn't a dream, and then I entered the room that had been his since the innocence of his boyhood.

IN THE MORNING HÉLOÏSE filled the three blocks to Galeries Lafayette with her exuberance, explaining that she had quit the Opéra because she couldn't bear to work for the entertainment of German officers. Instead, she had taken a job as a *secondaire* at La Maison Paquin. They had just received an order for twenty gowns from a single customer, so they were hiring.

"Our ambassadors' wives needed to declare with fashion that France might have lost the war but Paris couture still held the admiration of Europe. The German government was preparing to move the whole French fashion industry to Berlin and Vienna. We were outraged. Lucien Lelong famously defied them and instantly became the hero of every seamstress in Paris. I posted his response, which was printed in *Vogue,* above my sewing machine and read it until I had it memorized: 'Couture is in Paris or it is nowhere. A Paris gown is not really made of cloth; it is made with the streets, the colonnades, the fountains. It is gleaned from life and from books and from museums and from serendipity. It is no more than a gown, and yet it is as if the whole country has woven this gown.'"

"And so the Germans relented?"

"Indeed they did. Whoever runs the world, we said, Paris intends on making his wife's clothes."

"Who ordered those twenty gowns?"

She pursed her lips. "Oh, Lisette. We weren't told until after the gowns were delivered. It was that lizard, Hermann Göring. I felt savagely tricked. Germans had infiltrated our businesses and institutions. Unemployed artisans could be forced to work in German industry. There were many shades of collaboration, some of them unwilling." She turned to me, and the smooth skin of her face tightened into fine lines. "I hope you don't judge me for this."

"How can I judge when I don't know what I would have done in your situation?"

"Right after liberation, I went back to work at the Opéra."

She opened the brass-and-glass door of Galeries Lafayette, and a flowery fragrance surrounded us. Balcony upon balcony rose ten stories under a circle of wide gilded arches around a glass cupola.

"There were days in Roussillon when I thought I would never see this again."

She squeezed my elbow, steering me to the Art Nouveau stairway. "Let's go directly to Dior ready-to-wear."

Dior's new softness was positively voluptuous. I loved the bows, fabric knots, and rosettes. Héloïse pulled a day dress off the rack and held out its lavish ballerina skirt.

"Eight meters, I would guess. I can see you proudly swinging that skirt down the Champs-Élysées. Try it on."

"Oh, no. It's much too—"

"Flamboyant?"

"I could never wear that in Roussillon."

"You're not going to live in that village forever, my dear. Pick out three more, any color but military gray, and try them all on."

I chose two fitted suits and another dress and modeled each one for her. After much gay discussion, we both agreed on a blue crêpe suit with a flowing skirt cut on the bias, black velvet piping on the collar, and a black velvet rosette at the shoulder.

"It's the blue of the Mediterranean, I'm sure," I said.

"And Maxime's eyes," she added.

Héloïse carried the suit box, and I carried a Galeries Lafayette shopping bag containing my old wooden-soled shoes, a pair of stockings, and a scarf for Louise as we walked down avenue de l'Opéra, both of us in leather shoes, my left one bought by me, the right one by her. We angled onto rue des Pyramides, continued on through the Tuileries, and had a lunch of a salami-and-anchovy baguette on a bench overlooking the Seine.

"Paris has emerged from the abyss," Héloïse said. "The beauty, the grace, and the wit of centuries bred along the banks of this river have not disappeared. The city is engaged in an act of revitalization, and we are its actors and actresses. You too."

"Me? How?"

"The swirl of your new blue skirt is an act of freedom."

"It's more than I expected. Everything is more than I expected."

"I want to tell you something, but I don't want to say it in front of my son. In 1937, we went to the Exposition Universelle and saw some paintings by Picasso."

"I know. He wrote to us about that."

"Maybe he wrote about *Guernica*. We saw it again in the *Art and Résistance* exhibit here after he returned. That pile of bodies in grotesque postures in black and white, like a cinema newsreel, depicted the rawest human emotion. Against my will, I was mesmerized by the horror. I imagined my son in it. I am certain every mother in the exhibit hall did the same.

"And *The Weeping Woman*. A tortured face, the woman stuffing a sharp-edged handkerchief like jagged ice into her mouth. Her eyes floated out of their sockets because of the flood of her tears. Do not let that be you, Lisette. We can destroy ourselves by grief and disillusion as surely as by bombs, only our life erodes more slowly."

After a few moments, she placed her hand gently over mine on my lap. "What Maxime wants, I want for him, and I would move heaven and earth for him if I could. Honesty compels me to tell you one thing, though, and I don't want it to upset you. The night before you came, Maxime had a nightmare again. He hasn't had one for a year."

My chest collapsed, and all my breath leaked out. "I am the cause of it."

"No. War was the cause of it. The prison yard was the cause of it. This is precisely what I am saying. Don't take it upon yourself. Some men would take to the bottle. Others might turn cold and uncommunicative. Still others might live bitter, revengeful lives. We can be grateful that Max has been spared those fates. He's melancholy at times, when he misses the men he lived with in prison. It's a loss that I cannot assuage. I have to tell you, though, that sometimes fury erupts in him when he thinks I pay too much attention to inconsequential domestic things."

"I feel inadequate to help him."

"Just be prepared, and understand that if he rages, it isn't meant to hurt your feelings. Go gently. That's all I mean. His heart is open but fragile."

I nodded, understanding. She seemed an angel, guiding me with wings of steel.

My vow number seven slid unwanted into my mind: *Find André's grave and the spot where he died.* I would cross it out when I got home and never mention it to Maxime.

CHAPTER THIRTY-THREE

PARIS, ENCORE ET TOUJOURS

1947

T HE NEXT MORNING, SLOWLY, WITH EXTRAVAGANT CARE, I put on the luscious blue suit. I heard a knock on my door and opened it to find Héloïse, so I turned in a pirouette to swirl the skirt.

"Splendid, Lisette. A perfect fit. That means you'll have a perfect day, the natural consequence of Paris fashion."

In the parlor, Maxime was waiting for me.

"*Oh là là!*"

"Is she not a Dior woman, the very picture of the New Look?"

"*Bien sûr. Sans doute.* A portrait of loveliness, with the shapeliness of a Dior model."

The charming Maxime who had teased me with his dalliance so long ago, alive again.

"The blue is exquisite on you."

"That's because it's the color of your eyes," I said, then glanced quickly at Héloïse to see if I had revealed too much. She nodded in agreement.

"Where are you off to first?" she asked.

"To breakfast in place Saint-Germain, then to pop into the galleries of rue de Seine until the Jeu de Paume opens."

"I can walk there," I said, pointing one toe forward in my new shoes.

"No, *chérie*. You'll be on your feet all day," Héloïse said. "Take the *métro*."

We three left the apartment together and walked to the Opéra, where Héloïse went in through a side door, to work, and Maxime and I descended into the *métro*. We came out at Saint-Germain.

"What's your pleasure? Café de Flore or Les Deux Magots?"

"Café de Flore. Maybe we can eavesdrop on an argument of existentialists." I laughed at myself. "Let's get an outer table on the terrace so I can see the spectacle across the street at Les Deux."

I spent a few enthralled moments watching the corner live and move and have its vibrant being *encore et toujours*. Again and always, it would be so.

"In Paris, one's home is in cafés, in squares, on bridges, don't you think? They allow us to lay claim to the city," I said, utterly happy.

"Truly, my erudite one."

"You call me that here, where intellectuals toss philosophy over their coffee cups? No, no. I'm just trying to get over being a provincial by wearing a Parisian suit."

"You were never a provincial, Lisette."

"You haven't seen me milk a goat. I got pretty good at it."

"Yes, I have. You've forgotten."

The memory sent a tiny bleat of sadness through me. Maxime rested his hand over mine as it lay in a shaft of sunlight slanting in under the scalloped awning. Despite my urgency to find *The Card Players* and to meet Monsieur Laforgue, we lingered in the warmth of the sun and of each other. Beneath our casual conversation lay the deeper issues—what we both thought about in solitary moments, and how revealing we ought to be.

I ventured an opening question. "Are you doing better? Are you more at peace?"

"Most of the time. When I'm busy with people in the gallery or

poring over documents of provenance, yes. But when I see something unexpected that reminds me, like an amputee, I'm thrown
into despair about man's hunger to hurt."

"It's not right that it lasts this long."

"Monsieur Laforgue still remembers things from the Great
War."

"You are not Monsieur Laforgue."

"True, but I am also not the same man you knew years ago."

I placed my hand on top of his, which was on top of mine, a
lumpy tower of knuckles. "Yes, you are. You showed me that this
morning when I came into the parlor. If a man is pushed and falls
into a mud puddle and is covered with muck, he is still the same
man."

He thought about that for some minutes.

"On second thought, you're a *better* man. We have to acknowledge that those waiting years have served to ripen in us the qualities
we need to go forward."

"Us? You also? Are you at peace?"

"Of course I miss him, especially during long evenings with little to do other than think where to search next. At other times, I'm
quite content. I have Maurice and Louise and Odette and her little
grandson, Théo. We make a family out of odds and ends."

"And the constable? No more throwing shit on his boots, Lisette." Maxime's crassness made me chuckle. It was so unlike him.
"Not that you have to make him a friend."

"He wants to be. In fact, more than a friend. He invited me to
go to Paris with him. I said no, of course."

"Were you tempted to say yes?"

I remembered the wreath, his venturing a truce, his revelation of
his sorrow, the fleeting mutuality of our griefs. "For a fraction of a
second, when I thought of Paris. But I wanted to be here with you."

"Lucky for me."

"Let's go." I set my napkin on the table.

—

THE ART IN THE galleries between the secondhand bookshops of the rue de Seine was widely varied. I was seeing work new to me, and I began developing opinions. I liked Matisse better than Léger or Duchamp.

Outside Galerie Laforgue, as aware of my unpreparedness as of the odds against me, as hopeful as I was doubtful, I strode across the threshold, knowing that I had a trump card in my handbag.

An older man, his thick, silver-white hair swept back from his forehead in a perfect wave, was talking on the telephone. While we waited, I was drawn to the paintings of Pierre Bonnard and Édouard Vuillard. Bonnard's paintings of the life of the streets and cafés made me feel a part of the grand sweep of Paris again. Maxime explained that Bonnard was a transition between Impressionism and abstract art. I tried to see it, but I didn't know enough. Vuillard's depiction of claustrophobic parlors and bedchambers and bathrooms—Parisian private life—piqued my curiosity but did not move me as much as Bonnard's streets and intimate domestic scenes.

When Monsieur Laforgue was free, Maxime introduced me as his good friend. "Remember before the war we spoke about the possibility of Madame Roux training to be an assistant?"

He thought awhile, as though it were an effort to remember such a little thing after all the catastrophes that had taken place. There was a mistiness in his eyes that suggested the losses he had suffered. He was on the razor's edge of saying no, he didn't remember, so I leapt in and said, "Just being in this room is a dream and a pleasure, monsieur."

"Ah. You like the Nabis and the Symbolists? How about the Intimists?" His eyes opened wide. "I saw you looking at them."

Did he notice my embarrassment at my ignorance? Those terms were as foreign to me as Arabic and Swahili.

"I . . . They're beautiful. I especially like the colors and the patterns of the fabrics."

I liked the nudes too but was embarrassed to say so. Despite my blank look and inane answer, Monsieur Laforgue treated me with the graciousness he would show to a wealthy client. That must be what Héloïse meant by the power of couture. His refined manners emboldened me to say, "If you will permit me, I would like to show you something that might interest you." I laid Pascal's pages of the wives' conversation on the broad desk in front of him.

He read for a few moments. "How is it that you have this, madame?"

I explained, then gave him time to read the rest.

"You say your grandfather wrote this?"

"My husband's grandfather. Yes. He knew both of the artists and their wives. He traded the frames he made for paintings."

Monsieur Laforgue cast a glance at Maxime. "Extraordinary. If this can be documented, it may be worth something. Did he keep records of his encounters with them?"

"Only a few notes. He was a simple man. He just told me what he could remember."

"So you know more of his conversations with Pissarro?"

"I know what he told me."

"And Cézanne?"

"Yes."

"Write it down, madame, as much as you can remember. Maxime, make sure that she does this. Firsthand recollections of these two great painters are of inestimable value."

He put the pages in a large, stiff envelope and handed them back to me. "Keep this safe."

"I may be able to find more of his notes."

"Excellent. Keep them all together and bring them when you come again."

Maxime tapped his index finger on Monsieur Laforgue's chest

and said, "Another day, when I bring her back, ask her about Chagall. She knew him during the war, and she knows his work."

I thanked Maxime with my eyes for supporting me.

"*Formidable!*" Monsieur Laforgue declared.

"Do you happen to know, monsieur, whether he and Bella are safe? I've had no way to find out," I said.

"They made it to America safely."

"Oh, thank you, monsieur. I've been so worried."

"In fact, there was a large exposition of forty years of his work at the Museum of Modern Art in New York."

"How wonderful for him."

A scowl of thought passed across Monsieur Laforgue's forehead. His penetrating gaze rested on me for a long moment, which made me uneasy. What did he know that he wasn't telling me? He added, "I may have kept a clipping. I will look in my files."

"Yes, please do. Marc—I mean Monsieur Chagall—gave me a painting that I believe he painted expressly for me."

"Astonishing! Is it signed?"

"Yes, with the words *May it be a blessing to you.*"

"*Merveilleux, madame!* I must see it someday."

Monsieur Laforgue came to the door with us, and Maxime went back to the gallery owner's desk to write something down. Monsieur Laforgue said, just to me, quietly, "Maxime is a great help to me. I rely on his spirit to keep me from discouragement."

"I'm glad to know that. It's my deepest wish to help you too," I said, "even if it's just dusting the frames."

He gave me the kind of gentle smile an uncle might give a niece, and on the strength of that, I swung my skirt and stepped out the door with Maxime following, my new shoes hardly touching the sidewalk.

CROSSING THE SEINE ON Pont des Arts, the iron footbridge linking the École des Beaux Arts to the Louvre, we observed its damage from an aerial bombardment. Despite this reminder of war, I was heartened by Monsieur Laforgue's report about the Chagalls. Maybe some wonderful day, I would see them again. I tossed a leaf off the upstream rail, and we hurried to the other rail in time to see it emerge. "See? That's a sign. When the Seine is flowing, life is flowing," I said.

We walked along the quay to place de la Concorde and the Galerie Nationale du Jeu de Paume. It had been open for only a few months, Maxime said.

"You've been in it?"

"Of course."

The ground floor displayed the precursors of Impressionism. Of them, I liked best Corot's fishermen's cottages at Sainte-Adresse. On the floor above, Maxime took me a roundabout way through the Impressionist galleries.

"I'm saving what you want to see most for last."

The way his eyes sparkled playfully made me hopeful that *The Card Players* would be just around the corner.

It didn't take much to sweep me up in the parade of color and inviting locales. In the Monet gallery, watery reflections quivered, regattas gave the Seine over to pleasure and sport, clouds of steam puffed out from Gare Saint-Lazare, and a black-and-white magpie sitting on the rail of a gate reigned benevolently over the tranquillity of a snowy field.

"It's the one you thought of in my courtyard, isn't it?"

He nodded, rapt. "It gives me peace."

In the ballet school scenes of Degas, slim dancers in frothy skirts held their raised legs in arabesques at the practice barre. In Caillebotte's snow-covered roofs of Paris, quietness and somberness prevailed, and in a scene of an empty room, floor scrapers prepared the wooden floor for refinishing. An unusual perspective, I remarked, and Maxime seemed pleased.

In front of Pissarro's Louveciennes cottages there stood the washerwomen and farmwives who had used his precious canvases as aprons. Still outraged, I told Maxime about it, feeling proud that I knew something he didn't.

"Do you understand now, Lisette? Even though you don't have an academic education, you have information and insights that trained dealers and critics don't necessarily have."

"Only of three painters."

"But that can build. You have deep feelings. And you have curiosity. I can help you. We can make contacts with painters. Here. In Paris."

"After I find my paintings."

I turned, and there were red roofs behind trees, looking very much like Pissarro's orchard and red roofs.

"Truly, Maxime. It looks like the same place as in Pascal's *Red Roofs, Corner of a Village, Winter.* He loved it for its warm colors."

"Do you see now what an important painting you have?"

"*Will* have, if I ever find it."

I GRASPED MAXIME'S ARM in excitement as we entered the large Cézanne gallery and strolled along Cézanne's rocky cliffs above the Mediterranean Sea at L'Estaque, through the upward reach of a grove of poplar trees, and in the countryside of the desolate *House of the Hanged Man.* With Maxime's guidance, I was seeing more— the wideness of Cézanne's brushstrokes, thickly painted passages alternating with thinly covered areas, vigorous reworkings, hesitations, corrections.

Two walls displayed still lifes. Apples, pears, peaches, oranges, even onions. A flowered pitcher. A figurine. The same white compote. The same green olive jar.

"Look at the spread of the paintings' dates. They show that he studied his whole life to give shape by color gradations," Maxime said.

I turned around, and there it was. *"Les Joueurs de Cartes!"* I burst out in a voice too loud for a gallery. "You knew it was here all along!"

He grinned. "You said you wanted to find it yourself."

Two players in profile seated at a small table faced each other and studied their cards in absorption. I could see that the bottle of wine between them on the table divided the scene into symmetrical halves.

"Those rustic touches convey that they are in a spartan farmhouse or a tavern," Maxime said.

"What rustic touches?"

"The table leans to the left. The sheen and stiffness of the table covering suggest that it's an oilcloth, not cotton. Even his brushwork is rough."

"Is that bad?"

"Not necessarily. It conveys his passion. Even though it's a simple composition, it shows the character of the men."

"They do look like *Provençaux*. Rumpled trousers. The hat of the man on the right. Pascal had a chamois hat just like that, the same yellowish tan with only a small curved brim, and a beige cotton jacket too. It *could be* him!"

My words spilled out in a tumble of syllables. "Just before he died, he said he had posed for this painting. I took it to be a dream or a fantasy, but it could be true, couldn't it, when he was younger? Pascal's droopy mustache must have been brown once, like this man's, under his pointed nose. His eyebrows *were* shorter than the width of his eyes, just like they are in this painting."

"We'll probably never know."

"Is there anyone we could ask?"

He smiled down at me indulgently. "I'll look into it."

It didn't matter what he would find out. In my heart, I knew. This was the painting Pascal had gone to Aix to buy. The card player *was* him. Someday I would tell *that* to Monsieur Laforgue.

CHAPTER THIRTY-FOUR

WINGED AND VICTORIOUS

1947

THE FOLLOWING DAY, WHEN MAXIME AND HÉLOÏSE BOTH had to work, I had several destinations on the Left Bank to visit alone. At place Saint-Michel, I passed flower sellers, fruit carts, postcard vendors, and stopped in front of an old man selling handmade wooden toys. I chose a *bilboquet* set, a cup on the end of a handle and a ball attached by a string, for Théo. The man took great delight in demonstrating a perfect plonk into the cup.

Strolling pleasantly through Saint-Germain-des-Prés, the quarter where I had grown up, I bought a *pain au chocolat* at Maison Gérard Mulot. The pretty counter girl seemed so young, but in truth, I had been her age when I had worked there. I asked the proprietress if my friend Jeannette, who had claimed she was a Gypsy, still worked there. No, the woman said in disgust. Jeannette had gone off with a German soldier and was never heard from again. I was momentarily stunned. Had she been apprehended? Was her head shaved? The pity of it overcame me as I left the shop.

The corner of boulevard Saint-Germain and rue des Saints-Pères, where André had gallantly given me, a stranger, his umbrella, opened the floodgates of lovely memories: the ease with which he had steered me around the broken edge of this very curb—there it was still; the leap of my heart when, after passing this corner on a dozen afternoons, I caught sight of the jaunty tilt of his black fedora; the excitement I felt when he recognized me, smiled broadly, and hurried toward me as I stood motionless, and said in his warm, slightly teasing voice, "I'm not going to let you get away this time"; the smooth way he ushered me into Debauve et Gallais, on rue des Saints-Pères, the elegant shop of the legendary chocolatier of His Majesty Charles X, where chocolates were displayed as though they were crown jewels, hardly to be eaten, only admired; André's invitation to pick out some to fill the dainty basket he placed in my hand, not knowing that I worked for the rival *pâtisserie et confiserie* a few streets away; that first lingering walk along the quays; that first *café crème* in the Bois de Boulogne, where he shared that he was a frame maker and an officer in the Guild of Encadreurs, and where we discovered that neither of us had siblings, that he had been raised by grandparents, and I by a nun. Through it all, like a magical thread of spun sugar, ran the delicious sense that a rainbow arched over us and that we were falling in love.

Approaching the Daughters of Charity of Saint-Vincent-de-Paul, on rue du Bac, I panicked. What if it had been bombed? I walked faster, my thoughts riveted to Sister Marie Pierre. I couldn't count all the words she had taught me or how many times she had rapped my knuckles with a spoon for biting my nails. She kept the spoon on a string in the folds of her habit for that express purpose. I used to tease her by saying that she was trying to steal the orphanage's silver.

Once, returning from an errand, I had said that the carved faces on Pont Neuf were ugly. What a mistake that was! She made me return to it every day for a week until I could clearly express what I found so ugly in them.

"If they are truly distasteful," she said, "defend their ugliness with facts. Don't just call them ugly out of mental laziness. Give me word pictures."

A week later, I gave her my report. "They are grotesque and exaggerated. Some are scowling like mean kings, some screaming like monsters, some staring with oversized eyes like flies. Some have pointed ears like the devil or horns like a ram. They're all different and all ugly," I insisted.

"Fine," she said. "What is another word for difference?"

I knew she was leading me to a conclusion I didn't want to admit. *"Individuality."*

"Good. Individuality is a beautiful quality."

"You tricked me!"

La Maison des Filles de la Charité Saint-Vincent-de-Paul was not damaged. It was just as I remembered it. In the public room, where parents could visit the children they had abandoned, I found her. We hugged instantly.

"Oh, bless you, child. I'd despaired of ever seeing you again." She shook her head, and the points of her starched white headdress jiggled at the sides of her head.

"And I you."

She guided me to a bench, and we sat close together. Her natural beauty and smooth, rose-tinged cheeks had not faded.

"My, you were an incessant questioner, always asking things like, Why do you have to wear those blue-gray habits? Wouldn't you rather wear pink in the summer? Does God care how we dress? How do I know if God cares about us at all? If He cared about me, why did He let my parents abandon me? Will I ever be loved by a man? And all that time I was loving you with all my heart."

"I know. I always felt that. You were like a mother to me."

She took my hand. "And you were like a daughter to me."

"You remember my husband, André? He was killed in the war.

I've been without him for seven years. And now I think I might be loved by another man, his closest friend."

Out spilled my tale of the last decade, all of it, including André's death, Maxime's tribulations in the prison camp, and my friendship with him. "My affection for this man is growing deeper. I feel such powerful stirrings that it seems there's no bottom to them. It's almost frightening to think where it might lead. I fear what André would think."

She listened intently, leaning forward, her hands clasped on her lap as though she was praying to know what to say. She had always been like that. Most of her devotions must have been spent in listening.

I summoned my courage. "Is it wrong for me to love again?"

"It is wrong for you not to love, under any circumstances, even those you explained. Sorrow can paralyze a person. Don't succumb to that temptation. Love broadly and deeply, Lisette, without demands, without expectation of love returned."

"But I do think it's returned."

She nodded. "That's good. I'm happy for you. But there must be discretion in love, and there must be honesty and action. Grief can be stubborn, and it can be perfunctory and can lead you to mistake something as love when it's false and only serves to assuage the vacancy you feel. However, if you feel joy when you do something unselfish for him, and would just as soon do it in secret as openly, then that rings of the true metal."

"Do you find it strange or wrong that from something so horrible something wonderful and loving can grow?"

"Not at all. That is God's mercy. Such an experience binds people together. Trust it."

She stroked and patted my forearm, her customary gesture of comfort. "Do you know why I'm here?"

"No."

"It's because I could not trust myself on the streets of Paris. They made me want too much. Their beauties and allurements trampled on discretion. That's why I sent you out on my errands."

"You mean you . . . ? I thought you sent me because you have crippled feet."

"I can walk perfectly well, but you needed to learn to walk the streets with discretion and alertness and your own joyous observations."

"But what a sacrifice—"

"Isn't that what we do for our children? As I said, love requires action."

"Yes, but . . ." I let my astonishment settle. "You helped me develop a good conscience. And you taught me to see."

"I taught you description and metaphor and appreciation."

I kissed her hand. "I appreciate *you*."

"God is with you, Lisette. I can see His most bountiful gift, the bright and morning star, in your eyes."

"It must be love that makes them shine."

MY NEXT DESTINATION WAS in Montparnasse, 182 rue de Vaugirard, the address on the paper from Marc Chagall, where I now imagined I might enter the art world and participate as a gallery assistant if Monsieur Laforgue wouldn't have me, or a seller of art supplies, or the housekeeper of a painter, or even as a model. Wearing my magical blue suit, swinging its flared skirt, clutching the scrap of paper, I walked with a firm step toward my destiny. Maybe I would find out from Marc's friend where the Chagalls were living so I could write to them and tell them how much I treasured Marc's painting. If they returned to France, maybe I could even visit them someday.

From Saint-Vincent's, I took boulevard Raspail and stopped at the corner of rue de Sèvres to pay my respects to Hôtel Lutetia, the glorious building that had housed returning prisoners of war after the Gestapo had been ousted, the building in which Maxime had begun his recovery, its beautiful rounded stone balcony overlooking the busy intersection itself a survivor.

On rue de Vaugirard, there were still huge bomb holes and damaged buildings in between structures that were being rebuilt. I began checking the addresses, my concern growing because more destruction was evident the farther I walked. The building at number 164 was intact, 168 partially intact; at 174, the façade had been blown off, and the roofless building was an empty shell; 182 and the rest of the street, a pile of rubble. Any remains of a sign with a name lay buried in fragmented stone. I put the paper with Marc's handwriting back in my handbag. I would keep it, a generous gesture from a famous painter.

With nothing else to do, I walked toward the street one block over, where André and I had lived, rue du Rennes, at an angle from rue de Vaugirard, and marveled that our building remained intact while others were in ruin or were being rebuilt.

I wandered through Montparnasse as a *flâneuse,* a social observer, watching Paris put itself together again, greeting plasterers and stone masons and shovel-bearing laborers with words of gratitude. I stopped to think at Le Select, on boulevard Montparnasse. I poured milk from a tiny pitcher into my *noisette* and concluded that whatever and whoever survived when the building or the being adjacent did not survive would always be beyond human understanding.

I would not let the lost opportunity of number 182 defeat me. There were other ways to gain entrance. Besides, the time wasn't right. I still had five paintings to find in Roussillon and the notes to write for Monsieur Laforgue.

MAXIME CAME HOME FROM work looking glum.

"What's wrong?" I asked.

He gestured to a sofa in the parlor, and I sank into its cushions. He unfolded a clipping from a Paris weekly and laid it on my lap. It had been written by Marc Chagall.

To the Artists of Paris,

Thirty-five years ago, as a very young man, like thousands of others, I came to Paris to fall in love with France and study French art.

In recent years I have felt unhappy that I couldn't be with you, my friends. My enemy forced me to take the road of exile. On that tragic road, I lost my wife, the companion of my life, the woman who was my inspiration, due to lack of a simple medication, all supplies having been sent to the Allies on the Continent. Thus, she was a victim of war as surely as any fallen soldier. I want to say to my friends in France that she joins me in this greeting, she who loved France and French art so faithfully. Her last joy was the liberation of Paris.

In the course of these years, the world was anxious about the fate of French civilization, of the legacy of French art. The absence of France seemed impossible, incomprehensible. Today the world hopes and believes that the years of struggle will make the content and spirit of French art even more profound, more than ever worthy of the great art epochs of the past.

I bow to the memory of those who disappeared, and of those who fell in the battle. I bow to your struggle, to your fight against the foe of art and life.

Now, when Paris is liberated, when the art of France is resurrected, the whole world too will, once and for all, be free of the satanic enemies who wanted to annihilate not just the body but also the soul—the soul, without which there is no life, no artistic creativity.

Dear friends, we are grateful to the destiny that kept you alive and allowed the light of your colors and your works to illuminate the sky darkened by the enemy. May your colors

and your creative effort have the strength to bring back
warmth and new belief in life, in the true life of France and
of the whole world.

October 19, 1944

The print blurred, my hands trembled, and I wept.

Max took my hand. "I am so sorry. I know how you loved her."

"He adored her."

"I am sure he did."

"How could this have happened? After the trials they must have faced to escape, it's so unfair."

Max cradled me in his arms. "Life isn't always fair."

OVER THE NEXT SEVERAL DAYS, Maxime did all he could to lift me out of the depths. We whirled around Paris doing the things André and I used to do. We rowed in the lagoon of Bois de Boulogne and Maxime sang the barcarole; we danced in the Bar Américain, the basement of La Coupole; we rode the carousel in place des Abbesses in lower Montmartre, thrilled that it had not been damaged. In the funicular up to Sacré-Coeur, Maxime encircled me with his arms in case I lost my balance, teasing me by not touching me.

As we walked the perimeter of Île de la Cité, Maxime pointed out the bullet holes in the Conciergerie, the notorious prison of the Revolution, where modern-day *résistants* began the battle that liberated Paris. We were solemn, respectful, but he was not morose. I took that as a sign that he was liberating himself. Perhaps now was the time for me to do the same.

I insisted that we climb the long Daru staircase in the Louvre, pausing at each step to appreciate the full marble glory of Nike of Samothrace, winged and victorious. Her commanding presence, well over three meters high and set on a tall pedestal, demanded that we look up in adoration. I was certain that I felt the wind ruffling her gown.

"What a victory it was to remove that for hiding," he said. "September third, the same day de Gaulle declared war. We volunteers gathered to watch, holding our breaths as she was lowered down the steps on runners and held upright by ropes. More than twenty centuries old, she is. It does me good to see her back in her rightful place, undamaged."

In the Musée Rodin we stood transfixed before the two entwined white marble figures of *The Kiss*. Equal partners in ardor, and on the cusp of passion, they were forever chaste.

On a stone bench just outside the museum, Maxime and I had the same idea, and we enacted it instinctively, without words. My arm curled around his neck; his hand grasped my hip. We brought our faces close, our lips a breath away from touching, imitating the eternal love of Rodin's lovers in our stillness. We held the pose, waiting for passersby to guess our play, which was not entirely play-acting. An older couple coming out of the museum holding hands stopped and whispered, catching on, chuckling gently at first, then laughing outright, sending all four of us into gales of robust laughter. We were part of the theater that was Paris.

In all the other things we did, André was our shadow companion, a gentle presence, neither raw nor guilt-inducing. I had Sister Marie Pierre and Maurice to thank for that. But our moment of playing Rodin's lovers was ours alone.

For our last night's dinner, Héloïse took us to Café le Procope, in Saint-Germain, the oldest café in Paris. Countless times I had passed under its sign, which announced that it had opened in 1686, but I had never so much as rested one toe on its threshold. We walked through a red room floored in black and white tiles, past red upholstered antique chairs, up a sweeping marble staircase past portraits in carved oval frames, marble busts, tapestries, fireplaces, framed letters from famous writers and philosophers, all beneath chandeliers that threw a soft light onto the floor-to-ceiling gold-and-red striped drapery.

"We have just stepped into the eighteenth century," I said.

"I adore this place. Robespierre and Marat ate here," she said in a hushed voice, as though an emissary of Louis XVI might overhear. "See that red table? Voltaire used it as a writing desk. This place is history and theater and intrigue and philosophy. Despite the woes of Paris, despite suffering, to me it spells permanence."

Maxime rolled his eyes. "Enough, *Maman*. Think about what you want to eat."

"I don't have to think. I already know. *Truite meunière aux amandes*. You must have it too, Lisette. It's the fish of the gods."

I didn't object. The trout arrived browned in butter under a scattering of toasted almond slices, complemented by white asparagus and potato sticks *pont neuf,* arranged like a bridge over a river, and garnished with a stuffed tomato and a radish tulip, dramatically composed, an art form framed by the wide gold embossed edge of the white china. Whenever she spoke during the rest of the evening, Héloïse cast a spell as alluring as the meal and the room itself. As a result, those were moments in which I did not think of Bella so sorrowfully.

I recounted to Héloïse how cleverly Maxime had told Monsieur Laforgue to ask me about Chagall.

"What was it that you were writing at his desk?" I asked.

"Your name. So he wouldn't forget when you come again."

"You have visited Maxime; now Maxime must visit you," Héloïse said, glancing at him. "I'm sure Roussillon is lovely this time of year."

"Will you come to help me look in the bories? There are so many, and those stones are so-o-o heavy." I said it with a touch of a whine, just how Maurice would have said it.

"I would help you if they weighed only a feather, but not until I make a sale for Monsieur Laforgue or find one of his stolen paintings. I'm working on a good lead for one. Thousands are lost in France, Belgium, and the Netherlands. It's overwhelming. I'm determined to help him."

"When might that be?"

"Impossible to say."

I slumped back in my chair.

"You must understand it as my way to set things right."

I had to yield to that, his attempt to emerge from his dark journey by an irrefutable act. And I had to get on with my own search, my own resurrection of French art. Marc would have wanted me to.

HÉLOÏSE LEFT US TO walk home alone through rain-washed streets glistening in the honey-yellow glow of the lantern-shaped streetlights. All of Paris seemed to belong to us, enchanting us, blessing us. Crossing back to the Right Bank on the ornate Pont Alexandre III, I felt so exquisitely joyful that if I did just a little hop there on the bridge, like Bella in Marc's painting after the Russian Revolution, I might be carried up horizontally over the Seine, over the sculpted cherubs and nymphs on the bridge, over the double row of lampposts, their globes splendid with golden light, over the four Fames on pedestals, winged and victorious. Feeling Bella's exultation allowed me to grieve for her less sharply. I dared to think she would have wanted it so. Was it being with Maxime or being in Paris or being with Maxime in Paris that did this to me?

A beautiful thought winged its way to me on that bridge. In André's dying cry of "Lisette!" he had given me to Maxime. So in Maxime, I still had André. There was no greater love than that.

CHAPTER THIRTY-FIVE

YET

1947

As soon as I arrived home from Paris, I began to search the house for any more of Pascal's notes. I dumped everything out of the desk and found notes of his encounter with Cézanne in Aix. I did the same with his dresser drawers and the pockets of every article of his clothing that was too tattered to give to the collection. I felt jubilant when I found in his satchel his account of what Pissarro had said about Pontoise. Certain lines struck me as significant:

> When a man finds a place he loves, he can endure the unspeakable.

I suppose he meant the desecration of his home by Prussian soldiers or the women of Louveciennes wearing his paintings as aprons. What had I endured? The loss of André. Also isolation, deprivation, loneliness, heat, and cold, but I doubted if Pissarro would have even been conscious of those things in his passionate moments making art.

> Pontoise was designed especially for me. The random pattern of cultivated fields and wild patches, the orchards that

have given their pears to generations, the rich smell of this earth, the windmills and water wheels and smokestacks, the stone houses all akilter, even the pigeons dumping on the tile roofs—everything here moves me.

Yes. I could imagine Pissarro thinking up that list. I found myself listing things in Roussillon and its surroundings that moved me—the panorama from the Castrum and the view from Bernard's house as well, the humped rows of deep purple lavender in July, the grapevines heavy with fruit in September, the cooing of doves in pairs, the village after a rain when the colors of the buildings were intensified, the fragrance of fruit trees in blossom in spring, the times when I picked cherries and grapes, the calm after a mistral, even the quiet in autumn on the day each year when I realized that the *cigales* had stopped their scraping noise. And, of course, the people.

Isn't there a hunger in every human being to find a place in the world that gives to him so richly that he wants to honor it by giving back something of worth?

Yes again. I felt the seed of that hunger growing. Listing those things I loved about Roussillon, as I had done once about Paris in a letter to Maxime, made me realize that I adored this village even though I had just come back from the only city I had once felt was worth inhabiting. Surely a woman, not just a painter, needs a place where she can nurture her individuality, where she can *become*.

Pascal had told me more than what those scraps of notes revealed. I realized I would have to try to remember for myself all that he had said, so over the next days, I wrote down everything I could remember in whatever order the memories came to me. I sliced my pages into snippets, then put the slices in an approximate chronology and wrote them again, in order. Later, I found that I remembered more, so I went through the process once again, thinking often of Marc's hope for the resurrection of French art, and my own longing that assembling Pascal's memories would contribute to the art heritage of France. Finding my paintings was now more than a personal goal.

I HAD TO FORCE MYSELF to wait through July and August, when the glaring sun made place de la Mairie into a heat trap, and the Sentier des Ocres a dangerous, scorching cauldron.

But now, the first of September, I couldn't wait any longer. Carrying Maxime's battery torch and the pair of André's shoes I had saved, I left home in the morning coolness, wearing my old wooden soles as if it were any other day, except that I wore a pair of André's work pants rolled up above my ankles, the pockets stuffed with socks. Now I did feel like a *Parisienne* disguised as a peasant, as Bernard had called me on the day of the flying sausages. Nevertheless, I walked with resolution down to the village center, up the incline at the other end, past the cemetery, to the Sentier des Ocres.

This first time wearing trousers, I was annoyed by the itchy sensation of the seams rubbing against my inner thighs. I wondered if men felt that itchiness or if, like many things, one just grew used to minor irritations. But losing the paintings, part of the patrimony of France, was no minor irritation.

I had very little to direct me in my search, except that the places where I had found two of them were essential to the character of Roussillon and its surroundings. The mine certainly was, as were the windmills that had once ground local wheat and olives. I wondered if a thief would have even considered the connection. Regardless of that, I went forward, since the ochre canyons made Roussillon unique.

At the beginning of the treacherous descent I put on the two pairs of André's socks to make his shoes fit and hid my own shoes under a purple sage bush. Not long after André and I had arrived in

Roussillon, we'd explored a little way into the canyon, just as far as the wide basin, but I couldn't remember seeing any obvious hiding places for paintings there. It was just a continuous sweep of rock. I knew I had to go deeper into the canyon than André and I had gone.

It was early enough that the slant of light made the cliff appear to glow from within. The wide swirl of rock in the basin was grooved horizontally, the lowest part a swath of golden ochre, which became salmon-colored above that and was followed by a wide band of orange, red-orange, cinnamon, and maroon at the higher reaches. Occasionally there were splashes of bright, egg-yolk yellow, broad streaks of creamy white, and, for contrast, deep green pine and juniper foliage growing impossibly out of the rock. Was this modern art or ancient art? I stood and gawked, a tiny creature in this enormous, wavy bowl beholding its grandeur.

I descended deeper where the canyon narrowed. A tall tapered pinnacle reminded me of the obelisk in the place de la Concorde. Quarrymen had scraped both sides of outcroppings, making them into thin, undulating walls, appearing sharp-edged at their tops.

Farther down the canyon, openings in the cliffs could once have been mines. Some had iron grates across them. Others were too high for me to reach. I crawled up to one that I could reach by grabbing pine branches and trunks to pull myself up. I turned on the torch to peer in and it slipped out of my grasp and tumbled down to where I had stood. I had to slide down carefully to get it and crawl back up. I might as well have saved myself the effort. Nothing was inside.

There was no single path for me to follow. Lesser paths and narrow passageways branched off to the sides. I went up each one as far as I could, shining the light into caves when I could get to them, and into vertical crevices of the fantasy formations, and then re-traced my steps and pressed on. I lost track of time. The midday heat made me swoon, and the *cigales* making screeching noises in the hot air were jubilant about the headache they gave me. Rivulets of sweat ran in pathways through ochre dust along my bare arms. Would that they were a map leading me to a painting.

Discouraged, I entered the mouth of a cave a little way up an incline just to rest in the coolness. Leaning against the rough wall, I dozed until the plaintive cooing of a mourning dove roused me. Just outside the cave opening, a pair of them were going about their sweet pecking business together, always aware of the whereabouts of each other. For a few moments, the world felt complete and harmonious. One flew off, and the other followed. Heartened, I proceeded with my search, crawling on hands and knees deeper into the cave.

A pile of creamy rocks, either ochre or limestone, shone in the shaft of light from my torch. I crawled toward it and began to dismantle the pile. At the level of the ground, I touched rough cloth. A burlap sack! In it, the texture of a painting on canvas. I thought my chest would burst. I felt like shouting, like dancing, like flying. I chuckled at the absurdity that not only had I randomly wandered into the thief's hiding place for shelter, but the evil thief had graciously provided a burlap sack. I brought it to the cave opening and took out the canvas. My ecstatic squeal brought bats flying out of the mouth of the cave. Cézanne's *Quarry of Bibémus* hidden in a quarried canyon! How droll. Was this just blind coincidence, or was the thief teasing me?

Clutching it against my chest in the sack, I slithered down the incline, landed on my derrière, and started off at a delirious trot. After some minutes, I stopped, bewildered. Nothing looked familiar.

Retracing my steps, I couldn't even find the opening to the cave. I wandered in one direction and another until I had to admit that I was utterly lost, confused, overheated, and frightened. The different angle of the sun had changed the colors and created unfamiliar shadows during the time I had been inside. The shadows of pinnacles now stretched across paths like grasping fingers. A dozen times

I turned in a circle, panicked, feeling that stinging sensation behind my eyes that comes just before tears, and then I forced myself to stop and think. I would have to walk uphill to get out. With that logic, I took any opening between trees and rocks that was inclined uphill.

The afternoon sun hammered on the top of my head, making me squint against its glare. Sweat dripped into my eyes and plastered my cotton blouse to my back. I rolled André's trousers up above my knees for some relief from the heat. I felt nauseous, dizzy, on the verge of fainting. Then I saw only swirling gray shapes against black, and my mind went blank. I came to, sprawled on the ground, with my face buried in a clump of gray rockrose, not knowing how long I had been there. Slowly, colors emerged from the grayness of my vision, retreating, emerging again, pulsating. I put my head between my knees until the dizziness eventually cleared, and tried to swallow moisture to ease my parched throat, to no avail. What good was a painting when I could die of heatstroke?

I remembered Pascal telling us to let the paintings care for us. All right. I would. I took the painting out of the sack to diminish the weight, held the stiff canvas over my head for shade, and rested until I felt steady enough to go on, stopping to catch my breath often, my upraised arms aching.

Eventually, far ahead, the pinnacle that resembled an obelisk stood like a beacon. I let out a cry of relief.

"Lisette!" I heard. Or was I hallucinating?

"Lisette!"

I kept climbing, holding the painting above my head.

"Lisette!"

Bernard came running downhill toward me, slipping and catching himself, holding an open umbrella and carrying an earthenware jug.

"Oh, my darling!" he cried as he reached me and lowered me down onto a rock. "I saw your shoes and I hurried down. You should never have come here by yourself. Didn't I warn you?"

I set the painting aside while he poured water into the cup of his hand, and I slurped it up. He poured it over my face and head and throat and swished it down my arms, and I let him, vaguely conscious of a new intimacy.

"I've been crazy with worry at the thought that you had come to harm."

I drank out of his palm again.

"Not too much," he warned. "You'll need it as we go up."

"I found a painting," I said weakly.

"I see that." He puffed out a breath and shook his head. "And I also see that you will go to extreme lengths—"

"I have no choice."

"At least I get another look at those pretty knees."

Instinctively, I glanced down at them and found that bat guano had stuck to my knees and shins. "Ugh!" I cried, pulling my pant legs over them. His soft chuckle did not offend me. My exasperation with him was milder this time. In fact, I was grateful. When my breathing returned to normal and the water had cooled me, I let him pull me upright. He put the jug in my right hand and the umbrella in my left hand, closing my fingers around it. A memory of a man's hand wrapping my fingers around the handle of another umbrella streaked across my mind, but I refused to allow myself to make a connection. Bernard carried the painting and took the liberty of putting his arm around my waist to help me walk uphill. I was too weak to resist.

At the road up to his house I handed back the umbrella and jug.

"Don't think I'm going to let you walk home now. You're coming to my house to rest and to eat something."

He let me wash in the bathroom sink. A working faucet! Warm water! Oh, what luxury. I saw myself in the mirror and shuddered. My hair was caked with orange powder, and dirt striped my cheeks and arms. A fresh bar of lavender soap lay in a saucer, making me suspicious that he had put it there especially for me. It was stamped with L'OCCITANE, just like the bar of soap he'd put in my lavender pot. I tried to reason what this might mean. If Occcitan was the former language of Provence, as Maurice had said, then *occitane,* ending with an *e,* might mean "woman of Occitania." Was Bernard suggesting that I was that woman of Occitania? That he wanted me to see myself as such? That I belonged here?

I soaped my face and legs and arms, filled the basin and dunked my head in, rinsing it as well as I could. But what to dry it on? It would stain his towel.

"Don't worry about the towel," he said from the kitchen. "It will be my souvenir of today."

When I came into the dining room with wet hair and dirty clothes, he said, "You look radiant." I felt myself blush, knowing full well that I looked bedraggled.

He served us both *poulet fricassée* with small, whole onions, carrots, celery, and mushrooms in a lemon-and-nutmeg sauce. I ate ravenously.

"My chicken never tastes this good. You are an excellent chef."

"I've learned a few things over the last eleven years."

We passed some minutes eating quietly. There existed a harmony in this house that surprised me and allowed me to relax. I could hardly believe him to be the same man as the one who had been so insolent years earlier.

"I'm glad you found a painting."

Strangely, he did sound sincere.

He propped it up on the sideboard.

"It's by Cézanne. Pascal loved it because it's an ochre quarry."

"Is that so? Then whoever put it there had a devilish sense of humor."

The conversation came to an abrupt halt. I set down my fork, suspicious. His face was unreadable. Against Maxime's advice, I was tempted to ask him for permission to look in the two remaining windmills, but if he said no, that would only alert him to our clandestine intentions.

"You should have seen yourself tramping up the hill holding it over your head like the spoils won by a conquering hero. Or, rather, heroine."

We finished the meal but sat rooted to our chairs, unsure of how to move the conversation to other topics.

"Is this your favorite painting?"

"No. There is one with a girl and a goat on a path alongside her vegetable plot. I love that one. I feel a strong personal connection to it."

"But this one, any one, moves you one step closer to leaving Roussillon."

"That's one way of looking at it. Another would be that I have found my lost painting and can take pleasure in seeing it again, and I can give it its rightful place in the legacy of French art."

He seemed to consider that for a few minutes, as though the larger thought had never occurred to him. "Maybe I could think of it that way too if it didn't mean your time here is shorter now." He clasped his hands, leaned forward on his forearms, and looked silently at the table. Eventually, he raised his head and studied me. "Forgive me if I hope that finding them takes a long time."

That left us both thinking thoughts at cross-purposes. Hesitantly, I asked if he had gone to Paris.

"Not yet. I'm waiting for your answer."

"Once you said you were not a patient man."

"You remember wrongly. I said I *was* patient, but only up to a point. You are teaching me patience."

"It's a hard thing, isn't it?"

"Yes. A very hard thing."

"You have been kind to me."

"No. I have been rude. Worse than rude."

"I am putting all that behind us." At the risk of offending him, I added, "But my answer hasn't changed."

"Yet."

CHAPTER THIRTY-SIX

J'AI DEUX AMOURS

1948

"We'll be trespassing, you know," Maxime said to Maurice in his courtyard, under Louise's disapproving eye.

Maurice's bushy eyebrows crawled toward each other in an exaggerated scowl. With the speed of a thought, it changed to a grin. "No! We are the rectifiers of a wrong, just like the knights of Occitania. Are you prepared to fight with sword and dagger for our rightful booty?" He held up a long crowbar and a short, hooked pry bar.

"Don't clown around, Maurice," Louise said. "This is serious." She turned to Maxime. "If I didn't love him, I would whip him into shape, but whipping would have no effect."

"Serious, indeed. And we will be successful." Maxime raised a fist high with his index finger extended. "I will not go back to Paris until we find a painting."

"Is that a promise?" I asked.

"'The day of glory has arrived. *Marchons! Marchons!*'" he sang, saluting Maurice.

It was surprising to see him adopting the Provençal temperament. His playfulness, exaggerated gestures, and theatricality I took to be evidence of his exultation at having sold a painting for Monsieur Laforgue, as well as the result of Maurice's influence.

"'*Aux armes, citoyens!*'" Maurice sang, holding aloft the pry bar.

Louise shook her head at Maurice. "Tonight you *citoyen* of France ought to kneel and thank heaven for giving you a wife who loves you enough to put up with your antics."

"Oh, wonderful," Maurice said in the heavily accented English of Maurice Chevalier. "Wonderful to be in love with you." Then, with a little dance step, he launched into song, also in English: "Every little breeze seems to whisper Louise."

Maxime joined in: "Birds in the trees seem to twitter Louise."

Maurice held his hand over his heart and sang: "Can it be true, someone like you could love me, Louise?"

I applauded.

"Ouf! Go on, all of you," Louise said.

WE SET OUT AT MIDNIGHT with a ladder, a rope, and the encouragement of having drunk a bottle of Émile's rosé.

"Be careful," Louise cautioned at the doorway. "Don't do anything dangerous."

"Ha! Art must always be dangerous," Maxime said.

I was hopeful. The week prior, Maurice and I had driven by the Moulin de l'Auro and had seen the door ajar. Now we climbed into Maurice's bus, which was again working on gas, with the cumbersome firebox removed, and crept along by moonlight without headlights.

The Moulin de l'Auro, our first windmill, dealt a severe blow to our clandestine operations. Tonight the door was secured with a padlock. Something was afoot. Did it mean there was a painting inside? We had to get in. There was a small window about three meters above the ground. Maurice patted his round belly. It was evident at once who should enter. I had had the foresight to wear André's trousers.

As much as possible, we worked without lighting our battery torches and without talking. Maurice propped the ladder against the windmill, and Maxime rigged a harness of the rope around my waist and under my arms. He went up first with the pry bar to loosen a screen. It was so rusty that it fell off with a clatter that made us wince. He came down, and then it was my turn, with him close behind me on the ladder. Held steady by Maxime, I entered the window feet first, then turned onto my stomach while Maxime and Maurice lowered me down with the rope until my feet touched solid earth.

Aiming my torch downward, I peered into every crevice, looked beneath a pile of grain sacks, examined each one, upended barrels, and felt around the central shaft. My hands discovered levers, gears, wheels, ropes, but no painting.

I climbed the steps to the second level, where the two massive grindstones lay horizontally, one on top of the other. The space between them would be a perfect hiding place, but how would anyone get a painting in there? It would have to be the miller, who would know which rope to hoist.

Just under the rounded cap of the windmill near my house was where I had found Pissarro's *La Petite Fabrique*, beneath neatly piled wooden blocks. Here, the blocks were scattered. They hid nothing. I went back down, my hope punctured, and was reaching for the rope, the signal to hoist me up, when my head hit something soft that moved, startling me.

"Wait!"

I investigated what seemed to be a suspended canvas funnel. Nothing was inside it. I moved a barrel beneath the window, climbed onto it, and gave the rope three hard yanks. Slowly, I felt myself being hoisted up.

We had high hopes about the other windmill, Moulin de Ferre, where Monsieur Saulnier had found the study of heads, thinking that he might have overlooked other paintings. It was unlocked. Jittery because this windmill was visible from Bernard's property, we searched quickly, not overlooking any possible place. No painting. Afraid that Bernard would appear out of nowhere, I couldn't get out of there fast enough.

SPRING. APRICOT TREES BLOSSOMING with pinkish-white petals like flakes of the moon, and plum blossoms like the down of swans filled our nostrils with sweetness as Maxime and I walked to the bories. Along the roadside, wild purple irises lifted their regal heads. I felt a bashful pride that Maxime was finally seeing the Vaucluse in its glory. I only hoped a mistral would not blow through. In spring they were the most fierce. Everything seemed to have its opposite—sweetness and harshness. Yet with the spring came asparagus and sweet peas and my delicate, pendulous haricots verts, and, along with them, hope that things would right themselves.

Searching the bories was hard work—lifting off those flat stones that covered ovens and replacing them. From time to time, we rested on stone slabs and leaned our backs against the walls.

"I have decided that the primitive people who lived in bories had to have had some sort of language," I said. "To express wonder about mysteries. The phases of the moon. Bird calls. Rain. The mistral. Language was the only way they could confront the mysteries together. They must have hungered to understand them."

"What other hungers did they have?" he asked.

I thought awhile. "The hunger to explain themselves. Actions can so easily be misunderstood."

At that, Bernard leapt into my thoughts. What was I to understand about the time when he'd pinned me down among the pomegranates until it appeared that he was appalled by his own actions, then helped me up? What was in him that had prevented him from taking advantage of me right there in the road? What had possessed him to be so gentle in washing the blood off my leg, or in taking tender care of me in the Sentier des Ocres? Yet he had grabbed my arm forcefully when he'd asked me to go to Paris with him. If he were more articulate, maybe then I could understand him. As it was, whatever made him have such contrary natures was a mystery to me.

Maxime said, "Misunderstanding is exactly why people need words to communicate their feelings."

Exactly, I thought.

"Like *thank you*. And *I'm hurting*," he added, a mere whisper.

"And like *I'm sorry*," I said.

At that moment I realized that even *with* language, we struggle to say the unsayable. "Maybe that's why we have art," I ventured.

"But art alone can't tell the whole story. We need words to explain *why* that woman's tears burst out of her eyes like bullets in Picasso's painting. It requires context in order to be understood fully."

That was obvious in the case of the Picasso painting, but in everyday life, sometimes it wasn't obvious.

"We also need words to help along our hungers," I said, conscious of changing the drift of conversation.

He regarded me quizzically. "For example?"

"The hunger to be touched can be augmented by the word *please*. Please."

His hand came to rest on mine, and after a while, he murmured, "Imagine them falling asleep close together, those early people. Peacefully, in utter darkness, with a dome of stone above them."

"Or in front of their borie in summer, under the dome of the sky."

"Sprinkled with lights," he added.

"It must have given them a sense of the infinite," I said.

"And of their own smallness and vulnerability." He moved so his body was against mine and put his arm around me. "Being vulnerable together is less frightening than being vulnerable alone."

IT WOULD BE WRONG to say that we found nothing that day, even though we came home without a painting.

THE NEXT MORNING I told Maxime my idea that the hiding places might represent aspects particular to the region. I had convinced myself that there had to be a painting in a borie even though we hadn't found one in the borie village. Maybe that was too far from Roussillon. I mentioned that in the fields nearby, miniature bories used as toolsheds and shelters by farmers had wooden doors with hinges bolted into the stone. We set out on a long amble down dirt farm roads and found that they had no padlocks. How trusting were the country folk.

After investigating more than a dozen, Maxime said, "No more, Lisette. I can barely drag my feet."

"Oh, please, just one more."

Up the road a short distance, a path led to a small borie in the middle of a field of broad-leafed melon plants. The door had been painted the coral color of the flesh of cantaloupes, a Roussillon hue.

"That one. Look. It's special. I promise. It will be the last."

We stepped carefully between mounded rows of plants, found the door unlocked, and ducked inside. Cézanne's panoramic landscape astonished us. It wasn't even covered. It had been propped up in front of the handles of shovels and hoes, as if the farmer wanted to see it every time he opened the door.

"If this farmer loves it this much, I hate to take it from him," I said.

"Don't get sentimental. It's rightfully yours, Lisette. This art-loving farmer could be the thief."

Maxime brought it out into the sunlight. It displayed so much of

Provence—cultivated fields dotted with ochre farmhouses, a string of distant buff-colored arches of a Roman bridge, a narrow country road, tall pine trees on the left, their trunks bare, with foliage only at their tops, and the grand Montagne Sainte-Victoire in the distance, a pale lavender monolith, triangular and imposing.

I changed my mind about André's favorite painting. This was so beautiful, so true to the region, that it had to have been his favorite. "Look, André!" I shouted to the sky. "Your favorite."

Behind us we heard someone approach, startling us. I spun around to face a farmer.

"*Bonjour,*" Maxime said.

The man dipped his head in a nod, a slight gesture. "Adieu."

That disconcerted Maxime, since he didn't know the custom here.

"*S'il vous plaît,* monsieur, do you own this field?" I asked.

"That I do."

"And this little borie?"

"Mine too. For my tools."

We introduced ourselves and learned that his name was Claude and that he had painted the door to match the flesh of his cantaloupes. I liked his self-expression.

"We apologize for trespassing," I said. "We have been looking for a painting that we believed was hidden in the area."

Deep lines appeared in his tanned, leathery cheeks. "Then I conclude that you have arrived at the right place," he said, gazing sadly at the painting.

Maxime explained, "We found it in your toolshed."

"So did I one day."

"Do you have any idea how it got there?"

"Strike me dead if I know. It just strolled in one night, as far as I can tell. It's been here for a few years."

"Do you know who put it there?"

"*Bof!* How can I know? Somebody needing to hide it, I'm guessing. Did you put it there?"

"No, but the painting belongs to me."

The slow realization of parting with it seeped into his old eyes.

"Then you must have it, madame, but be sure I'll miss it fierce. It always made me content, seeing it there when I opened the door of a morning and the light angled in over it. It's mighty pretty, to my mind."

"Yes, I agree. Thank you for protecting it."

He took a hoe from the shed. "Adieu," he said and shuffled away.

Baffled, amused, and a touch saddened, we walked home quietly in the somber, pale, end-of-day light.

"I LOVE THIS ONE," I said that evening, seeing it framed and hanging on the north wall. We'd had to move Chagall's painting over in order to put the landscape exactly where Pascal had hung it near the dining table.

"You love all of them."

"Not like this one. This one I tried to imagine when I was looking at the view through the outhouse window."

"Yes, well, don't you see? That view is your own. You own it. You relate to it in all seasons of the year. In just that way, Cézanne owned this view." Maxime's voice became soft. "He must have coaxed the landscape to reveal its secrets to him, its hills and folds. It was his act of love that passed into expression."

"Listening to Pascal, I came to think that Cézanne was some sort of mystic."

"Perhaps you could say that. He didn't just see nature. He contemplated the *idea* of nature. To him, Montagne Sainte-Victoire represented the pristine natural purity of the earth. Seeing only the tip of this mountain, like an iceberg, like you see here, he imagined its geological root. It was for him a descent into time before human culture, beneath centuries of superficial civilization."

I couldn't grasp all that Maxime was saying, but I surely did understand the slope of Claude's shoulders and the angle of his downcast head as he had walked away with his hoe.

"All of what you just said is in this painting?"

"In all of his paintings of the mountain, to one degree or another. This one has to be an early painting of the valley and mountain, but the more he worked on this subject, the more abstract his work became—less of a depiction and more of a pattern of geometric shapes done in broader brushstrokes."

"So is this early one inferior?"

"Not at all. It's just early. But his later paintings show that the geometric shapes of his landscapes opened the way for Picasso and others to use flat, hard-edged forms to depict a figure."

"Like our stick drawings on the courtyard wall!"

"If you like." He smiled at the notion.

"Then these paintings really are a trail of the history of art, like Marc Chagall said."

"Once you find the Picasso, if it truly is a Picasso, they are."

"But Chagall doesn't fit in."

"Yes, he does. At the end. The *visible* reality expressed through the handling of light and color of Impressionism—Pissarro—moved into the solid geometric shapes of Postimpressionism—Cézanne—to the modernism of distortion and Cubism—Picasso—and finally to the postmodernism of the expression of the *invisible* personal reality of dreams. That's Chagall. You have an important historic collection here, one that should never be dismantled."

My thoughts flew to Pascal. Had he understood that?

"Besides the Picasso, there are still two paintings missing. Pissarro's red roofs and the first one Pascal acquired, of the girl and her goat on the ochre path in Louveciennes. I have lived that painting, Max. Remembering it kept me going during the Occupation years."

"They'll turn up."

"So you say now. I don't know where else to look."

"But you *will* keep searching."

"Of course. It may not mean much to anyone else, but to me, the Louveciennes is a painting of Geneviève and me."

"Ah. You think it's personal now, just from memory? Believe me, when you find it, the more you study it face-to-face, and the more private, the more personal, the more singular the experience becomes, the deeper it will enter your soul. You watch. It can't be forced, but if you are patient, it will happen to you, and you will awaken in front of that painting with new eyes and with unexpected appreciations. When that happens, it transcends the personal. That's when you will know that it's a great painting."

"Oh, Maxime, I can hardly wait to see it."

"Does that mean you won't come to Paris again until you find it?"

I hesitated a moment too long, and Maxime pulled his bottom lip behind his new front teeth.

"I don't know. It's possible that I won't come permanently even after I find it." My words surprised me. I had to continue gently. "It's complicated. You remember Josephine Baker's song 'J'Ai Deux Amours,' don't you? *'Mon pays et Paris'*? My country*side* is Provence. My people are not just Parisians anymore. They are *Provençaux* too. I have expanded, Max. Now I can sing, 'I have two loves, my village and Paris.' I'm not ready to choose. I may never be ready."

A shadow passed over his eyes and darkened them into some unidentifiable, watery, frightening color of hurt.

ON MAXIME'S LAST EVENING we walked up to the Castrum, the highest point at the north end of the village, just as Bernard's house was the highest point south of the village. Our conversation grew quiet in preparation for the spectacle to come. In the foothills below, not a leaf fluttered in Émile Vernet's cherry orchard, but high above us, the wispy wave of a silken Parisian scarf, all peachy and rose, gave evidence of subtle currents of air.

Lingering as long as it could, sunset's sad joy filmed over the day with a delicate blush as our dear earth turned and the mighty sphere slipped below our sight behind Gordes to astonish the Azores. We squeezed each other's hand, knowing we had no choice but to let it go, and stood very still until the western sky exploded in tangerine fire and slowly settled itself to mauve, and finally to a dusk of great beauty, soft as eiderdown. If anything could heal, it was such a dusk after a day of glory. Holding each other, we dallied until the sky became unfathomable ink. With our faces up, we watched the universe wheel, dazzling us with its immensity. A shooting star took us by surprise.

"Did you see that?" I cried.

"Yes."

"Did you *feel* it?"

"Yes."

That a spark of the universe had leapt for joy at that exact instant was beyond our wildest expectations, but for now, that we had both witnessed it together in a moment of unity—that was enough. We turned for home.

AS WE CLIMBED THE STAIRS, Maxime's hands clasping my hips behind me, he chuckled and said, "Like Monsieur et Madame Borieman."

"Like Rodin's lovers," I said.

"Like Maxime and Lisette."

He followed me into my bedrooom. There was no question of what we would do.

We indulged our shy curiosities, greeting each bared revelation of each other with kisses and light caresses, coaxing the landscape of our bodies to reveal their secrets in their hills and folds. Always asking with a look and a pause, we delighted in our findings, uttering soft, grateful noises, answering them with tender advances. Need carried us on, moving us as one. From first touch to peaceful sleep, all was harmony, all solicitude, all love.

A NOISE DOWNSTAIRS JOLTED us awake, and we lay frozen for a moment, all of our muscles tense. We heard it again, as though an intruder had bumped into a chair. Instantly Maxime pulled on his trousers and lunged toward the stairs. I quickly lit an oil lamp, ran downstairs, and saw Maxime sock Bernard in the face, ribs, stomach. Punches flew, arms flailed, legs thrashed in a tangle.

"Stop, both of you!" I screamed. "Maxime, Bernard, stop!"

Bernard let loose one last defensive blow to Maxime's jaw, caught sight of me, and went limp, while Maxime kept pummeling him in wild fury. Bernard lay still on the floor, staring at me with glazed eyes, even when Maxime went for his throat.

"Maxime, stop!" I yanked his shoulder away, and he let go.

"Bernard, leave! Please!"

He gasped, "I'm sorry. I'm sorry, Lisette. I didn't know. I did wrong." Hunched and holding his ribs, he staggered out the door.

Maxime collapsed on the bottom stair, breathing heavily, his head in his hands. I knelt before him. His single muffled sob rent my heart in two.

"Now do you understand? This is what happens when you see cruelty for five years. It becomes . . . instinctive."

"But you did the right thing, protecting me. He would have come upstairs. What if you hadn't been here? I'm grateful to you, Max. He won't come back now."

"I got carried away. I should have stopped when he stopped fighting back. I didn't need to strangle him. That's the instinct that was drummed into us—fight to the death."

I laid my hand on the scar just below his knuckles. What could I say to wipe away instinct?

"You may have swallowed that training, but you can spit it out."

Maxime turned from me, a gesture as hurtful as a blow. He pulled himself up the stairs by the handrail, padded barefoot into Pascal's bedroom, and closed the door in my face.

HE LEFT THE NEXT morning, silent in what I took to be his hatred of the violence that had been unleashed in him, waving me back into the house when I stepped out to walk with him to Maurice's bus, his swollen jaw glowing purple as new lavender.

I ached for a word of affection.

CHAPTER THIRTY-SEVEN

THÉO'S
NEGOTIATION

1948

ALL DAY AFTER MAXIME LEFT I DID NOTHING BUT WALK IN circles in the courtyard, devastated by his gloom. I hated to think what he would tell Héloïse. Thinking about Bernard was just as agonizing.

When Maurice returned from Avignon the following day, he knocked on my door, came right in, and held out his arms for me. Gratefully, I stepped into his comfort, and stayed in his embrace until I was able to ask him how Maxime had been during the trip.

"Morose. He stared down at his bruised knuckles and didn't tell me what had happened until we were approaching Avignon."

"Did he ask about Bernard?"

"Yes. I told him Bernard has been pursuing you. He asked if you cared for him. I said I didn't know but probably not. I told you adored *him*—Maxime—and that you were excited before each of his visits."

"Did he think Bernard broke into the house to take the paintings or to get to me?"

"He didn't say."

"If Maxime hadn't been there, Bernard would have come right up the stairs."

"To molest you?"

"To try to seduce me. At least that's how I'm sure he sees it. But how could he even think I would want him to after he broke into my house like that? And why would he want the paintings now? It just doesn't make sense."

"No, it doesn't. He has never been the same since his wife died."

"That doesn't account for what he did." I chewed on my thumbnail, trying to puzzle it out. "What should I do?"

I thought I was only thinking the question, not saying it out loud, but Maurice responded, "You should write to Maxime. He's suffering."

"Yes. I know. We all are."

"You're the only one who can make it right."

THAT EVENING, I WROTE,

5 APRIL 1948

Dearest Maxime,

You must not feel remorse for what you did. You were only protecting me or the paintings. I realize that you think you were being excessive. It was only the heat of the moment that made you keep fighting after he had stopped. Try to forgive yourself for that. I like to think of forgiveness as a dove alighting on your shoulder and clearing the air with a wave of her wings. Maybe that picture will help you to put the event behind you. Remember that I'm grateful to you for saving me from an unpleasant, unwanted encounter. Bernard has been an erratic presence—kind and chivalrous one moment and inappropriate and rude the next. Maurice says he hasn't been the same since his wife died. That doesn't excuse his behavior, though it might explain it. Don't let it spoil the joy we felt earlier. Please allow yourself to let my affection lift you

*from undeserved self-reproach. Please come again when you
are ready. I love you, Max.*

Your Lisette

I waited a week for a response and then went to the post office,
where Sandrine's son, Théo, greeted me proudly.

"Howdy, Madame Roux. I'm an American cowboy today. American cowboys say *howdy*."

"*Adieu*, Théo. Cowboys in our Camargue region say *adieu*."

"*Maman* lets me be in charge here," he chirped. "No letters
today, Madame Roux, so you can play with me." His impish grin
was irresistible. He ducked under the post office counter, his knobby
knees sticking out of his short pants, and skipped toward me.

"*Bilboquet*. I want to play *bilboquet*."

"Where is the ball and cup I gave you?"

With chest thrust forward, he reached around to his back pocket
and whipped out the little wooden cup on a stick.

"*D'accord!*"

"No, madame. American cowboys say *okay*."

We went outside to place du Pasquier.

"You first," I said. "Three catches in a row wins."

He swung the ball, attached by a string to the handle, and caught
it in the cup. It made a little clunking sound. "*Un.*" He did it again.
"*Deux.*" The third time he missed.

"You missed on purpose, just so I would have to play."

He didn't deny my accusation. I took the stick from him and
swung the ball neatly into the cup.

"*Un,*" he said, his choirboy voice making the word into two rising syllables. "*Deux,*" he shouted.

I missed the third try too.

"You have to practice, madame. Practice. Come back tomorrow,
and I will teach you." He galloped back into the post office, slapping his side like an overzealous cowboy on horseback.

—

THE NEXT DAY HE knocked at my door in tears.

"I lost my *bilboquet* ball."

"Oh, no, Théo."

Through sobs he explained that he had been playing with it on place du Pasquier and the ball had broken loose and had flown off down the cliff, perhaps far below.

"And you came all the way up here to tell me?"

I brought him inside, and we sat together on the wooden settee, my arm around his narrow shoulders.

"Losing something is hard to get over. I've lost some things that were very important to me. I've even lost a person. Maybe two people."

"I never knew you were sad."

"Oh, sometimes. But we can't sink into our sadness, or we may not find a way to get out."

"Sink like in the sea?"

"Sink like in the mud."

"Ugh."

"There is a nun in Paris, Sister Marie Pierre, who raised me. Oh, how I love her. Just before I left the city to come here, I told her I would miss her and miss Paris. She said that as long as we grumble over some loss, we won't be able to open ourselves to anything new."

"Like a new *bilboquet* ball?"

"Yes, or like a completely new game."

"What can we play without a toy?"

"We can play Sister Marie Pierre."

He tipped his head, intrigued but skeptical.

"I did errands for her, and afterward she always asked me what I saw. I had to tell her precisely, with picture words.

"'What did you see along the river?' she often asked me, and I told her that I saw a tugboat pulling a barge. 'What was it carrying?' 'Coal.' 'What is coal like?' 'It's like itself.' 'But what other thing is it like?' She always demanded a comparison. 'Like chunks of midnight when there is no moon.' 'Ah.' Then she was satisfied.

"But on the next errand she would surprise me and ask what I heard along the street. When I could distinguish in words the sound of a lorry's horn as different from a boat's whistle on a particular kind of boat, she tricked me and asked, 'What did boulevard Saint-Germain smell like?' "

"Why that street?" asked Théo.

"Because there are bakeries and cafés there and a shop that sells perfume and soap. I had to say whether the aroma coming from the bakery was cinnamon or vanilla or almond, and whether the fragrance coming out of the open boutique door was like carnations or roses or lavender. Practice that in your grandparents' bakery, okay, cowboy? Does your *maman* let you walk through the whole village?"

"Yes, unless it's cold or raining."

"Good. You are a smart boy, so you can do this. I want you to walk from one end of the village to the other very slowly tomorrow, as many times as you like, and then tell me everything you saw and smelled and heard. See if you can remember their colors, and tell me *what each thing was like.*"

I drew him close so that he snuggled against me, which felt indescribably good.

My mind swirled with remembrances of that dear nun. I thought of one Christmas in particular, before I had learned that my parents had died, when I'd burst out, "I hate my parents for abandoning me here."

"That's not hate. That's loss," she'd said. "Be precise when you use words. Hate comes from a different place in the heart than loss. Now think about it for a week, and on New Year's Day, tell me what you have gained from that loss."

That had seemed impossible, and I'd complained that she wasn't being fair. We'd eyed each other sullenly for a week. On the first day of the year I'd managed to say, in a begrudging tone, that had they not left to do their missionary work and died somewhere, they would still have been so involved with it in Paris that they would not have given me the time and education I'd received at Saint-Vincent-de-Paul. In that way, she had taught me to substitute gratitude and forgiveness for hatred and loss.

And now I had to learn even more about forgiveness and loss. Would it never end?

I felt Théo tugging on my sleeve.

"I've been asking and asking, madame. What was the thing that you lost?"

"Three pictures."

"How did you lose them?"

"It's a long story." I gave his shoulder a squeeze.

"I can draw you a picture," he offered. "What would you like?"

"A picture of a girl and a goat walking on a path."

"I'll draw that picture if you write the long story to go with it."

"Maybe someday. When I know how the story ends."

TWO DAYS LATER, THÉO knocked on my door, jubilant.

"Did you find your *bilboquet* ball?"

"No, madame. I found something better."

"A new game?"

"A picture!"

"A picture? Where?"

"In the dump. I went all the way down there to look for my *bilboquet* ball, and I found a picture. Maybe you will like it."

"Did you take it?"

"No, madame. It wasn't mine."

I was already putting on André's shoes. "Take me there."

He skipped and ran the whole way, so eager he was to show me. The dump was far down the road that led up to Roussillon, in a clearing hidden behind a forested area.

"How did you know how to get here?"

"I went with my papa once."

In among the remains of animal carcasses, broken wine bottles, sardine tins, and other refuse, there it was, partially covered by greasy rags—the study of heads.

"Théo! It's mine! One of the lost ones!"

He let out a squeal and climbed over the mound of trash to retrieve it.

"Why don't they have any bodies?"

"I suppose the artist was only practicing on heads."

"They're ugly."

"Maybe that's why someone threw it away."

I grabbed him and swung him around, thanking him a dozen times at the top of my lungs.

"If I ever get to have a son, I want him to be a hero just like you!"

CHAPTER THIRTY-EIGHT

FOR BETTER
OR WORSE

1948

Two weeks passed without a letter. Every time I went to the post office, Théo said, in his high-pitched voice, "No letter today, madame. Have you written the story yet?"

"No, Théo. Not yet. I still don't know how it will end."

I avoided Louise and Maurice. I went to the post office less frequently because Sandrine would see my disappointment and would tell Odette. I didn't want to be the object of pity.

Spring proved to be wet and long. *Cigales* spread themselves on rocks, waiting for the summer's warmth to signal to the males that it was time to vibrate their stomachs to make their mating call. How ironic. A mating call. Waiting. Also ironic that I longed to hear their jagged cacophony.

Once, when overwhelmed with the weight of Maxime's last night, I crawled into the bed he had slept in and hugged the pillow to my chest. He was cruel not to answer my letter. He must have known by now that I loved him. I had shown him in every way, besides telling him outright in my letter. How could a relationship so whole and lovely end like this? And if it were to dissolve, who would be at fault? Bernard? Me? What should I have said to either of them that I had failed to say?

—

THE RAINS OF APRIL persisted for days on end, even into the beginning of May. When it wasn't raining, it was misting, and when it
wasn't misting, it was damp. I ate only what I had in the house and
in the root cellar. My war widow's check was probably waiting for
me at the post office, and I needed the money for food. On Thursday, market day in Roussillon, it was barely drizzling. I put on a
coat and head scarf and headed downhill with my market basket.

"*Two* letters, madame!" Théo shouted in a voice bursting with
victory. He handed them over the post office counter—my government check in his right hand and an envelope with no return address in his left.

At home I noticed the water-smeared postmark. Roussillon. Not
Paris. It had to be from Bernard. The date was obliterated. Had he
carried it in the rain? I opened it to *Dearest Lisette,* presumptuous
as always. In his own mixed-up mind, though, I supposed he genuinely felt that way.

> *You must know how deeply I regret entering your house un-*
> *invited. It was the unbridled act of a passionate man, an*
> *awkward, desperate man of the country untrained in the*
> *niceties that you, a Parisienne and a lady, deserve. My foolish*
> *hope was that you might feel more comfortable and free in*
> *your own house than in mine. I feared that my time to win*
> *your affection was running out. I was oblivious to the hour.*
> *Please believe this above all—I came not knowing what I*
> *would do. In any case, I had intended to be tender, merely of-*
> *fering. Despite what I have shown, I do have that capacity.*
> *Discovering that a man was with you, I instantly felt embar-*
> *rassment and shame for my ill-conceived action. I would*
> *have left, but by that time, he was on me.*
>
> *I have been troubled ever since by not knowing a way to*

apologize and to have you feel my genuine sincerity. I have fi-
nally thought of a way, and if you come to the cemetery
some afternoon, I will see you and come down the ravine
and we can make a promenade together. I will watch for you
every day at two o'clock, hoping that you can find it in your
heart to forgive me.

> *Humbly, your devoted*
> *Bernard*

I read the letter twice, three times. In spite of his prior vacilla-
tion between aggressiveness and retreat, his apology struck me as
earnest. Sister Marie Pierre had always advised me to give others
the benefit of the doubt. Maybe I was naïve, like André had often
said. Maybe I too easily believed Bernard's protests of good intentions, but his tone of contrition here was different from how he
spoke before his declaration of a truce in his dining room. Except
for this most egregious intrusion, he had done nothing after the
truce to annoy or taunt me.

But to forgive him? If his intrusion had caused the ruin of my
relationship with Maxime, I didn't know how I ever could. Yet a
surprising seed of softness told me it would be unkind to deny him
his effort at reconciliation. If I didn't, then living in the same village
where I could run into him any day would make me nervous. It was
better to confront him by intention rather than by accident. I had
to see him, even if it was just to determine my feelings and to find
out how far I was from forgiving.

More rain tore through the village the next day, beating the roof,
pocking the earth, sliding down windowpanes in sheets. I would be
a fool to go out in it. The next day was the same. On the third day,
the sky cleared and the sun ventured out, and so did I. The plaster
walls had absorbed the rain, and where Louise's house was pale
yellow-ochre in dry weather, it was now a rich golden ochre. All the

buildings and surrounding cliffs had taken on deeper tones, even tangerine, ruby red, and burgundy, enchanting me with love for the village.

I arrived at the cemetery at the appointed time without mishap but with apprehension. He was there, standing on the edge of the red-orange cliff.

"Lisette! Wait just one minute. Don't leave."

He backed through the orchard and came out carrying a pair of tall rubber galoshes and an umbrella, then scrambled down the eroded ravine.

Out of breath, he said, "I had almost given up hope. I've been out here every day at two o'clock."

"Even in the rain?"

"Every day."

A tight knot of resistance loosened a little.

He asked if it was too cool to take a walk. When I agreed to go, he offered the galoshes. Too small for him, they must have been his wife's. Inside each one was a thick sock. He held me by the shoulders while I pulled them on.

He said nothing about his intrusion or the fight—too mortified, probably. That was good. I didn't want to have to search my heart to condemn or to forgive just yet.

He suggested going to see the Usine Mathieu, the ochre works where ore was refined into pigments. It seemed an odd thing to do, but since I had never been there, I agreed.

From the cemetery we walked toward the village a little way, then turned off onto a narrow avenue that inclined steeply downhill. The houses became sparse and were surrounded by fruit trees, whose damp petals lay on the ground. One last red-roofed cottage had a vegetable garden, but the lettuce and beet greens and onion stalks had been beaten down by the storms, just like mine had been. As we walked he named the trees—oak, buckthorn, Spanish juniper, pistachio, on the right side below the road. And on the hill above us on the left, maple, snowball tree, and Aleppo pines.

We turned onto a lane leading to a large estate.

"The owners are away and have left me in charge, so we can visit the garden," he said.

We followed a promenade lined with plane trees toward an octagonal pool, each side of which was a bordered flower bed, the plants flattened and wet. "I was hoping to show it to you before the rains ruined it." Terraces and a balustrade led to the main house, which was grander than any I had seen in Roussillon. When I exclaimed at its beauty, Bernard chuckled. "I could show you a dozen more, hidden from the roads by hedges and woods. There are big landowners here. When this family returns, I will be invited to a grand soirée, and I am permitted to bring a companion. You."

He gave me a sideways glance to ascertain the effect of his words.

"As *garde champêtre*, I have the responsibility to protect farms, orchards, vineyards, wineries, olive oil mills, mines, quarries, and factories, so I'm free to show you the Usine Mathieu, where Pascal worked. Monsieur Mathieu was not the first to make pigment from ore. The process was discovered before him, in the late eighteenth century."

He was obviously trying to impress me with what he knew, with his position, and with Roussillon.

We turned onto a gravel drive that led to the ochre works, two buildings and a series of large open concrete sheds, each containing a huge furnace. Men nodded to Bernard and went right on stoking the furnaces with wood.

"You can see by the powder on the floors and on their clothing what color each furnace is producing. Farther down the hill are the original basins. They haven't been used for many years, since the operation was moved to another part of the property. I'll show you."

As we walked through a forest of oak trees, he explained that the ochre ore, quarried or mined, had to be separated from sand. It was ninety percent sand and ten percent pigments, he said. Pulverized ore of each color was first flushed with water, which ran through large-diameter pipes. Managing the flow of water was done by boys called washers.

"Pascal worked as a washer when he was a boy," I said.

"So did I, a generation later. Almost every fourteen-year-old boy in Roussillon did, unless he was the son of a farmer who needed him. There used to be twenty such factories and a thousand ochre workers and miners in the area."

Every pipe we saw had once emptied into its own narrow concrete canal, and for every canal, lower down the incline, there were several different levels of large rectangular concrete basins, some of them now cracked and overgrown with weeds.

"They are the old decantation beds. Each evening a flux of ochre, sand, and water was sent through the pipes to the canals and basins. The sand is heavy and sank quickly, while the ochre in suspension flowed down the canals into the basins. Throughout the night, when the water was still, the ochre settled at the bottom. In the morning, the water on the surface was released through small locks. In this way, the basins were filled with successive layers of ochre. When the ochre attained a thickness of fifty centimeters, no more water mix was allowed in, and the ochre remained in the basins for six months in order to dry. Then it was cut into bars and sent to the furnaces, where workers refined the colors by heating them at various temperatures for different lengths of time."

Bernard seemed pleased to explain the process. He looked from one canal and its pipe to another.

"I think this was the one I worked." He went back uphill a few steps. "No, I think it was that one." He stepped over a canal and helped me across. "I know how to tell." He walked up to the pipe and looked back to make sure I was following. All the pipes had wooden plugs about the diameter of a dinner plate. He wiggled this one until it came out.

"Reach inside," he said.

"No! There could be spiders in there."

He peered in. "No spiders. Reach in."

I had a premonition, so I did reach inside and felt the familiar roughness of a painting rolled inward loosely. I tugged at the edge. It came out easily and fell open.

"Pissarro's goat girl! My favorite! This is no coincidence. You *knew*!"

He raised his shoulders. His expression of acknowledgment was unreadable. Was it sadness? Embarrassment? Shame? I couldn't tell.

"It was you all along! Hiding all of the paintings. Wasn't it? Wasn't it?"

"Yes," he said, barely audibly.

"How did you get them?" I demanded. "How could you possibly have known?"

"You have to believe me. I didn't steal them." He took a deep breath. "André told me where they were."

"What? I don't believe you. He never—"

"He thought it would be foolish not to tell a second person in Roussillon."

"But why you? And why did you take them?"

"He *told* me to. He had only a few hours to remove them from their frames and work them off their stretchers and hide them. He never intended for them to remain under the woodpile. He wanted them hidden in safer places, each one in a different place. That way, if someone found one, that person wouldn't find them all. I only did what he asked me to."

It took me some minutes to grasp the truth. In a way, it was a relief to find out that André had confided in the *garde champêtre*—in his mind, the proper person. He had trusted Bernard, the arm of the law, to return them.

"Why didn't you give them to me when the war was over and the Germans had left? That was wrong of you."

"I know. I know. Please try to understand. I couldn't bear the thought of you leaving once you had your paintings back."

I felt my cheeks flush with anger.

"I'm so sorry that I put you through this long, drawn-out ordeal. For a while, I actually didn't know what I would do with them, but I admit, I wanted the search to take a long time. You see, I was falling in love with you. There. I said it."

"And so causing me anxiety was your way of expressing love? Bursting into my house at night was your way of expressing love?"

"It was wrong of me. Both things were wrong of me. But then a strange thing occurred. I began to hope that you *would* find them, for your sake, even though that would hasten the time when you would leave Roussillon. I couldn't tell you outright that I had hidden them or had them—that would make you hate me. But whenever I discovered that you had found one, I was both happy for you and sad for myself. Do you see how conflicted I was? I was in a desperate state the night I came to your house. I thought I might confess everything to you, lay my soul bare, and then leave. I didn't come to molest you."

Stunned, I stepped back a step and shook my head.

"Did you perhaps notice?" he asked softly. "I put the paintings in places that represented a feature of the region—the mine, the ochre canyon, a little borie in a melon field, the windmill close to your house so that you would find it. But not in any sad, dilapidated house, or derelict *cabanon,* or smelly *pigeonnier.* Nowhere ugly or depressing."

"What about the dump? You put a Picasso in the dump!"

"No. That had to have been someone else. I would never have done that, Lisette. I put it in Moulin de Ferre."

"Why all of these carefully chosen places?"

"In my own clumsy way, I thought that your search might lead you to appreciate what we have here, and might make you want to stay. I don't know what I would have done if you hadn't begun to search for them. I would have had to return them all to you together, I supposed, but I kept putting it off. I felt sure that doing that would make you leave Roussillon forever."

"But now? What about now? Why did you lead me to this painting?"

"Because as I began to understand your love for the paintings, I couldn't bear the thought of you not having the one you love above all the others. I began to feel another kind of love, a better kind. I don't know how to say it." His mouth was drawn to the side. "I know I have ruined any chance with you."

Then a deeper issue crossed my mind. I thought of the silk stockings, the sausages, and the chicken.

"You had another purpose at first, didn't you? During the Occupation, before you came to know me? The paintings would be wanted by Vichy officials. You could use them to buy favor." I felt my lips purse. Accusation lay on the tip of my tongue. "You didn't care that the Nazis were taking over France? That meant nothing to you? You know, I could charge you not just as a thief but as a collaborator."

His eyes revealed the grave risk he had taken today. They asked what he did not dare put into words: *I trust you not to betray me.*

"The Germans didn't get any valuable information from me. I was able to placate the scouts with false leads, at my own peril. There was a reason I aligned myself with Vichy. If the Germans were aware that the constable of Roussillon was supporting the Occupation, that might save our village from the fates of Gordes and Saint-Saturnin-lès-Apt."

For the first time, the possibility of an attack on Roussillon struck me as real. Two important citizens had been part of the *Résistance*—Maurice with his bus and Aimé, now the mayor. "Do you mean to say that if Maurice or Aimé were known to have caused the explosion of a German convoy—"

"The Germans would have retaliated. Maurice was not terribly secretive," Bernard explained.

"No, I suppose not. His nature is too exuberant for stealth."

"German scouts had their eyes on those two British women and that Irish fellow too. One mistake by any of the five, and Roussillon would have been destroyed."

That Bernard had risked his reputation for the safety of Roussillon settled heavily on me. But was that equal to fighting in the *Résistance,* or in the war itself? This was too big an issue for me to resolve at the moment. I thought of Héloïse saying there were degrees of collaboration. I had not judged her. With my eyes, I said what Bernard needed to know: *I don't understand you completely and probably never will, but I do understand you enough now not to reveal any of this.*

"One more thing. I know you haven't found the last painting."

"How do you know?"

"You will never find it. I had to give one away. I chose the largest. I thought that would satisfy them. But you must know this. If I had not taken them from the woodpile, as André had instructed me, and if you had found them there and removed them, I am sure they would have hurt you to get them."

The rubber bludgeon flashed across my mind.

"So if you hadn't removed them, the Germans would have gotten them. But how did that officer know I had *any* paintings?"

"Someone told. Someone who could benefit by giving that information. Someone did that ransacking, don't forget. It wasn't me. I suspect Mayor Pinatel might have been the one. To ingratiate himself with the new regime, in order to keep his position or get a more important one. I'm sorry for what I've done, what I thought I had to do, but I thought it might be the only way to get them to leave you alone. I was praying that you would tell that lieutenant before he hurt you and that then, seeing your shock and disappointment, he would let you go."

I needed time to sort everything out. Bernard had put me through an unjustifiable sorrow, perhaps even the loss of Maxime, though he could not have anticipated that. And yet without him, the paintings would surely have been lost. He'd collaborated to the degree he felt would do no harm and would save his village and neighbors—

and yet he had sought to appease evil, not to fight it. His motives were both honorable and dishonorable. All I could conclude was that he was thoroughly human.

I gazed down at the painting.

"I'm glad you didn't give them this one. I have *lived* this painting, Bernard. It is my life in paint."

My tears spilled—because of the girl's innocent trust, because I had thought I would never see her again, because of the white goat in the painting, because of ending Geneviève's life.

I told Bernard about having to do that. He drew me to his chest, and I didn't resist. He was of the country, so he could understand, in a way Max never would, the sorrow of slaughtering a goat that had become a friend. What Maxime had to do to maintain his equanimity prevented him from contemplating slaughter. But Bernard knew a less complicated grief.

"It's not just the beauty of the painting that I love. It's more— the truth of it. See how the girl is walking along a path that curves? She can't see where it leads, but she has to go on anyway."

Gently, Bernard laid his hand on my head. "Like all of us, for better or worse."

CHAPTER THIRTY-NINE

THE LETTER AND
THE SONG

1948

9 MAY 1948

Dearest Maxime,

The first acquired is home at last. And the study of heads as well. I am on fire with them. You must come. I will disclose the last mystery of Roussillon only to you. You must promise to tell no one. This has to be handled with the utmost delicacy.

Do not berate yourself, Max, about that encounter. When I was a little girl, Sister Marie Pierre made me memorize this: To every thing there is a season. A time to kill and a time to heal; a time to weep and a time to laugh; a time to mourn and a time to dance.

Take that to heart and come for the Fête de la Saint-Jean-Baptiste, Midsummer Night, and we shall dance around the bonfire at the Castrum and look over the cliffs to see the small bonfires across the countryside. Even the shepherds in their mountain bories will have their little flames, and all of Provence will feel the healing time together.

I will host a veillée to celebrate Pascal's paintings, and you above all will know their meaning and their worth. It will not be complete without you, so put your dark thoughts away. Forever, dear Max. They are not in accord with your true nature.

A streak of impishness flashed through me, and I wrote,

I can't expect you to remember how to get here after nearly five long years—oh, I mean weeks. My mistake. With no letter from you, it only seems like years. So don't forget that mine is the last house on rue de la Porte Heureuse. Engrave that street name in your heart. In case you've forgotten, the house is rosy ochre.

I will not breathe until you arrive. Bring sugar— granulated and powdered.

Lisette Irène

I marched downhill with a purpose and strode into the post office.

"Howdy, Madame Roux!" Théo took the letter from me and peered at it. "I can read a little now. I have been practicing so I can read your story someday."

Such a darling, eager child. "I haven't written it yet, but when I do, it will have you in it toward the end."

He studied my envelope. "*Oh là là!*" he exclaimed, imitating his grandmother Odette. "This goes to Paris, so it must be very important."

"You are right, Théo. It is very important."

Holding my breath, I watched him slide the letter into the slot of the wooden box marked POSTE.

"Are you sad today, madame?"

"No, Théo. You make me happy."

"*S'il vous plaît,* will you make a promenade with me? Will you? Will you?"

"A very short one. I am only going to the cemetery." I glanced at Sandrine for her approval.

"That's fine," she said. "He likes to pretend to read the names on the tombs, just like he does with letters here."

"I do not pretend! I know how, a little."

"And every day, you are learning more," I said.

I took his hand in mine, smooth as an eggshell, a hand that had not known the vineyard or the mine, or the evil coolness of slick gray steel. It was a privilege to hold that hand as we climbed the incline to the graveyard. I let him open the iron gate, which squeaked on its rusty hinges. He led me to his favorite monument, the one adorned with a graceful angel.

"Anne-Marie—" he sounded out, then pinched his lips together for a *B*.

My heart took a plunge. "Blanc." I had never noticed.

"What else does it say?"

In hardly more than a whisper, I read, " 'Your loving spirit enchants me still.' "

How hard it must be for Bernard to look down upon that angel. I wondered how he had managed his loneliness for twelve years. We had that in common, as well as an aching heart.

Théo followed me to Pascal's tomb and helped me pick off every oleander leaf. He looked at the engraving curiously. "Pascal Édouard Roux—1852 to 1939. Is that a long life?"

"A very long life."

"Was he your *grandpère*?"

"No. He was my husband's *grandpère*. I wish he had been mine, but that doesn't matter. What we are to each other is what matters."

I gazed at Théo with what I knew to be longing.

He examined the tombs on both sides of Pascal's, as though looking for someone's, and then wandered through the aisles. His childlike voice sounded out a few one-syllable names, and in a few minutes I heard the squeak of the gate as he left.

"Howdy, Pascal," I said with a chuckle. "A dear little boy taught me that American word.

"Are you listening? I have all the paintings back except the red roofs of Pontoise, even the Louveciennes painting. I know how important that one was to you. You were living in Paris then, and the family vegetable garden in the painting must have reminded you of your mother's garden in Roussillon. The moment you noticed the yellow-ochre path and the mellow golden-ochre light bouncing off the cottages—the moment you recognized the ochre you mined— you must have felt elation, and a sense of purpose. That moment was the beginning of our story. All that has happened since then arose from that instant.

"I found some of your notes and have been writing down what you told me of your memories. An art dealer in Paris thinks they are important to the patrimony of France. That should please you."

Saying any more than that would be a foolish fancy. He was not there. But someone else was.

From the olive trees on the cliff I heard a baritone voice singing, slow and measured.

> "*J'attendrai.*
> *Le jour et la nuit, j'attendrai toujours*
> *Ton retour.*"

Such longing descended delicately, and was aching in its repetition.

> "I will wait.
> Day and night, I will wait forever
> For your return.
> For the bird that flies away comes back
> To search for the one it left behind
> In the nest."

He was holding the branch of an olive tree above him, as if to steady himself as he looked down at me. Again and again the refrain of desire and yearning glided slowly down the cliff. We had heard it every night on the radio in the café during the war. Rina Ketty had sung it then, and the heart of every Frenchwoman had pulsed with hope to its slow, rhythmic promise.

Now, hearing Bernard sing it to me so ardently, so sadly, I was overwhelmed beyond expression. At that fleeting moment, I thought that, under other circumstances—and without Maxime, of course—Bernard might have had a chance. As it was, all I could do was stand utterly still with my hand over my heart until he finished the song, turned, and disappeared into the orchard.

CHAPTER FORTY

TRUTH

1948

"BONJOUR!" CAME A JOYFUL CALL FROM THE STREET. "IS THIS the house of Madame Lisette Irène Roux? It's salmon-colored, what oil painters would call cadmium orange, not rosy ochre, but it's on rue de la Porte Heureuse. She will be happy today on the Street of the Happy Door because I am standing at that very door with a special delivery."

The voice, Maxime's for sure, kept on talking to the closed door even though it took me a few moments to reach it.

"Max! You've come!"

He was burdened down with five bulging shopping bags, his valise of clothes, and a bouquet of white roses wrapped in damp newspaper held under his armpit.

"What in the world . . . ?"

He let his packages fall to the floor, shook out his hands, and presented me with the bouquet, bowing a little on one leg and letting the other leg dangle behind him.

"I couldn't let that little man in Chagall's painting outdo me. Do I have it right? His right leg dangling behind?"

"Oh, Max. You're perfect. The roses are perfect too," I said, putting them in a pitcher.

"I would fling a fish like a crescent moon into the sky like Chagall did if I knew some invisible hand were there to catch it."

"Where did you get such beautiful roses?"

"From a flower stand at the Avignon station. I begged the vendor for fleurs-de-lis, telling her that lilies had all the glory and history of France's fleur-de-lis. She said, 'The truth is, young man, that the symbol of France is the fleur-de-lys, *l-y-s*, which has nothing to do with lilies, *l-i-s*. Fleurs-de-lys are yellow irises that grow on the banks of the River Lys in Flanders.'"

I laughed. "André thought France's flower was the lily, too, and that I was named after them."

"It's too late for lilies or irises. I had to settle for roses, and then had to beg her for a little pail of water. I gave her a pitiful look and said how far the roses had to go to a lady with a complexion like rose petals. She was an old woman, and so she understood."

"But where's the pail?"

"In Maurice's bus. I couldn't carry it. Open the packages."

I felt a-twitter, like a little girl at a grand occasion. Each bag was from a different department store. From the Galeries Lafayette bag I pulled out a beautiful salmon-colored brocade cushion and another, slightly different, in rose. From Printemps, there were two paisley cushions in golden ochre and bronze and cinnamon. From BHV, two embroidered cushions of yellow-ochre and pale orange flowers; from La Samaritaine, two with arabesques of burgundy and gold; and from Le Bon Marché, two broadly striped cushions in all the warm ochre hues of Roussillon.

"I'm overwhelmed. I never—"

His grin stretched wide across his perfect teeth. "If you're going to have a *veillée* here, you can't expect your friends to sit on those torturous wooden benches and chairs, which would bruise even Maurice's sitting bones."

I ran my fingers over each cushion to feel its silky smoothness and played with the tassles, fringe, and tucking.

"What rich fabrics. I can't imagine what they must have cost."

"I located one of Monsieur Laforgue's stolen paintings and arranged for its return, so he paid me a little extra."

"Wonderful, Max. I knew you would succeed. And you'll find more."

I couldn't stop admiring the cushions. "Each one is beautiful in its own individual way."

"It would be too common if they were all the same. *Maman* loved picking them out with me. They're from both of us."

I set out three on the bench and three on the settee, with the striped ones in the middle, and one on each of the four chairs. The cushions, the paintings, and the roses all together made the room glorious.

"I feel like I'm in Paris!"

I threw myself into Maxime's arms and thanked him. Ten little hello kisses traveled across my cheeks and nose, and down to my throat like moth wings, until he was out of breath and I was laughing.

"They are for sitting, Lisette, so sit."

"On which one?"

"Try them all."

I sat on one cushion after another, admitting that I had been resentful toward Pascal's mother for not furnishing the house with cushions.

"Riding here on Maurice's bus for the first time, we witnessed a farmwife offering duck feathers to Maurice for Louise to make a pillow. At the time, I didn't recognize the goodwill behind that act. Now, living here through the Occupation years, I see the kindness and generosity of her offering. It was made in the spirit of *la Provence profonde,* as Maurice would say."

I settled on a striped cushion on the settee, and Maxime sat down next to me.

"So what do you notice about the room?" I asked.

I had hung the study of heads by itself on the left side of the stairs and had moved the Chagall yet again, so that *Girl with a*

Goat could have its rightful place as one of the two central paintings on the north wall. On the space beside it, once commanded by Pissarro's *Red Roofs,* I had tacked my Chagall, where it would remain, its home at last.

"Ah! Two more paintings! Tremendous! Tell me about them."

"The head study first. Maybe you know that André's father, Jules, purchased it cheaply from the concierge of his Montmartre *pension* before the Great War. I remember André saying that as a small boy he liked to draw it."

That made me think that perhaps that was his favorite painting, a memento of his father and a reminder of his childhood. I cherished this glimpse of him as a boy drawing the outlines of those faces.

"What did he tell you about it?"

"Just that the concierge had said it was by some Spaniard who couldn't pay his rent and left it as payment."

"It *is* a Picasso, Lisette. Just as we had thought. He did dozens of sketches and studies similar to this for a final painting called *Les Demoiselles d'Avignon,* depicting the prostitutes of a Barcelona street with the same name. Look at the women's long, angular noses flattened to the side, their narrow faces and concave cheeks, their heavily lined oversized black eyes. Those distortions all appear in the final painting."

"Why did Picasso make them like that?"

"For expression, I suppose. He may have thought that sharp angles suggested the sharp experiences of prostitution. Hard edges show how such a life hardens the human spirit."

"To me, those faces are harsh and ugly."

"Do you think the life of a harlot is anything other than harsh and ugly?"

"All right, Max. Have it your way." I winked at him. "I concede the anguish in that one misplaced, mismatched eye."

"Then his purpose worked. He was trying out two styles here.

Cubism, which flattens shapes, gives them hard edges, and shows different angles of view all at once."

"And the other?"

"Primitivism. The long, concave faces suggest African masks. His preliminary studies like this one surface from time to time in galleries and sell for high prices because they show him experimenting, working out the principles of new techniques. *Maman* was outraged when she saw one thrown onto a heap and burned in front of the Jeu de Paume."

"Would you feel outraged if I said that a little boy here found it in the dump?"

"You're joking."

"It's the very truth."

"Then it might have been given to a German officer, who discarded it as degenerate art."

"More likely Gypsies took it from that windmill as they were scrounging the area for goods to sell along their way and, on second thought, threw it out as unsalable. We'll never know."

"What about Pissarro's *Girl with a Goat*?"

"That's a more complicated story."

Just for a moment, I considered hiding the truth. Its effect on Maxime would be unpredictable, and I had so much as promised Bernard that I would not reveal him. But Maxime had not lied to me about André's death when he could have. Nor could I lie to him.

"I didn't find it. It was *shown* to me. You must not tell a soul." I gave him a stern look. "This is no frivolous secret."

When he agreed, I took Bernard's letter from the desk drawer and gave it to him to read.

"'Your devoted, Bernard'? 'Devoted'?"

I chewed on my lip. "He did come to care for me."

"And you?"

"In his own rough, peculiar way, he has been kind to me."

That seemed to satisfy Maxime, at least for the moment.

"Let me finish about the painting. So, out of contrition for bursting into my house, he begged me to let him apologize by an act. When I agreed, we took a walk, and he showed me the factory where the ochre was processed. It was interesting, and I'm glad I understand it now. Seeing where Pascal worked and the steps in processing, from ore to pigments, gave me an appreciation for what Roussillon is all about.

"Bernard took me down a hill through an oak grove where the slurry of ochre and sand used to be piped down to canals that led to drying beds. He brought me to a particular pipe, about the diameter of a dinner plate, and told me to reach inside, and that was where the painting was."

"Had he found it there or put it there?"

"Put it there. He was the one who took the paintings from the woodpile and hid them in different places. André *told* him to."

"Truly?"

"Yes, Max. So André wasn't as careless about not telling someone where they were as we had thought."

"My speculation still could be correct. The constable's intention must have been to offer them to some German officer to court his favor. Then after the Germans left, he could not reveal that he had them. In a village this small, people would figure out that he had been a collaborator, and that would put him in danger of losing his position, at the very least, or, at the worst, his life."

"You think so? Even now?"

"Yes, even now." He spoke harshly. "People don't forget."

"So giving me the last painting was defying danger."

Maxime leaned forward, arms on his thighs, and didn't say anything for a painfully long time.

"He must love you. More than his own life."

"He says he's been in despair for years."

"And I haven't been?"

"Max."

He paced around the room. "And what can I sacrifice for you to compete with that?" He flung out his arm. "Cushions. How do they rate in comparison with the sacrifice of his reputation, his livelihood, and possibly his life?"

"Please don't compare. It's you I invited to the Fête de la Saint-Jean, not him."

"He'll be there anyway. And what should I do? Pretend that I don't know?"

"Yes. You must."

"Have you forgotten that it was collaborators like him who put men like me in prison camps?"

"Max, stop. Please. He *posed* as a collaborator to save Roussillon."

He stormed out the door before I could finish explaining. I let him go. He had every reason to be upset.

I looked again at every cushion, touched each one as though their colors could heal the rift between us, and then cast a glance at every painting. No matter how beautiful they were, no matter that they exhibited the movements in the history of French art of the last century, whatever it was that Maxime had said, were they worth the suffering they'd caused? Worth the sundering of the dearest friendship I had? Worth heartbreak?

Should I have lied and said I found the last one myself? Was it cruel to have told him? To have shown him Bernard's letter? Was truth really more valuable than love?

Two men, both wounded, both suffering—I had betrayed both of them. Bernard by telling Maxime, and Maxime by accepting Bernard's reason for collaboration. I had been disrespectful to both of them. In the harsh light of the truth, I felt as unworthy as a worm.

I went out to the empty courtyard. With no one to comfort me, I sat at the base of the almond tree and leaned up against it. When Geneviève was young, she would have leaned against me and nudged my hand. Even Kooritzah Deux, gone now into Louise's cook pot, would have helped by distracting me with some antic.

I should have left Roussillon when I'd learned that André had died, should have left the paintings too and forgotten I had ever seen them. Let Bernard hide them in his house until he died. The people of Roussillon would have found him out then, and it would not have mattered, and the paintings would now belong to the village. That would be the story Théo would tell his children, and the tale would become part of the sad history of Roussillon. The villagers would have wondered about Bernard and me, and André, who went off to war and was killed, and some Parisian dandy who drifted in and out of the story. They would wonder all of this as they gazed at the paintings in the town hall as reminders of the beauty from the earth of the Vaucluse gone wrong.

I HEARD A KNOCK on the door. It was Maurice, swinging a little red pail with a red rosebud in it from Louise's rosebush and singing a children's song about love and a rose:

> *"Il y a longtemps que je t'aime.*
> *Jamais je ne t'oublierai."*

Any other time I would have sung it back to him. *I have loved you for a long time. Never will I forget you.* It was a bittersweet song about a sad little girl who had lost her boyfriend. Its irony landed heavily.

"Do you like the roses and the cushions? *Oh là là*, there they are! Don't let madame my wife see them. She'll complain that I never buy her anything in Avignon."

He finally looked at my face. "What's wrong?"

"Oh, Maurice, I've ruined everything. I told Maxime that Bernard had led me to the last painting, and that confirmed for Maxime that Bernard had been a collaborator."

Maurice spread his arms wide and folded me in them. "*Non, non, non, ma petite.* There is nothing that can't be rectified."

"I should not have told even you right now," I whimpered.

"Shh. You didn't have to."

I pulled back. "You knew?"

"I suspected it. Even during the Occupation. We all did. Otherwise he would have been operating with Aimé and me. The night Cherbourg was liberated, he poured champagne for you and sat at your table in the café. He knew the tide was turning. By being seen with a war widow, he was proclaiming that he was not a collaborator."

"It was a ruse, then? He was using me?"

"That night he was. I didn't say anything because I thought it best to let sleeping goats lie. But now I say this. It would be wrong to consider him a bad man. It was Bernard who stood without a weapon other than words between those trigger-happy *maquisards* and the unarmed German soldiers retreating after the armistice."

"I never guessed. Unarmed, you say? He had no pistol?"

"Oh, he has one. A hunting rifle too. Apparently he chose not to carry them. In that act, he was keeping the peace that was only hours old."

"That puts him in a different light."

"It's time to leave the past behind us and let things heal themselves."

"I'm not sure they will."

"They will. Give Roussillon ten years, a plumbing system, and new stucco, and Germans will be coming here on holiday, and we'll be glad about it because they will fill our coin purses."

"But what about Maxime and me? He's distraught."

"Maxime is a smart man. He'll work it out. He knows what he has in you, and that none of it was your doing. The spectacle tonight will help. Prepare a good dinner, and he will get over it. Men are made that way." He patted his paunch. "Satisfy the belly, and the heart will follow. Nothing to worry about."

"What about the constable tonight?"

"He'll be busy making his rounds, making sure the fires in the countryside are tended and won't get out of hand."

Just as Maurice was edging toward the door, Maxime came in. Maurice gave him a manly slap on the back and went out. As he was closing the door, he poked his head back in. "She loves the cushions."

"What was he doing here?"

I pointed to the pail.

We stood caught in a tangle of emotions like a ball of fishhooks, not saying a word, wishing the other one would speak of what mattered first. The longer we were silent, the harder it would be to bring it up.

"The last thing I want is to cause you anguish," I said.

"It's not your fault." He sat down at the table and wrapped his hands around the pitcher of roses. "It's not anybody's fault. Maybe he was just an opportunist, not a downright traitor."

Hearing that, I felt a shred of relief.

"He thought that supporting the Occupation might save Roussillon," I explained. "*Résistance* activity in two villages nearby brought on brutal reprisals, and Maurice and other *résistants* were working here as well. He thought if the Germans knew that the constable of Roussillon was a collaborator, it might prevent our village from suffering a similar fate." Saying any more than that would cast me as Bernard's supporter.

Maxime considered that for some minutes and then said, "My mother remarked more than once that there were many degrees of collaboration. I wouldn't dream of condemning her for working for the Opéra or the couturier."

"Nor would I."

Hoping to put an end to the issue, I asked him if he was hungry. "I started some ratatouille this afternoon. There were some beautiful eggplants at the Thursday market."

He nodded and seemed willing to change the subject.

"I bought a *pain fougasse* for you," I said, holding up a flatbread slashed with openings to look like an ear of wheat. "See? It's a traditional Provençal bread with olives." Laying it on the table, I was glad I had something to do right then to prepare the meal.

When I sat down opposite Maxime with only the veil of steam from the Camargue red rice between us, he said, "I didn't come back just because I was hungry, I'll have you know." A mere glimmer of a smile passed quickly. "Actually, that's not quite true. I was hungry to be with you."

"I hated it that I upset you."

"You did right by telling me. Think what you would feel like if you had to keep that secret forever. It would eat away at you, and the longer you didn't tell me, the harder it would be to bring it up. I understand that only too well."

"What about the letter?"

"If you had not shown it to me, I would have questioned his motive in taking you to the painting. It makes him not a bad man."

"You won't see him tonight. Maurice said he has duties in the countryside, monitoring the bonfires."

As we headed uphill after dinner, I touched my hand to the back of Maxime's. He grasped it instantly, giving me the reassurance I needed. Villagers were already gathering at the bonfire on the plateau. Soon, a violinist, a horn player, and a piper began the music of the farandole, and all the villagers held hands and danced around the roaring blaze in jubilation, turning the Castrum—once the camp of Roman soldiers bent on killing—into a dance floor.

Théo ran toward me, and I reached out for his hand. The leader of the dancers broke open the circle, and the string of dancers, including the three of us, like a family, followed him in a sinuous line around the perimeter of the Castrum, down the hill past the church and the bell tower, then looped back on itself to reach the Castrum again, where the line split into groups.

Maxime kept hold of one of my hands and Théo the other as we walked to the railing at the edge of the plateau. Théo tried to count the bonfires, then skipped away to his papa. Some fires were directly below the cliff. Others were scattered in the valley. Somewhere down there, Bernard was going from one to another to make sure they were well tended, faithful as always to the commune of Roussillon. I imagined him looking up at our big fire, maybe even trying to identify the silhouettes passing in front of the flames when we danced.

To the west, we could see a light spot in the sky where Gordes had its fire, and a paler light up the mountain to the northeast at Saint-Saturnin-lès-Apt, both villages in need of healing from their losses. Shepherds in front of their bories in the higher elevations had their dim little beacons, signaling to us that they were there to be counted among the populace of Provence. I hoped their solitude was rich with thoughts of peace.

"It feels like a sort of communion," I said. "All those people gathering to commemorate John the Baptist heralding the coming of Christ with his message of grace and forgiveness for all mankind."

Maxime put his arm around me. "What we're seeing is the world in miniature. Vast darkness and spots of light where people gather. Some lights burn brightly and steadily. Others only glimmer. Some appear to go out completely, but the people are still there. And soon they will kindle new flames. That's history."

"And life."

After a few moments he added, "The thing to do is to stay close to the light. That's where love is."

CHAPTER FORTY-ONE

MY LIST

1948

IN THE MORNING BEFORE MAXIME CAME DOWNSTAIRS, I TOOK out my List of Hungers and Vows and read it over. It seemed an important day to take stock. If André were miraculously given to me again, I would hope that in telling him how I had lived, I would not be ashamed.

1.   Love Pascal as a father.
     I do, I wrote below it.
2.   Go to Paris, find Cezanne's *Card Players.*
     Done, I wrote.
3.   Do something good for a painter.
     Done.
4.   Learn what makes a painting great.
     Learning slowly. More to learn.

In addition to considering what makes a painting great, I wondered, shouldn't I also be considering what makes a life great?

5.   Make a blue dress, the blue of the Mediterranean Sea on a summer day with no clouds.
     Héloïse's gift has taken care of that.

6. Learn how to live alone.

    *Always learning. But maybe now was the time to
    learn how to live together.*

7. Find André's grave and the spot where he died.

    Crossed off.

Markers on a strip of earth pale in comparison to the marks left
on each other's souls.

8. Forgive André.

    No need. He was right to have gone to war.

    And forgive Bernard?

    Working on it.

I would know when complete forgiveness had come by the peace
it would bring. But what about forgiving God for not preventing
André's death? Who was I to forgive God? What did I know of His
intention for me, or for all of us? Commenting about Marc's painting of the beggar in the sky, Bella had said that the messenger bringing good news was held aloft by a spiritual force despite gravity or
any downward pull. By contemplating Bella's thought, I could
glimpse the idea that despite pain, despite cruelty, despite loss, the
notion of having to forgive God would someday dissolve.

9. Learn how to live in a painting.

    Done. Move on. Learn to live in life.

10. Try not to be envious.

    Of whom? No one. Not even Bella and Marc.

11. Find the paintings in MY lifetime.

    Done, enough to satisfy me.

12. Learn how to be self-sufficient.

    Always learning.

Self-sufficiency doesn't only have to do with living alone and providing for oneself. It's finding in oneself the qualities that make a person unique, and being content with them.

13. Do something good for Maxime.
     I have, and will.

Loving is a blessed thing. It blesses the giver as bountifully as the receiver.

14. Earn my way to Paris.
     Done.

I was pleased by my responses, which, I supposed, meant that I was pleased with my life, and I thought André would be too. But I certainly had more life to live, so there was always room for more items. I immediately added a line:

15. Bathe in the Mediterranean Sea.

Oh, wouldn't that be a thrill? I sat at the table thinking of what else to add, while loving the way the light of Roussillon slanted in through the south windows. New thoughts were born in that light, and I added to my list:

16. Do something good for Roussillon.
17. Love more. Love again. Love broadly. Love without res-
     ervation.

Maxime came downstairs carrying a three-kilo bag of sugar and thudded it onto the sink counter.

"What do you need all this for?"

"For marzipan. To give to my guests at the *veillée* this evening. To celebrate the return of the paintings."

He turned in a circle to look at them. "There's one missing!" he said in alarm.

"I know. Pissarro's red roofs." I felt a pang, knowing I would never see it again. "I'm content. Bernard had to sacrifice it to his German interrogators."

The blitheness of my response seemed to satisfy Max.

"You can help me with this." I got up and reached under the sink and drew out a pail of almonds I had harvested in November. "Let's shell them outside."

It was a beautiful summer morning. A pair of doves on the fence rail were cooing their harmonious lay; the passionflower vine was in its full, complicated bloom; and the branches of the almond tree were laden with a new crop of pale green velvet pods. To me, they represented continuity. Using the perfect flat rock and André's mallet, we progressed quickly with the shelling at the work table in the lean-to. I struck the almonds open against the rock, and Maxime peeled off the shells. I brought out another pail from the root cellar. "Save the shells in this. I use them as kindling in the stove."

I told him I wanted to give one of each kind of marzipan to Héloïse and Sister Marie Pierre and Monsieur Laforgue.

"And you want me to deliver them, I suppose?"

"No," I chirped and gave him a teasing look. "I will."

His eyebrows lifted. "Truly?"

"Yes. Truly," I said with intentional lightheartedness, as though I had said something of no consequence, and proceeded to go over the guest list for the *veillée*.

"Maurice and Louise, of course. Odette and René Gulini, the baker. We bought a brioche at their bakery. Remember her?"

"No, I can't say that I do."

"Maxime! These people are important to me. They're not just provincials with no names. René said he would make two *francesco* loaves, his Italian version of round fruit breads, one with apples, the other with pears. I asked him to use these fruits because of the still life, instead of the apricots and strawberries he usually uses. Both of them will be sprinkled with chopped almonds. My almonds. Their son, Michel, and his wife, Sandrine, who works at the post office, will come, and their little boy, Théo, who held my hand in the serpentine last night. He's the one who found the Picasso in the dump."

"Then we must honor him especially."

"I will. I already know of a way. Émile Vernet, the vineyardist; his wife, Mélanie; and their daughter, Mimi. We will drink their rosé this evening. He has already given me the residue from a wine cask to use as cream of tartar in the marzipan. Monsieur and Madame Bonnelly. Remember the vineyard we stopped at? She gave us pears. Aimé Bonhomme and his wife and son. He's the mayor and was a *Résistance* leader. Monsieur Voisin, who had to adjust to having women in his café at *apéritif* hour. Jérôme Cachin, the grocer. Henri Mitan, the smithy, who struggled so mightily to explain the workings of the gasogene conversion, and his patient wife. Father Marc. And Claude, the farmer who loved the Cézanne landscape and kept it safe in his little borie. I tacked an invitation to the door of his borie shed. It took me hours to find it again."

"And the constable?"

"I'll leave that up to you."

He tipped his head and drew in a noisy breath.

At the stove, I went through all the steps of heating and cooling the ingredients, not forgetting the almond extract. When the mixture was ready to be divided into balls about the size of grapefruits, one for each color, I reached into the *panetière*.

"Look! Real food coloring! Four colors."

"You don't mean to tell me that you found it in the cramped little grocery store here?"

"No. I bought it in Paris the day I was by myself."

With the four bottles, I mixed seven colors, drop by drop. Together we kneaded the colors into the marzipan and began to make the shapes of fruit. Maxime watched me and tried the simplest shapes, oranges. He rolled too much in one direction, and it came out like an egg. He made several attempts and found that all he could make was a banana.

"You had better do it," he said.

It was a pleasant time, doing this together, and we found ourselves laughing frequently. I worked at it until I had enough for each guest to take home one of each fruit, with plenty left over.

"My mother will think they are exquisite."

"Good. I want her to see that I have talent at *something*."

There was still some orange mixture left.

"Ah, I have an idea. An experiment."

I pulled off a small amount, rolled it into a ball, flattened it and stretched it into an oval, trimmed it to make straight sides and a straight bottom, with only the top rounded. Then I pressed an imprint of my thumb, to make a shallow cavity, and pressed in my thumbnail at the rounded end to make an arch. I did this two more times, top to bottom, each one with a smaller fingernail.

"See this, Max? This is the way the galleries look in an ochre mine."

I went to work mixing just the right orange-ochre by dulling the orange with the tiniest speck of blue and made one for each of the guests with a few left over. I smacked my sticky hands together in glee.

"These will commemorate Roussillon. Pascal would have loved them. Maurice will too."

"Everyone will, *chérie*, if they can pick them up without them crumbling. It will tell them that you love their village."

"My village too, Max."

After a moment in which a worrisome look passed over his face, he conceded, "All right. Your village."

—

WE ATE THE LEFTOVER ratatouille and rice, and while I cleaned up, Maxime went out for a walk. I dusted, swept, and put everything in order.

Then I had an idea. I ran down to Cachin's grocery to buy some chewing gum, but he had just sold his last packet to Théo, who was now across the square watching a *boules* game. I found him chewing a big wad.

"Théo, do you have any more chewing gum?"

"*Oui, madame.*" He slapped his pocket. "Half a piece. It's Hollywood gum. American cowboys chew it when they ride their horses."

"May I please have it? I need it for something fun. Come with me. I'll show you."

"Is it a game? Will we play a game?"

He galloped up the hill slapping his bottom.

Inside the house he cried, "Cushions!" and ran around the room plopping his little derrière onto each one. "Ooh, little fruits! May I have one, *s'il vous plaît, madame?*"

"A fair trade. One fruit for a half stick of gum."

He chose a cherry and produced a quarter of a stick of gum still in its wrapper.

"Is this all you have?"

With a grin, he pointed to his cheeks, bulging like a squirrel's. "I want to see if I can chew a whole packet at once, the way American cowboys do."

I chewed the morsel. "Here's the game. I want to use these candy oranges and apples and these two saucers to make a copy of this picture," I said, pointing to the still life.

I pressed half the gum from my mouth onto the back of a marzipan orange, stuck it to the saucer, and tipped it slightly. It held. Théo's face was ebullient. I used the other half on another orange. I set five marzipan apples and one orange in a row on the table. Now his expression grew serious.

"If you can read a little now, you must be able to count too." I pointed to the row of marzipans on the table. "How many more are there, not counting the pear?"

"Six," he said, his voice dropping, making the word into two mournful syllables.

Slowly, thinking it over, he took the gum out of his mouth, pulled it into two pieces, and placed one in my hand.

"Oh, thank you, thank you, Théo. You are a true chevalier on horseback."

I set the apples into a pyramid, securing them with gum.

"Why is there only one pear?" he asked.

"Because the artist thought that was all he needed. See how its top curves to one side? That makes it interesting and beautiful. There is no other pear in all the world exactly like that one. The same is true for little boys."

I worked on the remaining orange, the most precarious, until it was securely in place. I placed a teacup upside down on the cabinet, bunched up a white cotton napkin over it, and set that saucer at an angle. It slipped into my waiting hand.

Without my asking, Théo chewed one last time and, with only a brief pout, gave the rest to me.

"Oh, *merci,* Théo."

I pulled the gum into a length, wedged it between the edge of the tipped saucer and the cabinet top, and adjusted the napkin around it.

"It's magic! I'll be the only one who will know." He raised his arms like a champion and skipped out the door, shouting, "I'm the only one!"

Joy and innocence incarnate bounded down the hill, all arms and legs, naturally buoyant.

"There's no other boy in all the world like me!"

CHAPTER FORTY-TWO

LA VEILLÉE

1948

MY FRIENDS BEGAN TO ARRIVE FOR THE *VEILLÉE* AFTER the dinner hour, as was the custom. Maurice wore the traditional red Provençal sash and white shirt for the occasion. He winced the moment Louise saw the cushions.

"Oh! Lisette! Cushions!" Louise cried. "They're beautiful. I've never seen such cushions. Roussillon has never seen such beautiful cushions."

Louise was so focused on the cushions that she didn't even notice my blue suit or the paintings on the walls. She went around the room and made anyone who was sitting on them stand up. "How can I see them when you have your fat derrières flattening these plump cushions?"

She ran her hands over the fabrics, picked out her favorite, lifted it off the bench, sat down on the wood, and placed the cushion in her lap, muttering, "Did she buy these cushions in Avignon, Maurice? You never told me there were shops in Avignon that sold such beautiful cushions. And we're still sitting on wood like a couple of peasants."

He squeezed the tails of his sash and raised his shoulders to his ears, trying to bury his face between them.

"No, he didn't, Louise. They came from Paris," Maxime said. "I'm sure Maurice would have bought you cushions in Avignon if the shops had any like these."

She eyed him with exaggerated suspicion.

"Up to now, I thought you to be an honorable man, so I suppose I have to believe you."

Odette and René came in, each of them carrying a *francesco*.

"Oh, the suit from Paris!" Odette said in admiration. *"Très chic."*

Mélanie came in right behind her and walked around me in a circle. "You could make something like this, Odette, if you study the seams." She traced her fingers over the seams to show her. "You can practice on one for you, and then make one for me!"

When Claude, the farmer who had painted the door of his borie the color of cantaloupes, arrived, I welcomed him with much attention. Émile served the wine and raised a toast to the recovery of the paintings.

"Santé!" my friends said, in agreement.

They admired each painting. The Bonnellys and Henri's wife had never seen them before. Madame Bonnelly had tears in her eyes. "I have never beheld such beautiful paintings." She gave me a bone-cracking hug. "At last. At last. I'm so happy for you."

"I knew you would be."

Everyone was talking at once except for Claude, who stood speechless in front of each painting. He looked the longest at Cézanne's landscape. Would that I had two of them so I could give one to him.

There was a knock on the door, and when Maxime opened it, in stepped Bernard. They exchanged looks of acknowledgment, maybe even respect, but not surprise. I was the one who was astonished.

"I beg your pardon, madame. Maxime invited me, and I couldn't stay away."

"Oh! Constable! You're most welcome here. I'm glad you have come. Thank you, Max, for making sure of that."

They stood next to each other just inside the door. Bernard looked quite handsome in his trim, well-tailored jacket, red Provençal sash, red silk cravat, pomaded hair, and, of course, his freshly polished boots. I had to suppress a chuckle. In this instance, it was the *Roussillonais* who outdid the Parisian.

Recovering myself, I said, "I was just going to speak about the paintings, but first I want to thank everyone for your love and support in so many ways all the years I've lived here. You have stood by me during my bereavement and my search for Pascal's paintings. Now they are all found, so I wanted all of you to see them together.

"Notice that every one of them has an area of ochre hues. For example, the ochre wheat fields in this landscape around Aix by Cézanne." Looking directly at Claude, I added, "I have it on good authority that Cézanne had enormous affection for the countryside of Provence.

"Note the yellow-ochre pathway in this painting of the girl with the goat." At that moment I gave a grateful look to Bernard that I hoped he would always remember.

"And here. Look here. It's an ochre quarry near Aix. Cézanne was aware that the quarries and mines in our region are the sources of all the lovely warm colors. Just think! Pigments that you dug as young men are used on paintings by *famous* artists! Look at this modern one by Picasso. The skin of these women is creamy golden ochre, and their cheeks are tinged with rosy ochre. *Picasso,* I'm telling you! That should make us all feel proud."

"Us? So do you count yourself among us?" asked Bernard.

"*Oui, bien sûr!* I have spent eleven years here. I came unwillingly to take care of a dying man whom I had never met, but whom I came to love. Some of the most significant events of my life have happened to me here. And here I've found wonderful friends."

It took me a moment to go on. "Just before Pascal died, he told

André and me to let the paintings care for us, but he also said that some of them belong in Roussillon. I agree with him. The building in this painting is a paint factory near Pontoise. Pascal told me that he sold our pigments there."

"He told me too. A dozen times, at least," Maurice said.

"He was deeply moved that this paint factory was a bridge from our mines and our Usine Mathieu"—I flashed another look at Bernard—"to the great art of Paris. And one of the greatest painters, Paul Cézanne, Provence's native son, who was born and died in Aix, painted this ochre quarry in front of—*in front of,* mind you— his most adored mountain, Montagne Sainte-Victoire. He chose that viewpoint intentionally. He knew the importance of ochre."

There were murmurs around the room, my friends grasping the significance of what I was saying.

"The still life with pottery will always make me think of the fertility and crafts of Provence, and the oranges on the tipped plate will remind me of Théo, the magical cowboy."

He grinned, and I nearly melted into my shoes with love for him.

"And this one of a girl holding a goat and a chicken—"

"Geneviève and Kooritzah," Louise said.

"—was painted for me by Marc Chagall, a Russian Jew who was hiding in Gordes. He loved Provence and hated to leave our beautiful countryside."

I had to pause because my throat had tightened around what felt like a marzipan cherry.

"But these two paintings, the quarry and the paint factory, are part of Roussillon's legacy. I present them now, in front of all of you as witnesses, to the commune of Roussillon, to be on permanent display in the town hall. What was it all for, if not for Roussillon to take pride in them? Aimé Bonhomme, I call upon you, *s'il vous plaît,* as mayor of Roussillon, to be their guardian and caretaker."

"With pleasure. And with our gratitude for your generosity."

Applause filled the room.

"I know that Roussillon can someday become a site that artists will paint. It might even have a gallery to complete the journey the ochre takes."

Aimé's son whispered to him excitedly, and widened eyes around the room showed that minds crusted by hardship and isolation were opening to new possibilities.

"Nobody is noticing," Théo complained, tugging on my skirt. "Look, everybody. Look for magic."

Bernard, the tallest, peered over everyone's head. "The still life in miniature on the cabinet."

"*Oui! Oui!*" Théo squealed, hopping up and down. "It's magic. Look!" He went around the room tugging at sleeves and skirts, making sure everyone saw, and everyone marveled.

Maxime tipped his head toward Bernard and said something amusing just to him, perhaps about my marzipan efforts, and Bernard chuckled. Then he said, "The entire room is magical."

Maurice pretended to be weeping, and when no one noticed, he increased the volume, sobbing so loudly that everyone laughed.

"So now that you have the paintings back, you're going to leave us," Maurice whined. "You will come back sometime, won't you?"

"*Òc, òc,*" I said, and a cheer rose up around me.

"Aha! She speaks the Occitan of Provence!" cried Monsieur Voisin, the café owner. I felt redeemed in his eyes.

"How can I leave for good? I'll have to be back to harvest my almonds and to help with the *vendange* and"—I shook my index finger at Aimé and his son—"to celebrate the installation of plumbing." I glanced at Bernard. "It *is* possible, I know that. And I'll be here the next Midsummer Night."

"Don't forget. Don't forget," said Théo. "The little fruits."

"Oh, yes! Théo, my hero, who found the Picasso all by himself, will give out these marzipans. A toast to Théo, the magical cowboy."

I followed him, passing around the plate of marzipan mine galleries, which delighted everyone, even though they fell apart in people's hands. That didn't matter. They looked splendid on the plate, and people ate the crumbles.

Each person embraced me and thanked me, some of them overcome with emotion, others enjoying the paintings, still others enjoying René's *francesco*. They lingered awhile, then slowly began to leave. Claude appeared most reluctant to go, so I invited him to come anytime to see the paintings again. After surviving Madame Bonnelly's iron clamp around my back, I picked up Théo and swung him in a circle.

"You won't forget me, will you?" I asked.

"No, madame. I will remember you every time I chew some Hollywood gum."

"And I, *jamais je ne t'oublierai*," I sang to the tune of the children's song.

And very quietly, following Théo, Bernard asked, "You won't forget me either?"

"Never. You are engraved on my heart."

"You are a remarkable woman, madame," he blurted out, then ducked out the door.

MAXIME AND I STOOD ALONE.

"Thank you for inviting him. It was right that he should be here."

I sat on the settee and brushed a crumb off my blue skirt. Maxime came to sit next to me.

"This will be the last time we will see all the paintings together," he said.

That made us contemplative. I remembered what Max had said about what makes a painting great—its power to enrich us with a truth, to enlighten us so that we understand our lives more clearly. I felt a gentle warmth come over me as I saw that the yellow-ochre path leading beyond our vision had been leading me through the Roussillon years to my purpose, to André's purpose, to Max, and back to Paris all along, only I had not recognized it. With that thought, peace descended. André would have wanted it so.

Then my gaze shifted to Cézanne's fruit and Provençal pottery.

"I have to think it out to be sure," I said. "At times it seems selfish of me to hold on to two Cézannes, to keep the still life hidden in a house away from people who need its freshness and colors. It seems almost against my conscience. It belongs to France. Marc would agree.

"There will come a day, when I have come to know every brushstroke as I know the lines in my palm, when I have nourished my soul with these fruits and have set the lesson of the lone pear to rest and can value my own uniqueness, when I can cherish solitude and companionship with equal grace—then perhaps I will be able to part with it, if I were permitted to stand before it as long and as often as I wanted to. Do you think the Jeu de Paume would buy it?"

He drew in a sharp breath. "Oh, my dear!" His eyes swam with wonder, although his mouth tightened in concern.

"Then I could maintain a Paris apartment for us."

"For *us*?" His eyes glistened as they had so long ago.

"Yes. Us."

"You astound me, *chérie*."

"One more thing. The Picasso. It's yours, Max. Keep it or sell it to start your own gallery, as you wish."

"Oh, no. I can't accept that. It's too valuable."

His hint of a smile told me that some thought was stirring in him. He drew me to him and whispered, "I won't take it unless you come along with it."

"I'm already packed."

AFTERWORD

Lisette's List is a work of fiction. Fabled Roussillon does exist, truly deserving its designation as "one of the most beautiful villages in France," well worth a visit. The Sentier des Ocres, the Usine Mathieu, the Bruoux Mines, and Gulini's bakery are all still there. The *boules* terrain is still alongside the public toilet opposite place de la Marie, where there is still a café and the town hall. But the spirit is new. To the visitor, there is no evidence of struggle, only of the enjoyment of life in the warm south.

Except for the artists, the principal characters emerged from my imagination, and I assembled them like beads on a thread. Sentences, even paragraphs in two cases, can be directly ascribed to Camille Pissarro, Paul Cézanne, and Marc Chagall. I felt I was honoring them by employing these passages. For more about these painters, please see www.susanvreeland.com.

The question of the authenticity of the paintings is a natural one. At the suggestion of my former editor Jane von Mehren, who encouraged me to free myself from the limitations of biographical fact in shaping this novel in its early stages, as well as by following my precedent of a fictional Vermeer painting in *Girl in Hyacinth Blue,* I invented two of the eight paintings—Pissarro's *Girl with a Goat* and Cézanne's still life. The latter I assembled using items

borrowed from his other still lifes, which I needed for their significance to Provençal material culture. In the case of Pissarro's *Girl,* I
have spent frustrating months trying to relocate a painting that I
seem to recall in an art history book of a girl, a vegetable garden, a
goat, and a path, which inspired its role in the novel, but to no avail.
Therefore, I concede that it must have been a wisp of insupportable
imagination. I am dreadfully sorry if this disappoints you. To be in
accord with the novel, Pissarro's *Côte Jalet,* appearing on the cover,
has been altered. The painting given to Lisette by Marc Chagall is
titled *Bella with Cock in the Window,* aka *The Window* (1938, private collection). All the other paintings are verifiable using the
names I have used. Apparently, there are many studies of faces that
Picasso drew in preparation for *Les Demoiselles d'Avignon.* That
was my reason for being vague on the number and positioning of
the heads.

Into Marc Chagall's historic letter addressed "To the Artists of
Paris," I have inserted the actual cause of Bella Chagall's death.
The event of her death was already in the letter, reprinted in its
entirety in *Marc Chagall on Art and Culture,* edited by Benjamin
Harshav (Stanford University Press, 2003), some of which I did not
use. Bella's description of coming to Chagall's studio on his birth-
day is taken directly from *First Encounter,* by Bella Chagall
(Schocken Books, 1983).

I am neither a visual artist nor an art historian. Rather, I am a
passionate lover of art, what the French call *une amatrice d'art.* I
am grateful to the libraries and museums that have supplied me
with information and images from which my imagination could
soar.

ACKNOWLEDGMENTS

My heartfelt gratitude extends to so many. To trace their influence from conception to finish, I wish to name the following people:

My former editor, Jane von Mehren, for encouraging me to seek a new direction, freeing me to invent, and helping me shape this story, and for being a gentle guide and friend through all my writing life.

Marcia Mueller, photographer and friend, whose enthusiasm for Roussillon prompted me to discover it for myself. I thank her for her beautiful photographs of the village and its surroundings appearing on my website, www.susanvreeland.com, which allowed me to remember and describe it.

Colin Campbell, professor emeritus of literature, Principia College, for introducing me to the female principle of which Lisette is an embodiment and to the two human hungers at work in literature and in this story: the hunger to hurt and the hunger to bless.

Hélène Albertini and Alain Daumen, lifelong residents of Roussillon, who were patient with my fractured French and were generous in giving me information about the community from 1937 to 1948.

Whenever I needed a detail on a subject unfamiliar to me, a

friend came forth with exactly the right information. For this I thank Ellie Gray for her advice on Lisette's vegetable garden, goat, and cheesemaking; Marian Grayeske for her advice on chickens; Barbara Scott for her advice on fruit and their seasons; and former U.S. Army sergeant Tom Hall for his advice on the battle scene. I thank Jan Thomas for her hospitality in Provence and her generosity in sharing books and recollections of the region.

To aid my leap into another culture, language, and time period, I thank Suzanne Ruffin, Hélène Brown, and Sophie Juster for their help in getting the French right; Rémy Rotenier and Isabelle Telliez for ascertaining details of domestic wartime history; Jim Farr for his knowledge of the events of World War II relating to this novel; and Clotilde Roth-Meyer for her instruction straight from Paris on pigments and painters' colors.

My gratitude also goes to Marna Hostetler and Karen Brown, my longtime library angels at University of South Carolina's Thomas Cooper Library, for their research into frame moldings, and to Barbara Brink, development director of University of California San Diego Library, for making available to me Marc Chagall's letter addressed "To the Artists of Paris," which gave voice to the theme of the resurrection of French art.

I thank Annabelle Mathias of the Musée d'Orsay for leading me to *Le Catalogue des Peintures et Sculptures Exposées au Musée de l'Impressionisme, Jeu de Paume des Tuileries* (Musées Nationaux, 1948); thanks also to Gary Ferdman, co-curator of the exhibition *Chagall in High Falls,* for tracking down *The Window,* Chagall's painting of a woman with a goat and a rooster looking out a window.

I gratefully acknowledge the contributions of two books in particular: *Village in the Vaucluse,* by Laurence Wylie (3rd ed., Harvard University Press, 1974), and *From Rocks to Riches: Roussillon—Time, Change and Ochre in a Village in Provence,* by Graham F. Pringle and Hildgund Schaefer (Middlebury, Vt.: Rural

Society Press, 2010). Some of the characters' names were taken from these two volumes.

My own *Dear Readers:* John Baker, Barbara Braun working over and above her position as agent, Angela Sage Larson, Marcia Mueller, and, especially, the writers John Ritter and Julie Brickman, who have given astute critical readings of the manuscript in multiple revisions and made the process fun—I cannot thank all of you enough.

I'm profoundly grateful to my new editor at Random House, Celina Spiegel, for her meticulous editing. I owe so much that is good in this novel to her advice, and I'm delighted to have her as the head of my Random House team.

And I'm forever grateful to my agent, Barbara Braun, for her guidance on matters literary, promotional, and business, and for her love and her constant belief in me through thick and thin since 1998.

To my husband, Kip Gray, whose steady encouragement, loving understanding, and ever-ready technical help are essential to me, I give my deepest gratitude and devotion.

PUBLISHED WORKS THAT DESERVE mention include:

Nina Maria Athanassoglou-Kallmyer, *Cézanne and Provence: The Painter and His Culture* (Chicago: University of Chicago Press, 2003)

Paul Cézanne, *Conversations with Cézanne,* edited by Michael Doran (Berkeley: University of California Press, 2001)

Norman Davies, *No Simple Victory: World War II in Europe, 1939–1945* (New York: Viking, 2007)

Julian Jackson, *The Fall of France: The Nazi Invasion, 1940* (Oxford: Oxford University Press, 2003)

Denis Peschanski, et al., eds., *Collaboration and Resistance: Images of Life in Vichy, France, 1940–1944* (Harry Abrams, 1988)

Irving Stone, *Depths of Glory: A Biographical Novel of Camille Pissarro* (Doubleday, 1985)

For a complete bibliography of works consulted, as well as for images, see www.susanvreeland.com.

ABOUT THE AUTHOR

SUSAN VREELAND is the *New York Times* bestselling author of eight books, including *Clara and Mr. Tiffany* and *Girl in Hyacinth Blue*. She lives in San Diego.

ABOUT THE TYPE

This book was set in Sabon, a typeface designed by the well-known German typographer Jan Tschichold (1902–74). Sabon's design is based upon the original letter forms of sixteenth-century French type designer Claude Garamond and was created specifically to be used for three sources: foundry type for hand composition, Linotype, and Monotype. Tschichold named his typeface for the famous Frankfurt typefounder Jacques Sabon (c. 1520–80).